DRAGON FIRE

R. C. Thom

Library of Congress copyright number: 1-175643321
Original copyright date 3/31/09 under the title "Of Mars and Men"
Final edit 2017

ISBN 978-1-7321459-2-4

R.C. Thom
Email: RC@RCThom.com
Web: RCThom.com

Editors: Angel Ackerman, Lisa Cross

Cover Art and Design by Rachel C. Thompson
Book Design by Gayle F. Hendricks

ONE

The Curious Child

The yearling dragon Mars stuck his snout inside the rock-cut passage and inhaled with unguarded curiosity; it smelled human and wizardly. Merilbe must have come by way of that tunnel. He had arrived just yesterday and strangely none of the brood saw his arrival. This morning Merilbe had examined the eleven hatchlings as before, yet this time his etched brow rose and fell repeatedly while the lock of white hair that cascaded from his otherwise black-haired scalp flashed bright to dull and back again much like a young dragon that had not yet learned to control his hue.

He is the oddest of all humans.

'Examine your scrolls,' Merilbe had said to Mother. 'I'm quite sure of the star-signs. The time of the Golden has come, and that can mean only one thing.'

Mother's crown feathers had risen suddenly, she put a finger to her snout and Merilbe fell silent. She then dismissed the brood. Mars raced off with the others but he kept an ear on their conversation when he flew near.

'Penelope, the predictions never mention two,' said the wizard, 'A hidden darkness is loosed. Things are clouded. How and when it ends, I do not know…the future is uncertain. There is no accounting for this…'

Mars looped in the air and lost their words. On the next return Mars saw Mother hurrying toward her study puffing gray smoke. She left Merilbe scratching his gray-bearded chin at the cave's arch with his long black hair and robes flowing around him like smoke. Mars had his eyes on the wizard and so nearly crashed into a tall standing stone. Reacting mid-flight, Mars twisted and beat his tail, thus missing the stone and in doing so he lost sight of Merilbe. Mars banked and touched down at the foyer, but Merilbe was gone. Mars stood there wondering about the wizard.

He must have gone in. No other human ever goes that way, Mars thought as he took another long sniff.

He edged nearer that small human-sized tunnel just behind the Teacher's Rock which was a low, flat boulder: Its top was worn slick and concaved like a grinding dish from eons of adult dragons perching there. Grown dragons, even the smaller ones the size of a pony, never entered that passageway. This tunnel was far too small for any adult dragon.

How does he come and go without riding a dragon?

Mars folded tight his wings, reared onto his hind legs, and stretched out his arms to measure the arch. Mars on his hind legs was as tall as Merilbe but a bit wider.

It's not too tight for me or any yearling, for that matter, except that oversized slug, Bullock. Mother is right. We smaller dragons have our merits. Ha!

The broodlings knew the legend of this cave well. The teachers say if any dragon child goes that way he would be struck fireless. This cave, it is said, goes out to the very edge of Rookery Top above West Gate. They say no one knows how Merilbe gets himself to and fro. The mysteries of a wizard's magic were incomprehensible, or so lore masters say. But Mars didn't believe everything his teachers said.

If I go, I'll be first among my broodmates to see wider Neff. Let Bullock top that.

Mars liked first place, and learning how Merilbe traveled without a dragon would be the best first place in school history. At the end of this cave Mars reasoned, were Merilbe's secrets.

Mars thrust his head into the shadows. No sunlight shown ahead. Mars blew a jet of fire into the darkness. The passage curved sharply right twisting upward unlike other common tunnels which mostly went down or even.

What could possibly go wrong?

Mars put in one quivering leg.

"Where're you going little bird?" Bullock asked as he landed with a plodding thump. "We're not supposed to leave the inner ring. You know the rules."

"You're not my captain," Mars said. "Besides, we're not to fly above the rim; I'm walking, not flying."

"I'm biggest. That makes me commander. Need I bite your tail? We're playing war. Come on! File in!"

Before Mars could answer Timor, Gordon, and Praxis who was the only lowborn Golden ever hatched swooped in and landed around Bullock. Bullock's command voice had drawn them. Gordon, almost as big as Bullock, stumbled on his tail upon landing, fell into Bullock, and bounced off. Bullock hardly noticed. Praxis and Timor laughed with blue smoke.

"I won't file in," Mars said. "I'm not going anywhere. I'm not playing with you."

Bullock heeled on his hind legs and puffed a great cloud of black smoke. Red fire licked his snout. Bullock's tail nearly hit Praxis as he thrashed it like an angry cat. Bullock knotted his tail fin into a fist, bent his neck and laid down his crown feathers ready for a head-butt. Mars, who had no room to avoid Bullock's attack, made wide his legs readying for the beating.

This is going to hurt.

"Apologize! Give respect to your better, you, you, sparrow or suffer my wrath!" Bullock hollered.

"My better!? I won't! I won't heed any lowborn the likes of you!"

"Stop it," Praxis yelled as she hopped forward landing between them. "Bullock let him be or I'll tell. Dragon's don't hurt dragons! What about the Golden's Rule? Leave him alone or you'll get punished!"

"I'll beat him in every game, then" Bullock said. "Highborn, golden, or all what else, he's still a runt. Class doesn't mean anything in war-games. Come on, boys."

Bullock spun, his tail whipped past Mars's face. With one hop, Bullock left the foyer. Timor and Gordon turned with heads low and tails bent.

"Why do you follow him like dogs after a huntsman?" Mars said.

"Aren't we supposed to follow the lead dragon?" Timor replied.

"Isn't that the way of dragons?" Gordon said.

"Bullock is no lead dragon," Mars snorted with gray-black smoke, "He's a yearling like the rest of us. No school dragon is better than any other. I'll outrank him on Last Games Day. You'll see."

"Mars is right," Praxis said. "You don't have to heed Bullock."

"The Light gives some to follow, some to lead," Gordon said quoting the Scroll of Neff.

"Following is better than getting sat on," Timor said.

Bullock slapped his tail on the ground. He was in center field, tall on his hind legs with his hands on his hips like an angry pod mother. Gordon and Timor hurried off toward the Game Grounds.

"Aren't you coming Praxis?" Timor called over his shoulder.

"No," she said. "I'm going to be a healer. Healers are independent. I've decided I'm not playing either."

"Suit yourself." Timor called running after Gordon.

Praxis jumped onto Teacher's Rock and waved her tail inviting Mars to join her. Mars ignored it and proceeded into the upslope passage. He did not reach the third bend before he heard a dragon's footfalls behind him. It wasn't the heavy steps of Bullock. It wasn't Gordon; His tail always slapped the deck every third step. It wasn't Timor; His stomach was forever growling. The other broodlings weren't around.

It's got to be Praxis.

"What's the use," Mars said sitting on his curled tail. Mars's eyes were not yet used to the dark, so he felt for the notch. Every tunnel had them. When he found it, he lit the candle with a lick of fire-breath. When Praxis appeared, Mars was suddenly glad for her company. This was a scary place, rough walls full of cobwebs and spattered bat dung, most unlike a proper dragon's tunnel. Mars wasn't about to admit his fear, though, not to a girl.

"Just because we're both Golden doesn't mean you have to follow me around," Mars said.

"That's not why I'm here," she said. "I'm protecting you."

"What?" Mars slapped his tail on the wall. "I don't need some dumb girl watching my back. I can take care of myself!"

"My mother says a healer must protect the weaker. Isn't that why we've watched over the humans for thousands of years?"

"I don't need protection. I'm small. So what? That doesn't mean I'm weak."

"Then follow Bullock and take your knocks instead of hiding in this hole. What if you get stuck in here? Coming here alone isn't smart, you know. I'd say your mind is what's weak."

"I don't need help."

"Maybe you do, maybe you don't. But if I'm going to be a healer, I'd best follow you. The way you're going it's only a matter of time before you get hurt."

Mars blew a jet of white fire. He could make fire here, technically. They weren't in a common area where fire-breath was restricted. He couldn't accidentally cook a passing human here.

"Come along. I need a witness to my glory, but keep quiet."

"Mars Hammertail, you are a rogue. What in the Light are you doing? You know the high-up winds are dangerous."

"I'm walking, not flying. I want to see the overlook above West Gate, that's all," Mars lied. "The Brimstone brothers are on guard duty, it's safe. You ought to go back. This is no place for a girl."

Praxis blustered and puffed out her chest, her scales blue-gold hue rippled. Black smoke rolled from her nostrils. Whenever Mars wanted Praxis to do something, he simply told her, 'this is not for girls.' It always worked before but Mars guessed by her stance she had had her fill of it.

"I'm no ordinary girl. You're not the only Golden, you know. I'll do what I want."

Mars grabbed the candle, flicked his tail and started up the tunnel. Praxis quelled her fire and followed. The tunnel opened wider, to Mars's relief, and there was room for her to walk beside him. The spiral ended at a switch-back then the passage meandered five hundred feet further climbing gradually.

Finally the passage opened into a domed cavern just behind the mountain's face. There was a wide slit in that thick wall five feet above the floor. The window-cut slopped upward showing nothing but blue sky. The air was heavy with the smell of Puffin and Dar guarding West Gate landing below.

"Room enough to wiggle up there on my stomach," Mars whispered. "I'll push my head beyond the edge and have a look."

Mars crawled into the window resting his belly on the wide sill. His feet were tiptoed at the floor. Praxis nudged her way forward and together they stuck their necks out. The top of Raven's Rock was ten feet below them, and twenty feet below that was the West Gate Landing. Praxis suddenly pulled back and hissed. Mars pulled his head back, too.

"It's that old crow, the one with the star on his head. He'll see us," Praxis whispered into Mars's ear. "You know how crows are, he'll blab."

"That's dumb, nobody believes crows. The wind's blowing. He won't hear us. Besides, he's watching them so he won't see us. Come on, let's look."

The wind screamed above Rookery Top Mountain, but near to the mountain's side, the air was calmer. Mars popped his head out again this time exposing his mane. Mars closed his flight lids to protect his eyes from whatever small bits traveled on the wind. The Brimstone brothers lay upon their tails against the mountain thirty feet from the landing's edge. The teachers told of how the winds blasted up the mountain and how tricky flying was around Rookery Top. That was no teacher's fable.

"The pod mothers are wise," Praxis said into Mars's ear, "See why we aren't permitted to fly here?"

"I can handle it," Mars said, but he knew she was right. As small as he was, the wind would toss him like a leaf in a storm. Bullock would do better with his greater weight.

For that alone Bullock would surely be chosen first to tour with the renowned
warlord Draco.

Great, Mars told himself, *everyone says Bullock even looks like Draco.*

The wind carried the voices of Puffin and Dar. Mars cocked his ear.

Back to the mystery, Mars thought. *Where did that wizard go?*

Before Mars could catch their conversation, the crow sprung up, jumping like a dragon launching to fly. He nearly hit Mars's snout as the crow passed. It landed and clung to the rock protrusion above and between the two dragons.

How strange for a crow.

"Mars Hammertail and Praxis the Healer's daughter! Well, I never! This is a first… two Golden dragons and not half a brain between them. Best you go, a storm is coming, and you'll not want this storm to find you here."

Mars puffed black smoke which floated only a few feet before it was captured and destroyed by rip-winds.

"I'm not abiding any stupid, old crow," Mars said.

"Smart dragons abide wisdom nary its' source." Praxis said.

"We're staying."

"Have it your way." Praxis said.

The crow began to squawk and cawed loudly. Mars shooed it with his hand, but there was little room to move. The crow easily avoided Mars's swats. Praxis slapped Mars's rump with her tail.

"The guards will hear. Let's go," she said. "I've not heard of crows speaking warnings. This is very odd."

Mars thought about it. He hated to admit it, but she was right—again. Crows don't give warnings, only riddles and gibberish, so the teachers say. Still, Mars wasn't worried about weather. The sky stood clear and as blue as a sky should be. There was no danger except for this crazy, old crow giving him away. And if the crow revealed them, the guards must report what they saw. He was chaffing his tightly folded wings anyway. The rock slit was rough and the fit tight.

"All right Crow we'll leave. I've figured your riddle," Mars said. "You are the storm and you won't stop howling while we're here. Good day!"

They withdrew and made their way out of Merilbe's passage. Mars tapped the walls along the way back looking for hidden doors and found none. After emerging, having no explanation for Merilbe's disappearance, Mars left Praxis and joined the male broodlings for a rock spitting game. Mars soon forgot his quest and that strange crow.

The females gathered to watch the game. And as everyone knows, it's a young male dragons' pleasure, if not his duty, to impress the females with masterful flying and fine rock spitting. Mars was not the largest dragon, but size meant nothing in fire-rock games.

The sun shone on Sky Top's gaming grounds causing everyone's scales to glow. Mars noticed that Mother was back in the foyer, a signal that recess would soon end. Time was short.

"Tail tag! Tail tag," Zandora called. "I call healer."

At once, the females took flight and scattered.

"Last one up is it!" Charlotte squeaked.

In a flurry of wings and tail beats, the males went airborne. Mars was first.

TWO

The New Brood

Draco held his great leathery wings wide ensuring his magic's full lift potential. With tips turned up, his wings caught the howling wind and drove him forward while his tail-fin, turned vertically, steered him. Six miles high in the South Stream, Draco needed all his magic to stay aloft and his belly's fire to stay alive. His prized dragon's gold breastplate was wind-pressed against his heart warming his soul but not his red-brown scales. Draco heard naught but the icy wind rattling the tokens woven into his mane like house charms. His trinkets were not of the kind that sang children to sleep. The Warlord Draco was mindful against sleep. One thousand years of practice did not guarantee his survival on these currents. When dragons slept riding this wind, they froze, fell up, and became stars.

Draco flexed his muscles to break ice from his wings. *At such heights a dragon flies by magic and wind alone. Wing flapping wastes energy.* Draco likened himself to a great ship on rolling seas. But, he felt no pleasure on this flight. His mastery of wing-sails and tail-ruddering did not help him steer within the human tides below. Human winds, often contrary, confused his course.

Draco folded his wings by half and descended to a lower stream before extending his wings once more. He surveyed the lands around him as the Eastward blew him toward the Rookery. To the west and south lay civilized men: Hammond's kingdom a land of livestock, gardens, forges, wine-making, and merry cooking hearths. Draco's stomach pleaded for recompense on the thought. To the north lay the Steppes and wheat fields, beer-making; sod houses, horses and some argue…danger. His nose read everything, perhaps even clearer than his eyes.

The odor of unwashed Outlanders assaulted his snout from the distance reaches of most directions. The Warlord's chill deepened. Dragons who flew into that smell were the warriors headed for the endless border wars. Draco preferred his duties as dragon patriarch and right hand of the king to fighting as of late.

I must be getting old.

While successful and honored as Warlord, Draco wanted to abdicate...should a suitable replacement hatch. Draco's thoughts drifted to Penelope.

Love burns long and now with Atmere dead...Dare I hope? 'When I retire, we will bind.' I gave not my word lightly. Yet, duty still holds me. Warlords cannot marry and I cannot retire, not yet, not until...

Strong scents came on the wind and drove the old dream from his heart. Draco smelled his responsibilities—the King's keep mixed with the Rookery air. The freshly-tilled soil of Vineland filled his nose as last year's produce cooked within the Rookery's kitchens. Draco's gullet rumbled for the King's friendly table. What Draco did not smell was Hammond's war industry. No forges smelted. Grinding wheels did not sharpen blades. Where was the slag and brimstone? This pleased him some and worried him more.

Could this be the peace foretold? I pray the Light this recent-hatched Golden of Penelope's proves suitable. He is an orphan, as the scrolls predict. My matchmaking was keen. Atmere, stars rest his soul, was a stout, highborn dragon. Mayhap retirement is near—a wellborn Golden dragon has hatched.

Merilbe's news brought Draco to the Rookery years before his traditional first inspection of the new pod. The exception was necessary: This golden hatchling's scales bore an impression which was a perfect rendition of the Crest of Neff. Merilbe had reread the scroll at spring breakfast: "When dragon-stars fill the sky then a golden crest-bearer will descend, be him a peacemaker born of the Light. He will lead the dragons to life without strife."

Draco blew fire into the wind. Practicality bespoke a great Warlord, not another spindly priest of the Light. What Draco needed was smart fighters to maintain Hammond's truce. But dragons were becoming fewer and rider-sized dragons were rarer still. The scribes and Penelope, a storyteller herself, advised a withdrawal of dragons from war. Too many are lost, they say. Peace cannot come while dragons fight for men, they say. War cannot end otherwise.

Such nonsense. Where there are men there is war always. Soothsayers think we dragons will leave. More foolishness, why would we go? King Hammond gives us much and cannot do without dragons. Will the turning of the calendar make the wastes of Neff green again?

Below, the wilds of Neff bore no sign of its lost glory, only tangled black trees and haunted swamps inhabited by fowl creatures remained. The historians say that Neff was once a garden of plenty where Golden dragons tended the new race called man until the dragons sinned and became like men—wanting. The Giants cursed the garden and went away many thousands of years ago, since then many generations of dragons' long lives pasted. Most dragons thought the tales true. Draco thought otherwise.

Nothing green in Neff. I believe what I see. The King's Tapestry gives usable signs. Those omens win battles. The living Tapestry hasn't shown the King any legends coming alive, no Golden Savior or a revived Garden of Neff, or the coming of the Golden Warrior.

Yet, even as he considered it, Draco knew the Tapestry's usefulness was fading. Hammond complained of fewer and less clear visions and the Tapestry did not foresee the ruin of Atmere. This failing caused bitterness to well in his throat. Draco spat the acid out not wanting to honor it with fire.

I need replacements, not legends.

Few dragons were as gold as Atmere. In the end, his color did not help him. Draco would train any large dragon with potential, regardless of color. Skills of battle and state were learned in War Camp. There weren't any born leaders, among men or dragons, except, perhaps the first long-dead Golden Warlords whose likenesses were stitched into the King's Tapestry from a time out of mind. Whatever good prospects hatch this season, highborn or lowborn with half a brain or twice-wise endowed, Draco would take that one under wing. Draco would not fulfill promises he made a thousand years and as many dead dragons ago, until a clear leader came forth.

Retirement and Penelope. Get that out of your head, you old fool. You can't predict how any yearling will do. This inspection is nothing but a spark in wet tinder. Ah, but this highborn Golden...Gold trumps a large measure of sins, perhaps...And dragons fly under sea!

Draco snorted black smoke at his hopes. Rookery Top Mountain drew nearer; he sensed it in the way the air currents were disturbed. This hallowed place stood alone in a vast, low, flatland. Rookery Top was a steep flat-topped cone half a mile high snaked with caves, grand galleries and culverts. The lower winds thrashed against it and deflected upward. The majority of topmost caves had long ago collapsed opening Rookery Top Mountain to the sky. Thus, the peak had earned the name 'Sky Top.' It was a place of safe dead-air to raise dragon children. Sky Top was the gaming ground from time out of mind. Draco opened his secondary eyelids to spy the newest dragon children flying below the rim. He belched his pleasure in blue flame.

A flutter of crow's wings pulled Draco's attention to the West Gate landing. His initial joy flew south. Footmen could not march to Rookery Mountain. Horses cannot tread in Neff. The Rookery was safe, yet, Draco ordered Puffin and Dar to guard that landing. They were not vigilant. These two dragons at age twenty were long past school-age. They should be at War Camp, not among the children. Draco cocked his ear and sharpened his eyes as he hovered high above.

Puffin and Dar lay on their haunches with tails as tripods, arms folded over breasts, basking in the sun with the gray mountain at their backs. The warm spring sun lighted their iridescent scales, their hues glowed in each one's natural colors; a sign of self-contentment. Puffin and Dar waited on either side of the entryway, no doubt avoiding the cooler air pouring from the tunnel. Before them, the parapet platform, side-edged with standing stones, was littered with small fallen rocks, weeds and grass. Draco had ordered them to keep that landing dressed! There was room enough for six harried dragons to dismount their riders but no room for disorder born of ignored orders, not in Draco's accounting. Draco opened wide his famously long reaching ears.

"Shouldn't we watch better?" Dar asked. "Draco said..."

******

Puffin snorted green fire and gave the common answer. "Nobody passes below. They'd get lost, enchanted, or dead. Even if they reached the base, they couldn't make the climb."

Puffin put a fresh rock into his mouth and called a small fire. Blue and red smoke escaped his nose while fire licked his mouth's edge like a campfire tickling meat on the spit.

"There's naught to look out for," Puffin said.

"I suppose you're right, then," Dar said. "Like they say, 'No dragon brings war upon this birth place.'"

Puffin put his hands behind his head and spat a fiery rock. It arched and sizzled and whistled thought the air before disappearing over the edge. Puffin popped another rock into his mouth.

******

So confident are you, Draco thought. *However, war dragons must be ready for anything and always.*

"I mean," said Dar, "the closest border is thirty miles and its Hammond the Dragon Friend's land."

"No worrying…," Puffin's voice drifted with the wind. "What could happen?"

What could happen? I'll show you.

Draco snorted blue flames. He was not without his sense of humor, however much he hid it. It was past time the Brimstone brothers learned this lesson—never disobey Draco's orders. Draco called up red fire.

A demonstration is in order.

Draco folded his wings and fell from the sky like a hunting eagle. Seconds before smashing into the ground, he hacked his tail and burst opened his wings which sent him racing along gnarled treetops faster than the King's champion horse. Draco rode his momentum a tail's stroke above death. The trinkets of his mane clanged against his breast plate like angry bell clappers as his black contrail rose. Even within this wind, Draco still monitored the Brimstones' conversation.

They should hear me by now, what slugs they are.

From many miles away he heard them, but they did not hear him. This did not bode well with Draco.

******

Puffin recalled King Hammond's watch-wall guards and counted himself fortunate. He saw them while on tour with Draco. Hammond's men were stiffly grim. And, no wonder; girded with iron head to toe or with chest-plates made of dragon scales, or, if from a poor family, leather and wood armor. How could they not feel grim so clad? Hammond's walls had not seen war in forty years. *There's no need for such disharmony among the men on the walls—Light forbid one should live so unhappily.*

The wars hadn't gone so deep in-land in two human generations, but King Hammond's sentries watched keen-eyed and worried nonetheless.

"Naught but worry itself to worry about here," Puffin said.

"What's that, a crow's riddle?" Dar said leaning forward.

"Idle thoughts spoken aloud, nothing more," Puffin said.

Dar relaxed his tail and leaned back again. He folded his spindly arms over his breast, thick fingers interlaced. His crown feathers rested a lazy half-mast.

Puffin spat another rock into the abyss. "Not long now, Dar. We'll join the fray, outlanders on the west border they say, and I'll be a front runner. I'll carry a great fighter!"

"A good place for you, brood mate. Your red hue is made for war," Dar said, words marked by white smoke. "You'll make a fine target for arrows. Alas, I, with my golden scales, will remain in reserve for breeding. Oh to suffer the fate of a golden breeder," Dar said feigning a sigh. "Tis ill, but I must do my part."

"More like yellow, I'd say."

Puffin spat his rock at Dar with a grunt. The rock bounced off Dar's forehead and rolled into the grass along the outskirts of the landing. The grass smoldered. Puffin's crown feathers shot tall.

"You've got green in your scales!" Puffin said, knowing full well that his brother sported desirable colors. "You'd be that unlucky. Cavorting with females while battles rage? You'd miss the glory. What good is that?"

Puffin popped another rock into his mouth and put his hands behind his head, fluffing his growing mane. He rolled the rock into place on his tongue and fired it.

"What female would want you?" Puffin mumbled. "Females want the greatest dragons, warrior-colored like me. I will sire first."

Dar laughed, blue flame curled around his snout. "I will be foremost in war and in love." Dar beat his leather breastplate. "My golden hue will dazzle the enemy. I will blind them with my reflections, and so the females will love me more. All whilst you languish as a rear guard. The humans will weave great awards into my mane, mark me."

"Rear indeed," Puffin said with false offense. "On guard, forge blower!"

With that, Puffin sprung to fight position, hands and feet on the ground and head low. Dar did the same. They butted heads, their loose crown feathers fluttering away on the wind. Stepping back, they thrashed their heads whipping their braided manes. Eventually, with the iron implements woven in their locks would become weapons, but for now the skirmish was quite safe. Puffin's tail swished back and forth like a house cat stalking an imp. Dar raised his tail, his fin a knot, but Puffin didn't cower. No sane dragon would bring his tail against another dragon. No matter the turn of battle or his captain's plea, dragons don't kill dragons. Tails alone were deadly enough, but, curling a magic tailfin into a fist transformed it into a stone-crushing mace.

Dar slung his tail over Puffin's head smashing onto the tall stone called Raven's Rock, jarring the old crow that often sat upon it.

"Fools," the Crow squawked. "You wonder why you are still here. "Tis fitting, children such as you don't belong in any trade much less the army."

Spitting fire had hardened Puffin's mouth but not his resolve.

"I'm not a child! I'm a war steed," Puffin said with a snort of red flame.

"Beware then," the Crow said, cocking his head. The white star on its forehead flashed in the sunlight. "War is upon you…even now."

The Crow ruffled his black and gray feathers and took flight. As the wind drove him over the mountain, he called to the dragons, "Take heed!"

"Crows," Dar said. "Never mind crows."

"I'm hungry," Puffin said. "I smell chicken."

"Hen feasts are for the courts, not our pleasure," Dar said. "There's no highborn here but Penelope and she's austere. There's no fine fowl in the kitchen for us, just sparrow pie."

Puffin's crown feather stood.

"That might account for Draco's foul moods," Puffin said with a puff of blue smoke. "He's been eating crows instead of pheasants."

The two reared onto hind legs laughing, while blue flames danced around their mouths.

******

Crow eater, am I? That is an insult I won't abide.

Draco reached the base of the mountain with fire in his throat. He spread his wings wider and twisted his tail moments before ruin. His scales flashed red in the sun, a call-to-arms beacon. Draco rushed upward along the perilous mountain's face. His wind sounded like angry pipers. He rose with a great red-smoked clatter, picking up speed with every tail beat. Draco flew his great bulk with the style and grace of a kingfisher. *This will make a lasting impression.*

The Warlord imagined the West Gate landing as an enemy stronghold and so exploded into West Gate's airspace a smoking terror. His war-worn wings, three times wider than his body, beat hard suspending him above the landing's edge. His wing-blasts dislodged small stones and shrubs which pelted his sentries. Draco landed like a rock fall.

"You fools!" Draco boomed in dragon's war tongue, a tongue only for battle and never before used there in anger. Dar and Puffin fell down and prostrated themselves, jaws on the ground, wings bent over their heads. They trembled like beaten dogs.

Draco folded his wings, forced his crown tall, and breathed red fire around his mouth. His point was made. As he calmed down, Draco looked on them with pity—two simple country dragons not hatched for highborn ways. Dragons such as these in years past would not have been considered. Only dragons of the Golden blood line fought, while simpler folk lived simpler lives. With so few dragons what choice did Draco have? He proceeded with his lesson at hand and switched to the softer dragon's high tongue.

"Don't cower! I'm no enemy. Your duty calls. Stand ready!"

The two youngsters reared to hind legs, tails stiff, necks bent, and eyes on Draco as the protocols demanded. Puffin looked sickly white while Dar shook so hard his scales rattled.

They answered in unison, "Yes, Draco."

Woe to us all should dragons ever come against dragons. May it never be!

Draco balanced the girth of his great body on massive hind legs like a warhorse posed to strike while his tail cut to and fro like an angry school teacher's switch. Draco then splayed his wings and puffed out his chest, many arrow and spear tears suffered his wings. His long, black braids hung from the nape of his neck. One spiked iron ball hung on either side. Above the maces were woven awards made of costly dragon gold. Battle scars striped his arms, undersides, neck and jaw. Draco's famous vanity, a breast plate made of purest dragon gold was lashed onto his chest with blood-stained leather thongs. The Fall of Neff was carved into it. Draco knew himself a fearsome sight.

These two will remember this day.

Draco softened his voice further. "Come now lads, is this how you prepare for a soldier's vocation? Harden your hearts, games are over. You may one day face each other on the borders.

Dar lowered his head, speaking to the ground. "Draco, will we not be together. We are brood blood, hatched together. Will Puffin and I not fight in fellowship?"

"Where you fight and against whom, it is not time to say. The twelve's estates wax and wane. Price decides where you go, but it is mine to say when."

Draco flattened his crown feathers and stopped the billowing of black smoke seething from his nostrils.

"Are we to leave, then?" Puffin asked. "Off to War Camp so soon?"

"I've naught come for you today. There's time enough; steady your hearts. Next spring, I'll review your applications. I'm here to see last spring's hatchlings. Step aside."

Puffin's color improved and Dar trembled less. Draco allowed himself a puff of blue smoke and dropped onto fisted hands and entered the West Gate tunnel. Ten yards from the archway, the cave opened into a wide foyer and parted three ways. He chose the up way. Silent as a long-tooth cougar, ears standing, Draco made his way seeking rumors. The pod was assembled on Rookery Top, he knew. *Good. I'll appear unannounced and see what I may.*

THREE

Penelope Teaches

Penelope looked upon the children at play as she hunched on the Teaching Rock. *Only eleven dragons—the smallest brood in centuries and an unlucky number at that.* Sky Top was three hundred feet around and there was room for three dozen dragon children at play. *Three highborn pod mothers this hatching and three is a lucky number, but not for me.* Only one of her three eggs had hatched. The yearlings looked so small in this huge space and her Mars was nearly the smallest of them all, surly the smallest high born of her life. *Leading dragons ought not to be as small as he.*

Sky Top Gallery was on the perimeter of Sky Top and situated along a wall overhung by a rock shelf. Sky Top capped the subterranean dormitories, libraries, eateries, and treasure rooms which held the accumulated wealth of dragon kind. Teaching Rock was within sight of the game grounds where children raced the gauntlet and counted the stars at night while visiting human and dragon scholars likewise pondered the sky. Penelope thought Sky Top's hatchlings the most valuable of treasures on or under the mountain. Every young dragon loved this place where sun and starlight bounced off polished mica tile floors and onto smoothed crater walls like dancing fireflies. Here children had no cares of the wider world. This was not the center of dragon life however much it seemed so to the children.

This place only, Penelope thought, was her true home. No matter that every court in the land had housed her in turn and honored her as Dragon Matron. Her courtly ways were welcomed everywhere, yet her wisdom regarding these latter days was less welcome. The Lore of Light glowed dim in the wider world. Here, too, at Sky Top, the Light was fading like so much exhaled smoke.

I should not be sad while the light of dragon's play flashes about. Her students twisted in the air casting joyful magic everywhere. Yet, her heart was heavy. She lowered her head toward the glossy floor and saw her disappointment in her reflection, sad golden eyes amid gray-gold scales that gave no hue. *The children must not see me out of sorts.*

She raised her head and jetted gray smoke at the nearest standing stone, one of many blackened by students spitting fire. These pillars appeared as ghosts on foggy nights. As these walls protected Penelope's flying charges, so, too, would she protect their hearts and minds. *Yes this place is safe, but not safe from him.* Draco's ways, passed from warlord to warlord, is why dragons die. Penelope cursed the contracts between men and dragons. The very notion was a black fire in her heart. How long must dragons swallow human bile?

Penelope fluffed her crown feathers and stood on hind legs to call the brood. She had determined to teach the Lore of Light. Draco forbade it, saying of it, 'It is naught but filling their heads with fanciful distractions.' Such lore stood counter to his warrior ways. *Mars and his brood mates will know the Way of Light.* Penelope prayed they'd keep it well.

"Children come around," she called, her voice sweet.

From behind rocks, within nooks and from the sky the collective lament of her students sounded.

"Play time's over? It's too soon," they cried.

"Come at once, children," Penelope said in the high human language, her voice melodic. "I will tell you stories of Neff. If you come quickly, and listen well, I'll suspend afternoon lessons."

A stampede of yearlings cascaded from above and below. Those not flying ran like galloping horses on ice. Timor slipped on a patch of spiting stones, tumbled like an acrobat, landed on his feet and never slowed. Mars, racing Bullock for first as usual, slid the last twenty feet and bounced off a sidewall before coming to rest. Blue flame curled around Penelope's snout. She hunched upon the teaching rock like a dagger-toothed lioness, such dangerous creatures were gentile with their young. The pod gathered, each to his or her usual place.

"As you know, it is your first year's end," she said. "To celebrate, I'll let you decide the story."

At once, the brood called for their favorites. "Tell of the giants!" "How men came." "Spit rocks for first! Best aim first!" "Tell us about the fall!" "Tell the White Raven!" "The dwarf massacre of the Lowborn."

"Hush, no shouting," Penelope said. "First hand seen is served first, and Praxis was quickest. What will you have me tell?"

Praxis had potential in Penelope's reckoning. Rarely did a lowborn dragon have such a long neck, long legs, or the blue and gold of highborn lineage. She was also, so far, the best student and forever full of questions. Penelope saw greatness in her. This one could serve the courts, another thread stitching the Estates and Vineland together. Courtesans required cunning and intelligence, flying between so many suspicious vassals. Penelope thought she could make use of one such as Praxis, once the dragon child learned to keep guard over her thoughts. A courtier must be contained. Overt honesty, a common trait among country dragons, was undesirable and even dangerous at court.

"Pod mother," Praxis said, "it is not a fable I want. Tell us true tales."

Penelope raised her head high. Her crown spiked straight as she exhaled rainbow smoke. Penelope's ancestors were the storytellers of old and so the love of lore coursed within her blood. Duty had taken her from her beloved craft. As eldest female, she was obligated as the foremost courtier. Now her duty wrought living stories for peace, not stories of wisdom and history. *It is time they learn the truth.*

"It once was that storytellers enjoyed high status for they were the keepers of truth," Penelope said. "Storytellers are not honored today as truth-speakers and yet every story still speaks truth. Lore made fanciful may be considered entertainment and no longer good counsel for kings, but remember this: lore contains great wisdom. However, the importance of lore-learning is not recognized by the King's right hand."

Penelope, lowered her head, her long neck brought her close to the dragons on the floor. She spoke softly. Some others that lived on Rookery Mountain were Draco's ears. Even trusted Wren, although well-meaning, was too loose with words. 'Country folk are plan talking folks,' the old saying goes.

"I will tell you a secret, but you must not repeat it," Penelope whispered. "Not to the other brood mothers. Not to Draco. Not the teachers. Will you swear on your fire?"

The brood was mesmerized by Penelope's promise and her unusual countenance. Each yearling whispered in turn, "By my fire I shall not tell."

"Good then, I will confide what warlords and kings rather you not know. The legends of Neff are all completely true. They are not fables at all. They are histories told in parables so they are remembered. Human influence has driven out the importance of dragon memories, yet in every tale a golden thread of truth still remains."

"Like the Tapestry." Praxes said with aw.

"What?" Gordon said. "All the teachers say they're just fables. Everyone says it!"

Penelope brightened her hue. "Not everyone. The wise, such as the King's wizard Merilbe, keep the scrolls dear. King Hammond honors the scrolls, too, more so than folks know."

Praxis raised her hand."Why can't high dragons bond by love as is common with humans and country dragons? There is no answer in the tales I've heard."

"Why, indeed," Penelope said. "We higher dragons cannot mate for love as our numbers dwindle. We must reestablish the line and restore the Golden Order. Recall the story of the dwarf's war against the country dragons? So many ground dragons were lost that flyers and walkers were mated to rebuild the population. Now, of course, the low flourish as golden blood prospered them, but the rebuilding has long been subverted."

Penelope almost choked on her own words. She took a moment to compose herself.

"Draco makes matches for war. As such, he works less to reestablish the pure Golden Line, the line that will bear a savior. Draco is more for blending the best qualities of dragon lines for fighting. Even Draco admits the purest golden dragons make the greatest leaders. Undoubtedly golden skills are also useful in war, but war is not, it is not the way of dragons."

Tears filled Penelope's eyes. *Mars is pure gold.* Her tears loosed. The brood watched as drops ran along her snout and fell to the floor. They had never seen a grown dragon cry, least of all Penelope. The eldest of dragons is not supposed to cry, everyone knows. Important figures never cried, so says common lore. Penelope could not help herself. The brood fell silent for a time.

"How did we come to such a state?" Tiny Charlotte said.

Penelope raised her head higher and shut her eyes, answering in whispers. "Twenty thousand years ago when every flyer was golden we high dragons were charged by the Giants to bring up man in wisdom. The Giants made the lands hereabout to help us in our task. The Garden of Neff was made a place of plenty were strife could play no part. For the Giants knew the childish hearts of men and so provided no reason to want. However, as men grew in number they also grew in greed. They fought over possessions. They lorded over the possessions of other races. They were jealous for dwarf's gold and started wars against some and traded with other dwarf kind. Such endeavors began our downfall…The slaughter of the land dragons…the return of the Giants eleven thousand years ago whereby they destroyed the garden and forced men out. Thereafter, slowly, dragons came to serve, instead of lead, and so the needs of men remade us for war. Thank the Light that Hammond's truce stays this madness."

"But, in war is glory," said Mars, puffing much smoke. "Dragons lead men in war!"

"The only true glory is the glory of Neff, dear Mars," Penelope said with bitter disappointment in her voice. "Wisdom is no more. Men brought us to this state, Charlotte."

Penelope motioned to the empty room with one wing. "The Golden Thread has failed, lost and tangled in man's patchwork. And now, the end of the age is nigh. The Dragon Constellation is nearly full. Only the Great Golden Dragon can restore the Light. He will bring us peace, a new land, and restore reason. So it was written."

Penelope heard her self say it, but she did not have much hope. The purest gold dragon alive was her young son, a dragon on a false flight path already tainted by lust for war, a dragon already taken by Draco's far-reaching influence.

No, it can't be my Mars. He is too little, too smitten, and it is too late.

There weren't any recent omens showing that an astounding dragon was born or forthcoming and time grew short. Doubt filled Penelope. Then, she caught an old familiar sent and her fire burned colder. Penelope's bile rose and her heart raced. She reared up high on the teaching rock.

"Remember your oath, and mind my words. The stories will save you, all of us, not the ways of man. Now be gone, fly off until the dinner bell rings. No more classes today!"

With that, the brood scattered and resumed their game playing.

Penelope smelled Draco. Courtly dragons were not known for keen scenting, but it did not take a hound-dog nose to know when Draco was near. The smell of war was always upon him. Even in times of peace he reeked of acid, brimstone, blood and death.

To think I loved him! She would not abide Draco this time, no, duty or naught. She accepted Draco's judgment before, but not again, not this time. *Not my only son and likely my last egg.* Draco had set Atmere to fighting for Hammond's kingdom and so she let her husband go. Draco would ask likewise of Atmere's son. *For what? All to stitch patches together for Hammond's kingdom however tenuous the threads? That's not what the Giants taught us.* She crinkled her nose, twisted her neck and spit acid into the cave against Draco's odor.

She slipped from her perch to meet Draco meaning to turn him away. Her only hatchling, perhaps her last, was more than colored for greatness. All highborn dragons have the mark, but Mars had the finest Crest of Neff upon him that she had ever seen or heard told. Only Emerald's crest was as fine, although Emerald was all wrong, and not only in his color. Draco would not resist a dragon such as Mars, sure as gnomes walk on quicksand.

FOUR

Stopping Draco

Twenty yards beyond the foyer's arch, the tunnel bent and widened into a small room before closing again and going onward. The voices of the children playing echoed a sweet song down the tunnel which covered Penelope's movements. She heard Draco's breathing like a wind blowing through the desert. Penelope headed to the small familiar anteroom because she knew it was a favorite spot of Draco's. The ceiling there housed a mica skylight which conveyed soothing warm light even in winter. Draco often paused there and closed his eyes, enjoying this sun-treat. Penelope did not think she was perceived. Her scent was so prevalent on Rookery Top that Draco wouldn't pay it any mind.

Penelope quietly advanced. Finding him as expected, she became a stone. Sunlight illuminated Draco's dark scales. His hues were alit with earthen colors: red ocher, green-black mica and bog-iron-browns flashed along his snout and back. Gold light reflected from the tokens woven into his top mane. He was beautiful, she thought, but these adornments were war badges that bore the scent of blood. Penelope stiffened her neck and entered the anteroom.

"Rookery light is best suited for eggs, not the trappings of war, my Lord," Penelope said in high human."

Draco's slowly opened his eyes. His red hue fell onto her. Penelope felt his warmth but she shivered cold nonetheless.

"You mock me," Draco said in vulgar human speech. "Is this how you treat the broker of your pod? Show respect."

"A broker of spear fodder, Warlord. It is not my place to disrespect you, but it is my place to speak truth."

Draco's stomach rumbled. Black smoke suddenly steamed from his snout. He was not one to suppress the bile that accompanied emotions. This was a bad place to stoke fire. This anteroom was too small for smoke. So Draco spat his acid, careful not to ignite it. The hard rock floor sizzled and fumed.

"They say womenfolk have no sense of war. Yet, you stab me with pointed words. I did not come to fight but to parley. Is it true? One of yours bears the mark?"

"Not 'one' of mine. He is my only. What of his mark? You cannot have him!"

"Don't be a fool. The one egg rule doesn't apply now. I am lacking flyers. Refuse me and you will never lay eggs again, unless of course, you want Emerald. He is a free-actor."

Draco let out a low growl. Blue fire licked his snout.

"Better him than you," she said.

"Emerald?" Draco snorted. "Emerald the prophet! Emerald the fool! He does have a fine mark. Perhaps he's of your liking? My dear brother has good blood. I'll arrange the bonding for you."

Draco's upper lip raised showing one, long, eye-tooth fang, the only part of his mouth not ruined by fire. Draco spoke human remarkable well for one who had spat fire-rocks for so long.

"Matching is not why you've come," she said.

"Then show me what I've come to see." Draco called down the tunnel. "Puffin, Dar, come here. Come, get me out of my flight bags."

Penelope rumbled within, glad the sentry's rush covered her noise. *Hold your smoke. Don't give him satisfaction, offer no sign of anger.* She bit her inner cheek and watched Draco with forced cold, golden eyes as the Brimstones unlatched him. They worked with reverence. Draco's composite saddle and flight bag, common to war dragons, not only housed Draco's effects, but carried the King as well and no other human.

"The scent of Hammond is less on you, I am glad for that," Penelope said.

"He has duties on Vinetop. He trusts his generals."

"He improves with age," Penelope said. "He grows in wisdom and Light unlike you war-dragon. Hammond accepts wisdom. The end of the age is nigh and so he made his truce. The King knows that dragon magic will end in this land and he makes ready. Our magic can only fail in this way. Either we leave here, or we'll die here."

"Foolish female, this land is safer now than it had been for many years. I am duty bound to keep it that way. We aren't going anywhere, not while I am Dragon Lord, not while the King's peace requires us. There will be no slaughter of dragons. Hammond's borders are secure. I do my duty."

"Your duty?! Your duty is to lead us away. Your duty is to save dragons. You must muster the people—."

"Enough! I will not revisit this old argument. Now show me Mars. It is my right."

"The children are playing. Will you see all eleven? The pod mothers are near. I can—."

"I don't need the mothers," Draco said. "I'll inspect the eleven. But, this golden... Let me see how he measures."

"I'll see to it that he measures by the Scrolls of Neff," Penelope said.

"Hold your tongue," Draco said snapping his jaw with a crack, his brown crown feathers thrust tall.

Penelope lowered her head and answered as decorum demanded.

“Yes, Lord, this way.”

Draco dismissed his attendants. Penelope brought Draco into the foyer, but he took her elbow and halted. Side by side, they watched the children at play from the shadows of Sky Top’s edge. The broodings soared like whirlwinds, dodging one another, nipping at each other’s tails. Their wings and tails beat while they belched white and blue smoke with nary a finger of fire.

Penelope felt proud of how well they honored the rules. She did not let her hue radiate her pleasure, not while Draco brooded in the shadows with his red eyes darting after the action.

Does Draco even see what good dragons they are?

During air play, fire breathing was not allowed. Fires breath was only permitted during fire lessons or on the fire-rock spitting range where the males shot stones at every chance. Yet today, with the sun so bright and such a bold blue sky ideal for warming iridescent scales, the yearlings couldn’t help but ignore ground games in favor of flying with fiery joy. So, fly they did with playful smoke, accidental fire, and carefree abandon. The children did not see Draco the Warlord or Penelope the Dragon Matron. Penelope followed them with ears wide as Mars eluded his foil, Praxis. Praxis flew aside Mars and called to him.

“You did not make the promise! I heard you. You swore by your finger, not your fire! You had better keep Penelope’s oath!”

Draco made no sign that he had heard.

Mars rolled in midair and dove between the rows of tall standing stones escaping Praxis. There was only room for one flyer inside the obstacle course. Penelope eyed the exit, and so as Penelope expected, Praxis met Mars as he emerged on the far side of the colonnade and out of ear shot.

******

“Why’d you lie!” Praxis yelled, “Tell, or I’ll bite your tail!”

Mars slowed, still puffing white-brown smoke. Praxis flew closer. Once aside the colonnade, Mars spoke.

“I won’t swear on my fire! I need my fire or I cannot be Warlord! I won’t risk it! A dragon’s got to have fire!”

“How will you keep true? Look what happened to Emerald. You should not withhold a white promise!”

“Warlords need no oaths,” Mars replied and flipped head over back midair.

Praxis nearly crashed into a pillar. She turned hard and scraped her rear leg causing a rain of blue-gold scales. She swooped in pursuit. Mars was not easy to catch. He was the smallest among the boys, but he had oversized wings for his body making him fast and maneuverable. ‘Big wings do not make for big brains,’ Penelope taught. Praxis embraced that lore. Praxis used a series of aerobatic maneuvers she had learned in class while Mars daydreamed. She caught him unaware and tugged his tail.

“Best be careful, Mars Hammertail,” Praxis taunted. “Warlords eat dragons that lie or refuse white oaths.”

“Never mind that. Where’d you get that move?” Mars called.

“In class. It’s a classical warrior’s ploy. Do you ever pay attention?”

"Course I do. When it matters, like when they teach soldiers stuff."

"Well, you missed that one."

"That's handy for battle. Show me."

"You're too small for battles. Only the big browns and reds like Draco go to war! Forget it. Penelope's calling. Race me to the black stone."

FIVE

Draco's Inspection

Penelope called the youth. Draco waited in the shadows while they raced toward the foyer. Draco decided to make his usual first impression. He reared to his hind legs and bounded forward fifteen yards in one jump. Before he could command attention, an especially small dragon dodging a tail bite veered sharply crashing into Draco's breastplate. The child bounced and rolled away, a tangle of wings balled like gold-brown yarn. The little imp stayed where he landed still as a log.

"Dragon down! Hurry, Zandora!" shouted Praxis, "Make way for the healer!"

"Zandora, dragon down! Dragon down! Make way the healer!" chanted the broodlings.

Zandora, a squat bodied country dragon of green and brown, instantly bounded from behind a standing stone. She played rescuer as Mother Wren, the Rookery healer, must have taught them to do.

"Make way the healer!" She also called like the others. "Make way the... the..."

Zadora stopped mid-step before Draco.

"Hey, everybody, look," she yelled. "He didn't hit a wall. He…Oh bothers."

All at once everyone saw a great, dark, foreboding dragon, the likes of which none of them there, except for Penelope, had ever seen before. No war dragons had yet graced the Rookery. Draco stood there, a statue of ruin, doing his best not to release blue smoke.

"Don't eat us," Zandora whimpered, backing away.

The children froze. Some floated down, wings half cocked while others closed their wings and fell like stones. He had hoped that Penelope had continued her famous bedtime stories of evil warlords who ate misbehaving dragon children. From the quivering before him, he determined the answer was yes. Several of the children began to cry.

"Silence!" Draco boomed.

His upper lip curled showing his fang-tooth. The children didn't know of his softer humors yet. Draco was delighted that his smile was misinterpreted as a sneer. His one toothed smile, a sign of good will, magnified the rumors that Warlords have a taste for disobedient broodlings. Draco blew a jet of white smoke with a decidedly blue undertone, rather enjoying himself. He dared not laugh. Draco was intent on keeping the tradition of a strong impression when meeting a new brood for the first time, albeit he never inspected a pod so young before.

"What unfortunate dragon dares fly against me?" he said.

The tiny dragon played dead after he'd hit the ground, as the game goes. Draco's gruff command jerked the young one to his hind legs. Wide golden eyes appeared from under brown wings as Draco glared. The little one cowered into his wing-robe, trembling, but he did not retreat. Draco growled. Yet, this child did not retreat. *He's either brave or a fool.*

"Broodlings," Penelope said in a soft but firm voice fraught with magic so to soothe the hearers. "Line up, quickly, now. Draco has come sooner than usual to marvel at you. He shall not eat you, no, not this day nor ever."

The young dragons scurried making a racket borne of nails scratching floor and tails slapping warm stone. They lined up away from the shadows. The dragon that had lain at his feet arrived first in place but stood furthest away in formation still wrapped inside his wings.

Draco moved into the sun. His mass swallowed the light like a ship's sail catching broad winds. He reflected red tones, although his resting colors, those of the living earth, were normally associated with country dragons. Draco let loose his hue for effect and glowed in the color of spilled blood, a hue of war and power. He reined in the shine before it got too bright. There is a fine line between making an impression and scaring them witless. The children could not show this much light so early. The magic of one's hue grows with age.

Draco quelled his display and paced the line on four limbs. He traveled to and fro several times before finally stopping at the right end of the line at the largest broodling.

"This one's a fine young specimen, a warrior in the making," Draco said. "Good colors, perhaps a front runner."

"He is Bullock, my Lord," Penelope said. "One of Isis' clutch."

Isis the agitator, her ears serve me well.

Draco clasped the youngling's wings and spread them to better show the youth's brown-green body. The child's breast inflated full upon Draco's assessment until Draco vented unhappy black smoke.

"However, he's a bit short-winged, less good for speed and agility."

Draco moved to the next student, an average-sized youth who was green with gold-tipped scales. Draco shook his head rattling his tokens.

"What of this one?" Draco asked.

"He is one of Becka's children; she is from hill country," Penelope said her voice tight. "He is Nedell."

"Hill country, eh? Too bad. Hill dragons aren't much for wing fighting."

Nedell's breast deflated, his green-gray scaled shoulders slumped and his eyes fell to the floor. Draco moved on. Penelope's gullet gurgled with acid as he passed by her. Penelope hated this 'demoralizing' ritual as she called it. Draco knew differently. His words would inspire the children. Nedell will become a fine flyer, if only to prove the Great Warlord wrong. Draco stopped and scratched his chin.

"A rare beauty this one… A golden-blue and come of a lowborn's egg?"

Penelope nodded.

"How unusual. How wonderful. I'll match her with my finest warrior when she's of age," Draco said. "Your name is?"

"Praxis, Lord." Praxis's white crown feathers stood and rippled pink. Her hue, although muted, shown forth more gold than blue.

"See to it that you don't show your emotions at court. Quell your feathers!" Draco demanded. "You are bound for court."

Praxis's feathers instantly lay down. Draco went to each young dragon, poking and prodding, making complaints and judgments. "This one will be a messenger. Yes, fine swift wings, but he's a bit too plump…This one's a healer. She has her mother's colors, but such big hands…This one has the eyes of a sentry, too bad his color is so green."

Draco marked the good, the bad, and most importantly the possibilities, knowing well that each dragon would chase whatever dreams Draco sowed. However much Penelope disdained Draco's 'undermining games,' the game would go on for as long as Draco was in charge. Penelope's concern was always the same. 'Your compliments or criticisms make war games more important than study. That is no way to inspire young hearts,' Penelope had once said. No doubt, she thought as much now as she stood chewing her cheek. Draco took his time and inspected each child as if they were perspective War Camp cadets, however premature this exercise was.

By the time he finally got to the careless little flyer that toppled into him upon his arrival, Draco heard that Penelope's gullet was nearly boiling over. To Draco's surprise, the little one threw open his wings and thrust out his breast displaying the Mark of Neff. The child's crown feathers stood rippling golden pride. The mark was there. This one's scales were gold, but he was not what Draco expected.

This one is Penelope's precious Golden, Mars?

The deep rumbling laughter let loose with a mirth he seldom expressed unless for raucous courtly sarcasms. He slapped his thigh and billowed blue smoke.

"What is so funny?" Penelope asked.

"He's a runt! The Great Golden? What vanity my fool's dreams were! Where is the great warrior of lore, a large and strong dragon of exceptional size and power? I am waiting for he who will take my place. My wait is not over. Gold and marked well this one is, yet he will not do, no, not at all."

"So that is what you seek," Penelope said. "Even you hope for the prophecy however much your hope is skewed."

He did not laugh at Mars, no. Draco laughed at the joke he played on himself. *In my rejection, let Penelope's hope take root. She can have her priest.*

"This bearer of our sacred symbol is only half of a dragon! Did he paint it gold as Emerald did? Mark my words he will keep company with Emerald one day!"

The breath Penelope had held so long erupted into a jet of hot, black smoke. Draco had never seen her countenance change so fast. His crown flayed. He quickly pondered. *Penelope is the master of intrigues. What is her game?* She was clearly out-of-sorts.

"Emerald doesn't have half Mars's ability…" Penelope snapped her mouth shut.

She thinks the runt able. I must watch him closely.

"Emerald had size, intelligence and the mark," Draco said. "He'd have been here in my stead if he made natural fire and was less likened to conniving ways. No dragon is perfect. This little golden at least makes fire. He has potential, I see, if not proper size. Work hard, boy, and you may succeed me."

Draco rumbled. He had had enough. It was time for a bite. He walked across the game grounds toward the far tunnels. He heard the brood exploded with chatter as he entered the kitchen tunnel. He looked over his shoulder once from the dark. The children were in disarray. Some cried. Others latched onto Penelope. Mars held his place.

There is something about that boy…

******

Penelope breathed silver-smoked relief. Before Draco had traveled twenty feet down the passage, the broodings fell out, all crying or near tears. With Draco gone, she could heal some of the damage. Her crown feathers glowed as she set about soothing her charges with hugs and soft words. Her feathers dulled when she spied Mars. He visibly swallowed his bile while biting his inner cheek warding off tears, a trick he learned from her. Mars stayed at attention until Draco's footfalls faded into the mountain.

"He's gone," Lolandra said with a tear dripping from her snout. "Hey, Mars! You going to stand there all day?"

"Nothing is going to make me cry, not any smelly Warlord! I will not be defeated!" Mars cried. "I will become the best of all dragons."

Mars lifted his feathers higher, puffed out his breast and stretched and straightened his neck. The brood's attention fell on him. The boys snickered with hot breath.

"You'll never measure up," Bullock said.

"Already I've gained an inch," Mars retorted.

"Mars, you've made me proud in many ways," Penelope said. "The Light doesn't want you for war, no matter how much you desire it. There are higher callings."

"I'll show, Draco! I can do anything!" Mars said. "He will eat my scales!"

Mars blasted into the air. The others took after him. In seconds, a game of tail-tag ensued leaving Penelope to her thoughts.

No dragon achieved so high as Draco without a myriad of intellectual and physical skills. So, Penelope resolved to teach Mars the greater skills of wisdom, foremost the folly of human wars to offset Draco's passions. *Mars is more than his size. He'll have a place in war should Draco ever learn of my child's passion.*

Penelope mounted the teaching rock as the dinner bell rang. The brood ran toward the eatery tunnel. Penelope remained on her perch, not thinking of food but of ways to spread rumors. She would lead the court to believe that Mars was clumsy and stupid, qualities Draco despised. It would be difficult. Mars was neither and her pride in him was great. Visions of the fire in Mars's golden eyes filled her soul. He had proven himself the bravest of the brood, though smallest.

Wren, the dragon who cared for the children's health, and Isno, the human teacher, emerged from a nearby side tunnel. Wren was docile and respected Penelope's place. Isno's three hundred years, an age granted her by living so long among dragons' magic was obstinate toward the pod mothers and respected no dragon overtly except Draco.

Isno's grumblings behind Penelope's back were famous. Penelope marveled at how one so thin and frail could be so hard.

"Wren, please check on the children. They're at meal," Penelope requested. "They've gotten out of wing with Draco afoot."

Wren obeyed. Isno gathered her fine white hair, knotted it, and put it behind her to avoid loose fire.

"You're not telling more of them unholy stories, are you?" Isno said. "End of the age, bah, horse dung! Filling their heads with such nonsense, setting their minds on false hope. Draco won't tolerate it. The Kingdom's salvation rides in Draco's saddle."

Draco decreed that broodlings should not know the greater legends. Draco insisted on tales of war and bravery. He favored the 'realities of life,' Isno's specialty. Even at court Draco cringed at entertainment lore. While the hearers laughed, Draco brooded.

"That is not my perspective," Penelope said. Penelope's crown rippled indigent. She reared over Isno, who did not flinch. "Draco's ways will destroy us all. Mark my words. The tales of Neff are not to be ignored! Dragons must leave this place and soon."

Isno laughed, shrill and pointed. "Don't be a fool, Matron. There will be no Golden Savior. There is no light in such dark times. There is no better land than this. Draco and Hammond will protect our kin. Best you put your faith in them! That mark Mars bears is no omen. It's nothing but fool's fodder."

"I am no fool," Penelope retorted. "The Scrolls speak truth."

"That's your interpretation, Matron, and you are entitled to believe it. But, telling it to the children is treason. Be careful, Penelope. Draco has punished greater dragons than you for less."

Penelope loosened a jet of red flame into the sky. She jumped from the rock, over Isno's head and set out for where Wren would gather the brood for bedtime stories.

If teaching the children truth be treason, count me a renegade.

SIX

The Wizard and the King

Hammond entered the War Room from the residence door. Merilbe was close behind and made no indication of his presence by way of sound except for the chatter of the crow that sat upon his shoulder pruning its feathers. Hammond stopped short at the Dragon Wing Table. Merilbe glided around him like a down feather on rising air.

"I am grateful for your council," Hammond said. "Yet I shall never get accustomed to your ghostly ways."

Hammond placed a loving hand on the table. It rocked like a boat on a windy lake. Hammond whispered the calming incantation that Merilbe had taught him. The dragon wings that gave the table motion ceased straining against their tethers. So by Hammond's touch, the table rested.

"What disturbs them?" Hammond asked about the wings.

"It's a sign of the end age," Merilbe said, smoothing his beard. The crow turned its star-marked head toward the table. "They will fly again and join the Dragon Constellation. They sense the time draws nigh."

"Or is it that the wings feel my fears?" Hammond asked. "They know my quandaries. One of which is due to arrive today. Are you sure inviting the Green Wizard was expedient?"

"He is not so much a wizard as an inventor," Merilbe answered. "Even so, useful or not, or how much of his magic is earned, stolen or found matters little. You must gather the dragons together, even him. I do not know exactly how or when the age will end, but it is better not to have him loose in the world. Keep him under your thumb. He could do us much harm."

I have no time for it. Hammond is well-suited for this task.

"Of course," Hammond said. "Keep your friends near and your agitators nearer still. He is tricky, but I'll handle him. I'll use his mischief against him. He is the smallest of my worries."

Eyes wide oh King. Emerald is no easy mark. Careful or he'll become your biggest worry.

Hammond paced to and fro before the textile oracle, one hand behind his back, the other hand scratching his trim gray bearded chin. His riding boot heels clicked on the stone floor. The dragon-winged table rocked with each clack-clop.

"What of the Goldens? What part will they play?" the King asked.

"The scrolls are ambiguous: Many possible outcomes. I cannot say. The clouds of change are unexpectedly dark. The scrolls never mentioned two, and the boy is… shall I say somewhat underpowered? We cannot rely on the legends for details other than to say the scrolls rightfully predicted the Golden's hatching as the dragon-stars alignment comes full. Those predictions prove right. But something is askew. The constellation is not finished yet. We must prepare for a great fall."

Hammond returned to pacing. Merilbe hovered and allowed his black robes to flow on the breeze. Hammond finally stopped near the inlayed badge on the floor called Starstep. The King raised a hand to the Tapestry.

"I've had one hundred and thirty years of good counsel from it," Hammond said of the textile oracle, "but no longer, not since my wife died. I was full of hope then. So many ravens attended my daughter's birth."

I must keep the King's hope high.

"Omens said hers was a blessed birth," Merilbe said. "Your queen was the purest of all past king's wives. Your daughter will follow in the same vein."

"No ravens came to see Rogsin born. That child is cursed," Hammond said. "Who will inherit my kingdom? The Lords of estates? None are worthy. None! The boy? Rogsin is least worthy of all. Now in theses our waning days, the Tapestry of Neff speaks nothing but riddles."

No ravens at his birth, now there is a puzzle. There is something in it. Ravens won't speak of the times, but their actions do.

Hammond lowered his hand and resumed his pacing. Merilbe waited in silence.

"This sacred relic, made by dragon and human weavers, guided worthy kings and beguiled the pretentious for thousands of years. My line has always read its truths well. I honor the Light in my heart and deeds. It never failed me in all my years. But now, every year, it tells less and less. Am I too old and it fades with me?"

"People allied with dragons live long," Merilbe said. "The longest a king has lived is one hundred and sixty years, and the Tapestry's power did not waver."

"I will reach that age in ten years." Hammond said. "I need a rightful heir. A new king will revive the Tapestry's magic. I'll ask it to show me a wife while it still has power."

"Only questions concerning the kingdom will be answered," The Wizard said. "Common magic such as love it will not provide."

"Its magic wanes," Hammond said. "I have no heir except Onyx, last blessed of my line with her raven-attended birth but a girl, a fragile girl."

Do not discount her. Her mother's blood was as stout as your own.

Hammond knelt upon the Starstep and raised his hands. Looking to the Tapestry, he spoke.

"Show me my wife!"

The images on Tapestry swirled. *Nothing recognizable.* Hammond held his hands skyward until his arms shook with fatigue. Having no answer, the King rose and resumed pacing.

"Only the blessed tame swirling images," Hammond said. "What sin have I done?"

"I suspect it is not your sin. The Tapestry tries to speak. All is not lost," Merilbe said. "It shows well enough for mundane concerns. A glimpse is enough. It has not abandoned you."

"Yet, it gives me so little. Nothing of importance," Hammond said with bitterness.

"Even so," Merilbe said, "We need not the Tapestry. We have resources, especially for war: spies, dragon sentries, and merchants trading news along with wares. Gnomes are easily hired. Messengers come from beyond the Outlands."

"Beware the garden gnome. Beware the gnome's path," the old crow squawked.

Merilbe quieted the crow by placing his hand over its eyes. *The King should not have hired gnomes to guard the cliffs.*

"I do not need predictions for crops," the King said. "Common lore tells me plenty. I know how the land fares, but how will I make ready for the end time without great visions?"

Hammond stopped. Standing near the Starstep, he grasped Merilbe's thin shoulders with bear-paw hands.

"What will befall the kingdom? You say yourself that the Age of Dragons will soon pass. What of men? How shall we live without dragons? How shall I keep my oaths? It is for me to keep the lands of Neff whole. Will it become undone?"

"No one in my five thousand years had received such clear counsel or has made such lasting peace as you, my Lord. Be glad. You are apt for the task. Your people will go on."

Hammond released his Wizard and paced faster. The table jostled frantically. Hammond ignored it. Merilbe sent his crow to soothe it with bird's whispers.

"Now, in this hour of endings, it gives me no war counsel," the King said.

"That may not be so. Recall your last vision. What did you see?"

"Strange sights. Dragons flocked like birds, some with riders while others flew with over packed flight-bags. Their manes were cut close to their necks. No breastplates or rock-bags. No armored riders and no Draco. They flew toward the Steppes. Dragons don't fly there."

Hammond saw the departure. There is no comfort in that for him.

"What does such evil mean?" Hammond asked the Tapestry.

"It does not speak evil," Merilbe chastised. "It gives a Lighted path: Always a way to peace. Sometimes a hard, bloody road, but nonetheless, it bespeaks the Light."

"Darkness overcomes it," Hammond said. "The greater Light cannot shine."

"I have hope," Merilbe said. "Only the blasphemy of an unholy touch may render it useless. We have time to make ready before the end. I will seek the answer and overturn this spell against you."

"So be it," Hammond said. "Seek as only a wizard can. I will fight bad tidings my own way. I'll even use Emerald, if I can. Evil knows evil, they say."

Hammond spun on his heel and walked quickly away. Merilbe glided after him.

SEVEN

Rogsin Invades the War Room

Eight-year-old Rogsin, son of Hammond the Great, pressed his ear against the garden door and heard the heavy foot steps of his father fade. Everyone says that the year of Rogsin's birth overflowed with good luck, but it was whispered to be good luck for dragons and not for Rogsin. It was the same year Mars the Golden hatched. Golden dragons are lucky indeed, but he had his share of luck, too. Rogsin tried the King's Garden door and his luck prevailed once more. The door was unlocked.

Rogsin peered into the War Room, his heart beating like humming bird wings. He had visited here once before. Father brought him, as none may enter without the King's leave. Today, Rogsin entered anyway. There was much for him to learn.

His eyes shot right and left. He surveyed the room with baited breath. The ancient suits of armor below the high glassless windows did not stir. Each ghost knight stood with sword, shield, dagger and a dragon-gold tipped pike, all wrought by uncommonly fine craftsmanship. Between each suit burned torches mounted on stone pilasters. The pillars and walls also hosted shields hung with crossed swords, axes, long-knives or maces in accordance with the traditions of the giver's homeland. These shields and weapons came from different estates or outland chiefdoms, each recently presented to Hammond as a token of truce.

Yet another sign of Father's folly. He was a fool to accept them.

Golden dragons' breast plates hung on sliver chains behind the King's table at the head of the room. 'All these relics,' Father said, 'belonged to long dead kings and dragon lords. These devices were bequeathed to Vinetop and set in place to guard the Tapestry of Neff.'

Satisfied no living guard was about, Rogsin released his breath. The nearest suit had what he came for, a souvenir. A small dragon-gold knife was tucked into the calf-guard of the suit nearest the garden door. He had seen it when Father told him the lore of each knight's gifts. Father named every weapon and spoke its glories, but father did not name the small dagger. Barely a glimmer of it showed. *He must not know of it,* Rogsin thought at the time, as he marked it in his mind.

'Each artifact must remain in its place so long as the Tapestry lives. We honor the fallen that died protecting it and so the Tapestry gives counsel to its protectors,' Father had said.

'I wish a gold blade of my own,' Rogsin proclaimed that day but Father said he was not yet proven worthy. 'Only the fittest fighters are permitted a rare dragon-gold blade,' Father said. Rogsin decided his own worthiness and returned to the War Room to fulfill his desire. He fingered the handle of the little dagger. It was loose in the boot sheath. Rogsin withdrew his prize and shoved it into his belt's leather pouch with nary a mouse-sound.

Bad enough that Rogsin trespassed in the King's Garden, but worse punishment awaited him if anyone found him in the War Room without a chaperone. *I should go, but first a quick look!* It was hard to see much from the door so he stepped over the raised threshold and slid sideways into the shadows. An idea stuck him.

I'm in! Take advantage! Find out Father's secrets.

Rogsin moved deeper into the room, carefully avoiding the light from the door or wherever the archer's windows cast sun-slivers. He studied the War Room. Its weapons bespoke power. *All this will be mine and 'Iron is power,' as the dwarves say.* Rogsin decided to see his future wealth, too. *By right of my inheritance, the Tapestry must show me what I ask.*

For his sneaking, Rogsin wore soft leather slippers perfect for light footfalls. Any noise would startle the Dragon Wing Table and if the table moved too much, the candelabra could well crash to the floor. Guards would investigate the racket. Rogsin slinked to the center of the War Room quiet as a gnome. He stood on Starstep, the best place to see the Tapestry. Father said not to look at it directly, for reverence sake, look from the out to the in. So Rogsin first searched the Tapestry's borders. The textile hung from thick wooden poles fixed on stone pilasters with iron brackets, strung with red ropes ending with tassels. It protruded several feet forward of the infill wall and ran thirty feet top to bottom and thirty feet side-to-side leaving only a sliver of shadow between the wall-hanging and the floor.

R*oom enough for me.*

Within the great wall hanging, Rogsin looked next to the legendary creatures, kings and dragons stitched within its twelve sections. Rogsin looked inward and the images whirled wherever the sunlight struck it. The figures looked at him as if they were alive. 'The unlearned are unworthy and go mad if they ponder it too long,' Merilbe once advised him. Rogsin turned away afraid. Fancy embroidery bordered each section with geometric patterns of every color although blues and reds dominated the weave. Each section held a familiar legend, stories of heroes and evil beings. The Garden of Neff showed greenly lush at the Tapestry's center where unicorns, dragons and Inowise shamans danced under the White Raven.

But Rogsin was not satisfied. He looked more closely and everywhere within the weave he spied golden threads woven together with common threads.

"Dragon's gold," Rogsin whispered. "So that's how it works."

The story of how the giants built the seat of Vinetop was Rogsin's favorite story. Now, he saw it pictured in the Tapestry; a tale that unfolded before Vinetop became a fortress. The mighty chair remained, but it now formed a section of Hammond's Keep. The seat's stone planking served as the roof for the better part of the Great Hall. The front chair legs guarded public entries. The rear hollow legs became citadel towers. The royal residence was built against the chair's back.

When Rogsin looked from his bedroom window, he saw the stone carved rattan which the giants had made, that same pattern he recognized in the Tapestry's borders. A section of the giant's seat below his room was now the Queen's Garden, but with no queen to tend it, it grew wild.

Mother died the day I was born. The dragons born that year were also under an unlucky number-eleven is a bad omen. Yet eleven proved lucky for dragons; two Goldens born. Dragons' bad luck had gone somewhere, that's what killed her, they sent it to Vineland. Curse the dragons!

Rogsin turned from the Giants and again visited the center of the Tapestry depicting the Garden of Neff. The White Raven, bearing a golden wreath in each talon, hovered above the heads of a Golden dragon and a gray-haired Inowise. Each figure reached for the gifts. The dragon's mane was cut off, no braids or tokens as is the custom. The primitive man bore no armor, no weapons, only a vine-woven loincloth and a crown of green leaves.

How strange. How did they kill the bird and take its gold?

The center swirled. Fearful, Rogsin tried to look away but could not! He dropped to his knees upon the Starstep, his eyes fixed on the White Raven. A vision took him all at once.

Men were fighting on foot, a golden dragon was shot from the air, a pale and gaunt woman with long black hair was in labor and she had Rogsin's own dark eyes. A little girl, Rogsin thought his sister, stood by the woman's bedside. Onyx was crying and her long black hair was in disarray like a brier patch.

Onyx was no more than three years old. Her younger face was plump unlike her later thin features. The woman looked with kindly eyes at Onyx, smiled, pushed a tangle of Onyx's hair away from her cheek and said, "My life now ends dear one. Do not be afraid. The King has naught any legitimate male heirs. You must be queen."

Next, Rogsin saw an old man, weaponless. He soon recognized himself in the man's coal black eyes. A flash of gold fire engulfed him. A golden dragon blotted the sun. Dragon fire rained. The White Raven sat upon the golden dragon as it flew. Rogsin spied a funeral. A man of the Steppes dressed in deer hide leggings and hemp shirt stood over the pier, the final resting place of a knight Rogsin didn't know but the man's face was in ruin. The knight's bloody armor was raked by the claws of dragon's feet. The foreigner said, "So ends the dragon slayer, his enemies victorious!" The man stabbed the ground over and over with a rusted long-sword. Each stab felt as if it pierced Rogsin's own living heart. "His pursuits paid death!"

"Curse the gold dragon, curse them all!" Rogsin cried.

A white light beam shot from the Tapestry of Neff and struck him like a blunt lance. Rogsin fell backward, hitting his head on the polished blue-rock floor. He bit his tongue and rolled over, spitting, and splattered the Starstep icon with his blood. The dragon carved within the floor's star looked right at him. He spat again. His blood spattered the white limestone dragon but as soon as it landed, his blood gathered together and seeped away like a snake. Rogsin spit again. No matter how much he tried, his blood did not stain the carved white dragon.

"No dragon will best me, no! No dragon will see me to my grave!"

Rogsin rose to his knees outside the carving and dabbed blood from his mouth, rubbing it upon the carved dragon.

"By my blood, no dragon will ever rule over me."

The white stone turned black. Foot steps echoed from the King's passage, a hall leading to the royal residence. The door was behind the King's half-round wing table. Only the King took that way. Rogsin rolled under the woven oracle and into its shadow where he lay with his stomach on the floor. He was between pilasters. He pressed as deep into darkness as he could. His face was to the cold stone but Rogsin saw little beyond the veil. The King's footsteps became sharper until his leather boots stood upon Starstep. The King rocked on his heels as he often did stroking his short beard while in thought. The King addressed the Tapestry.

"Your power's fading was long ordained yet not with such discombobulating! Why do you fail me so?"

There was a flurry of wings. The ravens on the upper sill must have fled. One bird remained, responding in bird-speak.

"Ah, Merilbe, right on time, come give me counsel," Hammond said. "What have you found?"

There was a flash of light and when Rogsin could see again, Merilbe's sandaled feet were beside the King's.

"I have traveled far and read deep. I've learned much in these last nine years, dear King. The marvels of the Rookery Library! I've read books written in lost scripts that even dragon scholars cannot read. I have discerned much. I have stories to tell. Let me begin..."

How can that be? Rogsin asked himself. *Merilbe is here more than away.*

"Yes, yes," the King said. "Share your complex tales at court, but now I desire simple answers. I will hear of your puzzle-fitting later. What do you conclude from your study?"

"It is as Penelope says; she reads the scrolls correctly; this age will soon end. My order has not seen the planets align so in twenty-six thousand years."

"Yes, yes, I know that, but what of this current faltering of omens? I cannot change the stars but I will usher this kingdom into the future whole and safe if I can. For that, I must know what spell clouds my vision and how to proceed, omens or not."

Hammond's stance was now wide. He planted his feet as if ramming a pike into a dummy on the practice field. Rogsin saw no sign of Merilbe's emotions from this low vantage.

"Tis the seductions spell; that same spell which your brother cast unto your wife—."

"I won't hear of it again!" King Hammond interrupted. "If there was foul magic afoot, that spell died when I killed my wife's rapist."

"You must hear me! The spell is real and it lives on, and not just in your bastard son. There is more."

I have heard the rumors before. I'm no bastard, I'm the rightful prodigy. By split blood or by heritage I will be King. None can stop me.

The King dropped to his knees upon Starstep, never had Rogsin seen the King humble himself. A tear fell to the floor, or a drop of sweat, which he could not be certain.

"Tell me Wizard. I will hear you," Hammond said with a voice uncharacteristically contrite.

"I've learned the nature of the spell and it proves true in Rogsin. His intelligence and ambitions are unnatural. As long as he lives, clouds will obscure the light of prophecy. And you had a part in it. When you killed the spell-caster, in anger, you sealed his magic."

"What should I have done?" the King said sadly. "Mordune was a traitor."

"Had he lived, we may have found his partner and undone this travesty. This spell is two-fold, a double spell, one side light, and the other dark. It took two to make it. But Mordune's accomplice I cannot find. No scent of him rides the wind. He is dead, gone or not human."

The King pressed up from his knees and paced.

"There is no hope of Lighted counsel? No doubt Mordune's accomplice is as evil as he."

"Not so, my King," Merilbe scuffed his foot on the Starstep. "How odd... This magic required that at least one of the seed-sewers possessed a measure of good in his heart. In any event, because Rogsin was born, so too was his counterpart: Balance is the way of this sort of magic. Where and who that child is, dragon or human, we may never know."

"Find that child, and you solve our puzzle," Hammond said.

"Quite so, King. If the father is found I can undo this spell and if the perpetrator cooperates, all the better. He need only speak the truth to remove the curse. Then, you will have your oracle restored. Meanwhile, it tries to speak. Good counsel will break through dark clouds. Keep watching and seek small omens. When the age turns, it will speak no more."

"How long?" Hammond asked.

"That is hidden. Ten perhaps fifteen years."

"We have work to do, my friend," the King said.

Hammond turned and walked briskly toward the Great Hall, his heels clacking a military cadence. The slap of Merilbe's sandals followed. Once Rogsin heard the War Room's door latch, he rolled from behind the Tapestry and ran for the garden door. Once closed, he sat with his back to the door, breathing shallow, ears cocked. The garden was hemmed in on three sides with high walls, the fourth side a sheer drop. Three feet below the cliff's edge was a narrow shelf, a gnome path which wrapped around the mountain, just wide enough for a fleet-footed child. Rogsin heard the thunder of his father's footfalls again and so slipped over the cliff's edge thus escaping.

EIGHT

Rogsin and the Gnome

Rogsin hid on the gnome's path until his curiosity spurned him to act. He climbed over the edge and pressed his ear to the oaken door of the War Room. The King and his ministers were crossing the hall. No doubt Hammond made for his office with his scribes. Rogsin deciphered little of the talk except one line that the King said before leaving earshot.

"I have no rightful heir!" spoke the King. "Onyx is last in my line…"

Rogsin pushed away from the door. In the distance, a complement of armed dragon riders flew in formation. Their golden implements gleaming in the sun hurt his eyes. He brushed his black hair in front of his eyes to guard against glare. Once the glare abated as the riders turned, Rogsin picked up a stone and hurled it toward the distant dragons.

"Death to you all!"

Rogsin then sat upon a low, stone stool. Head in hands, he felt crusted blood on the back of his scalp; he had hurt more than his tongue when the Star Step ejected him. Rogsin never allowed himself to cry. Not even the school master's switch moved him. Kings don't cry, he often told his befuddled teachers. But now, alone, he let his tears fall.

"I will be king. I will. I'll fix him. I'll fix Onyx, too!"

Rogsin beat his fist on the rock. A small but deep voice laughed. Rogsin whipped his head in every direction, wild-eyed, fearing he was had. None were allowed here except the King or his blessed gardener. No one was near. He was out of view of the guards on the walls above. He realized the voice of a gnome was what assaulted his pride.

"Show your self," Rogsin demanded. "You have no business here."

"My business here is none of your business," was its answer. "What's more, I should kill you for trespassing."

"I am the King's son, I've a right."

"Hammond the Great would say otherwise."

Rogsin jumped to his feet and grabbed a large stone. He rushed from path to path, from vegetable patch to herb plot pushing over every stalk.

"I'll crush you!"

"Kill me if you can," a jovial voice replied.

The voice taunted him as he ran from place to place. His pursuit yielded nothing but small foot prints and surprised toads. Rogsin's anger grew with every false ambush, yet all Rogsin managed to kill was the parsley he trampled. Rogsin finally plopped exhausted onto the ground. A little man leaped over his head and landed on the stoop where Rogsin had sat earlier.

"I have you," Rogsin said coming onto his knees while raising the rock to strike.

The gnome's calm demeanor startled Rogsin and he hesitated. He had never seen a gnome before. Few people do. The creature was as tall as his knee but as thick as a stout club. He wore a long white beard tucked into a leather waste belt, pointed green hat, red shirt and brown knickers with no shoes. He looked much like a dwarf but unlike dwarves, his feet and hands were far too big for his body.

"No, I have you," the stranger said.

In a flash, the gnome pulled a machine from over his back, a bow mounted to a stock. The gnome let fly a bolt. The bolt hit Rogsin's rock with such force that the rock flew away as if thrown by a sling. While Rogsin stood blinking, the archer reloaded faster than any long bowman ever could. Lore said that gnomes fought ferociously with clever devices, engines that could kill a person ten times their size. Rogsin had not believed that lore until now.

Rogsin, realizing the danger, resisted the urge to wet his linen breaches. He squeezed his knees together like a determined toddler. The small man lowered his weapon and loosed a laugh. He winked his eye and slung the device over his back.

"By blue Dragons teeth, that was good sport! I'll not kill you. As we gnomes say, 'Good games beget mercy.' Now be gone. I'm here by the King's leave, as long as his money holds, that is. I take it you are the one who's often trodden my route uninvited?"

"By that you mean the ledge below, yes I've traveled that way," Rogsin said, steadying his voice to show no more fear.

"A hard one you are," the gnome said. "I like that, I do, aye. That path is not easy, even for me. So I can't have it no more. Your weight weakens the trail. You must not come that way again."

"How will I go? I can't go by way of the War Room."

The gnome's brow furrowed. He dropped upon the stoop, his legs dangling over the edge. He scratched his cheeks and pushed back his cap showing a bald head and bushy eye brows.

"Suppose not," the gnome said. "Take my path once more. Next time you come my snares will save me a bolt. Yet, if I show you another way, a secret way, will you visit me? I could use some company, a good story, sweet foods and wine from time to time."

"You are sneaky," Rogsin said, "Why not help yourself? The lauder is vast and you are small."

"I'm not invited. It's in the agreement. We gnomes abide our contracts, 'til a better one comes along," he said with a wink. "Nor do we go quietly on carved stone. Earthly places we travel. Nothing inside is natural, most unappealing. Make me a deal. Think on it a moment."

The gnome reached into his waist and brought out a long, stemmed pipe, filled the tiny bowl, and snapped his finger to flame. The gnome puffed with no concern. Rogsin thought to attack, but then recalled the gnome's quickness. *No, that's no good. I may need him. Father hired him, so how may I trust he'll not tell? If I support him, I'll learn why Father keeps him although gnomes under contracts never tell their terms. Good wine will loosen his tongue.*

"I'll do it," Rogsin said. "I'll bring you what you ask, every tenth day until I am 18 years, but you must show me all the hidden ways."

"Every fourth day," the gnome said.

"Every seventh day," Rogsin said.

"Done," the gnome said. "I will forgive an occasional lapse, as when you travel by the King's bidding, but if you cross me, I'll shoot your eye out."

Rogsin extended his hand, the gnome did the same and so Rogsin took his first step against the King. Rogsin puffed up his chest with a proud, and to his mind, a justified heart.

NINE

The Outcast's Invitation

Emerald flew an indirect route from his lair in the Forbidden Mountains and approached Vineland from the southeast. The easy way went far too near Rookery Top. Emerald was forced to flap, there were no favorable winds. It was hard labor for one who seldom flew, but Emerald was not unhappy. Hammond's invitation was a keyhole to pick Hammond's lock, an opportunity Emerald could not resist.

I'll gain the King's favor, Emerald thought as he flew. *I'll pit him against Draco and strike a path to my rightful place as most honored dragon. Let Draco languish in the Outlands eating roots and scratching for trade gems. My mind is mightier than any Warlord's flame or fortitude!* Emerald's tired wings felt lighter on this wind of possibilities.

Emerald spied Hammond's southern stronghold. On a clear day, Rookery Top was visible from the King's Keep at Vineland Emerald recalled. Vinetop was situated twenty five miles northeast of the badlands he just flew over. He crossed Hammond's boarder when Rock Point passed under him. The island of sunlit rocks called Rock Point floating above the swap mists now below him and it looked inviting. Basking in the sun proved a fine temptation for any dragon, but Rock Point was deadly. Emerald flapped harder.

Hammond's fort was not the strongest in the land but it was the most visited and therefore most important. Hammond's ancestral home lay among the fertile hills and dales of Southern Vineland where every crop grew abundantly except wheat. This was a place of vegetables, grapes and fruits. Vineland was famous for its wine and preserves put-up in fancy ceramics. The King acquired great wealth and also earned the jealousy of lesser Lords.

Oh I know this kingdom. Whoever controls Vinetop controls the money. The King will give me a great share before I'm done.

The richness of cauldrons cooking and smoke houses savored the air and caused the wizard dragon's gullet to cry. Gaiety also rode on the wind. Peasant farmers sang as they toiled. Children played. String music wafted from the town's inns. *Hammond is a fool. His bounty should build armies not prosperity for common folk.*

"They deserve nothing!" Emerald cried.

Emerald would have spit fire, but born without the sparking-gland, all he could do was spit the black acid that fueled a healthy dragon's fire. Emerald contained his angst. Anger made more acid, which in turn digested food faster, and that would burn flight reserves sooner. Emerald had miles to go. He tuned his mind to scheming, a pleasure of which he never tired.

I must get close. Short puppet strings work best. Hammond's want isn't conquest. What will entice him? Rather than take the lands about him, the fool befriends his neighbors. He's built wider trade but not a wider kingdom. Outlanders and robbers from every quarter harass his borders. Hammond will not expand. He honors the Giants' decree, but he still must fight. He'll want war engines.

"How long will you last, oh King," Emerald asked the wind. "Outlanders all around and your people increase yearly. How long can you honor the Border Mandate?"

Emerald's spies told much. While black magic and dark omens told what else. Emerald looked long and deep for ways to unseat his brother Draco. Emerald knew more of the courts than any outcast should. Hammond's twelve counties were not all loyal by preference. Hammond and Draco went to their aid when called, true, but those Lords were no friends of Hammond.

When city-states warred among themselves, Emerald secretly supported each side. *And now I'm invited to meet with Hammond?* Emerald was glad that he reserved his best tricks for this day.

Hammond's protection cost the Lords more than a share of wealth. The gazes of Penelope's ambassadors, dragon extensions of Hammond's eyes, were upon them. Hammond shared his vineyards and forges, but not his best armaments or wines. *Be careful. Hammond is soft-hearted, not stupid.* Hammond's Court of Lords at Vinetop welcomed the Twelve Estates, but the Lords who embraced dragons in their courts were most esteemed. *Who will embrace me? This will be fun.*

Emerald licked the bugs from his teeth and swallowed. He had needed a meal on the wing. For once the stars were shining his way. He was close now. He beat his tail and climbed. Tradition had dragons circle high above the palace. The messenger had told him to look for the green flags sent up by the Captain of the Guards. The Captain himself provided the signals and directed incoming dragons.

Emerald circled Vinetop, a place far older than humans or dragons, a gray rock mesa surrounded by rolling green pastures and farms. The guards green flag went up. Emerald banked wide over the town.

Hundreds of humans and dozens of dragons lived below the Keep. A wide road came straight through the town's center with stone-built shops, homes and inns on either side. Lesser roads radiated from Main Street, further away were foot paths going to poorer homes of logs and earthen tuft. Dwellings of stone or mud-brick were at the crossroads. Merchants, Emerald thought. Clay tile roofs for the richest homes, thatch or sod for the poorer. Every home had a garden and livestock. The town proper was surrounded by a wet moat and earthworks. Beyond the town were fields, creeks and orchards stretching into the distance until stopping at thick forests.

A train of brightly-dressed people and dragons led by men carrying standards on long poles marched up the Keep's only ground approach, a mile-long earthen ramp from ground level to the west side cliff edge. *I'm not the only guest.* Emerald glided in and touched down lightly.

"Most dragons' that land here shake the timbers," the guard said. "This is Warrior's Gate, how is it your landing is so light?"

"Warriors eat better than I," Emerald said.

The guard, suddenly recognizing Emerald, clutched his sword hilt.

My reputation precedes me.

"My good man," Emerald said pulling a parchment from his neck bag and handed over the invitation, "I've flown long. I'm starving, I require refreshments. Where is your master's famous table?"

A well-muscled older man sporting a flowing blond mustache approached. He wore the fine armor of higher rank.

"I'll take it from here," he said. "I am Boomax, Captain of the Guards. The King bade me bring you direct, if you be the dragon wizard. No doubt you are, follow me."

The Captain led Emerald into the Great Hall through the landing door which was a door built over large for fat fighting dragons. Emerald fit easily. As he did everywhere, Emerald searched the Great Hall's interior seeking ideas to steal. He looked to the heights of the roof's structure and noted an oddity.

"Clay pipes," Emerald observed. "The roof collects water for your cisterns?"

"Quite right," Boomax said. "You are a clever observer."

"More so than you know," Emerald replied.

The public entry to the banquet room faced west, with the outer courtyard and defensive wall situated beyond. Two thick oak doors bound with iron straps stood open, each side wide enough and high enough for three dragons below the arch. Six lit cooking hearths ran the length of the hall between giant columns. The room was empty except for the staff. One hearth had a baker's oven with a sideboard dresser holding breads, rolls, sundry-preserved fruits, jams, nuts, honey and raisins. Cooks roasted a pig at one fire-station, a fawn at another, and rabbits and hens, all on spits while vegetables boiled in iron pots over the coals. Three long wooden bench-tables were placed in the center of the room far enough apart for dragons and humans to sup together. On every bench table were ceramic wine jars, flatware, cups, salt and crooks of butter.

Hammond knows well the advantages of keeping a good table. Dragon warriors relish gold but not as much as they relish food. Booty does not fuel the engines of flight. Yet I require more than food. Draco is bribed too easily.

The smell of rabbit stew, his favorite, watered Emerald's palate. He wiped his mouth.

"The Lords' Court is a place of comfort and good will," Boomax said with a sweeping hand. "In years of good harvest, that is."

Emerald's long hind nails clicked against the polished stone floors as he followed Boomax. Bright tapestries hung on many walls. Some showed forests with birds, stags, fairies, and lesser country dragons. Others represented the legendary deeds of Giants: oil lamps on tall stands cast gold light upon them. Between tapestries, shields and weapons of artistic make were wall-mounted.

The fireplaces stole the better part of Emerald's attention. Each hearth was tall as a man and tended by bustling cooks. The plenty was more than Emerald could stand. His stomach rumbled loudly. Most unlike himself, Emerald gave away his thoughts.

"I must eat," Emerald cried.

"The feast is not yet ready. Do not fret. One station's always fit for flyers," Boomax said. "Messengers came at all hours. There's food enough for you after the King's query."

"The flyer is worth his wages," Emerald said quoting common lore.

Boomax quickened his pace. Emerald stopped mid-stride half down the long room. For the first time, Emerald saw the dragon wing table which had been moved out of the War Room for an occasion. A usually large table, it curved wide half around but not sharply like a horseshoe. It was built for humans and dragons to eat together with room for twelve men and six dragons. The table's polished legs and stiles were carved in garden motifs. On each end was lashed a dragon wing, tied closed yet flexing against their tethers.

"Why are they restrained so tightly?" Emerald asked.

"Should the wings be loosed," Boomax said, "the table would float off. It wishes to sore of late. A bit of trouble getting it down form the rafters, I'll tell you."

The trek resumed. Emerald recalled his scrolls featuring pictures of wagons pulled by wingless dragons.

No, the dragons in the scrolls did not have wings cut off, Emerald thought. *Land dragons never had wings. The wings of the table must have been bequeathed. The only other way would be law-breakers and wings taken from lawbreakers have no magic. Without consent of the owner, cut wings are useless.*

His mind's eye flashed. Emerald envisioned war-wagons drawn by wings alone. Emerald's crown ruffled at the possibilities. They came to the twin oak doors behind Hammond's table. Two guards clad in chainmail over green hemp shirts and leather britches stood on either side. Each man stiffly held a war ax fixed on long poles. Sheathed long swords hung from their belts. Steel-clad boots made of interwoven scales like dragon scales covered their feet.

Emerald's escort called, "Make way the King's guest."

The guards stepped aside pulling and splitting the twin doors open in one smooth motion. One sentry put a hand to his sword hilt. The other began to protest but Boomax raised his hand. The doormen snapped to order standing taller than before, grasping their pole-axes tightly. Their grim expressions twisted into dismay.

"Yes, Captain!" they said together.

Emerald made his way around the King's table past the guards and into the War Room's foyer but he did not get far.

TEN

Rogsin Spies

The gnome proved good to his word, though in the end Rogsin felt cheated. The gnome's secret passages were nothing more than voids between walls used to vent air or remove black water. That mini, man-like atrocity showed Rogsin the cavity between the War Room and the Great Hall, which got him out of the King's Garden via the kitchen's drain system. *I should have figured this out for myself.* But the deal had been struck. *I'll think twice over before I make any more contracts with gnomes.*

Yet, with the gnome's idea understood, Rogsin had the better part of the exchange. Within the day, he found that Vinetop had small grated openings near the floors everywhere and often hidden behind wall hangings or furniture. His slight body fit places where only vermin traveled. Rogsin quickly found great sport in these dark places. He waged war on his co-tenants and quickly established his kingdom. The void's residents were not ordinary animals either. Each was uncommonly intelligent as was usual for natural creatures living in magic places.

Hunting the voids was good sport and a challenge at first. The dragon imps and wing frogs were especially hard to kill. He made gruesome totems of the creatures he found inside the walls and gardens and left dismembered bodies where his foes would see them as a testimony to his pleasure. He killed so many imps, owls, rats and cats with his golden dagger that the survivors took warning and fled only a fortnight after Rogsin's war began. *How sad, the fun ended far too soon.*

Rogsin also discovered passages built for men but disused or forgotten. He spied far and wide unabated. He even found a direct way into the War Room. Behind the Tapestry of Neff, between pilasters, was a foot square vent in the double wall. The opposing hallway wall had another grate. There was room enough for him to slither in, turn, travel a few yards, and so go from one hole to the other. Rogsin also found the secret escape-stairway that was made for the King's residence. That passage led to the base of the tower where the stair spilt. One passage led to the valley far below, the other led up to the King's armory, a room stuffed with weapons, trophies, and spoils. The King seldom visited there. Rogsin went often and sat there, alone, lusting after the horde.

One day, while he thought the King away, he entered the War Room again. Standing on the Starstep he pushed away his unruly mop of black hair and squinted at the Tapestry. Rogsin found the perfect spot. He brought out his magic knife, went to the oracle and cut out a parcel within a tiny square. He returned to Starstep and looked again. He could not find the eyehole that he himself had just made. The slit blended with the black border pattern. He could now see what he heard while hiding behind the Tapestry. Touching the cloth was forbidden and he knew why. Cutting it caused him to surge with a strange excitement and power. Rogsin stuffed the fabric scrap into his charm pocket. Power seemed to drain from it into him and he felt oddly better for it.

"I am greater than Hammond. I will be the first dragon slayer."

Rogsin, hearing distant footsteps, slunk under the Tapestry, careful not to disturb it. He groped in the darkness and found the eyehole. He sat on the floor before the cutout, his forehead against the textile, quiet as a gnome.

"I knew you were spying on Father and now I know how," Onyx whispered.

"You!" he hissed like a snake. "How did you find me?"

His eyes could not yet see but he knew by her voice where she was.

"You are not as cleaver as you think, I'm telling Father," she threatened.

Rogsin reached into the dark and grabbed her hair. He yanked her closer.

"I'll kill you," he warned.

"Touch me again, I'll scream. The guards will come."

"Scream and I'll squeeze you…until…"

"The guards will come first," she said confidently. "I'm bigger. You can't hurt me."

Onyx twisted from his hold and scrambled out of reach. Rogsin swiped at nothing.

"They'll catch us," Rogsin said, forgetting to whisper. "Favored or not, you're in as much trouble as me. You touched it, too."

"I'm wearing gloves," Onyx said. "I made no offense."

Fear flooded Rogsin. Drops of sweat suddenly stung his eyes and his chest tightened. *Did she see me cut it? I must take drastic measures.*

"I'll kill you before you scream. I have the means."

Rogsin pulled out the dragon gold dagger. Magic blades glow like fire in dark places. Even courtly girls know such a blade kills by the slightest thrust. The gold light plainly gave her hiding place away. She had no defense. Onyx pressed herself against the wall. Her white-skinned face was stark against the stone wall.

"Now see the source of my power," Rogsin said. "You've seen my handiwork, too, dead animals with entrails spilled. I'll do the same to you. Hold your tongue and you'll live."

Rogsin rotated the dagger, its hilt brown with blood stains. *Father keeps his implements clean. She won't mistake this for his knife.*

"I won't tell," Onyx said, quivering. "Mark me, you'll slip. He'll discover you without my help. Father's wisdom is great."

"Mine is greater. Father loves lizards too much. Quiet! Someone's coming."

Rogsin directed Onyx to the hole by pointing his blade. Her face shown in the murk, pale as swamp mist, her teeth chattered. Rogsin witnessed another's deep fear for the first time and he liked it. *Onyx may have discovered me, but she'll never tell. I'll see to that. She will fear me forever!* Rogsin decided then that he would never share power with her, or anyone, certainly not any dragon.

"Stay there," Rogsin whispered. He sheathed his knife, returned to his spot, and peered through the eyehole.

Hammond entered the War Room and went to the scribe's table, a simple oak table set edgewise along the garden wall. The dragon wing table had been moved into the Great Hall for the feast, giving Rogsin a straight line of sight. The King took the desk's chair between two oil lamps, unrolled a scroll and bending his face to it, he read. The garden wall windows lit the Tapestry, not the room. These high windows also provided a perch for the ravens that came to watch the Tapestry. The clanking of the door guards armor and the heavy footfalls of a dragon caused Hammond to lay down his scroll.

Draco? No, this dragon treads light. This is all wrong.

Draco's illumination was unmistakable red. The color that splashed Father's face was green and light enough to see that Father's temple pulse with anger.

"Stay your place," the King said. "I will see him at court. Only Draco may come hither. See him out!"

"As you wish, oh King," said an unfamiliar voice, far too soothing for a war-dragon.

The green light withdrew and the King followed after a short time later. With the way clear, the siblings made their exit. Onyx, although three years older and taller was thin and fit through the vent openings with ease while Rogsin, with greater girth, had a harder time of it.

ELEVEN

Emerald's Day at Court

Emerald was led from the War Room before he had time to think, much less learn anything. He barely saw the man hunched over a scroll. Boomax had next brought him to the flyer's hearth for food but Emerald barely had his first bite of cold smoked ham when a barrel of a man, really too tall to be so wide, with trim gray bead and braided black and gray hair burst through the War Room doors and hailed Emerald with a wave. It was the King. Emerald beat tail and went to Hammond's wing table. Emerald bowed low with eyes fixed on the now seated King, not wanting to miss a twitch. Merilbe the renowned and with his crow on his shoulder, stood aside Hammond's chair.

"Greeting, oh King," Emerald said. "I'm at your serv—."

"Go careful," Hammond the Great interrupted, stern-voiced. "I'm taking a risk allowing you here. My allies know you as a misfit. Come nearer and speak quietly."

Emerald heeled. Hammond drew his golden dagger and stabbed it into the table. Reflected lamp lights cast Emerald's deep green about the King. Emerald enjoyed casting his hue over others but he did not like the look of Hammond's mistrust illuminated in green.

"Your duplicitous ways are well-known," Hammond said, "Betray me, I will cut off your wings and send you to the forges a living bellows. Do you understand?"

"Certainly, oh King," Emerald said with perfect restraint. "But what risk am I? You are King, you invited me...It is said you fear nothing, none of your under-lords, certainly not me. Not Draco. So why would you fear the brother of your dear pet?"

"Do not word-game with me!" Hammond said. Rage edged his voice.

Hammond leaned forward in his chair; balling a fist. He hammered the table once. Emerald flinched. The guards behind the King rippled as if Hammond had cast a stone into a moat.

"Draco is my collaborator, not my servant. He is my friend," Hammond continued. "You are not. Insult my friends and you'll have cause to fear me."

Merilbe put a hand on the King's shoulder and Hammond relaxed back into his chair. Hammond's continence changed as quickly as flame blown out from a candle.

"But let us start on level ground," Hammond said. "Frankly, I'm surprised you even answered my call. I don't rule dragons. Dragons rule themselves. My messenger made no demands. I asked you here to negotiate your services, for business. Tell me, why did you come?"

"The signs are in confusion. Birds flock out of season. Black clouds ride high winds. Dark creatures venture from cursed places. Fortune tellers receive no wisdom. The age ends soon. Surely you know that darkness is upon us, and from wherever it comes even I do not know. Theses are uncertain times. I thought we might help each other. I have magic and ways not even Merilbe knows."

Hammond sat straighter furrowing his brow upon the word "magic." Merilbe did not respond. The star-signed crow upon the Wizard's shoulder bobbed its head rapidly.

Omens fail the King. That's his game. He needs a watcher at his back door.

"That is true. Second sight fails the soothsayers," Hammond said it as a mundane fact. "As such, I need whatever advantages I can hire."

"I only wish to enhance your greatness, my Lord" Emerald said, his voice soothing. He sat on his tail and lowered his head. "That is reward enough."

"Come now. I am no fool," Hammond said. "There is more. You'll want your price. Let us make terms."

Soften him, old boy. Emerald told himself, the real pay off comes later.

"To give you aid is to help myself. My desire is that your kingdom stands against these uncertain times."

"Pretty words," Hammond said. "You are the slippery one. You have no love of man or dragon. Why help me?"

"My good King, it is simply self-preservation," Emerald replied. "As long as peace holds, no one can bother me. Yet peace is fleeting. I have my fears. What of the Steppes? Will such hordes rest? Armies must fight. Will they sack my home? They could. Who is to say that your majesty will not seek treasures in my lands, too? If I help you, I gain your protection. You gain my wizardry. Of course, I have material needs. I can't serve well without your patronage. I can't make something from nothing."

"Ah, that's the rub, material needs you say. Two wizards are better than one," Hammond said, scratching his beard. "What have you worthy of my patronage?"

The fool thinks I care about his trinkets. He is still fishing. There is something more he wants, something Merilbe can't or won't provide.

"My mind is better than my magic," Emerald said, "There has never been a wizard cleaver than I. I'll make you engines of war. Even now, I have begun work on devices the likes of which no one has seen before. In the face of my industry, none will overrun you. Your army may one day even march against the Steppes. The Outlands will no longer be a hindrance to your movements. You'll defeat all comers."

He likes the bait on my hook.

"A tremendous boast. You have engines in your cave besting Merilbe's devices? Prove your worth. Words alone I cannot abide. Show me."

Merilbe is no war wizard. Hammond is interested. With my engines, he won't need Draco, either. This is my way in. I have him.

Emerald reached into his flight bag and removed a rolled velum parchment. He laid it before Hammond who studied it intently for a long time. All the while Emerald's gullet cried.

"Very interesting," the King said.

"It pitches rocks a great distance, my gift to you. It works like an artillery man's sling, only it throws much larger missiles by mechanical means. Dragons become fewer every season. How do you attack high walls without dragons? With this device, is how. With it you can throw stones or fire pots over any wall. Build it. Have your craftsmen do as I instruct. You'll see I make no boasts."

Hammond fingers traced the scroll as Merilbe and his crow looked over Hammond's shoulder. Emerald had heard of devices like these used in far-away lands. The inventors of such engines were thousands of leagues south. Hammond had never sent emissaries there. The Southern men are too far away and no threat, but not too far for Emerald's spies. The Outlanders walls were unsophisticated but strong. The King's fighters could bring one down without dragon's fire, but the cost would be great.

Hammond can ill afford wasting his precious dragons, be it men, he will waste. I need an angle.

"Such a tool could bombard ungrateful estates or foot solders at a distance without risking dragons," Merilbe said as if he read Emerald's mind.

"You give me this so easily?" The King said.

The crack in his wall is his love for dragons.

"Yes, oh King, I have many more engines, many better. This one is my gift to you, to show my sincerity. Once you are satisfied, become my patron. I have ideas that make this a child's toy."

Hammond took the parchment into his hands and pressed his face closer. Squinting, he examined every line and letter. "Yes, yes this could work. You have me curious."

Hammond stood and pulled his dagger from the table with a grunt and sheathed it. He leaned forward on fisted knuckles over the table's edge. He searched Emerald's eyes as if seeking true intent. Emerald was a master of hiding.

"I will not cut your wings off this day. You will need them. My men will build it and I will send for you. But you must do better to gain my ongoing patronage. This device is not unknown to me. Men have built such things elsewhere. What do you name it?"

"The dragon-sling, my Lord."

"We have a deal," Hammond said. "Tis a fitting name."

The guard at the dragon entry sounded. "Clear the landing. Clear the Warrior's Way."

A page-boy ran to the table, bowing low. He said. "Lord, Draco is landing."

"Good, good. Green Wizard, not a world of this in open court. Our doings are our own for now. That is, until I'm sure our arrangement will be honored."

"Of course," Emerald said as he backed from the table bowing. His black-green crown feathers would bristle with disdain for his brother but Emerald kept them still.

This is no time to give away the game.

"Stay and eat," the King said. "My nobles are due. They may as well get used to you. I believe we very well may do business again. Make yourself at home."

The King turned away, walking briskly toward the rear of the hall. People and dragons dressed in fine, brightly-colored attire of gold, green, red and yellow filed in. Emerald followed at a distance and palmed a wheat roll as he passed the baker's hearth. He then situated himself along the south wall and stuffed the small loaf into his mouth.

Draco swooped into the Great Hall a storm of white smoke and blue flame; Emerald instinctively took a step backwards. Draco landed inside the hall never touching the exterior landing and he slapped the stone floor with his tail after touchdown. *My brother loves to show off.* Draco was famous for stealth but he did not always go lightly.

Emerald waved to his brother knowing well that Draco would not like it. Draco's crown stiffened. *He is not pleased; how predictable of him.* Draco shot a quick glance at Emerald as he approached Hammond and lowered his head to the King. Draco greeted Hammond properly then backed a step and snarled. Black smoke suddenly curled around Draco's head.

He's not one to hide his feeling, the fool.

"What bad omen brings my brother the outcast here?"

The cloud of black smoke hung in the air. Even the guards stationed at the farthest door heard the question. Every ear leaned in.

"My King," Draco said. "I cannot abide this trickster. He is an embarrassment. Giving him quarters belittles us dragons."

"Draco, my dearest friend, I know of this Wizard's dishonor, but, he comes offering aid," Hammond said. "He came with low crown in peace. Tradition extends hospitality as such. He is welcome."

"He is a danger," Draco said, straining to keep a civil tone. His scales deepened to amber red. "There is no peace in him, only trickery and malice. Beware his words. He is crazy and a friend of darkness."

"Madness lies with genius and partaking of it benefits us."

"If Emerald is a genius, then I am a pod mother," Draco replied.

Emerald, born without fire and thus soft-lipped, could smile much like the humans. He seldom did, not wanting to show his mood. But now, Emerald lay back on his tail, arms over his breast, he let his teeth reveal glee. Draco did not miss the gesture.

Can I avoid such fun at Draco's expense?

"You would make a poor pod mother, dear brother," Emerald said, allowing mirth in his voice. "They give life, you deal death. However, you are as bulbous as a sow bearing eggs."

Thicker smoke steamed from Draco's nostrils, his tail fin clenched into a tight ball.

What joy!

"Steady, Draco," the King admonished. "Come now, the feast is made. The Countries are here. There are vitals to quench your fire. Spitting flame and cruel words can wait. Today's fire is for food. Let us indulge my hearth keepers."

"Of respect for you and the Tapestry, I'll hold my tongue, but I cannot disguise my countenance," Draco said with eyes fixed on Emerald. "He should not be here."

"I trust you, Draco," Hammond said with a hand on Draco's neck. "You must trust me."

"I'll swallow my fire," Draco grumbled as they walked away together.

Emerald bowed low, a hand on his crest as they passed, but the King ignored him. Emerald dropped to hands and feet and went for food. He got a dragon's bowl and filled it with a large portion of rabbit stew. Emerald waited bowl in hand to be seated but he was not invited to the wing-table among the estates' ambassadors and Lord's seats.

"Enter my lauder," Hammond bade the men and dragons at his own table with an outstretched arm. "Fill your bellies."

Servants appeared and the King's place at table was quickly set with dragon-gold plate, goblet, fork and knife. The servants also set a place for Draco on the King's right and next to Draco, a place for Penelope. More people and dragons came carrying their own plates or bowls. Servants set glass goblets of wine for human places and great brass drinking tankards for the dragons as each settled into their spot at table.

Emerald had a good vantage point from his lowly seat at the end of a common table where the servants had placed him. Of course, this table was also for important people and they that sat with him reacted to him with jeers and whispers. Emerald paid it little mind. One thousand years on the outside made his scales hard. It was not long before Emerald was forgotten and the Lords or ministers freely spoke. The stew tasted good, yet Emerald was contented more by the food for thought. He opened his ears for harvest. It did not take long to reap a bounty. The fare was not simple dinner-talk. Concerns of state were passed like bread-rolls.

Torney, a representative from Barber, went so far as to stand up with agitation. Torney did not look much like the King's relatives. He was tall, thin; clean shaven as was the odd tradition in Barber, and his brown hair was shorn as if his mother had placed a bowl over his head before a hair-cutting.

So much for the fashions of men. Torney has not changed since I sold him my gate-trap plans.

Torney had rolled the sleeves of his blue linen shirt as to keep them clean. But, when he thumped his fist on his chest for attention he left greasy marks upon his red vest.

"Hammond, we must have more sentry dragons," Torney said. "Our croplands are forever visited by thieves. My Lord's resources are in peril. I suspect the raiders come from Longland—."

A very old dragon with gray mane, green velvet vest and very few crown feathers pounded his fist on another table which was his and nearby.

"See here, if any estate needs more sentries, it is Longland," the old dragon said. "We border the frontiers. Our border is far longer and far more vulnerable than any inland country."

If your landlord had bought my spy-crystal, you would not have the need.

"I'm tired of your first defense argument, Groundthumper. What if the unicorn folks attack from Highland or Hilland?" said Torney. "The Outlanders are the least of our problems. If the Steppes should march, they will fly over you and burn Barber's fields. They could come from any direction. We are the first farmlands. We need protection more."

"The unicorn folk won't attack," Groundthumper said with a smack of his tail on the floor. "Our truce is three thousand years old. Why would it change? As agreed, no dragon has flown their lands in generations. They have no reason to attack, unless of course, your countrymen are the ones robbing the Steppe's trade caravans."

"I must agree and disagree with Groundthumper," said the Highland representative, who looked much like Hammond, but squat, with forearms like twisted snakes from years of hammering stone. Lord Meric's man was known for ambiguity. "The Unicorn's Queen Lea was good to her word. The robbers and raider beyond our borders cannot be attributed to us. They are Outland tribesmen. The kingdom is quite safe."

Easy for him to say, no one is fool enough to attack Meric's stronghold.

"Not all highwaymen are Outlanders," said King Bormore of North Borderland. "I've had local robbers on Neff Road for years. Many black dragons as well, criminals all and escaped from the greater kingdom's punishment. They care nothing for our safety. Such interlopers could spark a war. We ought to stockpile now. King Hammond is too generous. What if we have a bad harvest? We should move on the unicorn people before they move on us…"

They have no cause to fight each other so they will attack the innocent instead, if Hammond lets them loose. Matters not to me, I'll have my share of their goods either way.

Merilbe came to the table with a crow on each shoulder, one pecking at his ear. Merilbe went behind Hammond and whispered something in the King's ear.

"I have it on good authority that Queen Lea has no intention of warring," Hammond said. "There are no signs that she musters her people."

"You don't know that," Torney said. "No one has seen Lea in three hundred years. So the traders tell. Merilbe, must you always have those filthy crows about you all the time? I wish you would refrain, people don't care for crows."

Torney is such a kill-joy. What is so bad about crows? They are not bad roasted in a pie.

The debate continued, each human or dragon with his or her own rational for war or peace or having further arguments as to why their estate needed a greater share of Hammond's support. Emerald grew tired of it and opened his ears for subtler tells. The two most important dragons at the King's table, he realized, refrained from these arguments. *I wonder why.* Penelope sat next to Draco, as the decorum demanded and right of Hammond. Emerald thought it unlikely that these two dragons were removed from the debates. Were they considering what was said between them secretly? Emerald opened his ears wider. They spoke in long-speak, the language only dragons can hear. Had Emerald a co-conspirator he would have done the same.

How clever, I almost missed it. I thought I was hearing far-off dragons.

Neither one gave any sign of their conversation. Draco chopped whole pheasants as fast as the servant brought them while Penelope quietly sipped her tea and nibbled bread and cheese with her ears standing erect and proper.

Neither misses a tick, I'd wager.

"I'll see to it that my ambassadors convince the Lords to spend more time protecting the trade roads," Penelope's said in the low-pitched grunts of long-speak.

"The like you will," Draco grunted. "The Lords won't abide your tactical concepts. They don't deserve my counsel, either. Let them act like children and be repaid likewise."

"Then do it for me, will you not keep the peace? We must have secure roads. Take away their reasons to fight each other. Our purpose is to keep the peace."

"Yes, I know. The way your treated me last we met, why should I do for you? Don't answer. I'll do it for peace's sake, though you make it difficult for me. I'll set Dar and

Puffin to road duty once they're ready. They won't be auctioned. I'll retain them for myself. Satisfied?"

"I'll have my girls convince the Lords to accept your offer."

Emerald found it hard to contain his laughter. Penelope and Draco were famously and forever at odds yet they always came to the same conclusions like two halves of the same mind. Fight as they may, Emerald heard far more in their words that either one accounted for.

The love birds are still at it. Nothing has changed from my Rookery years, I see. They've played so long they've forgotten it's only a game. Clearly, they love each other, another crack in Draco's scales.

Hammond clapped his hands above his head and the doors to the Great Hall were opened. The meal was then given over to lesser courtiers. The important people had had their fill. Dozens of minor courtiers, human and dragon piled in. They soon filled the long tables. Some were from the Estates, some from Hammond's house. Some were likely town merchants or others well-to-do. Having ate long and well, Emerald decided to indulge in the one human fancy he favored.

He went to the table where men got tobacco and long-stemmed clay pipes. Emerald enjoyed the custom. His unburned palate easily distinguished tobacco's subtle flavors. He lay against the wall next to a service table, watching and puffing. A dozen human men and women circled three young female dragons of whom were a courier, a storyteller and a messenger, Emerald judged by what they wore. Emerald made a smoke ring and whispered, "Sharpen my ears."

His phantom crossed the room and hovered above the speakers unnoticed.

"Why in the Light did the King invite him?" One dragon said.

"Nobody I know has ever seen Emerald in person," a human said.

"Did you see how that Green Wizard took the King's best without reserve?"

"Appalling just appalling. Simply outrageous," they murmured.

"What need could Hammond possibly have for him?"

Emerald cast his breath toward the King's hangers-on and dismissed his spell.

This is what I've missed away in my retreat. Hammond's table is indeed generous. The King even feeds leeches.

With most now fed, the folks mingled about. There was a circle of friends around Hammond that noticed Emerald's attention. Emerald raised his tankard toward the gathering and tipping his drink to the group, saying, "Bottom feeders eat well, indeed." He puffed on his pipe and blew a jet of red smoke at them. Hammond took no offence and moved on to another group. One of the female dragons, a young messenger no more than 100-years-old and wearing King Meric's colors exhaled black smoke as the King departed. She moved to Emerald facing him with blazing green eyes and a tightly wound tail.

"You insulted us!" She said.

"Nothing of the kind," Emerald said. "Where I come from, that's a compliment. Don't make hard-eyes at me, messenger. Where's the respect for your elder kin? Haven't you noticed that you have my colors? We very well may be long-lost cousins. You should respect me better."

Emerald took a long drink while the messenger backed away.

"Respect, you don't know the meaning," Draco said as he lumbered into the space between Emerald and the offended group. "I'll show you..."

"Now Draco," Emerald said. "You know attack-speech is not tolerated at court."

Before Draco could answer, Penelope shouted, "Clear the way, they're landing!"

Two human youths were in front of the open landing's door directly across from Emerald's position. The dark-haired boy faced skyward, unmoved, while a thin girl struggled to remove her hand from his. Barely a moment passed when Hillguard, a dragon favored by Penelope, came in fast on half wing. He quickly folded his wings, slid through the doorway, and hopped over them. The boy did not move.

That must be Rogsin, the spawn of my deceased friend, and his sister.

Hillguard screamed, "Crash landing!"

A young dragon was coming in too fast. Finely controlled landings were the warrior's art and not child's play. She came on like a war horse and flashed through the archway catching a wingtip on the door-jamb. She spun just enough to avoid hitting that pair of human children. She rolled into a group of bystanders knocking some of the humans to the ground. Guards and servants ran to the scene. There were people strung all about but Rogsin emerged from the chaos unharmed. Emerald focused his keen ears on the children as he moved toward the mayhem. The boy roughly pulled his sister by the hand bringing her ear closer to his mouth.

"See, Onyx," Rogsin said, "no dragon can harm me."

A housemaid ran to Rogsin and his sister. Rogsin stopped the maid with a raised hand. Emerald detected relief on the women's face. Rogsin marched away dragging the taller Onyx. Emerald followed. Rogsin stopped and faced him. Emerald let red tobacco smoke curl from his nostrils.

"Be gone else I set your hair to flame," Emerald said to the girl.

Rogsin let Onyx go and she slunk away.

"Rogsin," the King bellowed. "Don't ever drag your sister that way!"

"Yes, Father," Rogsin replied, bowing his head with black hair falling into his eyes.

Onyx ran to her father and buried her face in the sleeve of his linen shirt.

"Father, he is so cruel," Onyx whimpered.

The King stroked Onyx's head. "Out of my sight Rogsin! I'll deal with you later."

Rogsin shrugged and spun away. The room soon returned to calm as no one was hurt bad at the landing. The lad Rogsin stayed near, Emerald noted, the boy watched the room from the shadow of a chimney corner.

There's a boy after my own heart.

Penelope and that young crash-landed female dragon came forward and bowed to the King saying the proper greetings. *That must be Praxis.* Onyx glared with anger at the little dragon that nearly cut her down like autumn hay. Praxis and Penelope then joined a group of ambassadors.

Rogsin appeared forgotten, but not forgotten by all. Emerald made a smoke sculpture shaped like an eye and sent it out. His mind's eye traveled by smoke seeking more. Emerald had the courtier's skill for discerning the nuances that faces told, but no skill or smoke-eye was needed to recognize Rogsin's hate. Emerald wondered what made the boy so angry. Emerald's smoke followed Rogsin's line of sight.

"Father," Onyx said in a small, bold voice, "May I sit upon Draco?"

Rogsin seethes at the mention of Draco. I like this boy. The enemy of my enemy is my friend, indeed.

Hammond slapped his knee saying. "Young lady, Draco is his own person. Only he may give such leave. Draco bears me by his generosity, not contract or orders! You must ask him."

"But, Father, he is so fearsome."

"I am," Draco said, his upper lip curled, "That is true. Only enemies need fear me, however. Come, come and sit."

Draco thrust his arms forward making himself as low to the ground as he could. A practiced rider mounted dragons with the dragon's head held high. For Onyx, Draco laid like a repentant hound. Onyx would reach Draco's saddle more easily by climbing his neck.

She took hesitant steps toward him but stooped and stroked his massive head just as Hammond had done upon arrival. And like her Father, or any rider, she said the words tradition required of the first mounting.

"By your leave, oh master of the sky, may I join you?"

"I give my leave," Draco said with blue smoke.

That is rich: Females never ride dragons. My brother still has his sense of humor, I see.

Rogsin sprung forth.

"NO! It is my right," he yelled.

Rogsin jumped upon a table upsetting plates and goblets. He leapt again and onto Draco's wing. Draco intuitively reared backward, flexing his wings, which tossed Rogsin head over heels. He landed well, rolling away as riders are taught. Rogsin was bruised, Emerald guessed, but his pride was damaged beyond reckoning by the look on the boy's face. Emerald knew what that boy felt.

"You'll pay, Draco. You…you lizard!" Rogsin cried. "You'll pay."

Before Draco could utter a word, Hammond bounded from his chair.

"How dare you!" the King boomed. "How dare you dishonor this house and my friend? What of my guests! Off now, off to your room!"

The King loosed his wide leather belt, slid it from his waist, and laid it on the table. Rogsin, wild-eyed, ran for the residence door.

That boy is far too old for spanking. His embarrassment is more punishing, I'd say. The King is calculating.

"My apologies, Draco, the child has no wits." The King said.

"No need," Draco responded. "He is still a child. Come now, Onyx. I am a dragon of my word."

Onyx had scurried away and stood behind the wing-table trembling.

"Sire," Onyx said in a timid voice, "I wish to take my leave."

Onyx, not waiting for an answer, ran for the nearest door. It wasn't the way Rogsin had gone. She moved past Emerald with her long black hair steaming behind her like a rider's cape on the wind. Emerald placed his pipe on the table. Walking upright, Emerald went before the King and bowed.

"It seems a good time to take my leave," Emerald said. "Your kindness, oh King, is far better than what lore proclaims."

"To enjoy it further," Hammond said, "and to prevent harm; keep your word."

Draco walked Emerald to the take-off in silence. On his way, Emerald spied the crash-Lander. Emerald, isolated as he was, did not see many dragons. Yet he suspected that Praxis must be the most beautiful dragon in the land. Emerald did not expect to see any Goldens in his lifetime. Yet, there was Praxis, blue radiance but very much golden. Emerald stopped, his jaw hung slack.

"Move along," Draco said to Emerald.

"What is she doing here?" Draco grunted to Penelope in long-speak.

"I'm touring the females. Have you forgotten?"

Draco's crown stood. Gray smoke engulfed his head.

"Females are your concern, not mine. The lads tour later."

"Will you take the male Golden first?"

"I'll take the best first. Your son's coat ill matches his size and skills."

Another golden! Penelope had laid a golden egg!

Emerald's jaw snapped shut. He strained to control his countenance. He licked his hand and smoothed down his crown feathers. As he edged onto the take-off, Emerald decided to fly closer to the Rookery on his return.

Times are changing, and I intend to change the times. Another Golden, this I must see.

Emerald had had his fill in more ways than one. As Emerald flew to the Forbidden Mountains alone, the winds were, for once, in his favor.

TWELVE

Lunch at the Rookery

The sound of dragons crunching at meal and the murmur of conversations filled the tunnel as Mars approached the main eatery cavern three levels below Sky Top. Mars pressed through the dark velveteen drapery at the entry and passed from a brightly-lit tunnel into an expansive, dark, and cool room. Despite the few candles, Mars knew there were more diners than usual, dragons and people. *Something must be going on,* Mars thought. *Too many travelers had arrived in the last few days.*

Even so, the guests upheld the tradition and lit no bright lamps. *How silly. Why sup in the belly of the Earth while the sky is so bright and the sun so warm?* Mars rubbed his eyes but he could not see well, yet. With flared nostrils, he smelled his way around the dozens of bench tables and to the students' table at the far end. The table was set with the rich and fatty fare required for growing dragon children.

"This is stupid," Mars announced upon bumping the students' tables, not sure who was where. "How does this sharpen our senses?"

"Yeah," Nedell agreed with a full mouth. "Day or night or blindfolded, I'll always find the food."

"The teachers say we must heighten our senses," squeaked Charlotte. "They say, 'A dragon must find paths in dark places.' A dragon needs sharp eyes."

"Don't worry, Mars. Draco doesn't need dragonflies, no matter how good their night-eyes," said Bullock. "You might be Mr. Golden Scales but squirts like you always stay home."

Mars ignored Bullock and found his usual place at table and reached for the common plate using his snout as a guide. Mars found the pork hot.

"I may be small," Mars said as he bit a greasy pork chop, "but I'm an altogether better war dragon than you."

Bullock pitched a bone at Mars hitting him on the snout. It stung. Mars swallowed his bile along with his pain, not willing to show Bullock any weakness.

"Prove it," answered Bullock. "Race me the gauntlet tomorrow after school, one to one. Or...are you scared little bird?"

"Why should I?" Mars said with a lick of red fire, "To prove how well you cheat?"

Bullock laughed with a low rumble. It reminded Mars of the big war dragons that occasionally came and went. *Bullock will grow to Draco's size, color and shape, but not Draco's intelligence. Bullock thinks size is everything.* All his broodmates thought Bullock would become the next warlord. Mars thought differently. Warlords needed more than muscle.

Mars saw how Bullock cheated on school work and at field games. He never played fair. Bullock rammed his competitors when the judges weren't looking or nudged whoever was spitting rocks, skewing their aim. Mars simply practiced harder and felt sure he was the better athlete, however much it was unrecognized.

"There is no profit in cheating," Mars said.

"All's fair at war," Bullock said. "Is it my fault you fly stupidly? Only a fool would go between me and the walls. If you get belted, it's your own fault."

No one offered any comment. Tails scuffed the floor nervously. Someone's stomach churned anger. Bullock used challenges as an excuse to inflict misery. Nobody ever accepted. Thus, Bullock freely used his weight to take whatever he desired. Disagreement with him resulted in a tail-slap harsher than the headmaster's worst. Bullock's insults became more insufferable the bigger he grew. The teachers taught restraint and forethought, but Mars had had enough.

"I'll do it," Mars said sternly. "I'll race you."

"No!" Praxis cried from the far end of the table. Red flame shot forth. "I go off on tour for two days and you suddenly become an idiot. Mars, he'll smash you. Are you crazy?"

"Listen to your girlfriend, dragonfly. She speaks the truth," Bullock said.

"She's not my mate," Mars said.

"You don't have to prove anything to that...that feathery brained raptor," Praxis said, her voice quivering.

"Light must overcome darkness," Mars said. "Charlotte is right. It is time Bullock changed course. He flies in shadow."

Bullock burst into laughter. His tail slapped the stone floor with a crack. "Light, what is Light? You sound like your delusional mother. Light is for the defeated. Children's fairy tales, just as Draco says. I am no longer a child. Shine all you like, golden boy. You won't best me."

The bell sounded for class. The brood immediately sprung from the table, many still chewing, and the group made for the exit where they lined-up as required. Bullock pushed toward the front of the line but stopped before Praxis on his way.

"You should treat me kindly," Bullock said. "I've time to sire eggs before I ascend to Warlord."

"I'd rather mate with an iron skin," Praxis said. "You are much the same, but, they're smarter."

The brood laughed as Bullock vented steam. Iron skins were nothing more than giant flying lizards, dangerous but dumb as rocks. Bullock marched into the tunnel. Everyone followed with Mars last as usual, but Mars held his head high. Once in the tunnel it seemed that the touch light gathered to him and sprung outward. His golden hue overcame the others' light, and so Mars' light illuminated the way forward from far behind. Draco's words reverberated in Mars's mind: "Cool-headed warriors driven by need get better results." *If Draco employs the wisdom lore so shall I.*

"Bullock is big," Nedell said. "Mars is faster. He'll take Bullock if he wings smart."

"Speed is important," Timor said.

"Spoken like a true Border-Lander. Your kin are always on the run. I would not wager against Bullock," Rowbert said.

"Woodlanders should know the value of maneuverability," Nedell said. "How can you say that, Rowbert?"

"Boys are so stupid," Praxis said. "Mars is about to get squished and all you can think...Oh never mind! What's the use?"

Praxis stormed ahead. Zandora, Lolandra and Charlotte scurried after her.

"Girls," Gordon said. "They don't know anything."

THIRTEEN
Penelope's Wish

Penelope perched on Teaching Rock basking in the noon sun as was her habit. A rent in the overhang above allowed this noonday pleasure. Her students exited the eatery tunnel in disarray, skipping, hopping or running across the playing fields in no particular order. Yet, when they reached her, each fell into their usual places according to size, the smaller ones closest as customary. Otherwise, Bullock would always push to the front. *He'll be the first of this brood killed, too,* Penelope thought. Bullock ignored the wisdom stories, another bad omen. *How many times must I repeat, 'the least shall go first?' That is how Atmere died, leading the charge right into a trap. A smaller dragon could not have been impaled by the force of his own weight on a simple wooden pike.* Penelope feared that Mars would one day take the lead from Bullock. This day her fears were less.

Penelope did not interfere with their order. Only amongst themselves could the children decide their place. Just as Penelope could not make honey from nectar, she could not force any of the brood to accept or ignore wisdom lore. Mars loved the Lore of Light, an advantage over Bullock, but the doctrine of Draco held greater sway. The popular, fanciful stories of the fairies or elves at war that the other males favored disinterested Mars. As long as Mars remained last among the brood, he was safe. Mars's only first among the males was in book study, which further reduced his standing. She thought his book-smarts was a sign that the Lore of Light took root in his heart.

"Wisdom will save you," Penelope whispered.

Mars settled in last. *Highborn dragons are born to lead, but he follows.* This hurt Penelope's pride. Every mother desired her children's success. Penelope swallowed her bile and reminded herself that "*My pride must not over match salvation's cause.*"

Last was safest. That pained Penelope, too. Mars suffered ridicule as last dragon. Mars did not deserve the humility of last-dragon. He grew in so many ways great dragons needed. His athletic ability was greater than his size, his fire passionate, his mind focused, and his heart brave. He only lacked confidence. Penelope did nothing to change that. Should Mars find his confidence, Draco's wish would be fulfilled. Draco didn't know Mars's potential. Penelope's ambition was to send Mars to Sage School. There he would become the leader dragons really needed, a dragon made after the scrolls, a dragon most unlike Draco. But Penelope knew the fire in Mars's eyes; she had seen that flame in Draco one thousand years before now and Atmere's fire-eyes more recently. Mars could be no scholar should war's fire spread within him.

"Can we have a game?" Zandora called snapping Penelope out of her thoughts.

"Tomorrow," Penelope said. "Time enough for games then."

Penelope straightened her neck and made her crown feathers erect as was her teaching pose. The brood did the same, ready to learn. Mars's neck was straightest.

"Rookery Top is for learning," Penelope said, "and not for games, although games have a place here too."

The females held steady, while the males crown feathers dropped in unison. Mars flexed his feathers, but his crown stayed upright—another good sign.

"There are many more things you have yet to learn," Penelope told them. "This is your ninth year, spring has come and so Rookery Top is full. They've come to give advanced teaching in diplomacy, human/dragon relations, hunting, history, magic, finance, and healing. They have come to examine you and perfect your special abilities, whatever they may be."

The brood whined in various version of, "Oh great more work."

"It's not so bad," Penelope continued. "There'll be hunting expeditions and work details at Hammond's estate. The males will tour with Draco. You are no longer children. It is time to learn survival skills, foraging and cooking, mastering your own fires." She paused and took a breath to expel what they would see as bad news. "Play time is over."

Her broodlings exhaled a collective sigh of black smoke. Tails twitched as the prospect of harder work and less play washed over them. Bullock's crown could not flatten more. Nedell brightened with the prospect. He'd rather read than lose at games. The girls also perked up, now they had opportunities to shine and more so, beat the boys often.

"Why would I hunt?" Nedell asked. "I'm not a country dragon. My father keeps an iron-smithy. We're town folk."

"You may be drafted," Penelope answered. "Remember my tales of my late husband Atmere, he was called out of retirement and went to arms. There is peace now, but peace is fleeting. We are told that a day comes soon when dragons will leave men. You must prepare. On that day, dragons will forgo luxuries. There will be no inns, no towns and nary a friend when we leave this place."

"Hunting and cooking is for warriors," Wedge said, "as is war games! How else can we sharpen our skills?"

"Yes, yes!" the boys cried with Mars yelling first and Bullock loudest.

"Tomorrow is Last Games Day," Penelope announced.

"Last Games Day!" Mars cried.

The other dragons followed his lead. Cheers raced skyward. Last Games Day was the greatest of Rookery holidays. Tradition was to thrust Last Games Day onto the brood without warning, like an Outlander's ambush, giving the young ones no time to prepare. In this way their fire was tested cold. Mars reared like a stallion, his hue brighter than Penelope had ever seen it. Her heart sank. The others cowered. Then, all at once, the boys joined Mars and let loose their hues. *Mars took the lead*, Penelope thought. The young dragons rippled colors and blue smoke.

"The greatest of all games days is upon us!" they cried.

Penelope had some solace. Draco was dealing with a boarder skirmish in South Highland and he would not witness the tests. The brood would make their best showing in the morning, a demonstration that dictated each dragon's future, and Draco would not see it.

"Yes," Penelope sang in heart and voice. "The greatest games day ever is tomorrow."

The brood sang about the glories of Last Games Day and Penelope joined them. She found her comfort in Mars' weakness. He was far from the best gamer. The most important game, the gauntlet, was a game of rock spitting and acrobatic flying. Mars excelled at both, but lately he performed poorly, as if he had no heart for the game.

The gauntlet winner's fame and self-esteem flies high indeed. Bullock will no doubt win and he has no need of the boost! Mars is more able indeed, she thought, *but Draco will not know it.*

A seldom read prophecy came to mind.

"Smallest among them though his fire the greatest, the humbled crest-bearer will lead them to a land of peace and plenty."

Once Mars loses the Last Games, he will fly out to the Sages without reservation. The Golden will fail in the sight of men and be humbled.

Only two more dragon ghosts are needed to complete the dragon-star constellation. The time is right. Mars must be The One who brings the end.

"Go and ready yourselves," Penelope said. "Class dismissed."

The brood scattered like joyful leaves on the wind. Not all of them bounded off like children. Mars and Praxis walked slowly, leaving a stream of thoughtful smoke.

FOURTEEN

Last Games Day

Mars didn't hear much at the fire pit gathering. As the elder dragons introduced the visiting teachers, Mars thought about how to defeat Bullock. Combined, the game points added to twenty. Mars was sure he could win two games, but he would need the gauntlet's double points to win all. The winner of Last Games Day usually toured with Draco first. *I'll show Draco*, Mars thought, *he will pick me and I will fly under his wing.*

No ideas came to Mars until Mother gave the last speech at the fire. Mother spoke first and last whenever she was home. Her duties had her away from the Rookery more of late, and after today, she said she would not teach them anymore. At the fire, Penelope spoke the legends of Neff as usual. Mars had heard it all before. He preferred the war stories traveling dragons told. He especially liked the stories of Draco's exploits. Draco, even outnumbered, always won.

"There is no weapon stronger than the mind," one retired dragon had said of Draco.

Draco is really something!

Mars's eyes wandered. Puffin and Dar had returned, on leave from sentry training. They listened intently. They never tired of Mother's stories. *That's why Puffin and Dar stayed behind while their classmates went off to War Camp. Those two just aren't much on fighting.*

But they gave him an idea. Not wanting to get hurt, the Brimstone brothers used tricks during the head-butt game, a game Bullock always won. Mars decided he would use one of Puffin's moves. Puffin hated fighting but he never lost at head-butting. That gave Mars some confidence as the games began.

The first game was fire-rock spiting. Mars won easily. Afterwards, Mars went to the butting field to plan his attack. As Mars backed out of the playing area, Bullock used his tail to trip Mars. Bullock spouted his usual taunts as he stood over Mars, who was now sprawled on the ground.

"You're really grown up, Bullock," Mars said. "Why don't you crawl inside your egg and start over? You act like a yearling."

"I'll crack you like the egg you are, little bat," Bullock replied. "Let's butt now! Come on, boys, let's take him out! I'll split my points with anyone who joins me."

Some females and Nedell came running on Bullock's threat. They watched while Gorgon, Wedge, and little Timor moved in to accept Bullock's offer. Nedell blew smoke at Timor.

"I need the points," Timor said apologetically as he approached the ring. "With Mars out, I could win the loop-course."

"Not fair, four-to-one!" Praxis yelled as she pushed through the gathering crowd.

"Nothing is fair in war," Bullock said, eyeing Praxis. "You'll be my spoils."

Bullock approached Praxis. Mars jumped to his feet and tail-swiped Bullock's reinforcements, knocking them off their feet and all over each other in one swing. Mars then sprung and landed between Bullock and Praxis with black smoke pouring.

"Leave her alone," Mars said.

"I'll do as I please," Bullock said.

"Stop it you two," Praxis cried.

"Let's fight," Mars said with a steady, smokeless voice.

"The fight is on," everyone cried as they rushed toward the ring for the best viewing spots.

The judges came running, too. Before everyone had settled into position, Bullock set his head and charged. Mars jumped straight up and landed behind him. Thus the game unofficially began. At the clatter of the charge, dragons circling Rookery Top swooped in. Within seconds, Bullock, his allies and Mars were surrounded by humans and dragons. Many exchanged wagers even as Bullock's reinforcements continued to fill the area. Mars paid the crowd no heed and focused on his strategy.

"What's your rule?" a human official cried.

"Winner takes all," Mars yelled. "Elimination!"

Great excitement rippled through Rookery Top. Free-for-all between multiple players in the ring was common, but many-against-one contests were rare. Rules for any head-butt contest were simple. Dragons faced off in a marked circle and head-rammed each other until a player got pushed out three times or gave up. No permanent damage was caused, but because it hurt, head-butting was normally last. The judges disqualified dragons that were notably injured. The only contact rule: No closed tail strikes. With multiple players, normally the player with the most head-butts in a timed period won, but Mars had called for elimination. That meant no time limit. The last dragon standing won.

Bullock charged while the others corralled Mars, but Mars dodged easily. Bullock stumbled across the line. As Bullock struggled unsuccessfully for footing before the out-of-bounds, Gordon merely watched. Mars rammed Gordon sending him out with Bullock. Gordon crashed into a pile of stones. Holding his ribs and gasping for air, Gordon was called out. Already, it was three-to-one.

"Little bat, you think you're fast. I'll show you fast," Bullock said from the sideline, as he waited for his ten-count to end.

Mars and the others circled each other. Mars dodged Wedge and Timor's half-hearted charge. With a well-placed tail-swipe, Mars knocked Wedge for a ten-count. Bullock returned to the ring. Bullock commanded Timor to press one side. Together, they pushed Mars against the standing stone in the ring. There, they each traded minor strikes. Wedge reentered, preserving Bullock's pressure on one side so Bullock could face Mars full on. Mars could not move without exposing his flank to Bullock.

"He's mine," Bullock called. "I'll bash him."

Bullock reared on his hind legs. Such a blow would end the game if Bullock hit squarely. Mars faced this dragon twice his size with no place to go, but he refused to surrender. He lowered himself like a crouching cat, mimicking Dar's move. His sides were exposed but he trusted that the others would not charge. No one was crazy enough to supersede Bullock.

Bullock's greed for glory is my advantage, Mars thought.

"Yield," Bullock snorted.

"Never," Mars answered.

"Have it your way!"

With that, Bullock charged. Mars roared. Praxis screamed. The witnesses gasped. Mars did not meet Bullock head-to-head. Rather, Mars pushed off from the stone behind him and shot under Bullock, slapping Bullock on the snout with an open tail fin, a legal move. Bullock could not stop his momentum and crashed head-first into the stone. Mars rolled and sprung to his legs ready to strike Timor. Timor shielded his face and yelled, "I give."

Mars did not hesitate. While Wedge stood blinking at his brother Bullock's ruin, Mars charged him and head-bashed the much larger dragon from the ring. The judges called for a count. Everyone counted to ten, even Mars, while Bullock stumbled and rolled in attempt to get up. He did not succeed and was eliminated. Wedge, stunned by Mars's blow, did not return to the ring either. The game was over.

"Bless the Golden! Hail the Golden!" cheered the spectators.

Bullock had never lost at head-butting before. He slunk away red-eyed mad. Black smoke poured from Bullock's nostrils as Mars accepted the medal for his mane. As the defeated bully skulked by, Mars realized that Bullock would be even more dangerous and more determined in the next games.

Use cunning. Make him madder. Let him flame out and waste his energy. Tired, angry dragons make mistakes.

"You surprise me, Bullock," Mars said. "I thought better of you. You are far less skilled than I thought. It is good I let you win so often in the past."

Bullock stretched his neck and roared. A jet of red fire exploded from him.

"Race me now," Bullock demanded. "While my gullet is hot and my wings tense, spit rock against me in the gauntlet now!"

This is going well.

Mars and Bullock closed on each other. Traditionally, the gantlet came after lunch with energies restored and competitors at their best. But Mars was ready. Bullock was primed for mistakes born of rage. Mars was focused, although his tail shook from peaked nerves. He was about to take the challenge when Praxis came between them.

"Let him rest. Make it fair!"

"Oh, you need your girlfriend to rescue you, little dragonfly?"

"I am not his and never will be!" Praxis replied. "When do low and highborn dragons bind? Don't act a fool, Bullock. He's an important dragon. I'm not!"

Her words were true, but still, Praxis was a Golden. It had not occurred to Mars before but she would make a good mate, no matter her status. Mars suddenly felt weak in the wings and desired rest. Praxis put her hands to her flanks like a scolding teacher. The girls shot angry glances at Bullock in support of Praxis. Bullock took a step back.

"Make it fair, Bullock," Praxis repeated.

"Fair? You know nothing of war-sport, girl. You want him your little bird unhurt that's all," Bullock said. "Girls don't understand war dragons, right Mars? You better learn or you'll never marry a warrior."

Bullock calls me a war dragon, never thought I'd hear that.

"War and war-dragons are stupid, every one of you!" Praxis said.

War dragons are great, Mars assured himself. *She's just messing with him.* Yet, Praxis's words stung more than any taunt Bullock had ever leveled. Mars thought he had better prove his prowess and fast, show her who the best dragon really is. She'll change her outlook. The thought of Praxis's approval made his tail twitch. Mars suddenly acquired new energy.

Too bad Bullock calmed.

"You can't beat me, fair or not. Come on, Bullock, let's race!" Mars said.

With the challenge accepted everyone quickly gathered at the start line.

Praxis moved to Mars's side and whispered, "You don't have to do this."

"I'll win. Too bad Draco won't see it."

"All Draco would see is a fool," Praxis hissed. "I can't believe you let that moron draw you into a contest unprepared. You can't win. I thought you were smarter than this."

Praxis blew black smoke and stormed toward the crowd. Her crown feathers were askew. Mars had to ignore her. He needed to concentrate. *I'll show her how smart I am.* Mars needed a running start to gain the air first. Against Bullock races were pretty much decided at take-off. Mars's gait was certainly less than Bullock's long strides although Mars was normally faster on the ground. Pushing off that stone wrecked his spring.

Bullock will get the better start. Good, let him run hard and burn energy. I'll hold back and look for openings where he can't see me. Fly his blind spots.

Mars had never flown as well as he could during this game before: it was foolish to fly the lead just to get bashed. It had never mattered before. No one on Rookery Top knew how well he could fly, not really. They had no idea how much faster and better he was. Mars settled on the starting line. This gauntlet could make his future. Getting past Bullock on this tight course would be hard, but not impossible. One benefit for Mars, with so many watching, Bullock could not afford to cheat.

The combatants waited. The sky was clear save one far away speck, circling far above. Human and dragon watchers perched on the crater's edge or climbed onto stones. The judges were satisfied with the course. The distant sentry would not land. All was ready. Mars wished for Draco as he flicked his tongue and tasted the tension. Mars and Bullock called "ready."

"Don't get killed," Praxis called in long-speak.

The starter called, "set." The mallet struck the drum rock and Mars sprang forth realizing he had forgotten to load rocks into his neck pouch. Bullock, ahead, had rocks in his mouth as he took the air. Mars must dip for rocks on the wing, a dangerous move, or forfeit the game. Bullock may well finish the ten laps first. A missed target meant Bullock would have to repeat the lap, and Bullock was known to miss. Mars had to hit every target. Plus, he had another plan.

FIFTEEN

Draco Above

Draco slowly circled Rookery Top careful not to cast his shadow upon it. He went so far as to darken his scales by muting his hue as far as dragonly possible. His red reflection would not reveal him. He was a dark speck in the sky. A good warrior would notice and wonder. Warriors were trained to note everything. By his design, there were no warriors below. Distant objects indiscernible to humans and untrained dragons were clear in Draco's practiced eye. He recognized Mars at once. The child's female-sized body, gold scales, and glaring crest were prodigious even at this height.

What is this? The diving move, where did he learn that? And he twisted well, as not to break the rule—very clever head butting. They cheer his name.

Hillguard, Penelope's primary messenger, delivered Penelope's reports of the brood's development as required and always on time. She wrote much. However, there was little news of Mars. She wrote that he was a good student, but nothing on his greater abilities. This concerned Draco. Draco's and Hammond's decisions required accurate reports. Penelope had lied by omission. Mars was far better a dragon than purported.

'I need take matters under my own wing,' Draco had told the King.

'Let us hope,' the King had said, 'that this Golden's magic can restore the Tapestry as Merilbe thinks.'

'Golden magic heals all others,' Draco had agreed, quoting wisdom-lore.

Below, the games drummer beat a start. Draco banked. The largest brooding raced the gauntlet against the smallest one-to-one. Mars dipped rocks on the wing, a difficult strategy that lightened his carry load giving him greater speed and agility. Bullock was onto Mars's game. Bullock slowed for aim and spat true on the first lap. Then, Bullock's smoke went thick, no doubt to hinder Mars's pursuit. On the next lap, Bullock flew faster but still aimed well, not dead-eyed but he hit the target.

That Bullock is not bad, indeed. Smart, too, not risking a miss.

Bullock blocked every passing attempt. Mars barely escaped the crush each time. Mars hit center every time he spat rock and managed to keep Bullock guessing, too. Mars flew Bullock's blind-spots like the Iron Skin hunters of lore.

Clever flyer that little dragon and hitting so well in the face of ruin. Steady nerves that one has.

On the last lap, with Bullock winning, Mars, while maneuvering to scoop rocks, folded his wings on the up-swing and dropped building speed. Half a second before crashing, Mars spread his wings, scooped rocks, and shot under Bullock. Mars twisted upside down mid flight. He must have kicked Bullock's underside, because Bullock curled in his wings as if protecting himself. Mars shot up as Bullock lost speed and balance. Bullock streamed raging red smoke and he bit Mar's tail, an illegal move. Mars held his aim, even against the dirty tactic, and fired the last rock first, making the tiny dragon the clear winner.

Now that is a dragon I can use. Well done, well done!

The runt he had examined years before had grown into a quick, agile flyer and an exceptionally smart athlete, perfect warlord material.

Maybe I will retire sooner than later.

The possibility caused Draco to belch deep blue smoke as he had not done in centuries. *Penelope is not yet too old to lay eggs. I may keep my promise yet.* The brood was too young for War Camp. He had time to punish Penelope and time for her to repent. Things were falling in.

Draco veered west and climbed. He sought the High Stream toward Vinetop. He must arrange the males' tour of the Kingdom. Draco decided not to send word of who would tour first. The judges will want Bullock, if he was not disqualified for tail-biting, or Gordon.

Once in the Stream to Vinetop, Draco's mind wandered to Penelope. His first and true love had deliberately kept Mars' abilities secret. As Draco's wings took on ice, ice also filled his heart. The Matron is high but no dragon is above the law.

Your feelings over-flew your duty. My duty comes before desire. You bore false witness.

Draco shook off the ice and descended toward Vineland. As he flew lower, the ice in his heart melted little. He could not let love sway him. The Warlord's greatest responsibility was to sustain the law and ensure order. The burden of it shot down his desire. Not for the first time, Draco wished he could retire.

SIXTEEN

Draco Restricts Penelope

Three days after Last Games Day, Draco landed quietly at one of the Rookery's lower service entrances. No guards were there, as none were assigned. No dragons were airborne. Everyone still celebrated within the mountain as usual after Last Games Day.

Draco paused and listened at the head of the tunnel. Mother Wren, identified by her shuffling gait, approached an intersecting passage. Draco waited. He had time. Dinner was hours away. Classes were suspended and the brood would be gathered on Sky Top just as Draco and his brood mates had done in his school years. Draco felt comforted on the memory of his youth.

Nothing changes on Rookery Top.

Wren did not detect him as she passed. Part of that may have been because he had bathed before arriving. Once she left, he slunk up the service tunnel toward the games arena. As Draco got closer he heard cheers echoing thought the halls. Last Games Day excitement often continued for weeks. Draco hid, his darkened scales blending with the rock. He quieted his breathing and watched. Mars was not jubilant as the winner of the Gauntlet ought to be**.** The young dragon's crown was down. He exhausted rainbow smoke. The boy was thoughtful and a bit uncertain Draco decided. The golden one paid no attention to the dice game at hand.

Mars seemed to look past everyone. *He sought someone—Praxis?* She was not among the throng. *Yes, must be. Mars is in love.* Draco's fang glinted in the dull light as he recalled himself as a youth in love. *He is not unlike me at that age.*

"Are you testing our alertness, my Lord?" a young female dragon said.

Draco's head snapped up. Praxis bowed, trembling. He rumbled with laughter.

"Forgive me, Lord." Praxis said bowing again.

"Nonsense," Draco said. "There's nothing to forgive. Well done, young beauty, well done."

She is better than half my sentries! I am not so easily caught unawares-this one has natural talent for stealth, and a female. What strange tiding.

Draco rumbled softly. Blue smoke escaped his mouth. Praxis relaxed a little and let her darkened hue brighten but her eyes were still attentive and her crown straight. Draco motioned for her to walk by his side. The two emerged from the tunnel together. Once in the open, he made for a spot away from view and stood still a while. Draco let the sun shine on his scales while he considered Praxis. He did not stir until he absorbed so much light he glowed the color of hot coals. Praxis remained near, quietly respectful.

"If my soldiers were as vigilant, I'd sleep easier," Draco said turning to her, he lifted her chin. "On my first assessment, I thought you a courtier. I judged too soon. You'd make a fine sentry."

"You'll draft no females for your campaigns, Draco!" Penelope's voice rained down from above. "Not while I remain Matron."

Penelope was perched on the crater's rim. She blew a jet of hot red smoke. The chatter of the crowd stopped. People and dragons forestalled whatever game or story teller's tale they partook of.

"That time may be at end," Draco said, coming forward. His lightened mood had suddenly fled.

She swooped down and glided to a halt before him. Draco held the cutting remarks that came to mind determined to meter-out the law with prudence. *She must understand it is my job, not my pleasure. I will not take her bait.*

"You have ignored your duties," Draco said boldly to Penelope. "Your reports cite none of Mars' exceptional skills."

"Praxis, everyone" Penelope said, "give us privacy. Go about your business."

Praxis bowed and made toward a group of guests gathered around a human story teller who had come to the target range to place wagers. The odds-maker and wager-placers renewed their squabble over payment odds for the next rock-spit contest. Draco's eyes followed Praxis. Mars, seeing her, suddenly took feigned interest in the betting.

Draco withdrew into a nearby alcove where their voices wouldn't carry to face Penelope's fire. The very suggestion of a female in war service never bode well with her. He'd long admired her strength and convictions, even directed against him, but he was not willing to make their conflicts public.

"My duty is to raise them in peace for the good of Neff—not for your ill-conceived wars," Penelope said as she followed him into the alcove.

You idealistic fool, Draco thought.

He stiffened his neck, determined to execute his duty.

"Hiding Mars' talent from me was treason." Draco said.

"How dare you! How can you say that?"

"Upon legal-lore spawned by the stories you love so well. He bears the Crest! He is highborn and must take his place in the ruling order. He will go to War Camp upon graduation."

"The scrolls say humans will turn on us. Your blindness won't admit the danger. The Crest is a sign of peace, not war. He must go to Sage School as the scrolls mandate."

"Mandate! You broke the law, today's law. What was written ten thousand years ago cannot supersede present realities," Draco said.

"The prophecy is the greater law. Who do you serve Draco humans or dragons?"

"Enough! I will not entertain prophecy or politics. Hold your tongue or suffer the fate of Emerald."

Penelope did not cower.

"To spare Mars, yes, I'll speak boldly and suffer anything," she said.

"You fly tempest winds. I can replace you. Many desire your place." Draco said. "You have everything to gain with Mars as my apprentice, even our love."

"Take Mars to war and forgo my love. More so, forgo the Dragon's Hope. He is the Golden. Take him and you will ruin us all."

Penelope's fire spilled. Flaming bile, the gold of truth, dripped from her mouth. It pooled on the floor beneath her and sizzled.

Draco sat upon his tail and relaxed his neck. She was so close, yet so resistant, so unwilling to reason, yet so beautiful and so strong: a whirlwind of puzzle pieces.

"Lasting peace is closer than ever before," Draco said softly. "Hammond is strong. The Lords are under his sway. He has trade and treaties with Outland tribes. Mars will reign in peace as foretold, something we both want. You cannot deny it. When I retire, your son at Hammond's side, I will fulfill my promise to you. I still love you."

Penelope jumped back, startled. Draco was not surprised. He was bold in battle, which cannot be denied. He never before was so bold with his feelings. He had not voiced this sentiment directly since they were students. *She remembers my promise,* he thought. Conflicted emotions radiated from her, every color rippled in her scales. Even her smoke was a rainbow. Draco had hope, but first came duty. He refocused.

"In the morning, I will have the first tour," Draco said.

His insides danced. He dared not loose his emotions, no matter what Penelope did. He had much work to do. Yet the old hope filled his heart. With peace, they could finally bond-mate. Should Hammond call him, as a reservist, he'd answer and with Penelope; he'd never hear the end of it. War is the humans' nature. How long will Hammond's peace last? How long will benevolent kings rule? Even in retirement, like Atmere before him, Draco would be needed.

"You tempt me to believe the impossible," Penelope said ignoring Draco's redirect.

"Do you still want me?" Draco said.

"At what cost? I cannot betray the Light. Hammond's peace is fleeting. His concerns are not of the dragon's way."

"Foolish female," Draco said. He rolled his head, spat acid and rose up, his neck stiff. Good humor fled his mind and reason returned like a hammer fall.

"I'm not here for the tour alone. I must punish your disobedience as required. For your trickery, you are restricted to Rookery Top. Move against me again and I'll banish you."

Draco headed for the eatery, leaving Penelope's mouth open, her tail twitching and naught but red light in her golden eyes.

SEVENTEEN

Mars Tours

As Draco taught flying the High Streams, Mars was filled with an unfamiliar apprehension. Sure, the importance of stocking one's stomach to keep the fires burning was common lore, but how to keep the inner fire burning as to not exhaust the reserve on a long flight was new to Mars and the other broodlings. Mars found it hard to concentrate, even though he knew someday this information could save his life. He could question the others later about what he missed, because no matter how hard he tried to focus, one question now swirled in his mind: Who will go on tour first? Even winning Last Games Day did not give Mars enough points.

"Once in the Stream," Draco said by way of long-speak, "twist your wing tips to push you faster but relax. Don't waste energy fighting the cross winds. Rather, adjust your sails."

Everyone practiced twisting tail and wings while Draco paced the ranks with suggestions. The girls stood nearby watching. They had their tours last year, but not by way of riding the Streams. Girls rarely flew that high, and when they did, it was not for very long. Girls didn't have the stamina, Draco said. Mars feared it had more to do with the female's size and he was no larger than the average female. His tail twitched with worry. Timor's tail stuck straight behind him and vibrated. Timor was not much bigger than Mars but weighed less. At the end of the line, Draco stopped and shifted to command voice, a deep guttural tone suitable for speaking into battering winds.

"Go fill your bellies and your flight packs," Draco boomed. "We go together to the heights whereby you'll taste deep cold. I will choose the first to tour by your performance. The rest of you will land as I instruct."

In a flurry, the males ran for the kitchen. They loaded their packs while simultaneously stuffing their mouths. Mars returned first, too nervous to eat much. He headed the line. No one seemed to mind, not even Bullock. *I'm in for it now,* Mars thought.

Flying the gauntlet is one thing. Flying the High Stream is quite another. Mars wished he had eaten more.

Once the brood assembled, Draco led the way to the jump-off and without hesitation, he launched from the West Gate landing. Mars and his brood mates jumped one-by-one after him. The first draft thrust Mars upward like an arrow. Soon, everyone circled Rookery Top, albeit haphazardly. The girls cheered from below. Draco had the brood fall into a"V" formation and led them into the updrafts that pushed them higher and higher. Mars had never before flown so high yet he felt strangely confident. As fear left him, Mars beat his tail to go higher faster.

"High flying is a patient thing," Draco warned in flight voice. "Do not flap until the updraft plays out."

Oh bother, I show enthusiasm and I get yelled at.

Once the flock had reached the windy heights, Draco commanded them to maintain station between the South and North High Streams. Draco remained head of the V formation; Mars was first behind him on the right with Bullock a dragon's length back on Draco's left. The four directional winds blew at different heights but here the wind swirled. The cold was staggering. Every bone in Mars's body felt like ice. He stoked his internal fire, and that helped but his scales felt as if they could break off like peanut brittle. His wings never felt so stiff.

After an hour, Timor turned blue and Mars felt his broodmate's pain. Timor didn't eat much and nether did Mars. Draco circled and flashed Timor with fire bidding him to descend into warmer air. Mars, happy to move his stiff neck followed Draco's movements. Gordon, Nedell and Bullock did not look much better. Everyone, except Draco, carried thick ice. Nedell continually flexed his wings. The bigger dragons hunched their backs casting off ice as Draco resumed his place.

Mars focused on Draco. The Warlord was as still as stone. When Draco's hue pulsed with the sunlight he absorbed, what little ice he had fell. Mars resisted the urge to move his muscles and instead attracted sunlight as Draco did. Mars reduced his fire and relaxed deeper. With half-closed eyes, Mars called his magic. The ice slipped off as Mars propelled warming spells from his mind to his body. He daydreamed of warm rocks and bright sunlight. Mars reveled in it. There was more to high flying than fire. It was as much a thing of the body as it was of the heart and mind.

Draco rumbled laughter and blew a jet of blue fire. Mars snapped out of his concentration.

"You've found it, Mars follow me. The rest of you, go down," Draco dismissed them.

Draco flapped beyond the Northward, leading Mars to the Westward wind. There Draco came about and made sails. Mars followed and fell into a wakening dream. Together, they flew five hundred miles west to the border of Neff before descending into the Southward wind.

Mars was aware yet felt as if in a dream. He breathed in the lands of Hammond fixing each order of each place in his mind. Draco spoke little. It was an hour past nightfall when Draco led them downward and landed at one of the lesser settlements. There, they ate smoked meats, drank brown beer, and sang songs at the Dragon Wing Inn until Mars fell prey to the day's journey and nodded where he sat.

The plump and jovial innkeeper brought Mars into the dragon's lodging, a structure like a barn. The man's rosy-cheeked wife had prepared clean rooms for them. The dry hay and fresh soft grass cast its spell. Mars immediately crashed onto his bed. Mars' body collapsed as his Crest of Neff shown brightly and lighted his abode. Draco's final words to him reverberated in Mars' mind.

"We go to Vinetop tomorrow," Draco had said. "You'll visit the Tapestry."

Despite his exhaustion, it was a long time before Mars slept soundly. In his restless dreams, Mars changed and became a frozen depiction of a besieged warrior woven within a great Tapestry. He and all the dangerous icons of lore and legions became alive: they attacked him and Mars bested all comers. Yet, he took no pleasure in the defeat off his enemies.

EIGHTEEN

Mars Returns

Vinetop was far more than Mars expected. It appeared below like a living story as he circled above waiting to land. The teaching scrolls had shown him every stone of it, yet no drawing could capture the true grandeur of Vinetop. The defensive walls were made of huge interlaced gray stone blocks stained with eons of rain streaks, the parapet brackets were carved like winged horses, trolls, gnomes or dragons and the terracotta roof tiles of the buildings within were laid in patterns of many colors that seemed to ripple as Mars flew. Even the messenger's landing was opulent—wide enough for six dragons with its archway stones at the wall carved to look like dragons holding lances over the doorway like honor guards. Mars almost skidded into Draco on his landing distracted and over awed by the feelings of age and magic that radiated from the Messenger's Gate.

With all its immensity, loud colors, and busy doing's of Vinetop's resident administrators, house staff and solders rushing about, Mars felt like he was in a whirlwind. Mars wondered how much more the place would buzz like bees if the King was there. Draco introduced Mars to many people and dragons and Draco knew each by name yet Mars forgot each new name in turn. Draco walked the grounds and gardens with Mars while speaking lore all the morning until they came upon the joisting grounds; there, a war-teacher called to Draco bidding him come to the far side of the practice field were fighters with wooden lances stood waiting.

"I am needed. Go to the Great Hall for mid-day meal. I'll come shortly." Draco said pointing to a gate that led through a garden toward the Hall.

The meal was in progress. Mars's entrance was noted with waves of greetings, mugs banged on table tops and voices of welcome. Mars was called to table by the wizard Merilbe who introduced his distant relation who was a houseboy named Simon. Mars rather liked Simon right off although it was hard to hear his small voice over the group of fat, scale-polished dragons and their well dressed human counterparts making merry nearby. They were minor courtiers whom talked and talked and talked all at once but said little that Mars could actually make out in the din. Mars strained his ears and chewed hardly but barely tasted his food. Everything was all so strange and wonderful.

Draco suddenly appeared at table just as Mars took a bite of mutton. Still chewing, Mars popped to attention like a submersed cork from a watering trough. Mars chastised him self for missing Draco's arrival. They stayed at table long and Draco ate much.

"It's time you see Hammond's glory." Draco said laying aside his napkin.

Draco and Merilbe brought Mars forward to the War Room's doors. The guards stiffened to attention as Draco and his party drew near.

Merilbe hailed the guards with a raised open palm hand saying, "The King gives leave to show this young dragon the War Room. He is here for Draco's tour."

The guards remained unmoved. Draco turned to Mars.

"Humble yourself," Draco said sternly in high human. "This is a holy place. Show respect and they will yield."

Mars bowed low and then stood at attention as he was instructed to do in his schooling. The guards reached together one to each handle and smartly opened the split doors like clockwork. Yet either man wasn't quite machine-like; Mars thought mirth danced in their eyes. The party stood back several steps and the guards waited.

"Only the King's advisers enter here normally. Yet guests may enter with the King's permission," Merilbe explained with a sweep of his hand.

Mars thought it disconcerting that Merilbe spoke first rather than Draco, but after all, the Wizard was Hammond's chancellor. Draco was a dragon of the wider lands and not court-bound.

"As we enter, keep you head low," Draco added. "Show respect. Do not face the Tapestry directly."

Merilbe signaled the guards with a clap of his hands and they called "Enter the Warlord, make way the Warlord." although the room echoed empty. Mars learned back in school that tradition held in all circumstances and so went the proof.

As Mars put his best foot on the threshold, a thin, black-haired, red-faced boy burst through the nearest side door into the Great Hall. Mars turned mid-step at the commotion. Upon seeing Mars, the boy's face went pale as he bounced away like he had walked into a wall.

"What's that thing doing here?" he said pointing at Mars still at the threshold.

"He is the first of the Brood of Eleven," Merilbe said. "He is invited."

"When I'm king, no lizards will enter there, especially the likes of him," the boy said.

"You are not king and never will be," Merilbe replied. "You have no right to treat the King's guests poorly. Be gone, Rogsin, else I tell your Father of your bad manners."

"I'll get you, Merilbe!" The boy yelled. "You think you're so great. Just wait, I will be king."

What a little rat-boy. He's as obstinate as Bullock.

Rogsin exited as he came. The door slammed behind him in anger.

Mars proceeded into the shallow foyer and onto the War Room. Draco had told Mars the lore of the armors and arms that hung there speaking as they flew the last miles toward Vinetop. Mars and every dragon knew of these artifacts yet now Draco recalled the brave men and dragons that once used them and he spoke with great pride as he explained each hero's life and arms in turn. Mars felt as if he had met each forbearer inside Draco's close telling. Mars' crest felt warm and thus joyful upon seeing the relics of glory that Draco's tales now brought to life.

Finally, Draco brought Mars to stand before the iconic winged table. Draco puffed and glowed especially bright as he recited the lore everyone knew, but coming from Draco with his deep ageless voice, the tale became more than legend.

"Mayson Wingbolt, the great Golden Warlord, had gathered the human people fleeing the Garden of Neff when Neff's magic failed," Draco began. "The people were without purpose, hope or homeland. Mayson, not willing to forgo the Giant's commission to protect the people, reestablished the surviving humans under the departed Giant's very own seat of power; the Giant's Chair."

Draco paused and quieted.

"Mayson divided the lands that later became the Twelve Estates, the very same lands the Giants had given dragons on the condition that dragons guard it until the end of the age. It is our duty to protect the borders, and the people within."

To hear Draco tell it, it's an entirely different tale.

"Old Wingbolt gave his wings for the King's table so that the King's affairs would always remain lofty," explained Merilbe. "Mayson's star remains bound to Mother Earth until the end of the Dragon Age."

The winged table shook as Merilbe finished his sentence. The wings strained against their tethers. The Wizard went to the wings, muttering calming spells. Yet the wings would not relax.

"Draco, speak magic with me." Merilbe said. "One of us at each wing. I've never seen them so riled."

Mars backed away until he found himself in the center of the long room while Draco and Merilbe worked to steady the table. Mars' neck twisted toward the Tapestry, though he knew he shouldn't look. His head spun against his will until Mars faced the Tapestry. The weaving swirled. Mars tried to close his eyes but all he could do was blink.

Drawn in, time stood still. Visions of golden dragons at war and peace flooded his sight. The lore came alive before him—familiar, imagined, strange and mundane images flashed like lightning bolts one after the other. He could not measure the meaning of any scene or fix any details.

"Mars," called Draco. "Come here."

Mars blinked. The Tapestry became a plain wall-hanging again. Mars lowered his head and as he did, he discovered an eye within the carpet's geometric boarder. It was like the eye of a human child. *Such a strange thing this is.*

"I saw it move," Mars said. "The Tapestry; it's alive. Did you see it? It has eyes."

"Nonsense," Merilbe said. "It has not moved in over a year. It won't speak again until the next king comes."

"But I saw—."

"Your imagination plays tricks," Merilbe interrupted.

Don't back-talk like that Rogsin kid. I don't need to bring troubles upon myself.

"Yes, sir," Mars said.

"I must take flight for Merilbe, he has need of a sage's potion to soothe the table," Draco said. "You'll go home. It is sixty miles and an easy flight. Tell your Mother I'll be along in a few days."

Draco immediately escorted Mars to the messenger's landing and flew him into the north-east winds. The clouds were low so Mars could not see his destination. Before turning back, Draco explained the way home.

"Keep your nose sharp," Draco said, "Eye the setting sun for bearings. The Rookery is north east. You will smell it before you see it. Trust the Stream."

Mars found no comfort in Draco's words. His tail twitched causing an unsteady flight-line at first. He had never flown so far alone before. There was fog below and clouds all around.

Mars, heeding Draco's words, let the Stream carry him home. He resisted the urge of fast flying and relaxed. His quiet pace allowed him to reflect on the vision he had seen. *What did it mean?* Try as he may, Mars could not remember it. Pod Mother Trisha had taught that memories of visions only came when one's heart was ready and the need was ripe. Mars had thought him self ready for anything.

Why does the message escape me?

The clouds broke and the Rookery stood proudly before him like a beacon on a dark lake. Mars dropped out of the High Stream and sailed through layers of misty clouds. He spiraled in loops as he came in—for fun. His mind cleared as he descended. Mars focused on his classmates, several of whom watched him from below. He flew first under Draco's wing and was two days gone. Mars had visited the King's War Room! He had stories to tell. His was not the usual tour.

How many touring students return alone? I'll get respect now, I'd wager.

Mars lit as he glided in. His color had never burned so bright. He landed like a victorious king, setting down on the largest game field of Sky Top instead of a regular landing spot. The awe of his pod mates who were gathered on the field made the landing worth the risk. But as he drew near, his brood mates scattered and ran off the field, slapping their tails and flaying their crowns. The last thing he expected was Mother storming toward him trailing black smoke.

"Mother, what's the matter?"

"You broke the rules, landing as you did," Penelope said. "One crosswind and you'd have met your ruin! We have proper landings for a reason! If any harm befalls you—."

"Draco trusted my judgment," Mars interrupted. "He brought me to Vinetop. I saw the War Room, the Tapestry. He let me fly alone and so I—."

"Draco showed you the Tapestry?" Penelope's crown and ears leaned forward.

"Yes, Mother. Draco and I...Well we...I know I wasn't supposed to look at it."

Penelope stopped him with a raised hand and her smoke stopped. Her crown lowered and curled in despair. Her blue scales faded to ghostly white as she plunked down onto a grass mound.

"Draco...You've made your nest with Draco," Penelope said. "That is not what I wanted for you. I wanted better. You must first master the deeper lore. There are secrets you must learn. He knows that."

What is she talking about? Can't she share my glory? Mars guarded his thoughts. *No use agitating her.*

"What of my needs?" Mars said quietly. "Draco opened my eyes in a way the Sages could never do. The relics of the great knights' meant little until he spoke of the heroes that bore them. I want the officer's vocation. I want to stand with the brave."

"I had hoped there was more to you than that. Go and eat, you need replenishment," Penelope said before she turned her head away. "Please, leave me."

What more could I be?

Every dragon had a right to and need for post-flight food. Mars felt no desire for it. Mother's rejection had doused his appetite. Mars went to the eatery anyway. *A warrior must eat well. It is his duty to remain fit.*

Mars hardened his heart against Mother's disappointment. He had no choice. Before his tour, Mars was unsure about his vocation. Now, he knew his calling. He would become a war-dragon after Draco. Mars's future fell neatly into its place. His time to shine had come.

NINETEEN

Rogsin's Hunt

When Rogsin first saw it several years before, he immediately desired it more than any of Father's riches. Rogsin was nearby and ignored as usual on the day Emerald presented the device to Father.

He remembered the lizard's words very clearly.

'This can even kill a dragon. Think of it, oh King, your men armed with my device. Every King's man, every archer, equal to a dragon.'

Emerald had notched the strange device by way of a ratchet gear and let loose a bolt. It struck a hard rock pillar and stuck fast. Father had reacted with amazement; even that lizard-loving Merilbe had never seen anything like it. Yet Rogsin had. He knew its source. It was a gnome's bow: A gnome's bow in human proportion. Emerald modified the design to make it bigger and possible for a man to load.

How clever, Emerald is not so much an inventor but a thief. He adapted drawbridge gears for that device. Father, the fool, did not even rejoice for having it.

'This must never see the light of day,' Father had said that day. 'I'll pay for your service and more for your silence. Never speak of it. I will not provide machines so dangerous as to harm our steeds. No other dragon or man will know of it. Dragons do not kill dragons, nor shall I.'

Oh but I will, Father, Rogsin thought as now an older boy remembering that day. *I'll use it if you won't.*

Father assigned a trusted house servant to accompany the green-scaled conniver to his abode. No doubt the man was to keep an inside-eye on the misfit, as if Emerald wouldn't detect the ruse. Father then put the machine in the high armory tower and therefore into Rogsin's hands. Rogsin had long ago found the secret escape staircase that bypassed the main stair and the tower guards. In that way he obtained the device.

Now, at age seventeen, Rogsin relied less on gnomes' paths and crawling through vents and rather used stolen keys, servants' stairs and seldom-used passages to move undetected. In the case of the armory, the key lay on the lintel above the Armory's door.

His key is safe in plan sight. Who would dare enter but me?

Having gotten his prize in advance, Rogsin made his way off Vinetop's heights to ground level by way of the maze of servant's passages. He first crept to a seldom visited storage room. From there, he followed a crude stairway beneath a floor hatch. It was a narrow, wormhole of a stairway chiseled through solid rock. This screw auger shaped stair was tricky. No two steps were the same height. The deer-hide pack slung shoulder to shoulder on his back made the journey through darkness even more difficult. Emerald's device, 'crossbow' as he had called it, was nearly as wide as the winding staircase walls. It got jammed between side walls many times before Rogsin reached bottom.

Father will never know. I'll put it back when I'm done.

Once outside, Rogsin rushed to the grain barn as to remain unseen. He leaned the crossbow behind the open door, hidden well enough until he got his horse. Something stirred inside the barn. It was the house boy Simon, one of Merilbe's relatives who earned his way by cleaning and washing. Simon was taller than Rogsin despite being two years younger.

How can anyone have no ambition for a better trade?

Simon's family was prodigious in the mechanical arts such as making pulleys and engines for the King. Simon's brother Rolo was just as foolish—working as a huntsman for the King's table. Rolo appealed to Rogsin even less than Simon. At least Simon was entertaining. Simon quietly sung while sweeping loose grains into little piles on the wood plank floor, all the while scratching his soft bristled-broom in time like feathers on a drum.

As much as Rogsin hated household staff, he needed someone with him on this journey.

"Simon," Rogsin called. "Carry something for me."

Simon went stiff. Simon's fear pleased Rogsin. But, Simon, like the servant fool he was, continued sweeping. Rogsin couldn't let such insolence stand.

"A moment Lord," Simon said as he swept. "I...I...I'm nearly done. I was told to finish…"

Drawing his dagger, Rogsin heaved it toward the boy. The deadly knife hit the broom handle splitting it asunder. The knife then stuck into the floor. Simon fell prostrate to the ground, his eyes on Rogsin unwavering. The sunlight poured through the door, reflecting off the golden dagger and sending sparkles across Simon's terrified face. Rogsin laughed.

Yellow. Befitting a coward.

"You're done laboring," Rogsin said. "Get my horse and your pony."

Rogsin seized his dagger and ripped it out of the pinewood floor. He held it up into the streaming sunlight as Simon climbed to his feet.

"We will hunt. Saddle accordingly," Rogsin said.

"But Lord," Simon protested meekly, "I don't know anything about hunting, that's Rolo's trade."

"Fetch Rolo, too," Rogsin commanded. "You can carry provisions. Go now, bring horses."

"Wherefore not fly? There are dragons in the guard—."

"We're riding! I hate dragons!" Rogsin bellowed. "Be quick. Bring plenty of food."

Simon hurried toward the door. Rogsin kicked him in the rear end as he passed. Simon stumbled losing his balance, but he recovered his feet and doubled his pace. Rogsin was disappointed that the boy did not fall on his face.

"No matter there will be sport aplenty today," Rogsin said to himself.

The house boy returned quickly, with Rolo, hunting gear, the food and the horses. The three were outfitted and on their way before breakfast. Rogsin lead them to the east service gate and threatened the gatekeeper not to speak of their passing, on pain of death. They exited the little-used east road and took the third left—the way to Rock Point. Rolo's horse balked at the turn while the huntsmen's face turned grim. The man and the horse knew of what danger lay that way.

Singing Rocks line every good road in the realm, but none appear on the east road. The old wagon-wheel ruts soon became thick with weeds. The further Rogsin ventured toward Neff, the more the road closed-in with thorns and thistles. At twenty miles, the road vanished completely. Simon's ceaseless singing faded long before the road did. Only a uniform line of old, gray trees once planted to dress the road told where the highway had been. Wagons had not gone here in a hundred years. On this entire ride Rolo, known as a quiet fellow, did not speak.

"Rock-crab taste sweet, but life is sweeter." Rolo said breaking his silence quoting common lore.

Rogsin watched Rolo seeking signs. Only nineteen, Rolo already had many seasons in the wild. His weathered skin, briar-scarred face and taut long-bowmen's arms made him appear ten years older and yet life in the wilds made him twenty years wiser: Such learning Rogsin would rather steal than earn.

Rolo and his mount were much the same, dark, lean and nervous. The muscles in Rolo's square jaw and his horse's neck twitched in tense unison. His sinewy black horse snorted and shook its head wildly in protest as the huntsmen took his long bow to hand and quickly pulled two arrows laying them across his lap and all the while never taking his darting eyes form the surroundings. Hunters and their steeds were normally a calm and steady lot.

It's his habit, that's all, he is watchful like any experienced huntsmen, Rogsin reassured himself.

"I don't like it," Rolo said. "This is a bad road. Nothing moves. No tracks fresh or old, the forest sounds only behind and that smell ahead is death."

"What should we do?" Simon asked.

"Go back," Rolo said.

"We go forward," Rogsin said. "Whatever greets us here, I have its match."

Rogsin patted the device in its sack that he had balanced on his fore-saddle miles before.

"I don't know what you carry," Rolo said, "but it won't work sheathed."

"Nothing wholesome lives here," Simon said, "so says the lore."

The birds flew fast and high, they were only other living things Rogsin saw. It was too quiet. A strange flutter traversed Rogsin's body. This place unnerved him, too. Rogsin thought the sensation a weakness and pushed it out of his mind. He tried to focus on his goal: the closest line of sight to spy the Rookery was Rock Point. The brood passed overhead here on practice fights. He wanted a better look at the Golden he'd met at court. Rogsin knew he must learn more if he were to stop it before it becomes a threat.

"What of it, lore master? Why should we recede?" Rogsin said, as causally as he could, not wanting to show fear or ignorance. "Tell us the tale of Rock Point."

Simon chanted.

"Their blessings are fair so they say.
In frostiest deep they once stayed.
When they rolled to roads that men had made,
They sang songs of happy days.
Living rocks that love sunlight,
Along the roads fit and right.
Before men found sun-warmed places
Singing-rocks brought luck to men's faces."

"I don't need the entire history of singing rocks," Rogsin interrupted. "Get to the swamp."

Simon lowered his voice. His tone mimicked a funeral-song.

"Rock Point's singers are treacherous.
Their magic causes unconsciousness.
Doze upon stone, fall between and die alone.
Below boulders is the cursed land.
Rock Point protrudes into mayhem.
Swamp crabs as big as wild boar,
Giant scorpions even more,
Leeches to match hunting dogs.
With fowl scavengers that live below.
Beware Rock-Point's every stone.
Men drawn by sing-song won't live long,
Sleepers tumble into the creases
Get eaten by the beasties.
The living rocks, so far from aid,
An evil pact they have made.
The rocks got sunlight in exchange
For luring prey to feed Neff's bane."

Simon fell silent. His brown pony shivered. Rogsin understood and felt no better. He almost authorized them to turn around when they crested a rise. A rocky peninsula came into view beyond fifty yards of dry marsh-grass. The trio stopped. Boulders the size of curled dragons sat close together and stabbed a quarter mile into a wet, dismal swamp. Although the day was bright, and the rocks shown with sunlight, the surrounding swamp was dark and misty. The place smelled of dead things, a scent Rogsin knew well.

There was an island of black tree a mile beyond the point. Above the tree-line, Rookery Top which seemed to waver in the haze. It was many miles beyond the point.

Dragons, specks at this distance, circled the mountain like flies around dung. Rock song, songs he had not heard on other roads, met Rogsin's ears. The hair on Rogsin's neck stood. His horse balked.

"What does lore say about how to stay awake?" Rogsin asked.

"'Travel by pairs and fill the air with watchmen, rocks-songs do rent despair.' Make noise and stay together," Simon summarized.

"Is this the game you had in mind?" Rolo asked. "Rock crab?"

Rolo strung his bow and took aim at the boar-sized crab, sunning itself near the edge of Rock Point.

"I can hit it, but this is no fishing bow," Rolo said. "I don't have barbed arrows or spooler."

"Don't waste your arrow," Rogsin said. "I have something better in mind."

Rogsin dismounted and hauled his package to the ground. He uncovered it. Rolo and Simon watched, perplexed. Rogsin cranked the ratchet handle, bending the laminated bow. The bow fixed to this device was many times thicker than Rolo's longbow. The hemp bowstring was wound with dragon-gold threads for strength. Rogsin fitted it with an iron-tipped, two-feathered bolt.

"That is a fearful thing," Rolo said. "Like the wall-breaker ballista. Why throw small arrows with such force?"

"Dragons scales," Rogsin said.

"Dragon-gold tipped points will do that even with my bow," Rolo said, puzzled. "I see no reason for it. Dragon scales are rare and costly, only rich lords gather enough to hinder gold points. Even the King's armor isn't fully protected. No one has ever layered armor with as many scales as natural dragon's skin."

"I mean to see if this device bests natural dragon skin." Rogsin said, fingering the polished brass release bar.

Rolo's tan face waxed white. Simon was off tethering the horses under the trees. Rolo opened his mouth in protest. Rogsin trained his crossbow on Simon.

"If either of you speak of this, you'll forfeit your lives," Rogsin said. "Care to test my resolve?"

"Your resolve is known," Rolo said with a dash of spite flavoring his voice. "I swear on the Light, you have my silence."

"I have your oath," Rogsin said. "I won't forget it."

Rogsin lowered his bow. The company moved onto the rocks, jumping from top to top as the rocks murmured soothingly. Rogsin kept Simon near to carry his quiver. Rolo slung his longbow over his back and trailed close behind. At about half way, the rocks raised their voices. Rogsin drew his knife and commanded the rocks to silence. The rocks ignored him and laughed. Despite their use of an archaic language, Rogsin understood their taunts.

"Command us not," the rocks said. "We make fishermen fall."

"I command who I will," Rogsin called.

Rogsin trained his crossbow at the largest boulder and let fly, splitting the rock asunder. Its core of boiling red liquid rock poured into the wet below. Steam hissed while the rock screamed. The other rocks fell into a low song of mourning. The cat-tail reeds swayed in agreement as if the wind blew time. Yet, there was no wind.

"I'll have no more singing," Rogsin said.

The murmur stopped.

"It is bad luck killing rocks," Simon warned, "even evil rocks. The legends say—."

"Shut up, Simon," Rogsin said, "or you'll be next."

They continued to the tip of Rock Point. Rolo made a blind of reeds over a hollow between boulders and the three settled in. After an hour, an enchanted frog appeared. Such creatures were common along Neff's borders. As common to its kind the frog was attracted by the hand mirror that Rogsin flashed as dragon-bait.

"I will hear your plea," Rogsin called to the frog before it made any request.

When the frog came closer, Rogsin glanced at his companions and seized the frog. He sliced its hind legs off with a single swipe of his golden dagger. The creature slowly bled to death and croaked out curses all the while until its final breath.

"That was entertaining, was it not?" Rogsin said but the brothers did not answer.

With the game over, Rogsin returned to his watch. The dragons were flying wider around the Rookery. Rogsin flashed his mirror. A dragon dropped out of formation and flew directly toward him. The other dragons followed. Rogsin worked the reflector in steady patterns. His crossbow stood ready.

"He comes," Rogsin whispered. "The male Golden."

"It is Praxis," Rolo corrected him. "Female. Gold and yet blue."

"Any will do," Rogsin hissed. "Quiet."

The glitter of reflected dragon light splashed the rocks. The rocks stirred. Rogsin's target approached—the sun at its back, just like in his vision. Yet, the sun caused unclear aim. The dragons closed formation. He could not tell one from another in the glare until they banked west. The female then broke ranks at one hundred yards.

Pity—she's the only dragon I remotely like. She was kind to me upon her visit. No matter.

Rogsin laid down the mirror and shouldered his crossbow. He gripped the cold trigger, aimed into the sun and let fly. Another dragon swooped into his sight-line. A horrible scream followed. Rolo and Simon scrambled. Rogsin halted them with a raised hand. Simon's eyes filled with tears. Rolo's face mixed anger and sadness in equal measures.

"Not a sound. Wait. It's still flying. Keep down," Rogsin said.

Two dragons came swiftly toward Rogsin's position. The others were close behind. Rogsin slid deeper between the rocks and tried to reload his bow but failed. The sound of chaos filled the sky with shouts and beating wings as Rogsin struggled with his bow. Finally, after stringing the bolt, Rogsin popped his head up. Praxis had not fallen. The male Golden's body was stilled. It hung mid air with his wings splayed wide. Two dragons held its wing tips outward. They began beating their tails while two others pulled on ropes tired to its flight bags. The bolt was lodged deep inside the Golden's neck. No smoke came out of him.

"The foul beasts of this place will not feed on Mars," Rolo said.

"Curse him," Rogsin replied.

The singing stones groaned. They crackled, scraped and shook as if they might split the earth. They cried out a dirge in rasping voices.

"*No harm to dragons must there be! Harm a dragon in my homestead and I will crush you dead!*"

The boulders around the blind squeezed in with great gnashing. Rogsin grabbed the bow and thrust it from the blind. Rogsin quickly crawled over the boulders with a boost from Rolo. Once on top, Rogsin reached down for the bow. Rolo handed him the quiver with barely enough room to pass it.

"Shoot, split the rock! Free us!" Rolo cried.

With the crossbow and quiver safely in hand, Rogsin paid them no mind. He jumped to a higher rock for a better view. The crack he escaped from closed tight, screams and then the cracking of breaking bones emanating from it. Rogsin's perch rolled. He leapt. More screams followed Rogsin as he ran, skipping from rock to rock until he reached dry grass.

Rogsin did not look behind or stop running until he reached the horses. Cutting the tether with his dagger, Rogsin freed the mounts. He tugged on their reins but the black horse and brown pony refused to move, even as the rocks raised their voices in a fearful chant of hate. The giant leeches fled their abodes worming into the marsh. Rock crabs scurried from the angry stones and moved ashore. They were surrounding him. Rogsin shook so much at the sight, fear muddying his actions, that he had great trouble mounting. Leaving the other two animals, kicking his steed's sides, gripping it's mane in one hand and his crossbow in the other Rogsin galloped away unharmed. Once safe away he laughed with glee.

TWENTY

Hammond Falls

Draco lumbered into the Great Hall from the courtyard with ears wide open. King Hammond paced, scratching his beard as he often did while searching his inner store for wisdom. The scribe sat at a long-table before a blank scroll, a quill between his soft fingers waiting for Hammond to speak. Gray and bent, Kendrick, much younger than the King at a mere ninety, had patience while the King did not.

"Kendrick," the King said. "When strong words are needed, my tongue wags free. Yet, this eludes me. How does a man announce that he seeks a wife?"

Kendrick set down his quill as Draco drew nearer.

"You wish to arrange your marriage?" Kendrick asked. "Most unusual. Only dragons do that. You seek an heir? You have a son of age, not yet given land. Unless you grant him an estate, Rogsin is next in line. This is all very confusing."

"He gets nothing," Hammond said. "I intend to circumvent his inheritance. Onyx, I'll give land."

"I saw her just now," Draco said as he reached the table. He bowed to King Hammond. "She was sword-playing with the guards. She would make a fine landlord and a good warrior, if she were not a woman."

Hammond dismissed the scribe with a wave. Kendrick gathered his writing implements and exited. The King opened his mouth and paused, surveying the room one more time before speaking. The ravens on the high windowsills and guards would not repeat what they heard. The King placed a hand on Draco's neck.

"I fear for the kingdom, old friend," he said.

"I, too," Draco agreed. "The Estates are restless. Nomads have raided southern frontier camps. Dragon and human robbers congregate in the east-wilds. The northern Outland tribes are most worrisome; they increasingly attack the Steppes traders.

The Long Way Road is unsafe." Draco lowered his head, "What If the Steppes should march—."

"Borders will always need defense," Hammond said dismissively. "The Steppes are no concern. It is too far and too costly to march an army to or from the Steppes. Emerald's engines are the best I've seen and having them makes us the stronger. Yet there is one in reserve so deadly, I've hidden it. The borders will hold. A larger matter of state worries me more."

"How so?" Draco asked.

"I have no heir. The Tapestry has not spoken in years. I must not be long for this world."

"What of Rogsin?" Draco asked.

"Even if he were surely mine, I would not let him follow me. You see his cruelty. A king must be stern but also wise. Rogsin cares nothing for Light. With Rogsin unleashed what evil will befall Vineland?"

The King slowly let himself onto the table's bench. He seemed too old for a dragon rider so young. Draco thought it past time they flew together. The King needed such renewal.

"I should not have killed Mordune," Hammond confessed. "My deed chased the magic from this realm, from the Tapestry. It would have been better to send them both away. I was rash."

Merilbe joined them, also bowing before the King.

"Nonsense," Draco said. "You are the rightful king. Black magic attacked the Tapestry, not wrought by you. Wed for love and so make an heir. You are not yet two-hundred-years-old, there is ample time. As long as we ride together, you will go on. Rogsin won't ride, not even to gain long life. You will outlive him."

Draco leaned onto his tail, straightened his neck and his crown feathers.

"Emerald wrought this black magic," Draco said. "He is the source."

"Emerald is the least of our problems," Merilbe said. "I've recounted the stars. There are greater issues."

"The stars cannot change our paths, "Draco replied. "Emerald must be the cause."

"I called Emerald because my sight failed," Hammond said. "The oracle fell and so I enlisted him and many others. He provided. I paid. He has no reason or opportunity to set spells against me. My man watches him even now. There is a hidden barb not of Emerald, I am certain."

Draco's gut rumbled. "We must find this thorn and remove it."

"Consult the primitive oracle," Merilbe said. "Only by confession do kings overcome black spells. Purify your heart, My King. The Inowise chief shaman will show you the way to new sight."

"I must make amends," Hammond said slowly. He bowed his head. "I have been a fool."

The King ripped open his linen shirt exposing his dragon-gold jewelry. To the floor, he threw down his gold—chains, bracelets and rings. All that remained was his dragon-gold chain mail under a torn shirt.

"I humble myself," King Hammond said. He called for the Captain of the Guards with a hand wave.

"Ready Draco for a long flight," the King ordered. "No armor or rock bags. We go as pilgrims." The King went off to his chambers.

Captain Boomax ordered the necessary servants to prepare Draco for humbled flight: the fitters of dragon's gear came, the maidens that weave and unweave dragon's manes and the leather smith came too. The women removed Draco's awards, only his Warlord's breastplate remained. The leather smith hid it with a rough leather cover made to fit. The gear-makers brought not Draco's fancy saddle but installed a mundane one instead. The King returned dressed in hemp shirt and canvas britches.

"Draco and I will fly until we find what I seek," King Hammond told Boomax. "Heed Merilbe until I return. I go now to deposit my dragon mail in my arms cache."

Draco watched the King leave with an odd feeling in his heart. Perhaps the King should retain his golden mail. Arrows fly unlooked for. Yet where they will go no archers can be. Draco shook off the feeling as he trusted his reason more than his heart.

*****

Hammond marched from the Hall toward his private armory. He had not visited the high armory since he placed Emerald's crossbow there years before. He kept his practical battle gear handy. This mail he wore under his shirt was a fanciful coat, suitable for display and a strong foil as well. He wore it more by habit than by need. He hadn't put it away in its proper casing for a long while, perhaps years. Light, strong and warm as dragon gold is made it a comfort to him.

This private armory stored ceremonial gear such as his dragon-gold chain mail, war trophies and heirlooms of Vinetop. It housed one of the most important relics of Vinetop, that is, the magic wheel old beyond reckoning which was used to spin the Tapestry's yarn from dragon-gold and human textiles.

As he climbed the stairs, Hammond thought of Emerald again and the crossbow Hammond had hidden within the armory. In this place no one would see it or know its potential as dragon slayer.

'There is no honor in dragon slaughter,' Hammond had told Emerald.

So Hammond had paid much gold for Emerald's silence. Even so, Hammond knew that Emerald did not receive what he desired most, his lost place of honor. That was yet another worry.

Perhaps Draco is right. Does Emerald's unfulfilled desire motivate him to mischief?

Yet, Emerald had proved his worth by creating other devices, such as a portable ram on a frame with wheels and protective roof. Why did no one invent this before?

The fear Draco had voiced nagged Hammond. Emerald was more than an engineer. He was a sorcerer like Mordune. How did Emerald acquire his magic-lore? Some would say that black magic lies hidden in the Forbidden Mountains, where Emerald now dwells. Did Emerald raid tombs for his skills as rumors told? Did he mix sinister potions? Mordune did, and Mordune was known to visit Emerald.

At the tower's topmost landing, clarity came to Hammond. *Mordune and Emerald must have caste the seduction spell. It is as Merilbe had said. Seduction spells require two conjurers. Mordune could not have done it alone. Emerald was a partner in Mordune's treason!*

As Hammond reached for the key, he noticed disturbed dust, especially near the door. The latch was turned, the door unlocked. The dust of the threshold revealed a familiar boot print.

Rogsin. He had invaded my sanctuary. Could he be inside even now?

Hammond gently pushed the door. The rusted hinges squealed. Sure enough, there stood Rogsin dressed as a hunter with Emerald's deadly bow in his hands. "You don't belong here." Hammond said his voice on fire.

Hammond entered the half-round with his face hot, his chest tight and his fists knotted like hammers. Rogsin, recognizing Hammond's rage, backed to the only window, which backlit him against the sun. Rogsin was dirty. His hair was wildly wind-blown except where his bangs matted to his sweating forehead. He smelled freshly of horse unlike the parade saddles stored there.

"Father," Rogsin gasped. "I only wanted to admire—."

"Don't call me that! My son would not dishonor me like this! My wife said it on her dying bed, the day you were born. I should have believed her. You are Mordune's son!"

Hammond thundered toward Rogsin, his hands outstretched. He covered the ten yards with bounding strides ignoring the arrows, iron sling-balls and bolts haphazardly laid about and not where they were left. He raised a hand to slap Rogsin but slipped on an arrow shaft as he swung. He stumbled. Rogsin side-stepped and swung the crossbow like a mall. The device's bow side struck hard between the King's shoulders and increased the momentum of his forward fall. Hammond crashed face-first into the window's stone jamb gasping for air he dropped the bundle of mail. With a gulp, Hammond the Great managed to straighten by half and face Rogsin.

"I banish you," Hammond rasped.

"No, I banish you." Rogsin returned with a victorious warrior's smile.

Rogsin swung the crossbow like a pick-ax striking Hammond below the heart. The King's breast bone snap like twigs under a dragon's foot fall. Ribs tore his lungs. He could not breathe. Hammond's legs went lame. He staggered and tried to stop his fall. Having no use of his arms, Hammond fell through the window on the next blow.

Hammond's mind was clear as he fell. He saw the ravens from the roof take wing and race after him. He felt as if he were swimming in molasses. He saw every good deed of his life in the clouds. A great light surrounded him and he blessed the sky.

"Into your realm I come."

Thus, Hammond the Great, Dragon Friend and Keeper of the Lands of Light entered the halls of his forefathers and took his seat among the stars.

TWENTY ONE
The Would Be King

It was the tradition of men that Kings and warriors should send their ashes to the sky and so the King's funeral pyre was lit the day after he died. The scent of the King's death would rise and not linger. Riders and messengers were sent bearing news of his death, but only those already in Vineland would see Hammond's remains burn. Mourners, dragons and men, wept openly as the King's smoke became a late morning haze and his ashes flew like phantom dragon wings. Only Draco and Rogsin spilled no tears. Onyx was nearest the fire weeping like a child, her sobs mingling with the sound of the roaring flames. Rogsin scoffed at the spectacle of weakness she made.

Rogsin remained in the shadow of a garden trestle, fingering the slice of Tapestry that he kept hidden all these years. This stolen relic was never far from his left hand. Stroking it provided strange delight, inner warmth, a deep sensation unlike any other pleasure his body had known. As such, Rogsin could not cry, not even to enforce his lie.

As his mind wandered a whisper carried above the dirge on the wind. It was the sound of bird speak the hearing of which the gnome had taught him.

"He was pushed from the nest, our brothers saw it."

No one acknowledged the voice except him as few knew how. He searched for the accusing whisper and found hundreds of ravens. Some perched on the trestles, others on roof tops. The nearest birds stood on the colonnade's lintels cocking their heads side-to-side while wagging their red tongues.

Ravens don't speak with men. Men and ravens parted ways centuries ago. They promised never to give council again unto the turning of the age.

Rogsin clearly heard them. Their words were not meant for his ears so he listened more carefully.

"Marks on his body tell the tale," one raven said. "The murderer burns him too soon."

"Look, no tears," another added.

"Look, the murderer spies us," said a third.

Panic welled in Rogsin. The lump in his throat nearly choked him. Ravens were considered good luck, larger and smarter than crows they were not unwelcome though largely ignored. They gathered at blessed births mostly. They watched but never spoke high human anymore. They had gathered for Onyx's birth, but not his.

"Murderer, murderer, murderer," the ravens chanted.

Rogsin began to sweat as if it were he lying on the pyre. His mind raced. His feet begged him to run. Rogsin could not let anyone see his distress. He backed deeper into the shadow where he reasoned within feverishly.

The truth will be found. Ravens always line the Tapestry's windowsills. How long before Merilbe hears them? What can I do? Destroy the Tapestry? Then, the ravens will leave.

Rogsin approached the pyre. The intensity of the heat and the smell of charred flesh washed over him but did not scrub his resolve away. He stared at the remnants of bone and ash that once was King in mock reverie.

"Look, he morns," someone behind him said.

Rogsin went closer and took up the unburned end of a burning branch. Boiled fat had transformed it into a torch. Rogsin extended his arm, holding the burning branch high.

"The Tapestry must be destroyed," Rogsin wailed as convincingly as he could. "It betrayed Father. It gave him no warning!"

The mourning crowd froze and silenced. Rogsin's false pronouncement made him feel powerful, in control. The people were overcome with grief and confusion. This was his moment to act.

"This for the King!"

Rogsin ran to the Great Hall's open doors unopposed with his burning branch held aloft. Merilbe chased him, the only person among the crowd able to escape emotional paralysis.

"Stop him!" Merilbe yelled from the courtyard. "Stop him, you fools!"

Rogsin now inside ran faster. Draco, his worst barricade, was farthest from the door when Rogsin took off. Draco could not catch him. He flew past the unattended War Room doors. Heavy, jingling footfalls from the Great Hall pursued him.

Guards in dress-gear can't run fast. None will stop me.

Rogsin slid onto the Starstep. His eye-hole had healed. The Tapestry suddenly swirled…alive. It was whole again and ready to speak…to speak against him!

"I am the King, give me council." Rogsin demanded.

The textile stopped moving. In its new image, the once white raven stitched into its center had turned black, the usual answer for unholy askers. The ravens above him squawked. Footfalls charged into the War Room's foyer. Rogsin surged forward and set flame to the oracle's tassels. The guards arrived too late. The icon was thirsty for fire.

Black flame spreads unnaturally fast. Fire and chaos ensued as the guards called "Fire!" People scrambled for the water buckets that were always at hand with so many fire-breathing visitors. Rogsin stood on the Starstep waving his torch and laughing in relief and for the joy of destruction. He felt like a victorious general.

By the time the first bucket came forward, nothing remained of the relic except white ash and a tangle of dragon-gold thread. The fire burned nothing but the Tapestry. Then, it ceased.

Merilbe entered the room and slowly moved to the Starstep. Rogsin backed away as if by command dropping his torch on the stone floor. The last remaining piece of the Tapestry, the scrap in Rogsin's pocket, grew hot enough to scald his flesh but it did not burn. Merilbe raised his hands. The commotion quieted. Those people still holding buckets set them to the floor.

"When true kings near death, the Tapestry oft-time stills," Merilbe said. "The Tapestry may have spoken again for the next King. Now it will speak no more. Display reverence."

Merilbe knelt with clasped hands. Those around him lowered their heads or knelt. The armored men stood at attention with one fist over their hearts.

No human had gotten a message from the Tapestry since Rogsin had his vision. The piece he cut from it ensured that. Nothing useful appeared for others, and no one but he knew why. "When true kings near death..." *Ha!* Rogsin's shoulders relaxed, he too lowered his head.

They'll never know. I'm safe. Next, I'll handle Merilbe and Onyx.

Onyx appeared at the doorway in her white morning dress like a pale specter. She walked stiffly to Rogsin and faced him with steely, gleaming eyes. Taller than him but slender as a willow sprig, Rogsin often hit or teased her when Hammond could not see it. Now, she showed no fear of him as she had not before. She grabbed Rogsin's shoulders, shook him, and then slapped his face, drawing blood from his mouth. He spat the blood clear. For the first time, Rogsin feared his sister. She had a new power in her he did not recognize.

"What did you do!?" she screamed hitting his shoulders with balled fists like blacksmiths hammering slag. The blows were painful but Rogsin did not cry out. "How will we know the next true king?" Rogsin pushed her away.

"I am your King," Rogsin replied. "I am his heir."

"You are not! Light of Light, you are no king!" Onyx fumed.

"The true heir must be worthy," Merilbe said sternly. "You have not proven so, Rogsin."

Rogsin surveyed the room. Nobles, merchants, guards and courtiers alike flinched at his words. Rage, or fear, or confusion consumed many faces and some all at once.

The people are not with me.

Before Rogsin could speak, the ashes of the Tapestry rose up and formed into a white funnel the height of a tall man. Lighting flashed as the whirlwind became solid. The others in the room backed away, everyone but Onyx and Merilbe cowered. The wizard approached it and pushed his hand against it. It did not yield.

"It is cold," Merilbe said.

A shout rose from the people. The mourners continued receding from the strange white form. Some ran from the room screaming. The apparition shifted, slowly dancing toward Onyx in the gentle spinning motion of a top. Onyx stood wide-legged as if bracing for a blow. Rogsin fell to his knees. His dread rendered him unable to move. Onyx raised her hands in reverence to this strange visitor. She did not waver as it approached her, not in body or in voice.

"Spirit of Light, I give myself to you," she proclaimed strongly.

The funnel stopped before her. She entered it and disappeared. Guards came forward hands to hilts. The funnel dissolved into white ash and again spun, burning white fire. The guards gave it space to pass and it continued until it reached Starstep. Once there, it spun faster and faster atop the floor carving a fiery pillar of lime-rock or salt, Rogsin could not tell. Then, like in his vision of years ago, the heat singed his hair although it was ten paces from him. Draco moved toward it with a great effort as if advancing against a mighty wind; his unbraided mane smoldered and flew behind him like a tattering flag in a terrible storm.

The whirling stopped. The odd funnel disintegrated, leaving a ring of fine powder on the floor and an unharmed Onyx. A coil of dragon-gold thread lay at her feet. Onyx's black hair had turned white with frost. Rogsin shivered.

"What does this mean?" Draco asked.

"She is a magic-weaver," said Kendrick, the scribe. "Penelope knows the tale. It tells of the original Tapestry makers. White fire chose them."

"Me? I can't," Onyx said. "I know no such handcraft."

"The Light has chosen you," Merilbe said. "I have need of consulting my scrolls. How did that song go, Kendrick?"

"It speaks of signs for weaving a magic Tapestry, such as we just witnessed. That's what she must do," Kendrick answered.

Onyx faded into her old self. The power in her was gone or hidden from Rogsin's perception.

"There is more," Merilbe said. "It's not that simple. I must examine the scrolls deeply. Only a true heir weaves magic. With these omens of the end-age, no new Tapestry can be made now. Did the Tapestry choose a queen as its last act? I must see Penelope's library."

Rogsin moved to the wizard and stomped his foot down saying "Look at all the scrolls you like old man, the age is new and I am the King. Writings of the former age no longer matters."

"I will see about that Rogsin. You are not king yet. I will answer this riddle."

You'll never get the chance.

Onyx collapsed onto her knees and wept before the Starstep. She covered her face with her hair. The ice melted from her locks and pooled on the Starstep mixed with her tears. The water became a shimmering mirage showing a new Tapestry for all to see. It was a very different reaction compared to the acidic bubbling Rogsin's spilled blood had wrought on the Starstep years before.

"I'm not worthy," Onyx muttered, "so unready am I. Oh Father, why did you leave?"

Rogsin came closer as did Draco each from opposite sides of the Starstep. Draco reached her first. Rogsin held his words.

How dare that lizard offer aid to my sister!

Draco gently presented his massive hand to her. She accepted it, rose to her feet and fell against Draco. Her slender arms embraced Draco's thick, scaly neck, two ghost vines on a tree trunk. Onyx's sobs increased while Draco patted her back. After a time, Onyx dried her wet cheeks with Draco's mane and whispered into his ear. Draco ignored the breach of manors.

Rogsin's anger at Draco and this entire display of affections between dragon and human caused Rogsin's insides to quake but he made no sign. He could ill afford emotional reactions that would make matters worse for him before witnesses. If he learned anything at court it was to hold back his true feelings when it mattered most. Still, he must establish authority.

"I will fetch Penelope," Draco said. "You need not act until we know more."

"Onyx will do as I say," Rogsin said evenly. "I am King."

"I am the Steward until the elders decide," Draco said. Onyx remained in his embrace. "More so, no king is seated until he achieves eighteen years. You won't be of age until spring. Onyx reaches queen's-age, 21, by then, too. We have time."

Onyx broke from Draco, kissed his snout. She left him, returning to the Great Hall for the feast prepared in memory of Hammond. The remaining mourners and guards followed. Draco, Merilbe and Rogsin lingered. Draco's and Rogsin's eyes met. The two eye-needled each other until Rogsin finally broke.

"You are not King yet," Draco reiterated, pressing his chest forward. Red fire filled his mouth. "Make no presumptions."

Rogsin cowered, turned and stomped away.

"They will pay," Rogsin swore under his breath. He left the room and climbed the stairs to the residence forgoing the funereally feast.

Merilbe first—I will lock him in the tower, quietly. I have guards loyal to me.

A plan for arresting and imprisoning Merilbe formed fully in his mind. With that, Rogsin's mood improved.

Late that night Rogsin ordered the King's counselor arrested. Merilbe was safely hidden away. No one knew where he had gone except Rogsin and the guards who did the deed. Next day and from that day onward Rogsin demanded that no one spoke of Merilbe. But the star-headed crow did not obey. The day after the burning that crow was heard squawking, "He's in the tower, he's in the tower," which prompted Rogsin's next decree: crows were not to be tolerated on Vinetop. As such, a royal bounty was placed on all crows but few hunters had heart enough to collect such rewards.

TWENTY TWO

The Ruin of Mars

In the mists of this emergency Praxis took the lead and sent Zandora racing for home. The call for help would reach Rookery Top far ahead of this make-do dragon flotilla. Praxis prayed the Light she and her band would hold together until help arrived.

Nedell and Timor pulled Mars by ropes in front. Twenty miles from home and with everyone already tired beyond reckoning Nedell's sharp ears heard it first.

"The horns," he cried. "The alarm sounds."

"Come on," Praxis called out, "not long now, redouble your efforts."

One after the other they all heard the horns and hope inspired them to flap harder. Every dragon panted brown smoke in exhaustion, a bad sign. Praxis held her doubts. Aiding the pullers Charlotte and Praxis struggled to keep Mars' wings spread by using their own extended wings to prop his while they beat their tails. It was exhausting. In this way, the brood managed to keep the wounded Mars aloft. Head winds made things worse. For the first time ever Praxis wished Gordon and Bullock were near. Big, strong dragons had their place. Brute strength was what the band needed. Carrying Mars was like spitting rocks up-wind.

"We're not going to make it!" Praxis cried between gasps of air.

"We aren't made to fly like this," Charlotte rasped.

Praxis' shoulder blades burned beyond fire. Her tail ached and her body shuddered with every stroke. Praxis' head drooped with fatigue. Charlotte flew with her eyes closed in grim concentration.

Charlotte fares no better than I.

"Don't give up, they're coming," Nedell called.

Just as she could bear it no longer two adult dragons charged in and took Praxis' and Charlotte's stations. The unconscious body of Mars suddenly lurched higher. Blood splattered Praxis' wing from above. More adults took Nedell's and Timor's positions.

The boys let go and drifted upward while the adults whisked Mars toward the Rookery. Praxis tried to keep up despite her exhaustion. Her fire went out. Her fuel gone, she made no smoke yet she flapped.

"Rest," a dragon warrior chided. The sky was now alive with dragons "Dangerous flying without reserves."

"I can't leave him," Praxis said.

"I will sustain you," he said as he latched onto Praxis's flight bags with his feet. He guided her in and let go on high allowing her wing-room to land. Praxis landed on Rookery Top's playing fields against all protocol. As Praxis flew below the rim, Penelope and Wren charged across the grounds.

"Make way the healer!" Penelope cried.

Praxis found her feet and rushed to Mars lying on the further field. She found him on his side. Wren was quickly applying a numbing potion on the wound. A thick, wooden shaft lay deep within his neck several inches below his jaw.

"Pull the spear," Penelope implored, her voice choked by tears.

"Nay," Wren said. "Pulled wrong, a barb makes a wound worse. It's near an artery. Barbs rip veins open. I need to know the nature of the point."

"Can anyone identify this thing!?" Penelope cried. "What is it? The healer must know." She stated pacing back and forth with her feathers askew and her hands waving in the air like a man fighting nats. Praxis had never seen her so out of sorts.

A dragon warrior came close and examined the shaft.

"That is no spear, nor arrow," he said. "I don't know its nature."

"This is beyond my skill," Wren said wiping the blood from her hands on a rag. "I can ease the pain, but he won't last long without a surgeon."

"The nearest surgeon is in Highlands. He'll die!" Penelope cried.

"Emerald," Isis said. "Forbidden Mountain is only eighty miles."

The mention of Emerald caused murmurs to rise among the gathered dragons and men. Emerald was banned from Rookery Top. If Penelope allowed him here, she would suffer for it. Isis knew it best. Such treachery in the face of disaster, Praxis thought. Should Penelope fall, Isis was first in line to replace her.

Penelope's crown flatted while Isis' feathers stood taller than Praxis had seen before. Tears glistened on the scales below Penelope's eyes. The crowd fell so quiet that everyone heard Mars' ragged breathing.

"Get Emerald, Hillguard," Penelope ordered. "By all that is Light, fly fast."

"He will not come without payment," Hillguard said. "What do you send?"

"My gold, my life, whatever he wants," Penelope replied. "If Mars lives by that wizard's arts, he can have anything I posses."

Hillguard, a fast flyer with powerful legs, leaped into the sky, wings half-wide, he stopped and hovered in mid-air.

"He will come, Matron," Hillguard promised, "or I'll leave him dead."

Hillguard flapped his overlarge wings and beat his tail with speed Praxis had never witnessed. Penelope collapsed, drawing her wings over her head. She sobbed. Praxis sat on her own tail next to Penelope and cried with her. Before long, all the females—except for Wren who was focused on her lifesaving work—wept, too, even Isis.

TWENTY THREE

Emerald and Hillguard

In the depths of his caves, Emerald poured water into a white stone basin. In its' calm water, his face reflected pleasure. He dropped a pinch of Rookery earth into the pool. The water bubbled and smoked until a haze condensed above it. In the haze, Emerald saw Hillguard racing across the northeast sky at tremendous speed.

The Inowise had crafted the seeing bowl in the Garden of Neff long before men came into this world. Upon his arrival in the Forbidden Mountains, Emerald stole it for his own use. The peaceful Inowise didn't expect such seizure and they would not recover it by force. To gain access to the bowl, the Inowise now paid Emerald a fee such as information on hidden travel routes and other useful bits. Emerald's henchmen criss-crossed Neff safely by these roads providing Emerald with goods, magic and secrets.

I am no proper magician. Yet, my deceptions are keener than magic.

The Inowise Bear Claw, a watcher set by his kind to keep an eye on Emerald, stood near. He brushed long, knotted hair away from his brown eyes. In the dark of the cave, Bear Claw's animal skin tunic blended with his hair and tangled beard. Emerald could not tell where Bear Claw's natural hair ended and the animal skin began. As an Inowise living close to the living Earth, Bear Claw read much more in the smoke. Emerald's only way to learn what his hairy companion saw in the smoke was to ask direct questions, but Emerald received only three answers in each moon cycle. That was the deal.

"Ah what brings you to me, Hillguard the swift," Emerald said, "and in such a hurry?"

"The Golden," the Inowise replied. "He is shot; he will die unless you go. Your first question is answered."

Emerald rumbled a low laugh but unlike other dragons, he made no smoke. He had no internal fire. Though perceived as weakness in dragon society, Emerald recognized his advantage. No one knew his intentions by his vapors. Lack of a sparking-glad was not a handicap as he had wired flints to his back teeth to spark fire when he needed it.

"This Mars is quite the prodigy. Even my dear brother, Draco, considers him a warlord-in-waiting. This young Mars may destroy me. Why would I help my competition?"

"He will not be warlord. He is no threat," Bear Claw said. "Besides, he is your son."

Emerald's balance faltered as his head suddenly swirled. Emerald blurted his last question unintentionally.

"My son! How can this be?"

Emerald cursed his outburst. He already knew the answer.

"You caste a spell and seduced Penelope. She thought you her husband, Atmere. The same stolen spell allowed King Hammond's brother Mordune to ravage the King's wife. Like him, the price will be your life but not today. I have spoken."

The Inowise crossed his arms over his massive chest, signaling he had finished his obligation.

"How will I die?" Emerald asked, knowing he would not get the answer. The very question was a taunt to the primitive man. He bargained in good faith while Emerald never did which the Inowise race found offensive.

Bear Claw straightened to his full height, slightly more than an adolescent human. He thumped his chest with a thick fist and jutted out his jaw, a jaw more pronounced than other humans. His heavy brow furrowed until the lines of his forehead molded rugged valleys.

"No more," Bear Claw proclaimed. "I read this moon's smoke. This I will tell is common wisdom. He who plants poison seeds eats bitter harvests. The vine will choke you. Its fruit is death. You will die by your own devices."

"Only if Draco finds out," Emerald retorted. "The defilement of my brother's chosen is a pleasure I will keep to myself and treasure. I'll foster wars and keep Draco occupied beyond his breeder years."

"What of the Golden?" Bear Claw asked. "The spell you wrought provides his inner power."

"Yours is not to ask questions." Emerald said. He considered the question and deemed Mars too immature a creature to earn Emerald's concern. "Tell my servants to make ready. Set fire to the beacon. We have an esteemed guest in rout."

Emerald smoothed his waxed crown feathers with a delicate hand. His crown would not inform Hillguard of his feelings. Bear Claw left the alcove and ran out into the main tunnel. He rousted Emerald's human servants. They set to preparing food and they lit the lamps along the landing path and into the mountain's entry. Few visited here so it was a strange sight to Emerald's eyes. Emerald went to the landing and paced before a freshly lit signal fire.

Customarily messengers ate and rested before giving deliveries. This was Emerald's opportunity to ply Hillguard with strong drink and potions, coaxing him to misspeak.

Hillguard is wise, a challenge. I hoped he is thirsty. Emerald chuckled.

Hillguard landed with such velocity Emerald moved against the mountain's face to avoid getting run down. He landed with a billow of fire. Emerald hopped forward and extended his hand. Hillguard refused it.

"No time for pleasantries," Hillguard said. "We need a surgeon, now. We must fly. Let us negotiate."

"Who sends for me?" Emerald asked. "Where do we go?"

"Penelope calls you to Rookery Top. What is your price?"

"Alas, I am banned," Emerald said his eyes downcast in false respect. "I cannot go."

"Penelope removes the ban—forever, if you'll come at once. That is her offer."

"Not much of an offer. Draco will pluck my scales for that," Emerald said.

"Penelope will placate Draco. What is your price?"

"Let me think," Emerald said.

Emerald resumed his song and his pacing. Hillguard waited, watching with trained eyes for magic, but Emerald had no tricks. Hillguard did not know that. Emerald could bluff but there was no point. Emerald wanted to go. He wanted a good look at his son, but he had to name a suitable price or he'd be suspected of cooperation. Opportunities like this were few.

Hillguard took from his pouch a magic rope. Emerald was no match for Hillguards girth in a fight.

"I want as much booty as I can carry from the treasure room," Emerald said.

"A standard messenger's pouch," Hillguard replied."

"Your pouches," Emerald said. "Yours only. I'll keep them, too."

Hillguard hesitated. His famous pouches were blessed with magic and lined with dragon-wings leather and thus carried twice the usual weight without the added burden to the flyer. Hillguard threw back his head and let out a great blast of fire.

"Done," he agreed. "If we go now, this moment."

Hillguard placed a hand on his long knife and loosened his grip on the magic rope.

"As you wish," Emerald agreed. "I need my medical implements."

"If we are too late," Hillguard said, "I will cut off your wings. Hurry."

Emerald called for his medical bags. His human servants brought them and fit him for flight under Hillguards close watch. The two departed within minutes.

TWENTY FOUR

Emerald at the Rookery

Wren continually bathed Mars' wound with clotting herbs and a numbing potion. Penelope never felt so helpless. As she watched Mars drift in and out of awareness her hope wavered with his state. He seemed without pain until he moved. Whenever Mars bent his neck, the bleeding resumed and he shook with pains. To prevent more damage, Wren finally applied a suave under his nose that made him sleep. With Mars stilled, Wren flopped onto a nearby rock as if a great weight drove her down. Penelope's heart felt as heavy.

"I can do nothing more," Wren said, her voice full of disappointment.

Praxis had not left Mars's side since landing. The other young flyers waited at a distance no doubt full of fears and heartaches. Penelope had to set the example. It was her station. She put on a face of clam although her guts were ripped asunder. She regretted her earlier display. Now it was time for answers.

"What happened?" Penelope asked Praxis in kindly voice.

"We were flying laps, like always…I…I mean…We…Mars…"

Praxis' head fell almost touching the ground. Her tears poured out and splashed on blue-stone. Penelope choked down her grief for the child's sake.

"No one is in trouble," Penelope said in her most soothing tone. "Praise the Light, you thought fast. I'm proud of all of you. Tell me what happened."

"We passed Singing Rock Point," Praxis said. "Mars saw some glitter on the Point. I told him to stay on route. I tried to tell him...but he broke ranks showing off. He's always showing off. We chased him. I cut in front to stop him. He raced past me. Suddenly, he was falling."

Praxis sobbed uncontrollably. Penelope gently patted her neck, stroked her crown and waited. The young dragon slowly stopped crying.

"Mars saved me," Praxis said between sobs. "He blocked it. I don't know where that spear came from but I saw a human running."

"Who was it?" Penelope asked.

"His back was to us. I saw a hunter's green cloak, green leggings, feathered cap. That was all I saw."

"Two dragons!" the Rookery Top sentries called.

Penelope's heart leapt. Emerald and Hillguard banked in, both dragons landing quickly. Emerald rushed to Mars who now lay like a dead rock. Even with sunlight fully upon him, Mars' scales did not glow. They were black.

"He has no hue," Emerald remarked. "Some help!"

Everyone except Penelope and Praxis stepped away from the green wizard.

"Give him aid!" Penelope ordered. "Remove his flight-bags."

Several humans rushed to assist Emerald with his gear. As they worked, Emerald shot questions at Wren about what potions she used. Emerald demanded they boil water and bring clean cloths. With that in motion, Emerald approached Mars and scrutinized the wound. Penelope drew close as well anxious to see Emerald's reactions. His countenance remained business-like but not grim. This gave her hope. Then, he noticed the barb and he stiffened. Was it recognition?

Then, Emerald's hue and feathers rippled every dark color in a flash, surely the mark of dread. His consternation disappeared in less than a blink, but Penelope noted Emerald's lapse. He unpacked his tools as if nothing had happened and made ready for surgery.

"He recognizes the dart," Penelope whispered to herself. Emerald was distracted. Praxis was the only dragon near enough to hear.

"How do you know?" The child asked.

"Not now."

"How could he—."

"Later," Penelope interrupted.

The other dragons stood mesmerized by the surgeon arranging his tools. A man pumping a hand bellows at the cauldron heating water covered their words. No one saw the deeper drama unfolding save Praxis. Penelope could not let her suspicions fly. Penelope knew then she must take Praxis into confidence. *The child must adapt the ways of the highborn sooner than later.* Slated to intern at court, Praxis would benefit from an early lesson. *Never volunteer information. Secrets prosper or destroy kingdoms.* Penelope's overheard words must be guarded.

Penelope quietly instructed Wren to keep careful eyes on Emerald, knowing Praxis was within earshot.

"He may do harm even while appearing to heal," Penelope warned.

Wren nodded and continued to layout the supplies Emerald had requested. Praxis peered at Penelope with startled, fearful eyes.

"Will he be all right?" Praxis asked.

Fresh tears rolled down her cheeks. Penelope raised a finger to her own lips and spoke so all could hear.

"Mars lives or Emerald forfeits his wings," Penelope snarled. "No tricks, Wizard."

Emerald whipped his head toward her and hissed, "Is this how your treat your savior, Pod Mother?"

"I have no savior but the Light, and there lies the chosen of the Light," she replied. "Mischief upon him is mischief against all dragons."

She seldom spoke her perception of truth so loud and harshly. Mars held great promise but was yet unproven. Some accepted the lore some did not but her words of power had its effect.

Silence consumed the crowd. The only sounds on Sky Top were Mars' labored breathing and the subtle pats as dragons and people shifted their weight from side to side. Penelope and Emerald met eye-to-eye. A low, knowing rumbling laugh rolled from Emerald's guts. He resembled Draco in that. Emerald removed scales from around the bolt shaft as Mars' hot blood dripped onto the cool mica rock floor.

"Spare me. This golden so blessed may help me, if he lives," Emerald said. "Little golden female, come here."

Praxis trembled. She gazed at Penelope, unsure what to do, her eyes begging for permission not to go, but Penelope would not stop any help Emerald wanted. She motioned for Praxis to join Emerald.

A wise move on his part. Her magic is closer to Mars' kind, she could help. She is, after all, golden. Like the saying goes, 'Gold heals Gold, Light begets Light.'

"I am no healer," Praxis cried. Her scales had gone pale on the suggestion. "I don't know what to do! Blood makes me sick."

"I will guide you," Emerald said as he worked. "I need your small hands."

Emerald had no time to mince words. Penelope thought Mars was fading. There was so much blood spilled, his breathing got worse by the second. Praxis backed away.

"By the Light, do it!" Penelope ordered. "Help Emerald!"

Emerald had cut an incision in Mars' neck, the skin was spread open giving room to work. Now he worked in earnest packing the wound with herb-mash as fast as Wren could prepare it, chanting a magic psalm while he worked. This kept the bleeding under control.

Lifting the scalpel again, he cut the incision deeper and had Praxis set the packing. Praxis overcame her well known urge to gag at the site of blood. Her hands were deep in Mars' wound, swimming in gore. Penelope thought her brave indeed. Blood spurted with each new slice and Praxis worked diligently to suppress it.

"Emerald knows his doctoring," Hillguard muttered.

Emerald focused on cutting. Praxis' color improved. Their movements grew smoother as they worked together. Emerald reached the shaft's end and called for his sewing gear. He worked a while at depth. Praxis held the tissue flaps stretched open. Finally, the blood stopped.

"His igniter glad is torn," Emerald said. "There's nothing we can do for that. I stitched what arteries were damaged. The point of the shaft is barbed. My hands are too large to remove it. Little golden, you must reach in and bring forth the point while I spread the incision. Do not let the barb turn."

With determination in her feathers Praxis reached in. She reported a snag as she carefully pulled. The barb came loose once Emerald opened the wound wider. With the arrow free, Emerald staunched new bleedings.

Then, he stitched the layers of muscle tissue working upward toward the surface. Meanwhile, Praxis packed herbs and sopped blood where needed. She seemed more at ease, and perhaps even enamored with the process. Penelope had seen such curiosity in her colors before.

Finally, they reached the last layer of open flesh. Emerald gave it to Praxis to sew and he couched her. Finally, he ordered Wren to make a cleansing potion for the wound. The last task was to apply herb-plaster. The familiar smells of Sky Top had twisted into the odors of blood and crushed herbs, unsetting even Penelope's well controlled gullet.

"Now, we wait," Emerald said.

The surgeon lifted Praxis' chin with his bloody hand saying. "Well done, little female."

Praxis pulled from Emerald's touch, cringing. Emerald grunted his satisfaction, much the way Draco did. The brothers' similarities disconcerted Penelope.

How could brood mates be so different in size, color and personality? Emerald a liar, Draco a leader.

"I'm for washing and eating," Emerald said. "Do I remember the way to the bathing springs and eatery? One forgets in a thousand years."

With a nod of her head, Penelope directed Hillguard to escort Emerald. Hillguard jumped down from the crater's rim. The two disappeared into the Lower Way tunnel with Emerald humming a merry tune favored at the lowborn's hearths.

With the wizard gone and the surgery complete, tension broke. Conversations ran through the crowd. Penelope unleashed pent up tears as she observed the slumbering Mars. A few others sobbed softly. Praxis, overwhelmed by her experience exclaimed, "Poor Mars, will he live?"

"He's all right," Charlotte said solemnly. "He'll recover."

Everyone cocked an ear toward Charlotte. She was a quiet one that only spoke when she had something important to say. All dragons had magic, each strong in one kind or another. Charlotte had a talent for seeing.

"Are you sure?" Penelope asked.

Charlotte stared into the sun. When Charlotte turned again, her eyes were sunlit pools of still, deep water.

"He'll live, but dark paths and long roads await him," Charlotte said.

TWENTY FIVE

The Time of Leaving

Penelope dreaded this day. Even her favorite sunning perch on the rim was no comfort—from it she saw Draco winging toward Rookery Top. She shivered. Even the warm fall sun could not warm her heart. The time of leaving had come six months too early. The brood was not ready, but Draco moved the release schedule saying he wanted them placed before Rogsin became King. Penelope knew Draco's real motivation; he needed steeds for his advancing armies. *He'll assign my students support stations and push the last brood's recruits into service.*

"They are still children in their hearts," Penelope lamented.

With King Hammond dead and his successor still under age, small opportunistic border wars erupted. The Twelve Estates' Lord's endless squabbles had proliferated—bad timing for her restriction to Rookery Top for her so-called crime. Outland countries lustfully eyed the Kingdom's rich lands as always. That miserable Rogsin was far from ready to take the throne yet factions already backed him secretly and freelance spies flocked to his service in anticipation of his rule. Rogsin's lack of wisdom in politics already instigated many conflicts. Mending relationships was her job, a job Draco won't let her do. He said it was his duty.

Duty, duty to that evil child?

Rogsin did not look or act like Hammond. Long had she felt the darkness within him, a curse she sought to expose to unseat him but it remained hidden. The burning of the Tapestry should have provided enough reason not to follow that impetuous boy.

Draco could have used this catalyst to lead dragon folks away to greener lands but he did not. Penelope wanted to hate Draco, but love's deep indwelling was greater. The same love-measure was not apparent with Draco. Once again he girded his heart with duty and thus forgoes the honor of Light, the prophets and the Patriarch's primary charge: Protection of dragon kind. All in all she could not hate him. Theses times were not Draco's doing. He was a dragon of his time.

"How did we fall so low?" Penelope said, exhaling black smoke.

Draco landed lightly below her perch.

"How indeed," Draco snorted. "We must deal with this reality."

"When dragons forget history, the Light fades," Penelope said.

She jumped from the rim onto Sky Top's floor.

"When the garden was green, when the Giants gave dragons humans to care for, the Giants warned us 'keep your ways first, least darkness invade your hearts,'" Penelope reminded him. "They did not intend us to become like them or serve them. We must leave them before it is too late."

Penelope, hopeful upon seeing reflections of light in Draco's eyes, continued.

"Humans were low creatures, greedy for power and land: Now we horde treasures, too. We once gave freely. Ravens brought us news and wisdom and we shared our gold and stones. The eagles hunted fish for us in exchange for our molted scales. Now humans kill eagles and make armor from our scales. The ravens watch but speak no more. We traded foolishly. This is not how it is supposed to be."

The dragons sweeping the floors heard Penelope's voice and stopped to listen, drawn to the magic of a story teller. She lowered her voice and broke the spell. Draco shook his head. His crown feathers stiffened. He rumbled that famous laugh.

"You've invoked my youth," he said, "a time full of fancies and hopes, but reality strikes."

"Reality is your bane, so here is a measure. Praxis desires the healer's trade, she rejects court. Rescind that assignment, you need healers."

"Rogsin calls for Praxis. He wants a golden in his court," Draco said lowering his head and scuffing his tail tip. "He will be King and if I cross him now things will not go well for the armies."

"Send Mars. By your own rule and the Scrolls of Neff, the infirmed cannot fight."

He will be safe there, away from battles, let the Sages educate him there.

"He can't spit fire, nor carry the weight of a suited knight, but he is stout-hearted, plus a fast and agile flyer. He will be my wing scout. Mars goes to War Camp."

"No!" Penelope cried.

Her flame shot past Draco searing his crown feathers.

"I won't let you squander his potential," she replied. "I am Pod Mother. I have a say. I invoke my right. Mars goes to the Inowise sages. He goes to the Collage of Light!"

Draco rose on his hind legs and extended his long neck. The maces woven into his mane swayed. Penelope held her stance. Black smoke rolled from Draco's mouth. His head bobbed as fire filled his mouth. Draco inhaled deeply. A barrage of flame-hot arguments would follow. She had seen this before and was not afraid yet every dragon and man near cowered. Even that old crow with the star on his head, Roecon it calls it's self, retreated. Penelope would not be moved.

"I will choose my own way," Mars said as he emerged from the West Gate tunnel.

"Only Warlords give vocations and only the head Pod Mother can say yes or no," Penelope said. "Unless you wish to be an outcast like Emerald—."

"I am already an outcast," Mars interrupted coming nearer. "My brood mates avoid me. They laugh at my infirmity. Cast me out! If I can't live as a warrior, if I have no fire, I am not a dragon."

Mars ran down the West Gate tunnel.

"You give false hopes, Draco," Penelope snarled. "He can't go to war. You know the law."

"What good is the law if Vineland falls? Vineland needs Mars. I need Mars." Draco said.

"Dragon kind needs every dragon and we need our Patriarch to respect the law. Will you abandon it now? Mars will find a place in the order."

Draco lowered his stance in the face of reason. He deflated and bowed his head.

"Go to your son, then" Draco said. "Soothe him; help him accept that he will not go to War Camp. We all have out part to play in these times. Let the Sages have him."

Draco turned and walked away. Penelope started down the West Gate tunnel with her ears open and hope in her heart. And, yet, Draco gave up too easily. She was not convinced it was over. More so, she felt something she could not square just begun.

TWENTY SIX

Mars on Raven Rock

Mars ran, blinded by tears, until he arrived at the West Gate landing. He jumped upon the Raven Rock, craving sun. It was a bright place good for thinking. The ravens were not pleased. Moving to the far edge of the stone, the ravens squawked at Mars. Mars gathered a handful of stones and spat a few at passing birds, missing widely. Raven stones, which were piled there, chosen for shine of color were oddly shaped and thus made poor projectiles.

"I will thank you to leave my collection in peace," the oldest Raven said. "Do I go to your nest and abscond with your scales? A little common decency, if you please."

Mars dropped the rocks he still had in his hand. Ravens rarely talked to dragons and never to humans. Still, he didn't see it as an honor.

"Fly off or I'll use you for target practice," Mars said. "Leave me alone."

"Mars, you won't hurt me or any innocent creature," said the old bird. "Hear my wisdom: Warmongering is not your true nature. I've said too much. I'll take my leave."

The bird flew off slowly.

Senile old bird.

"Soldiers do as ordered!" Mars called. "I'm a fighter!"

Half a year had passed since he was shot. He had made his recovery. Even his scales had grown back.

How can Mother be so happy? I was born to be a warrior. Now, Praxis, she's always preaching about the Light. All she talks about is becoming a healer. Big deal!

"What will I become without fire?" Mars asked bitterly, "Some dumb sage?"

Without fire, the other broodlings no longer befriended him. Except Praxis and she forever tailed him like he was a needy child. She helped him after his injury and for that Mars was beholden. She kept him company when the others spurned him. He had expected the others to warm to him when he healed, but they didn't. Worst of all and in the midst of her attendance, Praxis transformed into a little Penelope. He hated that. Even so, Mars was glad for one dragon on his side that wasn't his mother.

"Bad luck rubs off," the others taunted him. "A dragon without fire is unlucky."

How can they say that! I lived. That shot could have killed two dragons and I lived. How is that bad luck!

Mars knotted his tail-fin and whipped it against the mountain. A piece of rock hurled straight up into the air. It bashed it way down the mountain's face until all rumor of it vanished.

I've got the best tail-strikes too, not even Bullock can match that. I'm the best.

"You know Emerald's frustration," the old star headed crow said flying in. "He has talents, too and like you no one wants him near, either."

"That's just what I need; a crow's wisdom," Mars said dismissing the crow with a wave of his hand. The crow did make Mars think of the green wizard.

Emerald born without can make fire. He uses magic. Is that so bad? I could learn that. I'm true like Draco. I earned my way! How can I be so scorned? Natural fire isn't the be-all.

Before the accident, Draco had taken Mars under his wing. Then, he was the envy of every dragon.

Now even Draco rejects me.

Before today, the last time Draco came to Rookery Top was two days after Mars was shot. Draco forgave Mother then saying, "One dragon's life saved supersedes the banishment. It was a price well paid."

From a half-sleep on his bed of straw, Mars listened to the tenderness between Draco and Penelope, something he had never heard before. They agreed Mars would not regain his fire. Penelope and Draco lamented this. Draco spoke the war-code that day, referring to Mars as one of "the aged, young and crippled" that cannot go into battle.

Draco had found a way around that code and Mother stopped him.

Mother ruined it.

But Mars would not disappoint Draco.

"I must get my fire back," Mars told the crow. "I will have it or die seeking it."

Penelope emerged from the tunnel saying. "Dragon kind needs you, even as you are. A messenger or sage you will find your place outside war fields. Draco knows this, he relents. You cannot become a wing sentry. There is other help you can provide."

"I can't help if I'm not allowed to fight," Mars returned. "What good am I without fire?"

"Fire doesn't matter in the Lore of Light. With wisdom, you'll help us all. Don't you see that? Your golden scales, the Crest of Neff: These are signs. It's the prophecy. You are the beacon. You will lead us if you make the right choices. Fire is not a blessing. 'Black smoke makes shadows' not light."

"Fire is everything," Mars retorted slamming his tail. "If it wasn't, Emerald would be Warlord and not Draco. Green hatched first."

Mars crossed his arms over his breast. His chest felt hot as if his fires would burst. Yet, he had no flame. Frustrated, Mars spat a stream of bile over the cliff.

"That is not the reason," Penelope answered sadly. "Emerald is a creature of darkness. He lives in shadow. Finding fire so late in his life only burned his heart blacker."

Mars spit acid at his mother's feet. It sizzled but did not ignite. Penelope glared at Mars with blazing eyes. Red and black smoke billowed from her snout.

"How dare you," Penelope said with ice in her voice. "Disrespect brought Emerald low, would you bring yourself to such ruin?"

Penelope released a jet of fire over the parapet. She narrowed her eyes and snarled with a viciousness Mars had never heard.

"Don't try me young dragon," she said. "Go to your nest and consider this—either chose college, a trade or Emerald's black road, but you will not go to War Camp! I have the right to override Draco in this. He cannot have you. Now go!"

Mars, now glaring himself, hopped from the Raven Rock and entered the tunnel dragging his tail.

She doesn't understand- nobody understands. How can my own mother treat me so unkind?

TWENTY SEVEN

Mars Runs Away

Zandora rushed into the common-use library, where Praxis was reading medical scrolls. She breathlessly shared news of the argument between Warlord and Matron with Praxis.

"Mars heard them fighting," Zandora said after her recounting. "He fled in anger and that's never good. Do you think he'll do something stupid?"

Only Mars would get upset. Everyone knows dragons can't go warring without fire. Fire is the only defense against missiles. Of course Penelope refused Draco's offer. It was common sense. Yet there was more. It was the prophecy. Dragons were in peril.

"Mars must not get lost in human traditions or he won't be unable to lead dragons. The prophets and signs concur, the end of our age is nigh," Penelope had confided in her. "Mars is the dragon foretold."

Although Praxis supported Penelope's righteous hopes, she harbored her own selfish ones. Active warlords could not wed. Sages and healers could. She did not envy Penelope and Draco, their lives were not their own, their jobs never ending. As a result, little love remained between them.

" 'There is no Light greater that love,' " Penelope had once quoted to Praxis. "Don't let Mars go."

With the accident, everything changed. The obnoxious pride Mars had acquired upon touring with Draco dissipated once he was grounded. As the others prepared for life after graduation, Mars grew more distant and obsessed with fire. Determined to reject Penelope's fate, Praxis planned to follow Mars to college after her internship at court.

Akin to Mars' relationship with Draco, Praxis had earned a home under Penelope's wing. There she learned about the ways of court. More importantly, she learned the ways of Neff. To aid her dreams of becoming a healer, Penelope had Wren give Praxis classes in those arts.

'Follow your heart's desire,' Penelope had said. 'Consider this; it is not enough to treat wounds. Healers must treat souls, too.'

Praxis made it her goal to make Mars see the value in college. The more Praxis pressed him, the more he withdrew. Things were not going well between them.

'College is for weaklings,' Mars had said. 'I'm made for war. I'm the Golden. I have the Crest. Draco needs me!'

'I need you, dragon kind needs you,' Praxis returned. 'Let's go to school together. We'll help everyone. You don't need fire. We can bond-mate.'

'A dragon without fire is nothing,' Mars had said. 'How could I ever marry you if you don't understand that, my need?'

Mars stomped off spitting acid and hadn't said a word to her since. Praxis left the library, having heard the tale of Draco and Penelope's argument, and roamed the tunnels and galleries seeking Mars wishing to comfort him. She found him in the dorm, a great wide cavern with shallow depressions carved into the walls for dragons' nests. Sobs came from Mars' bunk.

"Mars," She called softly. "Can we talk?"

"Go away," Mars said.

"The sun is setting. Let's go outside."

"I won't go out until I've made up my mind like the scrolls say 'dark places for dark thoughts.'"

Praxis took the only lit torch from its bracket and sparked the other wall sconces. She could have used her fire, but out of respect for Mars, she did not. She also lit the hearth pit and silently sat by the fire with her tail curled under her. Mars descended from his bunk and joined her. Praxis poked one of the logs with an iron rod. As he sat she placed the rod back in the fire tender's stand. She then rested her head on Mars' neck. The hues of their golden scales increased together as one, the cavern's ambient light increased ten-fold; the clear crystals embedded within the rocks sparkled gold.

"Everyone leaves in two days," Mars said. "Draco will not wait."

"I know. Draco sends me to Rogsin. I will do as bid but I won't stay beyond my internship."

"Draco wanted to make me a wing scout," Mars said, "but Mother overrode Draco's offer. Now I have no hope...no way to glory."

"You can earn honor in many ways. Penelope is right. I think college would have many opportunities. There is always hope, Mars."

"Not for us, we the youth. Nobody asks what we want. Draco and Penelope have no idea what I want or need. I'm sick of them."

Mars went to his bunk. He pulled out his travel packs, bulging and prepared for a long flight, and flung them over his back. He slipped into the shoulder harness.

"Where are you going?" Praxis asked.

Mars' crown shot tall. He flexed his wings and rolled his head to loosen his muscles for flight.

"I'm going to find my fire," Mars said. "I'll seek my own path. Why shouldn't I? We aren't slaves. I am of age."

He whipped an about-face like a soldier. He had previously removed his mane charms and now dropped them and his well earned awards on the floor leaving his hair unrestricted in the style of a free wanderer. Praxis was taken aback. She didn't know what reason to put forth. She had said it all before. Every dragon had the right to free wander before taking up a vocation and she had no right to stop him.

"Mars you can't…I…"

"Just watch me."

He leapt across the cavern and darted into the tunnel that leads to the Supply Landing. This exit off the mountain wasn't very far away. He would be long gone before anyone could follow.

"But where are you going?" She called after him.

She received no answer. With a heavy heart and tail dragging Praxis made her way from the deep to the mountain's top seeking to give Penelope the news.

TWENTY EIGHT

Mars and Emerald

Mars hardly noticed his flight bags while climbing to the height of the Streams. He flew by nose in the dark, his snout alert as Draco had taught. Draco showed him how the scent on the Streams told the cardinal directions. Mars knew his way blind, but he wanted a different stream, a thin, strange wind layer that came from the east and flowed counter to the prevailing winds of that direction. Mars had learned of it from worming-over the library's oldest books.

Draco had not taught the way to the Forbidden Mountains, only how to go around them nor would he speak of what lay within his brother's adopted homeland. Mars only knew that beyond those mountains, rife with haunted graves and ancient mysteries, was a place where the Inowise and dragon Sages communed. Far north and east the Sages lived and taught pilgrims the Lore of Light. The common way to that place traversed the dangerous old Giant's Road, a road where robbers and Outland raiders often lay in wait; flying over it was safe enough but a long slow flight without good winds. None took the shorter route over Emerald's stronghold by choice.

Mars sought the Forbidden Mountains, not what was beyond them. It was the very place where Giants buried their enemies and mistakes. It was the place where the first golden dragons were interned: their undying magic staved off the evil of older, darker ages. In death the first dragons protected the later dragon races. Deep in the bowls of the Earth evil beings and dark magic lived still, or so the tales say. Mars had his doubts but he could not deny the adverse conditions.

The Forbidden Mountains is where Emerald made his home; but where exactly? Those mountains were odd, without known maps and no rhyme or reason or order like other mountain ranges. All Mars knew for certain was they were made at the end of the First Age.

It is said that Giants had dug out the bad earth in Neff in order to plant the purest dragon garden and afterwards they heaped the refuge upon buried evils making cursed mountains. The range held darkness but what lay below it was worse, or so the lore said. The earth torn from Neff was condemned ages before Neff it's self was made unclean. What remained after the great excavation was Rookery Mountain a dead volcano forged by the fires of creation.

Mars loved the stories Penelope told. He wondered which tales were histories and which were myths. In his mind he saw her telling tales. A tear formed in his eye. Mars shook it away. A frozen tear could blind a dragon. He closed his flight eyelids and flew higher.

Mother forced me to leave. Why doesn't she understand? I need to restore my fire. Emerald will know how.

Mars did not know how to find the Contrary Stream. The conveyor to Emerald's caves was hidden from students least one be tempted to do as Mars did now. With the sun down, Mars had no line of sight or sense of direction. He flew up, then down and around for nearly an hour over the wastelands, searching and thinking himself a fool.

I can't fly by beating tail and wings all night and no place to land below.

While very high, he caught the scent of ice and the dust of deep age. Nothing smelled green within it. His doubts vanished. This was the way. He could find his way in the dark.

I must ride the currents by magic or land and rest. I have no fire to keep me warm.

Mars turned into the scent, curling his wings into sails. He let the wind carry him. He traveled blindly deep into the night, fighting the drowsiness that cold inflicted. As the night wore on lack of fire took its toll. His body temperature lowered steadily and he gathered ice. His muscles soon became too sore to flex off his frozen overcoat. The cold forced his hand.

I must set down, but where?

Around the time Mars thought he had made a fatal mistake, a distant red light flickered in the gloom. Of the many lights in the sky that night, this one was different. It was not a star. From that direction warmer air flowed. Mars next smelled wood smoke and meat cooking. His stomach growled in complaint as he adjusted his tail. He drove on for the beacon.

That must be Emerald's fire. Either he calls me, or I've found a mountain troll.

The ice piled on his back began crushing his lungs. The weight pushed him downward without consent. Mars had no choice. He rolled and arched his back breaking off the ice. He tumbled loosing height and direction. By the time he regained level flight he lost the push wind. He was obligated to beat his wings against crosswinds to stay his course.

He flew on exhausted. The beacon grew steadily brighter: The smell of oven-bread attacked the fatigue that threatened to down him. *Trolls do not bake bread.* Whoever was cooking below, he prayed the Light they would not harm him. With the last of his courage, driven by an empty stomach, Mars pressed to the finish.

The mouth of a cave appeared on the side of a mountain near its top. The cave entry, sided by lit torches, was made of worked stone. The archway was either new or well cared for, parts of it were chipped and stained but no moss grew on it. A wide, long landing of mud brick and cut stone jutted into the night before the doors. A bright, smoky fire burned near the landing's end. It was tended by a human and an Inowise. A baker's covered pot was set on a bed of coals that had been raked from the larger fire.

The scent of fire, smoke, steam and stew rose from a meat cauldron that was likewise set on raked coals.

Mars folded his icy wings with a crunch. They would not fully obey. Mars came in too fast and short. He hit the landing's edge, flipped over and, bounced twice before sliding to a stop. The man and the primitive one ran to him.

"We've been waiting," the Inowise said in high dragon speak while standing over Mars with laughter in his eyes. "Let us break bread."

Mars blinked both sets of eye lids as he had never seen an Inowise before, save drawings in scrolls. Such archaic men were depicted on school parchments but no drawing could ever capture the depth of wisdom that resonated from those deep-set eyes, nor was there mention of how stark a contrast the primitives conveyed while speaking with sophistication.

The Inowise lead Mars to the fire. The man, dressed in the clothes of Vineland, called for more servants to bring meat, hot wine and table wares. In less time than it took to sing a welcome song, Mars found himself in front of the fire with a sheep's wool blanket over his frozen back dipping buttered bread into hot rabbit stew.

The offer of kitchen food in the wilderness had surprised Mars, but supping with an Inowise that spoke high dragon seemed beyond all reason. *How does he know the high dragon language?* Human fighters that lived and worked with dragons understood dragon-speak, but only to a point. This primitive man spoke the perfect academic version, not the crude war tongue humans recognized.

"This must be a spell, or a dream," Mars said in common speech.

"This is quite real," the Vineland man said. "More an oddity to find you here."

"Emerald's abode?" Mars asked, still shivering.

"Indeed," the Inowise said in common human. "I am Bear Claw."

"I have questions," Mars said.

"The master is taking his rest," Bear Claw said, "We must talk, before he comes, so that I may speak truth. Even so, I am bound. I can only say so much. Ask."

He folded his massive hairy arms over his chest and grunted.

"How is it that Emerald is so learned?" Mars asked. "Dragons are not wizards, only humans. Can I trust him? I've come to restore my fire."

"He dwells within the burial caves," Bear Claw answered. "The ancestors of all creatures—giants, dragons and Inowise—rest here with books and treasures. Their bodies long ago became mists, but their artifacts remain. He studies their lost arts, industries best forgotten."

Bear Claw paused. Servants brought spits of raw rabbit and quail, setting the game on an iron cooking rack that was erected near the edge of the fire. The servants tarried until the Inowise spat upon the fire. He pounded his chest and the servants scurried from the landing. Once the servants disappeared, Bear Claw pushed his long, matted hair from his face. His beard covered from his cheek bones to his ears. Bear Claw resumed in a lower voice.

"The green one knows too much but he is unwise. He lacks understanding," the Inowise said. "Trust not what he teaches. He only tells what benefits him."

Bear Claw took a sizzling quail from the fire, more raw than cooked. He tore it from the spit and stuffed it into his mouth. His massive jaws ground side-to-side. The fowl's bones cracked and crunched. He swallowed it in one gulp like an unfettered country dragon. Mars immediately liked Bear Claw. *Any man that eats like a dragon is a friend of mine.*

"Guard your speech. Liars know lies," Bear Claw said. He grunted. "He comes."

Torch light flickered from the cave. That Vinelander Mars had seen first stood just inside the cave, out of earshot, swinging his arms and patting his body against the cold.

That thin Vinetop fellow wore the attire of a court servant; black knee-breeched pants, green velour vest and white hemp shirt, but his clothes and person were dirty with black soot and cooking spatters. Servants of Vinetop were proud and alert, this one with his down turned mouth appeared much less fit than one of his station should.

Emerald must not have had people here long. There isn't a wash tub for men.

While Mars watched the entry Bear Claw disappeared. Emerald hopped onto the landing, gnashed his teeth, and blew a great jet of fire.

Showing off!

"Ah, the foolishness of youth," rumbled Emerald with glee in his voice. "I knew you were coming, so I asked Walters to bake bread. But…why sit in the cold while the kitchen is warm and well stocked? Servants' meals and signal fires are no place for the Golden."

Emerald glared at the thin man in the mouth of the cave. The man crumpled.

"Master," he said, his eyes downcast, "the guest desired it, to replenish himself quickly."

Emerald's crown stood stiff. He looked directly at the butler. The man cowered further.

The man must be Walters, and he made no mention of Mars speaking with Bear Claw. Perhaps, he had a friend in Walters. How did these two come to serve Emerald? The butler could only have come by royal order. Why was the Inowise here?

Best keep my mouth shut and ears open.

"True enough," Mars said. "I asked for food and fire. I couldn't fly another mile nor walk another step. Sorry for crashing in. I landed a beggar at your door."

"It would be crude of me to turn away a rare visitor and one so auspicious," Emerald said. "I have not forgotten my manners. Walters, show young master Mars to a room. But first, tell me, why have you come?"

Mars thought he heard affection in Emerald's tone and almost spoke freely, but he knew better than to trust Emerald. Emerald was famously full of tricks. *I must not let my guard down.*

"Draco grounded me for my lack of fire," Mars said using the courtier's technique; grains of truth sprinkled within lies. "Mother wants me for college. Neither suits me. If I can't follow my heart, where should I go but to he who saved my life?"

"Indeed, indeed," Emerald said. "Where should rejects go? In my case, I sought higher ground. Walters, don't just stand there! Bring him in!"

"Will you have more food?" the servant asked as they walked.

"No," said Mars, "I'm for rest, it was a long night."

Walters showed Mars to a small room cut from solid rock off the main tunnel deep inside the mountain. The servant left Mars at the door. Its entry was mud-bricked and set with a dragon-size wooden door. Mars stepped inside. There was a stone table, a niche with a lit oil lamp, an iron coal pot radiating warmth, and an inviting alcove lined with dry, clean hay. It was a welcoming room. But, a ghostly chill suddenly consumed him. Evil filled the air like a nightmare. He backed into the corner. He closed his eyes against the fright and then the feeling he was watched vanished. Tiredness redoubled. With eyes half shut, he crawled into bed and quickly fell asleep.

In his dreams, he flew the front line of a great charging horde of golden dragons and men. Above the din of war, dragon voices from the stars whispered funeral chants and warned of danger. Mars cried out, still in his dream, "It's a trap!" Then, he awoke and saw that he was housed inside a burial crypt remade for the living but that dream-drudge continued inside his ears.

This is a strange place, where Star Songs penetrate stone or do the ghosts that dwell here sing?

Deep in the night Mars pondered his place in the world. The dragons of his dreams were those same ones he saw in his Tapestry vision; imagines remember vaguely and without meaning until this night. He recalled a part of that half-remembered vision. In it he flew among the great dragons of lore, dragons every child heard of, dragons long dead now, and yet he was counted among them. That was a good omen. Thus, he laid down his head again unafraid of the ghosts within the Forbidden Mountains. *Dead or alive what harm will my ancestors do me? I am a Golden, too. Not yet great, but invited to greatness.*

Lulled by the songs of his ancestors, Mars slept in peace.

TWENTY NINE

Draco at the Gate

All of the landing gates of Vinetop were closed for the first time in one hundred fifty years. Draco circled until the dragon horn sounded, but no landing signal followed. No landing doors opened. Entering Vinetop over the walls was considered an act of war. Draco wasn't interested in dodging arrows. He had sent word of his coming, there should have been flagmen at the Warrior's Gate, not guards with pikes before a shut door.

Draco descended trailing black smoke and landed on the road just beyond the moat's gate house. There was no one to greet him at the draw bridge but a guard nervously eyeing him. Draco crossed over and walked the mile-long steep ramp to Vinetop's main gate alone. Once inside, he crossed the Colonnade Courtyard spiting acid with every step. He entered the Great Hall from the public entrance bowing to fit under the arch. Draco found no fires and nothing on the spit. He marveled at the emptiness.

So soon after Rogsin's birthday and subsequent crowning, Draco expected the celebratory cooking fires still lit. There should be commoners, courtiers and other guests feasting. Draco's gut rumbled for a meal. He had missed the coronation, busy looking for the runaway Mars. When Hammond received his kingdom, dragons and men came for weeks. Now only Captain Boomax and two servants washing the floor occupied the place. Boomax met Draco near the door.

"What is this?" Draco asked.

"The King says an attack is nigh," Boomax replied. "He reserves his stores against siege."

"My sources bring no such news," Draco said.

The Captain's square jaw unlatched. His tight mouth opened to speak but he thought better of it and snapped his mouth shut. Boomax's eyes directed Draco to the King's winged table. Rogsin's squealing laughter filled Draco's ears. The new King sat alone, not filling his step Father's chair. His dark eyes and black hair blended with the ebony wood. With his shadow-colored robes, he was a shapeless blot. *Wizard's robes*, Draco thought. *Where is Merilbe?*

"Could it be?" Rogsin called. "My spies are better than yours?"

Draco approached. There was no space for him on the King's side. An empty dwarf chair stood there. On Rogsin's left rested a human chair. The table had no places set for dragons. Just three weeks ago the table was arranged for the Steward's Council, this interim ruling body was traditionally made of men and dragons with space for six of each. The Steward's Council ran the affairs of Vineland whilst the throne awaited Rogsin's coming of age. Dragon stewards from time out of mind had always sat with kings at this table.

"Our agents are one in the same," Draco said.

"Not anymore," Rogsin said. "I don't trust dragons. I have alternatives."

Draco swallowed his bile. *Let the fool give him self away.*

"You must earn your place, and already you have disappointed, dear Draco. I asked for the Golden. He is not here."

"A golden comes. Penelope escorts her. They will arrive within an hour. The Matron will train Praxis here."

"You defy the King? I want both Goldens!" Rogsin said hurling a silver cup into the Hall.

Draco waited for the clanging cup to quiet and said, "Dragons without fire cannot fly for the King's service. The law prevails."

"Of course," Rogsin said, his dark face flashed with a bright white smile. Rogsin's eyes shifted in a most particular way. Draco bit his tongue.

"Well, then," Rogsin said in an oddly cheerful voice. "Let us see to our guests. Servants, stoke a fire. Send for Onyx. Let us hold court!"

Rogsin jumped from his chair. He gave instructions to the guards that came running from the side door. Rogsin then entered the War Room and called behind, "Let no one follow."

For the first time since becoming Warlord, Draco was not invited. Voices were within. Draco's stomach rumbled and not from hunger. The court horns blasted. Servants filtered into the room. Unusual guests followed. None were dressed in the garb of the Twelve Kingly Estates. They that entered weren't traders or merchants, they were mercenaries: some from the southern Outlands, others from the Woodland chiefdoms, hill dwarves and human highlanders from beyond the Kingdom of Vineland. The royal executioner entered, too, and took a place at Rogsin's table.

No courtly dragons appeared, only a dragon prisoner led by guards. The old country dragon had green scales the color of spring shoots and a yellow stripe alone his side, a farmer by his leather work harness. The poor soul's snout was strapped shut, his eyes wild with fear.

What harm could this dragon do to warrant such treatment?

Draco heard Penelope and Praxis but did not turn to greet them. Rather, Draco eyed Rogsin as he emerged with his sister two steps behind. Onyx's mouth was downcast, her eyes wet with sadness. She appeared, thin and pale as she wiped away a tear with her hand. She did not greet Draco with her usual cheer. She bowed stiffly like a puppet on strings.

"This is a fine way to introduce Praxis," Penelope seethed as she came near. "It is her first day and just in time to see an execution. Are you out of your mind, Draco?"

"This is not my doing. I've heard of no crime worthy of this."

"I've changed the law," Rogsin said, "but I am merciful."

Rogsin opened a scroll and read, "Bingon, for the offense of refusing my dear sister in her hour of need, for the food you refused her, you shall forfeit your life unless you agree to donate your wings, with full consent, to the King's armory. Even so, you will be banished to the Outlands until you regain flight. How do you plead?"

Onyx went silently to Rogsin's side like a ghost and stood expressionless. Thick black bangs hid her downcast eyes. Yet, she could not mask the fresh tears rolling down her cheeks. *What spell befell Onyx?* Whereas her cheeks were once plump and graced with the color of roses, her face was now gauntly ashen. So full of fire not long ago, Onyx was now a statue of fear.

"My wings, Lord. Take them," Bingon said in a low trembling voice. He laid low, spread his wings and closed his eyes.

"Any comments from the witness? Onyx? No?" Rogsin asked without giving her time to answer. "Good. Off with them!"

As the axmen unsheathed his weapon, Onyx ran from the room. Praxis spit fire.

"How can she beguile that simple dragon?" Praxis exclaimed.

Penelope slapped Praxis' tail with her own and whispered harshly. Praxis hissed toward the door. Rogsin appeared bemused. Praxis's black smoke billowed forth.

"Praxis, I'm not surprised you've come," Rogsin said smiling broadly. "You are the only dragon that's shown me kindness. We will make good allies. I appreciate your support."

Rogsin waved to two guards who came forward and spread the condemned dragon's wings. The executioner raised and swung his dragon gold ax. In one clean swipe, one wing lopped off with blood spouting and the dragon screaming. The axmen changed sides and in a flash, amid more blood, the other wing came off. The guards backed away, forgetting to pick up the removed wings. Only the executioner's apprentices rushed to Bingon's side but not to aid him. They gathered and bound the fallen wings before they floated away.

Draco stood with mouth agape. Praxis rushed to Bingon. She took a healer's kit from her flight bag and tended Bingon's wounds. Bingon wailed. The cry was not due to pain. The only thing more sacred to dragons than fire, was their wings. Draco raged inside but shown no sign, rather he turned and walked toward the exit. Draco needed answers and not what lies Rogsin would give.

"Don't leave, Draco," Rogsin called in a mocking, sing-song voice, "The fun has just begun. Court is in session. There're more wings to cut."

"I've business away," Draco said. "Court is Penelope's responsibility, not mine."

Draco left, and despite the rules, he ran across the courtyard gaining speed for take off. As Draco galloped and flapped, a guard yelled, "Stop or we shoot!"

Draco did not stop. No arrows came. Vinetop's guards were old friends. Besides, good fighters knew not to waste arrows. Draco flew from Vinetop leaving Penelope to sort what was happening in the kingdom. He needed the kernels of truth Penelope would find. Inviting Outlanders and other undesirables was an outrage; the cavalier taking of wings was an abomination. Draco had not seen Merilbe or any of the Twelve

Estate's representatives in Rogsin's hall. *Where is the wizard? None have seen him since the funeral.*

Draco flew for the west foothills. He dropped into a shallow valley, out of sight of Vinetop's watchtowers. From there, he could fly between hills undetected. For the first time in years, he did not know which way to go. Draco flew aimlessly between hill and dale until he sighted a circle of standing stones built by Giants. It was a place called Stone Crop made to honor the sun when the Earth was young. Ravens perched on the circle's massive lintels. He drifted toward them.

They chattered in bird tongue. Ravens only spoke other languages on occasions they deemed important, only to a very few, and had not spoken to mankind since man's expulsion from the Valley of Neff. Now, most folks had forgotten how to listen to ravens who were once the heralds of Giants. Ravens had not landed on the window sills overlooking the Tapestry since Mars' visit to the War Room. When Mars flew off, so did the ravens. Since Hammond's funeral, the ravens had not returned to any part of Vinetop, save only a few nesting with chicks in the high tower's eaves where they were out of reach. A bounty seeking huntsman could not kill one there mistaking it for a crow.

I must speak with raven-kind.

Draco swooped into the center of stones, landing carefully to not create wind. The ravens held their speech and with heads bobbing, they looking down upon him. Draco quickly folded his wings and lowered his head to the ground. An old gray bird came forward. It was one of the birds who visited on Rookery Top.

"Master Draco," said the old bird. "It is a good omen you've come. We were pondering you and this lost kingdom."

Draco stretched his neck. His head remained below the ravens. His crown feathers and ears stood. Like Merilbe's crow, this raven had a star on its forehead. *Could they be related? No, ravens do not associate with crows.*

"Lost kingdom?" Draco asked.

"Have you not seen the night sky? The star cluster, what dragons call Dragon Field, is nearly complete. Surely even you know the greater legends?" The bird cocked his head sidelong at Draco.

"I know the rhyme. 'When dragon's wings fill the sky, into light living dragons will fly.'" Draco quoted. "What of it? This is a child's riddle. It has no answer."

"The answer, as you call it," said the old bird "is upon your children. It is not for me to tell. Dragons long ago forfeited wisdom in trading our counsel for human desires. Woven into your very mane is corruption. I cannot impart onto you raven's word. Beware. Darkness comes before the Light. This you already know."

At once, the ravens took wing. They rose like a black cloud over the land casting a shadow in Draco's eyes. The ravens squawked as they climbed to a great height. Draco thought he heard the old raven recite a quote from the scrolls. Draco had last heard it as a child.

"Seek The Golden when dark horizons bid…"

The end of the old saying eluded him. Draco sat quietly there all that afternoon until near sunset. With sky lit red, he flew for War Camp. It was a place where the rules were steadfast and a dragon knew what was what. Draco sought familiar ground. In his deep heart he knew war was coming. From where and when, he could not say. With this admission to himself, he remembered the next line.

"War like no other, the enemy is within."

It was like so many other riddles, nothing more than hearth-games, but why did the raven speak it? Ravens don't play games.

THIRTY

Mars Departs

Mars peered over the landing with itchy wings as the cold December winds blew. Conditions were too dangerous for flying. Mars went back inside. With nothing much to do, Mars missed school. *At least I was busy. Winter book studies weren't much fun, but school work beats boredom.*

Mars learned more in one day at the Rookery than he had learned in three months with Emerald. Emerald's smooth tongue waggled much, but he said nothing that brought Mars closer to regaining fire. Emerald offered to apprentice him, but Mars could not accept. Three years was too long to stay in this loathsome place. His time here already felt endless. When Emerald pressed for an answer Mars agreed to earn his keep washing dishes, gathering firewood and other chores. In this way, Mars hoped to stay long enough to see how Emerald made fire.

Adding to Mars's mundane existence was the lack of news about the greater world. News flowed like quicksilver at Rooky Top. Emerald came and went many times but said nothing of his travels. No friendly messengers came, only Emerald's rogue traders. Walters talked little. Bear Claw came on each full moon, but Emerald rarely let the Inowise out of his sight and the few other servants there had left before the weather turned. Mars regretted his venture more each day. *I'm getting nowhere.*

Mars' anger waned as he felt more friendless and lonely. Still, Mars would not give up his quest. He wanted answers and if Emerald would not provide, he'd seek them elsewhere.

"I've come for fire and I'll stay until I have it," Mars declared to the ghosts whom he heard inside his room but never saw.

Even if he had fire, Mars could not leave in mid-winter. Without food in plenty, no dragon sustained fire. Emerald ate very little and expected the same of others, likely why Emerald was so thin for such a big dragon. Mars grew thin too, so much so he was sure that he was too weak to fly. Fire or not, dragons must eat to fly. As time passed,

Emerald flew less and less, too. Mars saw Emerald's wisdom in preserving his larder. Winter prevented new supplies from arriving.

From within the cave, Mars cracked open the door and watched a wind-blown snow twister spin until it collapsed. The wind had died out. There was enough clear weather for a short flight. Mars needed to satisfy his wings. He pushed his head outside testing the air. Walters touched his tail. Mars pulled his head in and shook the snow from his mane and feathers.

"It's deep winter. Flying is suicide," Walters warned. "The winter sky cannot be trusted."

"This day is lighter," Mars said. "I can almost see the sun. I'll go for wood."

"Sun rays hate these lands," Walters said. "Flying is not safe."

Walters shut the inner door. *No wonder Emerald is so dark. A dragon needs to fly. But, Walters is right, snow falls constantly. Even short flights are exhausting in such weather.* Mars realized he was trapped.

"Even college is better than this!" Mars closed the outer door retreated into the cave and slammed the inner door.

The next day, when Emerald disappeared into a deep mountain cave, Mars decided to question Walters. Mars was not convinced he could trust the man, but Walters wore the clothes of Vinetop and Mars was at his wits' end. He found Walters in the kitchen soaking salt-pork for the evening's meal.

"Come to nibble? There's a smoked-dried apple or two, I can spare," Waters said without looking up from the wooden tub. His voice was more dour than usual.

"I've come to satisfy my mind not my stomach."

"Good, there is hardly enough here to winter one dragon, much less a man and a young flyer on top of it."

"Why are you here in such disarray? Weren't you a proper butler to the King? Have you done wrong?" Mars inquired.

Walters laid the meat on the cutting board. He smoothed his dirty green vest and held his head high. His face was dirty but recently shaved.

"I should say not! The King sent me according his trust. I was to stay one season. But no one has come for me as expected this past summer."

"Tell me, how can I leave this place?"

Suspicion glazed Walters' eyes. He put a finger to his lips and motioned for Mars to follow. They went to the dragon's landing. Walters brought Mars to a spot where the winds drove down from above. *Smart thinking—the winds carry our voices away from the cave, not into it.* Walters, although shivering in the cold, looked relaxed. Walters smiled for the first time and came close to Mars's ear.

"I've seen gnomes here young master, 'tis a bad omen. The King bid me bring news of Emerald and his doings. This spring, royal messengers stopped coming. Emerald hears worldly news, but he will not tell it. I fear the King is dead. You must flee. Emerald will make you his slave. He hunts for gems even now for that purpose, to cast a spell on you."

Walters pointed to a tiny foot path below the edge of the cave's abyss only large enough for a small child. The path twisted down the mountain and turned south before disappearing in the gray murk.

"'Tis a Gnome's path," Walters said. "Gnomes travel safe but secret ways. They cache food along their routes. So I hear tell. Has not a dragon the goodliest nose, better than a hound?"

Walters bowed and stepped away. The wind battered his waistcoat. A gust almost blew the frail man off the landing. Mars caught him by his arm.

"Ho there!" Emerald called from the door. "Are you mad? Come here, you fools."

Mars and Walters entered the cave with the wind sucking the door shut behind them. Emerald stood between doors on his rear legs with arms folded over breast. His green eyes squinted in suspicion. *If he had smoke, it would be black.*

"What of this? Tell me true, Walters, or I'll skin you."

Although ice lined his hair and his thin cheeks were fire-red, Walters answered in steadfast voice.

"We need firewood, My Lord. I pointed to where he should go. I heard a tree fall this morning."

Walters shows no sign of deceit, I mustn't either.

"It will keep," Emerald said. "Use the reserved wood, even he can't fly in this wind. Follow me, Mars. I've something to show you."

As Mars trailed Emerald, he marveled at Walters' ability to deflect Emerald. *That's why Hammond sent Walters and not someone else.*

"That man is foolish," Emerald said. "How can the King's butler have so little sense? No wonder the King sent him here."

"Right," Mars said. "I'm doing all the hard work. He's lazy, too."

Emerald grunted his agreement and led on through the caves. The front section of the tunnel system was natural but enhanced by handwork. The main tunnel had polished floors, smoothed walls, candle niches and chambers with brick-worked arches supporting wooden doors. A few natural cave-branches departed from the main tunnel but did not go far. One tunnel delved into the mountain's root. Emerald had warned Mars not to go that way. Mars needed no warning. That way smelled of death and the smell got stronger the farther they walked. Mars wrinkled his nose and sneezed.

"Giant bears live away down there. The valley caves give them access," Emerald said. "They don't come this far. My magic is great, they will not tread here!"

Mars read the gate spells inscribed on the floors and walls, but it was not Emerald's doing. The carved inscriptions were the work of dwarves. Mars had seen dwarfish letters in school. Dwarves created this place. Cutting rock and casting spells to bind the darkness was dwarf-trade. Lore said that dwarves were first to bring forth gold from the deep and in olden times they shared it freely with dragons, until the great falling out.

'In those days,' Penelope had said. 'There were many more dragons of all sorts, from tiny dragonfly to wingless grass eaters. Some were dumb, others were wild but intelligent. Civilized golden dragons had preceded country dragons and men who spread from the Gardens of Neff and, by our aid, made the Kingdom.'

'The simple folk, not given to worldly concerns, inhabited the wider lands. Thus, one day low-born dragons of one clan, celebrating a wedding, drank far too much wine. A rumor of gold spurred them to stampede through the iron mines. Less intelligent dragons of every kind followed until a great contingency filled the mines. No evil was intended so the gate spells failed. In the dark, dust and confusion many dwarves were crushed. Only the King's treasure house prevented a war, for dwarves love gold more than war.'

'Thus Dragons were first placed in the King's debt and tied to the rulers of Vinetop. Dwarves are stalwart fighters. Land dragons had much to fear. Dwarves could easily rend a flightless dragon. Highborn mated with the low to restore their numbers and so gave them wings as well. On Vinetop, in time, men and dragon created dragon-gold, an industry that bound our forbearers and binds us still. Although the debt is paid, dragons and men became interwoven.'

Mother believed that dragons should return to the Way of Light and live above men. That seemed impossible to Mars. Men and dragons have lived and worked together for more than ten thousand years.

Mother's voice faded in his mind as he followed Emerald deeper. Seeing this living history brought Mars new light. Even so, Mars had not found an answer in lore for his escape riddle.

"Ah, here we are," Emerald said placing his torch into a wall sconce.

Mars was deeper in the mountain than he had been before. There were many locked doors in Emerald's lair, doors Emerald set to divide his sanctuary and guard his secrets. This door was not new. It was of rough oak planks, not the local pine Emerald used. The door's iron fittings were mightily rusted. There was no lock. Carved glyphs of a kind Mars could not read were chiseled into the door's thick planks.

"What is this?" Mars asked.

"Firewood," Emerald said. "A tomb, perhaps an important dwarf, perhaps a dragon or even a man lay inside. No matter, we need wood. You'll find a pickax inside. Dwarfs always bury one grave making tool with the dead. Take down the door. Chop it up."

"You said you wanted to show me something, what was it?"

Emerald rumbled. "I wanted to show you that you can't escape your chores."

Emerald took the torch from Mars, turned, and started back.

"Don't disturb the bones, if there are any," Emerald warned. "You'll wake the ghost. I've enough to do without chasing new ghosts. Took years to flush them out…"

Emerald sang as he proceeded up the passage. The song faded as he climbed. Mars swung the door out. The hinges squealed. Mars spat bile on the wooden threshold, setting fire to it with his wall torch for more light. The tomb held nothing but a dusty floor, polished black walls, a rusty iron pickax, and a pile of fire-ash in the center. Charred dragon bones protruded from it. Mars looked at his gaunt reflection in the polished wall. His bones showed, too.

"What am I doing here?" Mars said miserably.

"Seeking light," a whisper came from everywhere.

Mar jumped, hitting his head on the ceiling. He looked around wildly. There was no one there, no sound, nothing moved. The air was still.

"Who are you?"

"I am a dragon of the lost garden." The whisper came from all directions. "The green one thought me gone. My grave goods he stole. My bones he burned. But he did not drive me out like my brothers. I remain, for I cannot go until the Golden comes."

"What's that do with me?" Mars cried.

"Cast down my door, burn it, scatter my ashes. Free me. The time is nigh. Will you help me?"

Mars had heard ghost lore and he knew the tales of evil men or dwarves bound to Earth. He heard that ghosts played tricks on people thereby doing mischief on the living. Ghosts relieve their misery by contriving ways to force the living to do their bidding.

"Let me think on it."

Mars searched his memory. Not all bound souls were captured by ill doings. Some had suffered undeserved spells from vengeful wizards. Others had spoken honorable oaths in life they could not keep. Mars had never heard of an Earth-bound dragon ghost. Good dragons became stars. Evil dragons were as rare as summer snow; no one knew what became of them, and could it be this is that?

"What is your oath?" Mars asked his voice unsteady with nerves. "Tell me how you were bound. Show me a sign. I will free you, if you prove honorable."

The face of a golden dragon appeared on the polished wall above Mars' own reflected image. The dragon was huge, like the dragons of his vision, easily twice his size. The spirit wore an iron helm. Dragons had not worn such armor on their heads since the fall of the garden. The dragon turned. Mars saw a broken arrow shaft embedded in its eye. Mars almost dropped his torch.

"I swore to defend the Light until the very end of the age," he proclaimed. "But alas, I fell in battle. Yet my wings continue to serve even now. My obligation is met; the omens are in place. I fulfilled my promise, release me."

"How can your wings survive, are they not stars?"

"You have not seen the dragon wing table?"

This must be a trick Mars thought. The wings of that table were younger than this crypt. Mars was at a loss. The wings were donated but there was no lore about the body of the dragon that gave them. Mars had to rely on himself to decide.

"Your dust lies behind sealed door," Mars said. "Your spirit was bound. Why is a good dragon bound if not to haunt the enemies of Light? How can you do so here?"

"I've guarded the wisdom and charms of the dead. Books of forbidden knowledge were laid here. I've driven out grave-robbers aplenty."

"Then why is Emerald still here?" Mars asked

"I cannot sway the first and only robber-dragon. He doesn't take and run. No, he lives among us. He is black magic. It is written: 'When the Green One revives the industries of yore, he will destroy dragon kind.' Your wound is proof. He makes forbidden weapons, best forgotten. The Golden is come but already defeated. The end of the age has come. My obligation ends."

The Golden? Surely, not me. Of course! The Golden must be Praxis. I may bear the Crest of Neff but I'm no good without fire.

Mars's wound throbbed on the mention of it as if the ghost loosed stored pains. He felt shot all over again. Dragons did not die easily. Slings and arrows did little harm. Dragons died by massive rock missiles or by an eye-shot or charging onto a pike trap as Sire Atmere had, impaled by his own weight. That device which shot him, whatever it was, could kill any dragon. Did Emerald make it? It had to be the work of a wizard. Did Emerald heal him out of guilt? Mars didn't wish to find out. Danger filled his heart. It was past time to leave.

"I will free you," Mars said, "if you help free me."

"Agreed."

Chilled air blew past Mars from within the chamber.

"What must I do?" Mars asked.

"Burn the door and destroy the seal. Take a piece lit to the open air. I will see you on your way."

A strong, cold wind blew, ripping the half-open door from its iron hinges. The door flew, hit a wall and was smashed into kindling. The air grew warm and still. Mars hoped he had made a good bargain. Mars never heard of such barter, the dead helping the living to gain freedom. What could the ghost do to aid him?

Mars filled his packs with the splintered wood and delivered it to the kitchen in several trips. The last wood on the pile made for easy burning. Mars, his travel bags still mounted, stayed in the kitchen while Walters stoked the fire. This dry wood would burn fast. Mars grabbed a long board and thrust one end into the fire. Mars had no plan. With dinner time so close Emerald would be near. Mars had no hope of going outdoors without being seen. His opportunity came moments later when a mighty crash heralded from one of Emerald's locked laboratories. A shelf full of ceramic jars and glass vessels had tipped. A faint childish laugh carried through the air.

"Walters, come here!" Emerald cried.

"Mind the strew pot," Walters said. "Imps are making mischief. I thought I heard imps."

With a wooden ladle in hand and such was a good tool to chase imps, Walters hurried from the kitchen leaving the door open. A cold wind blew the door shut as Walters disappeared down the tunnel.

"Fill your packs," a whisper commanded. "Quickly, take the burning wood!"

Mars stuffed his bags as fast as he could with dried apples, smoked fish and a stale loaf of bread. He took less than was wise, due to concern that Emerald might let Walters starve. He also stuffed a small pot and a flint and steel set into his bag. He hadn't emptied all the wood so that would serve him well. He grabbed the unburned end of the plank with the mark on it, the piece that he had just set on the fire and ran for the landing. Emerald called, chasing after him.

"Stop you fool!" Emerald yelled. "None survive the Forbidden Mountains in winter!"

Running with hunger and flight bags proved hard running, but Mars doubled his effort. Even so, Emerald's shouts drew closer. Emerald had almost closed the gap between them when Mars smashed into the exterior door. Emerald's teeth sliced his tail. With the door open, the flame on the board burst into brightness like a flare made of sulfur. Emerald retreated from the sparks and backed into the cave.

Mars's eyes burned from the light, yet he saw well enough. He ran to the edge of the landing, opened his wings and stopped. The snow was falling heavily. Torrential winds blew. Visibility was impossibly poor. He tossed the stick that burned like a torch over the side in hopes of illuminating the gnome path. The blizzard swallowed its light.

A mightier wind came from Emerald's caves howling like a dragon's war call. It blew Mars over the edge and the wind laughed. Mars peered upward as he tumbled. Emerald's shocked face was the last thing he saw.

The ghost had pushed him!

All became white. Mars fell blindly. His wings half-opened slowed him little. He began to wonder if this was all a strange dream, until he slammed into a protruding boulder. The jolt ripped a flight bag open but saved his wing from injury.

Mars, snapping out of it, spun his feet toward the mountain and kicked off. He opened his wings against the storm and hovered. He had fallen a long way. The climb back was impossible. His wings quickly took on snow. The weight soon made it impossible to keep his wings spread. He had no fire to melt it, nor any sun. He could not fly upward so all he could do was descend. Mars rolled in the air to eject the snow and began downward.

I better float down and nest for the night. I'll go home in the morning.

Mars was stunned by his thoughts, by home he had meant Emerald's cave, but that was not home. Homesickness filled him as he drifted lower. Emerald would look for him when the weather broke. If Emerald found him, he would cast his spell and make Mars a slave.

Mars would not allow that to happen. The blizzard became his friend. No one could track him in such a storm and there was no sun to shine on his scales to show him. Perhaps the ghost's betrayal was help after all.

Mars shook off the snow and folded his wings descending faster. Deadly obstacles such as sidelong trees and rock spires appeared in rapid succession. He twisted and turned to avoid them, bouncing off the slopes with each strike leaving him bruised and cut. He used what the gauntlet taught, but this was no game. The stones that bashed him were far less friendly than Bullock.

Mars heard sounds below, echoes. It had to be the valley's foothills. Mars could not land there. Too many creatures would make a meal of him. Mars flapped for all his worth. As he worked to gain height, Mars recalled the gnome's path and so he flew southward.

Exhaustion came fast but he gained height and distance. Mars searched for a crevice or outcrop suitable for landing. He found nothing. He hung his head in defeat, his strength waning. He noticed an odd line without snow squiggling along the rock face.

The gnome's path!

Mars dropped down to the widest section of the narrow path. He gritted his teeth and clawed his rear legs for footholds. Gnomes would wreak havoc on Mars if they found him. To counter their tiny stature, gnomes used magic weapons and poisoned darts able to kill dragons many times Mars' size. Mars shivered. If he met gnomes, Mars could not beg their help. Gnomes only helped in circumstances where they got the better of the bargain. A gnome required payment. Mars had nothing to pay. Mars prayed the Light that gnomes were not near.

Flapping his wings and using his tail to stabilize him, Mars inched along the trail searching for a respite. This siphoned his remaining strength. When the trail led to a great crack between a sheer rock face and an outcrop, Mars squeezed inside it.

Burnt charcoal, both in smell and presence, alerted him that gnomes had camped here recently. They had left firewood stacked against the wall. Mars inhaled and detected a food cache, too. As badly as Mars wanted fire and food, he could not take the risk. He threw himself on the sooty floor and let sleep take him.

THIRTY ONE

Unlikely Allies

Without Penelope near, Praxis faltered through her court season at Vinetop, alone and lost. As soon as Draco released her from her restriction, Penelope flew from Estate to Estate extinguishing fiery hearts lit with Hammond's death and Rogsin's decisions. Outlanders now traveled freely through Vineland. Merilbe was still missing.

What is Vinetop without its famous wizard?

Praxis filled her time dressing the wing amputations of hapless dragons or the flog wounds of equally unfortunate men. The prisoners whispered to her or spoke dragon tongues as she dressed their hurts. Rogsin dismissed their complaints as unworthy of his ears, so she listened instead. She served as friend and confidante to the unfortunate of the dungeons deep below Vinetop. In a sad way, her time in the deep as a mind and wound healer suited her better than court-life on the heights.

There were no courtiers or messengers to talk with. No other dragons at court. Rogsin only invited shiftless, crude men and dwarves from unholy lands where they obviously didn't like dragons. Her time was better spent where she was welcome; with the victims of the King.

Yet, Praxis needed a friend on Vinetop as her isolation there was great. The only female her age at court was Onyx, poor Onyx, sad, cold and aloof. Praxis understood Onyx's unyielding unhappiness. After all, she had Rogsin for a brother.

Praxis sharpened her ears and learned all she could about these atrocities. She also wondered how deeply the princess was involved. Praxis wandered the halls with stealth, a dangerous game of cat and mouse with Rogsin as the cat. On one such foray, she spied Onyx like a ghost, slipping past an Outland guard unseen under his very nose. The sight of a living ghost chilled Praxis from crown to tail.

What is that dragon accuser up to?

Also careful not to rouse the guard, Praxis followed Onyx. Praxis reflected on the doings of Vinetop as she stalked the empty corridors. She thought about the events of court. Onyx was seldom in the company of her brother. She sneaked around the castle as if she had the same worries as the prisoners and Onyx avoided the guards, too. She acted as if she were seeking something, but what?

I must question her. Is she a dragon's friend or foe? Her actions say she is no friend of dragons, yet she takes no pleasure in it.

Praxis lost Onyx's trail in the maze of hallways adjacent to the War Room. When Praxis reached the hallway opposite the Tapestry wall, she caught a fresh female scent. Praxis placed her nose to ground. She breathed in the remnants of Onyx's presence, quickly fading against the stone. Praxis tracked it to an air vent. There it stopped. This time she pressed her ear to the floor, discovering scuffling and foot patters inside the wall. Voices from inside the War Room interrupted her hunt.

"Gather your strength to mine and you'll share in my kingdom," Rogsin said. "Let us take up arms together against..."

The King's voice faded, replaced by the clacking of ceramic mugs against silver tankards. Muffled voices hailed Rogsin.

"What oracle's advice do you have?" a loud Outlander's voice called in protest. "The Tapestry is gone and so is Merilbe. Has the wizard joined another king? We cannot stand against him; it would go ill for you and us. Where's your advantage, your strength?"

"Emerald the Wizard Dragon," Rogsin replied. "Once winter breaks, I'll send for him and he won't refuse. He served my Father and he shall serve me. I trust you've heard of him?"

"Why should he help us? You're out to disarm dragons."

"What became of Merilbe?" Another voice inquired.

Still another crude voice said, "What of Draco and the Golden?"

"I'll handle Draco," Rogsin said, "as I've already handled Merilbe. He's not gone. I have him where I want him. As for the Golden, my hunters seek him."

The voices all spoke at once and clashed together. Praxis could not understand any more. Her heart beat a fearful rhythm on this news. This commotion continued until Rogsin angrily dismissed his guests. Praxis backed away and hid in a side hall to gather her wits yet still within sight of the vent.

The scent of Onyx approached, following by scratching from within the wall and a grunt. Onyx, on her belly in a black robe, emerged from the vent opening. She removed and folded the garment and stuffed it into the hole. She clapped the dust from her hands after closing the grate sending out a puff of gray dust. Praxes ducked behind the corner. The natural flow of air brought dust to her position and Praxis sneezed thrusting her head out of hiding. Onyx spun. She ran to Praxis, falling to her knees, even whiter than her natural pallor.

"Please don't tell him," Onyx begged. "He'll kill me."

Onyx hung her head. Her hair touched the ground like the manes of prostrated dragons awaiting her brother's punishment. The smell of human fear was thick on the air. Onyx had grown thinner, her face gaunt and sickly in the days since Praxis arrived. Praxis suddenly felt sorry for her yet the business at hand prevailed.

"Why'd you do it?" Praxis snapped thinking of the country dragons that lost their wings. The horror of her first day at court sprung to mind.

Onyx rose, but still hung her head.

"He threatened to cut out my tongue if I didn't," Onyx admitted. "I'm sorry. I had no idea he'd go this far."

Onyx fell on Praxis's neck and wept. Praxis then recalled her tour and how Onyx showed great love for each dragon she greeted at court that day, and how she spoke with deep affection for Draco. The signs Praxis ignored in her anger came clearly to mind: This girl was no enemy of dragons but one under the same thumb of destruction. Onyx regained some composure and spoke.

"My brother in his quest for power will destroy dragons. The kingdom will be lost, unless I bring proof of his deceptions to the Council of Twelve. Will you help me?"

"You have good cause for fear and so do I," Praxis said smoothing Onyx's hair.

"Will you help me?" Onyx entreated.

"If I can," Praxis replied.

Onyx collapsed on the floor, her tears renewed. Praxis lay beside her and cried, too. Her heart ached in the loss of Mars, for the innocent dragons that Rogsin hurt, and now, Onyx also. Even amid the sadness, a slight joy warmed her; Praxis had found an ally, and hopefully also a much needed friend on Vinetop.

THIRTY TWO

A Near Miss

Mars awoke slowly to strange, distant songs. He wondered if he might still be living in dream. Smoke rose from his mouth but it was not fire, only steam born of bitter cold. Mars shook his head and freed his stiff mane. Ice crystals rained like star dust. Mars looked past his narrow crevice in the mountain. The blizzard continued outside. He supposed it was early morning, but he had no way to confirm it while the wind roared like a wounded dagger toothed lion's threats of death.

Emerald will not seek me in this weather.

Mars unpacked his food and cooking gear. He searched his packs in vain for combustibles, when his outer flight bag pocket tore he had lost his wood and tinder.

No matter, I have flint, steel and the gnome's wood.

Mars arranged the wood. Although his gullet called as loud as the wind, he heard song again. This time, it was closer.

Gnomes!

He followed the sound to a small tunnel in the mountain that he had not seen before. It got closer with every frosty breath. Mars quickly stuffed and harnessed his flight bags. He squeezed through the crack and thanked the Light for disguising his noise by howling winds. Once outside, he half-flew and half-clawed to an outcrop above his former shelter. Mars gathered his wings around him. His mane whipped. He hoped to hold there until the gnomes moved on. He put his ear to the rock face.

"Emerald will be pleased with our news," one gnome said. "Rogsin calls him to court."

"Emerald will have to provide Rogsin his trophy," another said. "The head of Mars will make a fine wall-hanging."

"That green lizard had better pay well. Let's demand a bonus. No messenger should travel harsh winter without due recompense."

"Rogsin will pay us too, paid twice!"

The gnomes burst into laughter. The wind gusted and Mars lost his grip. He scratched for a foot hold with his hind nails and flapped for balance.

"What's that?" A gnome cried.

"An eagle!"

"Dinner on the wing! Top side, boys! Notch darts!"

Mars spread his wings and let go. He was torn from the rock like a leaf. Mars didn't know if the gnomes' arrows would find him. He had no time to look. The winds blew him downward faster than he ever dived.

He dropped below the snow clouds to find an unforgiving landscape of pinnacles and spires, nothing but angry, sharp rocks stabbing the sky. Touching down within that labyrinth was certain death. Mars had no choice but to flap harder against the storm. In his toil, Mars remembered a line from Mother's wisdom songs, 'Stone daggers are deadly perches.' Mars eyed the nearest crumbling spike and prayed the Light for a place to land.

Mars flew with the wind. He certainly couldn't fight it. He knew not how long or how far he traveled. He kept his flight lids down and his outer lids half-closed against the sleet. Soon, he was too exhausted to shake the ice from his mane. Every wing or tail beat became torture.

When he thought he could go no farther, he saw a flutter of white wings before him. Was it a bird or a dream? He was hard put to sort facts from fictions inside his weary head.

Birds know the safest roosts.

Mars followed. As he trailed after the bird, he remembered how the White Raven from the Tapestry was above all things. This bird, if real, did quiet the opposite Mars expected from a white raven. It shot downward into a queer fog. Reason barred Mars from indulging his desire to follow. He could not see the badlands below. The odd sparkle of the fog danced before him, inviting him, and it caused Mars to recall childish lore, 'Once in the fairylands time is lost. The few that come out end with remorse.'

His burning muscles would no longer heal to lore. His cramping wings folded unasked for and so he dove into the mists of time.

THIRTY THREE
Emerald's Commission

Onyx and Praxis helped prepare for the upcoming spring festivities by arranging the cookware and serving dressers at the hearths. The breakfast would soon commence. Praxis didn't feel happy despite the unusually warm April morning.

Mars was still missing.

Praxis breathed deep and smelled tilled earth and wildflowers. Already the farmers plowed and planted. The royal cooks counted their winter stores and declared them well preserved, not a single stone crock broken. The aromas of pickled vegetables, smoked meats, honey and jams floated on the early morning air. Barrels of wine stood ready to tap. A dead stag hung in the courtyard skinned and ready for roasting. There would be plenty to eat.

Praxis had no appetite. She began to understand Penelope's austerity.

Head Servant Martha directed her staff as they cleaned, set tables and brought wood.

"Dragons and men will start coming, today," Martha said loudly. "Quick about your work! Make good the King's hospitality!"

Praxis and Onyx worked alongside the servants and Martha treated them no differently. A brass, no-nonsense woman, Martha reminded Praxis of Penelope. So long among dragons, Martha served Vinetop for two hundred years. Her soft features and crinkled eyes gave evidence of her knowledge and kindness, features she hid from Rogsin but shared with Praxis and Onyx.

When the residence door swung open, Martha stiffened her spine and rolled back her shoulders. Rogsin came on and inspected progress. His red morning robe flowed around him like a firestorm.

"Praxis, Onyx must you do servants work?" Rogsin complained. "What fools you two are! Must you accommodate this fat, old woman?"

Rogsin's face twisted. Praxis did not respond. That would only invite more attention and draw his further wrath. Rather, she bowed low, as did Onyx.

Rogsin disdains house staff. Do as they do and he ignores us. He is the fool.

Rogsin marched on and found a boy to berate. He was especially hard on the house boys.

"Never mind him," Martha said quietly when the King left. "Tis wise to help where one may. Kindness repays kindness."

Praxis' allegiance was not accidental. Penelope had taught that staff knows more about the affairs of state then the King. Servants attended everything, yet Rogsin discounted them as mere furniture. Praxis had another reason to serve the servants, defiance. Simple kindness aggrieved Rogsin.

Besides, there is not much else to do while awaiting my internship's end.

The door guard called. "Messengers at the gate, Outland messengers coming."

Rogsin pushed a house boy out of his way and entered the War Room with his leather bedroom shoes slapping the stone floor. Rogsin only received messengers in private. But, then again, Martha sent a butler after him with hot root-tea. Praxis would get the news, but not the news she most wanted.

"Six months and no word of Mars," Praxis said as she placed an iron tea kettle aside the hearth.

Onyx, chopping roots and dried herbs for the pot, said, "He still lives. The only new dragon star appears in the origins constellation; someone's grave of old was opened. No young dragons have died this winter, despite Rogsin's pleasures."

Onyx put a hand on Praxis's neck and stroked below her mane.

"We'll find him," Onyx said. "After the spring breakfast, your commitment to Vinetop is done. We'll fly out together and find him."

"We have argued this before, you know it isn't safe. Female flyers and riders are against all law. Yet I would bear you if only it were possible," Praxis said. "I don't think I'm strong enough to carry a passenger."

"I am a feather," Onyx said. "Surely I weight no more than a travel pack. I have the evidence I need and Rogsin grows suspicious. I am next for the throne and a threat to him. If I don't leave soon I can't save the kingdom. It is better to leave with you than stay and die."

"Pray the Light that the Twelve Lords will rein in Rogsin's tethers," Praxis said. "We can't risk breaking the law, not yet. If we are hunted quickly your news may never reach friendly ears. We need a distraction."

"The Lords are forever squabbling," Onyx said. "Rogsin will make war on the Steppes. We must flee while we can. I've practiced war-arts and I'm ready."

Praxis resisted, but in her heart, she knew Onyx was right. There may never come a good time to go with so many Outlanders pouring in like smelting iron into a mold. Rogsin was a wildfire in a parchment-dry land. How long will the scrolls of law stand against Rogsin's flame? Time was short.

THIRTY FOUR
Rogsin's Spring Breakfast

Rogsin had sent out a decree calling all to court for Spring Breakfast and thus opened his gates. Penelope arrived in the town below Vinetop thirsty for news and also small early morning meal. She departed from the inn without satisfaction, took wing, and landed at the Dragon's Gate. There was none of the usual fanfare only the sad eyes of over-armed tower guards to greet her.

Have the heights of Vinetop fallen so low?

Once inside the hall she joined other guests awaiting new arrivals at the door. She ignored the gossip and surveyed the room. Highborn dragons and men milled, talking and drinking wine or beer while the human men smoked long-stemmed pipes. The Great Hall held many faces she knew, people from every court, and councilors from foreign but kindly realms. Many Outland chiefs and dwarf-tribe elders that she did not know were also represented.

This troubled Penelope, but the number of wingless dragons among the commoners troubled her most. Fire welled in her throat. Penelope took a goblet from a butler and gulped its contents.

Things are worse than I thought.

Very little news of Vinetop had reached her over the winter as Rogsin had shut his gates tight. Not even the ravens went near. She heard that Rogsin had his men shoot at them on sight.

The King had ignored all dragon affairs completely until his recent decree halting the search for Mars that also called court dragons to the Spring Breakfast. The announcement said Rogsin had important proclamations. The King apparently didn't think Mars important.

What madness lies in this boy's heart?

How could he stop the search while there was yet no sign of Mars? What were Rogsin's true intentions by ending the search for Mars? Was Rogsin hiding troop movements? Penelope wished on the Light Draco was near. She needed his expertise.

Rogsin's own runners were seen in every corner of the Kingdom yet dragons weren't called. What was he looking for? Penelope aimed to find out. Questions danced in her head like a whirlwind.

Praxis rushed toward her with pleading eyes from across the room. Praxes wanted her attention, but she delayed the child with a wave of her wing. Allowing the child to spill her content in mixed company was dangerous.

"Watch and wait with me," Penelope said quietly by long-speak. "I must gather news and your news must keep awhile. Join me in this. Times are critical, we must locate Draco."

"Yes Matron," Praxis said backing away with her head low as if castigated. Penelope lifted Praxis's head with a finger and winked at the child with her flight lids. It was a signal of Penelope's affection only Praxis knew. The child's hue lit brighter.

She has much to tell, but telling too much openly will not do. Foremost I must learn of Draco. Two missing dragons is two too many.

With each dragon that landed, Penelope asked for news of Draco. Hillguard thought Draco maintained the search alone. Others thought Draco had gone to the sages. Some believed the new dragon star proved that Draco was dead. None knew where he had gone.

As time passed, Praxis lost patients and rocked from leg to leg. She finally tapped Penelope's tail with her own. Penelope knew Praxis had wintered here and had important news but the child's timing was wrong. Penelope thought she had better let Praxis speak before the child gave herself away. The dragon child would be no good as an observer while so filled with expositions. It was time to restore the child's game face.

"Quietly, child what burns your attentions away."

"Pod Mother," Praxis whispered, "We must speak of details when ears are not so close. Rogsin's madness appears beyond all reason, but he is not inept as people may think; he has horrible plans."

Praxis let slip a small puff of black smoke. She was deadly serious and that same smoke gives away unguarded thoughts. A thing dragon-kind didn't do at court. Penelope needed a mental smoke screen. Bad manors were her ploy.

"Not now, child," Penelope snapped with raised feathers, feigning rebuke for the benefit of the many eyes that saw Praxis's released smoke.

Praxis, stung, lowered her head and trudged away, dragging her tail toward the main entry. Penelope excused herself saying, "Silly child," she said aloud. "I must have words with her. What is wrong with today's youth?"

Penelope joined Praxis outside in the colonnade garden. She grunted at the child in the uncommon high dragon's speech, something she rarely did. Praxis' ears and crown snapped to attention.

"I trust your concerns. We can't speak now, too many hearers. Keep your game face well."

Praxis blinked her clear eye lids in understanding, and changed her hue to brown and took on the demeanor of someone who had received castigation.

"I will deal with you later," Penelope said so nearby humans would hear clearly. "A week of kitchen duty will teach you better manors."

Praxis billowed black smoke and stomped toward the common entrance.

Good, that will cover the trail. Rogsin's men will think us at odds and Praxis a foolish child.

Penelope hid her pleasure. Praxis had acquired courtly observation skills past her years and Penelope's expectations. Once the child learned self control she would be better still. Leaving her at Vinetop would soon prove wise, Penelope was sure. Praxis's judgment of Rogsin's demeanor was as she herself expected; the brat was more than a spoiled half baked child proving his manhood as people thought. He was up to something more, much more. Penelope pivoted, slapped her tail like an angrily mother, and returned to her place among dignitaries.

The timekeeper blew the horn half past noon and the guards threw opened the common gate at the main wall, an old tradition whereby peasant dragons and ordinary men came for the feast. As the commoners walked the road toward the Great Hall Penelope remained among the dignitaries. The lowborn waited at the Hall's front door until it was announced that all the highborn guests had arrived. Such was court decorum.

As an intern, Praxis' job was to welcome the commoners. Penelope trusted that Praxis would keep her eyes sharp and her ears focused on court as she was told to do. Praxis had a heart for the lowborn, since she was of that stock herself and she was only elevated by the gold of her scales. Hopefully, reunions would not distract the child too much from her duty.

As the train of farmers, blacksmiths and craftsmen dispersed within the Hall, Penelope assessed the lowly lot. Far too many dragons wore horse blankets covering their wingless shame.

A rather large dragon, easily as big as Draco with like colors, was so shamed that he even covered his head and neck with a hood. This country dragon made her heart jump. Penelope closed her eyes against the painful realities of Rogsin's reign and so did not see Emerald land or Walters dismount from him.

"Is this how you treat the King's guests?" Emerald said slyly coming upon her.

Penelope's eyes flew open.

"What are you doing here?" she blurted.

"I'm called by the King," Emerald said. "You, my dear, are slipping. Bad form showing emotions."

Those around her had already stepped back from the landing. It was well known that Emerald had contracted with Hammond, but Emerald had never come to these breakfasts, nor did anyone suppose that Rogsin would follow his father's policy and host the Green trickster. Hammond, in his respect for dragons, only quartered Emerald when court was in recess. Emerald had not been seen anywhere since he saved Mars. Her crown fluttered as she searched for words to recover her status.

"Quite all right," he said. "Apologies accepted."

Emerald left Penelope with flared feathers and mouth agape. She chased after him when Rogsin's laugh rang so boisterously that all eyes turned to the King's table. The guards had not announced him. Rogsin had disrespectfully jumped upon the wing table. He stood on it with his feet wide and clapped his hands as if applauding a jester, complete with a ridiculous grin.

"Very good," Rogsin said. "The guest of honor is here. All hail Emerald! My feast is complete! Let loose the best of my kitchens."

Hesitant hails rose in the room, more for the food than for Emerald, Penelope thought. Everyone put hands together as expected, but the shocked faces of the high-born told another tale. No man or dragon demonstrated more surprise than Emerald himself. He shot tall on hind legs, his crown feathers stood despite the beeswax he had used to restrain them. He quickly bowed low toward the King. Not for honor's sake, Penelope thought but to mask his disarray.

"He hides his eyes," Penelope said to the Highlands Lord's attaché.

"Much else is hidden," said the Highlander. "Most odd."

"Unusual," Penelope said agreeing.

"So many traditions broken!" The Woodlands courtier cried. "Draco's not here. Outlanders are here. Rogsin has entered without announcement and Emerald the guest of honor!"

Penelope took a deep breath, quelled her smoke and steadied her twitching tail wondering what could possible go wrong next.

THIRTY FIVE

Mars in Dreglands

Amid the ease of sleep, Mars' Tapestry vision returned to him, this time calm and clear. Forgotten glimpses now played slowly. A beaded Giant clothed only in a waist-wrap sat on a great stone chair, it was Vinetop before men converted the Giant's Chair into a fortress. In the distance, Neff was lush with green trees. Where a spreading town is now there was a small cluster of huts. The landscape was alive with birds, lesser dragons, deer and goats. Some intelligent-race dragons flew above, while land dragons born without wings walked below. There was a man, no, not a man. He was taller than any man. He had pale skin, golden hair and pointed ears. He stood before the Giant.

"The Giants Age is over," the Giant said. His voice was mater-of-fact in tone as one that lived on despite the ages. "We will soon fade into the Earth, this I've longed for. As the last of our kind, we will soon rejoin our Mother, the Earth. The Age of Dragons has begun."

"Who will teach men? Men are children, foolish and dangerous. They kill, even my people, for mere trinkets," the golden man said.

Mars knew at once it was an elf that addressed the Giant, just like the ones he saw in library scrolls.

"Dragons are given charge over humans, to rear them," the Giant said, closing his great eyes, "and I give the counsel of the ravens to help them. Ravens will keep our wisdom in full."

"Who will prevent the dragon's end?"

"You will, at the appointed time. Fear not the Dragons Age waning. It is the order of things. In the last days, when the dragons' star fields are full, you shall bless the last Golden Dragon sage. The last Golden's fire-breath unlocks Star Gates. When that is, the fairies may then escape to the blessed heavens, forever free."

The vision jumbled and returned to the swirl of senseless images Mars witnessed that day at Vinetop. One of the voices spoke clearly, too clearly. Did it come from outside his dream?

"Make ready the feast. He awakens."

The smell of snow flowers and running water, early spring, filled his snout. Last he recalled Mars was lost in a blizzard. When Mars was first shot he had vivid dreams, so he raised his head, expecting to see his body dashed in ruin on an icy spire. Instead, he found himself on a bed of green soft ferns in a mixed-wood forest. Light streamed down between branches that were free of snow. Some snow remained in deep shadows on the ground under a giant fir tree.

"If this is death's door," Mars said, "'Tis a kindly passage."

"I think not, you are quite well."

Mars blinked his eyes and looked to and fro. The voice matched the voice of his dream and belonged to a man with like pointed ears but long white hair and white tunic. He sat on a gray brown-spotted toadstool as large as a man's bed had men round beds. Others of his kind were gathered around him. It was all very strange. Mars knotted his tail-fin thinking *was this an illusion to trick me?* The elfish man raised his hand in peace as if he knew Mars's fear.

"You are with friends, young golden. No harm will befall you," he said. "I am Begoth. These are my kin."

Begoth swept his hand and a dozen wispy men and women bowed low. Some had small dragonfly wings on their backs, too small for flying, wings that pulsed with colored kaleidoscope lights.

Mars was dazzled.

Each wore fine woven tunics that simmered the colors of nature like dragon scales and on their heads each wore a wreath of silver leaves and live flowers. Their skin glowed like a dragon in the sun, but there were no sunbeams on them. Mars thought them Imps, but these were far too large.

"Am I seeing Imps?" Mars asked. "That is my guess but Imps are so small."

"You guess rightly," Begoth said, "We are Imps as you call us, some say Fairies, and we have not grown, nor have you shrunk. We live in the Nederland, the place where pure magic and hard Earth meets. In your land we travel small to preserve our fading magic. These are my kind's last days. We help the Earthbound at need and the need called this past winter. We spent much magic to find you and bring you among us."

"I am grateful," Mars said. "How may I repay you?"

"The commodity we desire is magic, but you have none to spare for before the end you'll need all you have. I cannot ask magic of you. We are not like Rogsin and Emerald who steal magic, we only accept freewill gifts and that we will not accept from you. Your dreams paid us. Confirmed prophecy is no small favor."

Strange words Mars thought as he righted himself from his bed of ferns and sweetgrass. He had sweet, dry mint leaves ingrained within his mane.

Before the end of what, and what's this bit about dreams?

As Mars stood his legs shook like grape arbor-posts in a storm. He staggered a step or two. To weak to walk, Mars crumpled onto the ground. He felt his bones rattle. He had become very, very thin. He must have slept weeks by the reckoning of his stomach's count.

Questions must wait until after I eat.

"Sorry," Mars said, "I'll beg more of your hospitality. I wish for food. My bags are empty."

"The giving thanks feast begins," Begoth said in a voice like the stern voice of Mars's dream elf but yet turning sing-song.

Begoth waved his hand and all his folk sprang into a flurry. Cook fires were lit. Kettles and cauldrons were placed on and over the coals, stoneware crocks full of honey and jam as big as the Imps them selves were rolled out and cracked open. In no time…no time at all Mars had his wish.

Mars set aside his first questions. He thought it better to wait for an opportune time, and rather, question Begoth on achieving magic fire. *Surly Begoth has wisdom enough to help me find my fire? But first I must eat.*

And eat he did—Mars ate long and much as only a starving dragon can. All that day, Begoth filled Mars's mug with honey wine while others brought every kind of food and with each portion came a helping of songs, too. Tales and stories of lore were served with every course. Mars heard stories of the wilder lands in the world, histories long forgotten, tales of the Inowise and a great amount of Fairy Folk lore. Imps polished his scales and braided his mane as he ate. Mars listened and ate as if bewitched and forgot about his burning question.

At one point Begoth presented Mars with a stoneware honey pot saying, "Keep this jar well, for its golden content will never empty so long as its bearer seeks the Light. Keep peace in your heart and you will not go hungry."

"What of warriors," Mars asked, as Begoth stowed the jar in Mars's repaired flight bag. "How may we fighters keep the Light?"

Begoth through his head back in laughter saying, "Has not Draco taught you? Wars are for peace, not for glory, nor gain—Draco is too long among humans. That was the dragon's way…until this present time. All things change in the ends..."

Begoth became somber. Sadness filled his forest-green eyes, but only for a moment. Then he called for more bread, and nectar, and fish and butter.

Mars questioned no more. He ate until his body felt restored and it seemed to him he mended all in one sitting. Before the feast was done he felt 'as plump as a farmers child,' as the old saying goes. Finally Mars was satisfied. He set down his mug and leaned backward onto a young willow tree and folded his arms over the budge of his belly. There so reclined, he fell asleep dreaming not.

When he woke no one was there. He found himself in a green dale. Low hills surrounded him. The undergrowth was freshly grown around old hardwood trees. The evergreen trees usually found below mountains were few but immense. He heard rushing water. There was a little snow-melt brook behind the willow he rested under. The willow had grown new branches, the grass was lush and deeper, the tender ferns were an older green and the scent of flowers was everywhere. It was spring! Mars ate from mid-winter until spring in one day! The wise say, 'a day in Netherlands is as a season on Earth.'

Mother's lore was right—not all tall tales are fanciful. How many others of her sayings were true?"

Mars wished he'd paid more attention to lore-studies at school. Mars, reminded of his Mother, felt miserable for having run off so rash.

"Surly I am missed," Mars said as he stretched his neck taller and took his bearings."I must find my way home."

Mars located the Forbidden Mountains in the far distance; they should be in shadow this early in the morning. Only the high snowcaps would be lit. How strange. Only the setting sun lighted them from the Rookery's view and yet it is morning and the mountains are awash in light.

I could not have flown so far from Emerald's landing. It would take weeks. Not a day and half a night's travel, even on the wing. How did I get so far?

Mars puzzled and it dawned on him that he must be on the east side of the mountain range, perhaps five hundred miles beyond it. The far side it is said has no favorable winds, no good winds at all.

Mars climbed a nearby grassy hill with a rocky top. He stood tall on hind legs and spied an ancient stone-paved road meandering toward a black forest many miles away. It must be the old Giant's Road, Mars thought, it is that unguarded road of lore that goes around Emerald's mountains and eventually to the sages—a very long road indeed.

Mars could not fly the way he had came without fire enough to survive the High Streams over the Mountains. He would not fly that way again. The Westward was the highest and coldest way. There was nothing for it but to go around the mountains by that road. As the sun beat on him it felt like an old friend and he regained hope. He surveyed the lands with a new heart...until he confirmed the lay of the sun and his heart sank. He was much further north than he first supposed, almost at the foot of the Steppes and not far from college, and that was the last place he wanted to go. He felt that he could not find his fire there.

"This is Dreglands," Mars realized miserably, "A dangerous, wild place."

"No more dangerous than Rogsin's lands these days. He hunts to kill you, you know."

Mars spun about hoping to spy Begoth, but found instead only an old crow perched on a scrub tree at the hill's rocky crest. The Crow bobbed and twisted causing the starmark on its head to catch the sun. Mars spat acid. Crows talk much but only speak half true half the time.

"Good tiding," the old Crow said, "Begoth says, 'fly not.' Iron Skins, the great flying reptiles of old still hunt here. Iron Skins have no wit or reason. You can't barter for safe passage. They don't see well from far, but they'll see your gold from long off. March forest roads, I say. Keep wings over back. Stay in shadow. Hide your glint! Many fowl beings here would pluck your scales."

"Thank you," Mars said. The Crow was right. Remembering his manners and how crows love bright things. Mars plucked a loose scale and offered it to him.

"Nay," the Crow said, "I've payment enough seeing the Prophet alive. Fair well, head low, head low!"

The Crow suddenly sprung to wing and dove like black lightning below the hill's crest—most unlike a crow. Crows liked to talk on and on once they started, or crow, as people said. Crows were quiet different from their silent kin, the ravens.

"I am no oracle," Mars called after him. "Would a prophet be so lost?"

Mars got no reply except another "head low, duck!" before the old bird disappeared into the woods. Mars flopped onto the warmed rocks and wrapped his wings around him like a robe, as was his habit. He pondered the road ahead and reclined onto the same gnarled tree that the crow had sat upon.

A shadow fell upon the ground and raced toward him. Mars bent low. In the blink of an eye a great beast swooped down and clawed the air where his head had been. The top of the tree was gone.

The monster was twice his size. Its leathery body was small but it had great bat-wings forty feet from tip to tip. As it banked away Mars watched its long, low head bobbing as it flapped.

Lucky it can't maneuver as fast as a dragon.

Mars leapt from the hillock wings wide and flapped a few strokes while the beast faced away. He quickly grounded and rolled beneath a brier thicket and placed his brown wings over his back as the Crow advised.

The crow spoke true, at least, of the Iron Skin.

The Iron Skin circled high overhead. Mars waited. At noon the creature dove upon a stag that had broke cover to drink from the brook. This time the monster flew off with a meal. Mars learned about Iron Skins, or Dactels, as the highlanders called them, they were territorial creatures that hunted alone or so the lore said.

Mars now had his chance to move on, but fearing the sky for the first time in his life, he made for the distant road in a most peculiar way. Mars used his powerful legs to skip and hop occasionally flipping his wings open thereby glancing from low heights to high spots like a rabbit bouncing from tuft to tuft. He jumped, ran and ground-glided, always with eyes to the sky, until he gained the road just before dusk.

The Giant's Road was traveling the hard way. The paving stones, laid by Giants, were set far apart and required Mars to jump from one to another. Mars did not jump many times before exhaustion begged him to forgo the road. Mars found the ruin of a Giant's tollhouse. There a fallen stone pillar leaned onto a larger rock. Mars crawled under the lean-to, spun like a dog trampling the grass and made his nest. He fell asleep without eating, most unlike a dragon. Mars ended his first day in Dreglands the way he had arrived; tired, alone and hungry.

THIRTY SIX

Rogsin's New Cabinet

It was the custom that on Spring Breakfast the King would call the nobles to his table first. They took appointed seats in order of their importance with the King seated at center facing the Hall. With the Estates men situated, the King would then bring forth his best fare. In this way, the order was set so that the most important men and dragon's ate their choice first.

But Rogsin ignored that tradition.

Rogsin let loose his stores while the highborn milled about and were not at table. The poor and the Outlanders thrust forward and mobbed the cooking hearths. They stormed the serving tables filling plate and mug with the best fodder before moving on to the common tables while Rogsin slapped his belly and laughed. The tender yearly hart, still on the spit, was reduced to bone before Penelope's eyes. Nobles, rich merchants and other highborn watched dismayed whilst Rogsin's blood-relatives stewed like the contents of the cauldrons.

All but that big, sad dragon partook in the stampede. The covered dragon stayed near the door. Penelope supposed him so abashed at losing his wings he had no appetite. Penelope would question Praxis on what she heard of him and others at the public entry later.

He hopes to gain the low-born's support in this way?

Once the lowly were busy at table Rogsin jumped upon the King's chair and pounded his foot on the table.

"I've proclamations," Rogsin said taking a scroll from the old scribe, Kendrick. "As my first year has come full, I've picked my new cabinet, thirteen seats. My aid will read the names. Come and share my table as you are called."

Rogsin handed the scroll to a young scribe Penelope did not know.

"Marduc elder of the Westford Outlands, the 12th seat, Boron, highest dwarf of the Ground Sippers tribe the 11th seat..."

All the courtiers, Penelope among them, listened with mortified grumbling. The seats of the King's cabinet were established and reserved for the Lords of the Twelve Estates and the Dragon Warlord, not strangers.

This is blasphemy!

Shouts of protest rang yet the reader didn't pause until Rogsin raised his hand. Not one of the Estates was yet called. Rogsin sat unmoved by the malcontents; rather, he drank deeply from his golden tankard and laughed while everyone waited. Rogsin raised his drink motioning for his stuttering bard to read on.

It was then that Penelope noticed there was no place at Rogsin's right hand for a dragon. Draco had been the King's right hand for a thousand years through many Kings. Surly Rogsin will not break with that wisdom. Draco was her hope—he could tether Rogsin. Penelope appreciated Draco's station in a new light.

Yet there was one dragon-sized space reserved—the wizard's place at the table's end. Merilbe was still missing and likely dead. Vineland needed a wizard and engineer. Penelope's tail-end twisted into a knot on her realization.

The twelve that Rogsin named came forward, one-by-one and not one from the Estates. Dissent ripened into outbursts. Black smoke bellowed from dragons high and low while statesmen tore their robes in protest. Country folk said little between bites—being more inclined to keep to their plates and mugs well full, they cared little for the intrigues of court.

Voices shouted, "This is madness! What black magic is this! The King betrays us! You renege on your Father's promises! Won't dragons be represented?"

It was some time before it was quiet enough to speak without shouting although demands for Rogsin's explanation continued. And there was no mistaking that Rogsin enjoyed the mayhem. Finally Rogsin, appearing well pleased, stood on his chair again.

"You, my friends misunderstand me," Rogsin began, "My Father I do not betray, nay, I intend on fulfilling his word, especially where he fell short. That is foremost."

The room quieted. Penelope held her breath.

"For time uncounted it was given to the heirs of Vinetop to protect the gifted lands. The Estates were established as a perimeter for the Giant's Seat. It is my charge to keep this place well. Yet you the Twelve fight each other more than the enemies without. My duty is to the kingdom of old—keeping it whole. How best may I do that? How long can we fight the Outland invaders who grow stronger and better equipped? My Father fought for peace and so shall I. I aim to shoot well. I say, bring the Outlands into the fold, expand our boarders, and accept them as vassals."

The Outlanders at table flushed with pride and banged their mugs and stamped their feet.

Rogsin has them buttered like sweet-yams.

"I'm gathering all of Center Earth together against our greater enemy. My Father made trade agreements with them, but I know a better security. Even now they gather resources to march on us. I say, make war on the Steppes! Else they make war on us!"

The room erupted into lowborn cheers. Younger highborn men and some dragons cheered too. All but the eldest courtiers hailed Rogsin. Never before had a Vineland King called for war without common consent. Never had a King gone to war in the wider lands—it was against the Lore of Light.

The lowly folks first served and full-bellied celebrated Rogsin's words not understanding the ways of peace. Penelope shouted out disagreements based on holy scrolls saying such as;

"The Light will bless this land only so long as the land stays intact, the scrolls say. The way of Light disallows expansion by war! Sharing our bounty is the way of peace. Outlanders cannot co-rule! We must not preempt war. The Unicorn People are innocent!"

But the people jeered at her and shouted her down. Penelope called out until she felt faint and nearly heeled over for wont of air. She wasted her voice—mobs abhor reason.

It is not peace he wants, it is conquest and ruin.

"Rogsin's mind is in shadow," Praxis said quietly coming along side. "I've heard much of this talk all winter, and seen stranger things than this. But I've spied good news, too."

Penelope had no more pretense in her. Her hopes were dashed, her hue went dark and her feathers went flat. What good news Praxis had could not heal this, but it was noble of Praxis to try. Penelope put a grateful wing around Praxis and the intern was swept into Penelope's grief. Praxis shook with sobs.

"Let us hope there is no more mayhem this day," Penelope said.

"Least I forget," Rogsin called above the din, "in war, wizards and engineers serve best, not generals. So in one seat I call for all three talents, wizardly ways, invention, and wisdom. I name Emerald my wizard!"

And then another first took place in the Kingdom of Vineland, perhaps not the last of Firsts, the people cheered the outcast. All eyes were on Emerald, his green blazed like copper in a fire as he took Merilbe's place at Rogsin's table.

Penelope could not look. She turned her back on the King and faced the common door. There, the shamed, hooded dragon still lingered just inside the Hall. He turned away as she looked at him and flexed hidden wings. The hidden one withdrew suddenly. The blanket and hood he wore was throne down as he crossed the threshold to the outside. There in the courtyard Draco appeared with red smoke billowing into the sky.

"Is that your good news Praxis?"

"Yes Pod Mother."

"Good indeed, the new dragon-star is not Draco's, but hope is thin. I must go to him. Keep well all you see and hear and speak it to no one save me. Wait until I return."

Penelope made haste for the door leaving the fires of Rogsin to burn without her. But, she was too late. Draco had taken wing, and she could not follow. The day was young, and she had work to do, so Penelope reentered the feast with a hunger but one not of the table.

THIRTY SEVEN

The Unfriendly Inn

For many days Mar traveled the wilds of Dreglands below the elevated Giant's Road. He took heart as he travel—gathering and hunting paid well. Mars spit rocks and took rabbits or other small game as needs be. It was not fine fare, but he ate enough and the local herbs were good dressings. Lizards, frogs, rabbits, wild greens, honey and sunflowers sustained him like the prophets of old. He lit few fires, although he had suitable flints, and thus avoided the Iron Skin hunters. Mars even made a friction bow for starting fire and practiced other fire teachings he learned while under the Warlord's wing.

'Tis warrior's wisdom; observe your surroundings keenly whilst in far lands,' Draco had said. 'Make no smoke. Keep cooking fires hid. Never give away your position.'

Mars never seriously considered traveling stealth but the Iron Skins circling overhead forced the art. Whenever they flew they hunted. As such, Mars observed and learned; they never crossed each other's path. Where there was one there was no other near. Their undersides were sky-color with no natural glint or glow giving them away. Mars learned to track them by their ground shadows.

Mars unhappily took the Crow's advice and muted his hue. He made his color black. Mars didn't like it—his scales were his pride but here, his pride was a deadly beacon. Shadow-travel did not bode well with him. Changing color was a shameful thing for a warrior.

I rather fight openly than hide as lizards do!

Mars's heart struggled and Mother's saying came to his mind; 'Better to walk shamefully than fly foolishly and die.' She spoke of traveling Sages who walked from place to place teaching Light-Lore. She had said it to denounce Draco's offer. Her words were true in Dreglands—humbled as a sage, he preserved his life. But, she was not right on all accounts.

Flying as Draco's messenger must be safer than walking under Iron Skins.

Mars chanted the scout's spell as he flitted from shadow to shadow. He hated it. It was the same magic Emerald had used to recolor his Mark and discredit himself long ago when Emerald sought to usurp Draco's birthright. Two egg-brothers, each with the Mark, and the better color the greater rank. Emerald abused the spell and became an outcast.

Try as he did, Mars could not give this unpopular spell his all. Mars had to wallow in the mud to cover his stubborn underside scales. He covered himself with his wings and let the spell rest whenever the dactyls weren't too near.

"My Mark is well hid," Mars said miserably as he looked himself over in a still pool after applying a fresh coat of muck.

On the eleventh day—an unlucky number—Mars approached the south horn of the mountains caked in mud like a repentant lawbreaker. He smelled smoke. Not the smoke of war, but of a settlement. He flew to a hill top and saw the unexpected; a fortified encampment edging a distant pine forest backed by a low mountain. Mars quickened his walk into a run and flew the last mile.

Mars landed before the gate of a wooden-stockade. He figured it a frontier fort. He'd heard of such places. Hard, lawless enclaves beyond Vineland's reach where unsavory dragons and men avoided civil lands—havens for robbers and outcast. Mars's joy turned bleak. He chanted the spell and wrapped his wings around him like a cape regretting his haste.

"What's your business?" A harsh Dragon's voice called.

A huge black dragon's head peered down at him from the wall's top. This dragon was night-black, and not from mud, red flames filled his mouth like an angry forge. A slot in the gate slid open and the eyes of a man appeared.

"He's alright, another throw-away."

The dark dragon spit a great flame into the air and shook his head clearing away the black cloud about his head.

"Don't be so sure," the dragon said his tone angry "He's got wings! He's a sheriff's spy I tell you. We ought to roast him."

The eyes behind the door squinted.

"Look at him, all mudded up, someone's run him off...but why, that's the question, what of it boy?"

Many more archers' slots swung inward along the wall. Men with notched bows drew down on Mars. At this distance, scales or not, they could shoot his eyes out, or cause some other harm. Yet Mars, not wanting to lie, as he was no good at it, thought of a truth. Mars had no choice but to tell them his greatest shame.

"I've naught fire!" Mars cried in a country dragon's accent, "Every where, one such as me is unaccepted. Won't you let a fireless dragon be? I think not. I've gone about the lands in shame seeking refuge. Have you no pity for an outcast such as me?!"

"Never did I think I'd see the day a dragon with a shame worse than mine would knock on my door" The black dragon said spouting white smoke. "You have something we can use. Open the gate."

Mars did not understand the black dragon's words or shift in mood until he entered.

The rouge has no wings!

Nor did the dozen or so dragons gathered there, dragons of every Estate, look well and whole. As such it was plan that their condition was no accident of birth. Many dragons wore bloody bandages. Some had old stumps—they were wingless convicts. And the men were from the wider lands too as they were dressed in the garb of various places, but their offenses bore no mark other than tattered clothing.

Mars expected forest rangers, huntsmen and other woodsy frontier folk, who were also present and normally well fitted: yet, all were in tatters. Mars never heard of wellborn humans in such distress. Something terrible was afoot. Mars stood his place blinking his eyes.

"This is no play-camp," A scar-faced man said, "and we don't take kindly to visitors."

Dozens of rough men wearing crude armor and devices of mayhem eyed him maliciously. No doubt to see what they could steel, Mars supposed. The highborn gentlemen he saw in ruined clothes bore no weapons or dignity. Slaves, Mars realized, captured in highway raids. Mars scrutinized the dragons—highway robbers as well. They wore armored saddles and old battle scars. All were fighters save one.

"Argolis, come hither!" A man called harshly, "See to him, quick afore I pluck your scales and salt the wounds."

A most un-robber like country dragon came running at the call. Mars felt like meat that fell off the table and into a boiling pot.

THIRTY EIGHT

The Council of Rogsin

Rogsin sat long observing his spring feast. He watched the lowborn eating and toasting his generosity with disdain while the highborn whispered together with suspicious eyes. At first some Estates men attempted rousting the others to depart in protest. Emerald's seating was the last straw. But, Penelope rose to her duty and dashed from party to party successfully beseeching peace.

Penelope knows her work, but not how it benefits me.

Rogsin thought of her as a double headed ax. He could use her skills, but again, her skills could cut him low. And undercut him she certainly would on hearing his other proclamations. Rogsin had seen enough of her in his eighteen years to anticipate trouble.

"Penelope cannot be trusted," Rogsin said to no one. "Can any dragon be trusted?

"Nay," the man to his left said.

"Father was a fool for trusting so much to dragons," Rogsin said to the dwarf right of him, whose name he had forgotten.

"Whosoever holds dragons holds victory." The dwarf said reciting common wisdom.

Long had the hill dwarf clans lusted after the riches of the Highland mines, and with every foray onto claimed lands, they were driven off—standing against men on dragons was historically known as suicide to dwarfs.

"Whoever bests the dragons wins it all," Rogsin said to the dwarf.

Many of the Outlanders at his table were not well known to him. As such, they boasted between gluttonous bites to establish their worth. But Rogsin paid little attention. They would repeat their brags and pledges at War Council. Finally the doorman blew the horn and the room emptied of commoners. The courtiers remained sipping Vinetop's finest brandy and smoking his best pipe-weed.

"That went well," Rogsin said lighting his bowl with a candle.

Tradition was that the nobles assembled after the feast for the King's last word of the day. Rogsin hailed the nobles and called for their attention, as tradition warranted. They gathered before Rogsin as was usual while ending Spring Breakfast. Having said the formalities, words of thanks and appreciation, Rogsin ventured another announcement.

"As you all have heard, last year the Tapestry chose my sister as a magic-weaver. To satisfy the fears of my new councilmen, and to assure victory in the Steppes, I will redress the destruction of Vinetop's oracle. So, I proclaim: My dearest Onyx will remain within the Giant's Seat until such time as the Tapestry is remade. We'll have our war-adviser again."

Murmurs circled the room. The faces were not disagreeable. Only Praxis let slip black smoke. The Tapestry of Neff was sourly missed although it was no longer useful. Rogsin fingered the scrap of it that he always carried in his hip pocket—its temperature pulsated hot as though it were angry. Rogsin withdrew his hand and sucked his fingers. Penelope came forward with her crown upright and red flames in her mouth. She bowed slightly not yielding her full respect.

I will enjoy seeing your wings cut off.

"The Tapestry is…was not an oracle of war," Penelope said, "The lore is plain. It failed Hammond because he asked dark tidings of it."

Rogsin laughed.

"I know well what Father asked of it, your conjectures are untrue. More so, your lore is shallow. I have deeper lore. Emerald's learning came to Father and so it came down to me. Between Emerald's house and mine, dead knowledge flows like un-tasted honey. I tasted it. I will make a new Tapestry."

"Emerald's council failed Hammond. Those books of Emerald's were buried for good reasons," Penelope said. "He advises you wrongly. I don't know what black magic Emerald has, but Onyx cannot remake it alone or with Emerald's help."

"Quiet right, not without white dragon magic, Emerald tells me," Rogsin lied. "That is why I've decided to extend Praxis's stay. I hereby appoint Praxis Onyx's familiar. They get along well, after all."

"I'll leave you with this scrolls-lore." Penelope said evenly. "Another cannot be made." Penelope bowled. She went to Praxis whom smoldered with distraught smoke.

Rogsin's new cohorts appeared satisfied. Even the indignant Estates nobles gave nods of approval. The nobles were fools. Penelope's words were righter than she knew. As long as he held the last remaining scrap of it, it could never be made again. And Rogsin didn't care. Old magic mattered not. Rogsin needed naught but his wits. He cursed Dragon's Magic in his heart and did not fear them as dwarves did. He'd long decided to make his own fortunes without dragons. His pawns accepted the false hope of a new Tapestry—an appeasement that already repaid with loyalty.

This is almost too easy.

"A fine distraction," the dwarf said. "A dragon remaining here will bring bad luck!"

"Not so. Praxis, as my…guest, will keep dragons in check," Rogsin said, "and that Golden is useful…under my control. That's to our advantage, I'd say."

"What of the other dragons," several Outlanders said at once.

Rogsin looked around and lowered his voice so only those nearest could hear. Emerald looked on. He didn't care if the Green-wizard heard.

"Wing-cutting forces dragon's obedience. They can't stop us unless they forgo the Giant's Commission and that they will never do. We'll have our new oracle, and you my friends, will be woven into it as equal partners." And Praxis as hostage, Rogsin thought, but knew better than to say so aloud.

"You are wise and true, oh King," the man on the left said.

Outlanders only knew the legends of their own defeats—they had always feared the Tapestry's power that was set against them. Now the same power was theirs, or so they thought.

They already believe in this forthcoming but useless talisman. They fear dragons, yet I've proven my mastery over flying lizards. They'll march to my war-drum when called.

With the Lords in disarray, and Draco disbarred, it was time to plan, time to arm, and time to kill Mars. As Rogsin eyed Emerald at the table end he decided that Emerald must pay for letting Mars slip away—but not until Emerald's talents were used up. Rogsin nodded at Emerald and smiled thinking; *that dragon is my most unpredictable enemy. I'll keep him within striking distance.*

"Next I'll pull Draco's teeth," Rogsin said as he watched Praxis exit the Great Hall with Penelope. "Break the corner stones and dragon-house falls."

"What's that," Emerald inquired over the clamor. Estates men and Outlanders were speaking together, some angry and some in agreement whereas all day they had not conversed at all. Yet trust between them sprouted like spring seeds and Rogsin would water it often.

"All in good time my green-fellow, you will know all before I'm done." Rogsin said.

Rogsin abruptly stood and left the table. He adjourned to the residence leaving the Outlanders and Estate's men twisted together in a knot of his making.

THIRTY NINE

Mars Hits the Road

On the great black dragon's command, Argolis, the only unarmored dragon, came running with his crown low and tail slapping haphazardly like the typical country dragon he appeared to be.

"Argolis, show him around, make him comfortable. Be mindful of his wings. I need a flyer," the black dragon said.

The black dragon didn't wait for Argolis to answer. Rather, he snorted steam and walked away. Every footfall rattled Mars's teeth until the black dragon was twenty yards off. He was bigger than Draco.

"Right away, Mr. Black Bill, yes sir." Argolis called after him too cheerful for this dismal place.

Argolis was obviously a pure-bred country dragon—forest green with brown flecks, wide boned and short legged, and he had been fat, too, judging by his loose skin. Mars didn't think well of uneducated lowborn dragons, especially farmers. But Argolis looked as pitiful as Mars felt and Mars had far less in common with the shiftless highway robber dragons there—at least Argolis was friendly.

Argolis walked Mars around the camp and showed what little there was to see. There was only one proper building, a two story log-built structure with thatched roof. The entire gable-wall with fireplace was build of stone. Vines covered much of it while on the roof all kinds of fauna grew. The place was near ruin and not recently made.

"Was this once an Inn?" Mars asked.

"Aye, it was, it now serves as the fighting men's quarters and kitchen."

The rest of the town consisted of log shacks, deer skin tents and dragon barns strung here and there between stone ruins without order and otherwise haphazardly built. There weren't any proper houses standing or garden plots. Small corrals held goats for milk and cheese. There was a clean water spring edged with small stones behind the Inn next to a distillery. It smelted like they were making spirits from wild red-berry. A fire burned at the center of the compound. Mars searched every detail carefully, as Draco taught, looking for any advantage.

The enclosure's walls were made of top-pointed vertical tree logs twenty foot tall and latched together with hemp rope. The stockade surrounded the entire compound. A bowmen's scaffold was built onto the wall. In a pinch a dragon could jump the wall. That is, if the men on the wall or the ground-based archer's slots were asleep. A pike man on the ground could do a dragon great harm if a dragon should hop the wall. The arrangement was clever.

"There you have it," Argolis said, his voice happier than warranted. "Have a sit by the common fire whilst I get us some vitals. We can't eat in the main house. Only fighters are welcome at that table."

He's not a fighter. Their spy, I'd wager.

Mars sat by the fire thinking, *I am a fighter, golden at that! I would best any two of them!* Mars wanted nothing more than to let down the dulling spell and wash off the mud. But, no, he could not show his hand. The old crow was right again. They would take his scales for armor if they knew. Gold scales are the hardest, after all. All the dragons here sported dull, dark scales, and so did the men's armor that employed dragon scales—all here were dark dragons save Argolis who shown bright.

How long can I maintain this scale-muting spell?

Mars murmured the spell under his breath and waited. Dragons lose their colors by doing evil was the common lore. From what Mars gathered of Black Bill's gate keeping, Mars had no doubt the lore was true. The dragons hereabout had no wings and so cannot make spells like his muting spell. A dragon's magic was in his wings, after all.

They must truly have dark hearts.

Moreover, Mars recalled, dragons that loose wings grew new ones—but only if they keep the Light. Every dragon in sight had age-withered wing stubs—none were growing. Argolis's fresh wounds sprouted buds while the other dragon's wounds did not. Oddly, Black Bill's stubs looked natural and unlike old wounds. Bill was born a cripple. Mars drew his wings around him and shivered.

Argolis waddled up with a small iron pot and hooked it to the fire's rotating spit. Finally, a deep cooked meal. On the road he ate raw or quick-fired food not daring to keeps a fire long for fear of the Iron Skins.

"There we are, Sir, a nice stew, a bit of rabbit and wild pig, with taters and greens. They got good wild greens hereabout."

"Is it safe by the fire?" Mars asked. "What of the Iron Skins?"

"Safe enough," Argolis said. "Those monsters can't dive so sharp. They'll get hung on them pointy wall tops—they're not so stupid. And saying one strafes us, pulling up, she'd hit them yonder tress."

Argolis thrust a thumb over his shoulder. True enough. The town was built just below a stand of tall firs that climbed the mountain behind them. From a dive, even the best dragons would be hard pressed to pull up in time.

"Iron Skins is not as dumb as me, they don't go flying into traps."

"You don't look stupid," Mars said.

"Stupidity is how I came here," Argolis said, "if you take my meaning, Sir."

"Tell me—how'd you wind up here?" Mars asked.

"My tale is woeful, calamities one after another. I was hatched one brood before the Golden came but I never did I see him. That's begun my bad luck, if luck is what you call it. Not luck a-tall I'd say but foolishness."

Argolis took up a stick and poked at the fire.

"I washed out from the Rookery early on. No good for War Camp or schooling…I went home to work my Father's smithy and till his soil. Blowing hot air is what I did best till Rogsin's call for smithies came. I went to the forges of Vinetop with me dear old Dad. And I wasn't there a week when I spilled a cauldron of Dragon Gold. Well, Rogsin heard, and off came my wings! But without me wing's magic you can't blow no billows for Dragon Gold, or any other decent trade, for that matter. Rogsin tied his own hands, on that. So they banished me and I set off looking for frontiersmen's work and here I am."

Argolis picked up his stick again and poked the fire under the pot. The coals smelled as good as the stew. Argolis's fire tending seemed blessed; the fire was perfectly arranged for cooking.

"I fell in with this lot, came on as a smithy too stupid to see the blackness in them until too late. But that Bill, he's alright. I think he was a good egg. Still, it was stupid coming here."

"How so," Mars asked.

"I was made an outcast sure enough, but I've made it worse. Now, I'm an outlaw! Will you look at that! A pot and no ladle, no plates or spoons, I've got to get the service, stupid me again."

Mars' heart warmed toward Argolis. The country dragon was more out of place than himself. His colors were true; his wings unjustly taken. Mars figured Argolis a simple dragon and perhaps a clumsy one as well, but he was no highwaymen and not so stupid as to become one.

"No need," Mars said. He had not yet removed his flight bags. "I've bowls and spoons in my bags. Reach in for me and draw them out. We'll use mine."

Mars lifted his wings high exposing his flight bags for Argolis. Argolis ran his fingers along the fine leather work and admired the stitching before finding the eating implements. Argolis then served the stew while humming a song. Mars didn't know how good rabbit and wild greens could taste. The gravy was thick and spicy hot. So far removed from the kitchen-foods of the Rookery, Mars never thought he'd eat food that bested the King's table. It was not a big pot so the two ate without words until it was gone.

Mars allowed Argolis the bigger part of it: He did eat well along the road. Then Argolis fetched a bucket of water from the spring, drank a bit and poured the rest into the iron pot and began washing the utensils.

'"Fine bags you have," Argolis said while he scrubbed with a bit of chainmail. "I've only seen such good make on rich merchants. You have no dagger, sword nor even fire? How does a bandit do so well with no weapons? I mean, very fine bags, Sir—how'd you steal them?"

Mars, comforted by the fire and food, forgot himself and the game he played. Thus he cried, "I didn't steal them; they were a gift! I'm not a crook."

Mars curled his tail fin into a knot and beat his tail on the ground upsetting the wash water. Argolis rushed to grab the bucket and caused the bucket to splash Mars. The hot water ran down Mars's flank washing away a patch of black mud. A glint of gold shown in the fire light from Mars's underside—Argolis's crown stood up. Mars quickly covered the spot with his wing.

"You're him!" Argolis said shooting a blue flame. "You're the…"

"You mustn't give me away," Mars's whispered in a hiss, "I can do no good for dragons without my skin."

Argolis leaned back on his haunches and rubbed his chin. But, before he could speak, Black Bill jumped down from the wall, bounded three times and was upon them.

"What's this ruckus," Bill growled. " I don't like the sound of it."

"Sorry master," Argolis quickly said, "I've gone stupid again and spilled the water. Mr. Mud-flap doesn't like water on him."

"Mud-flap you say. Is that what they call you?" Bill said.

"Aye, I've been called that, and worse," Mars snapped his jaws. "I dragged my flaps in the mud a time or two. Too often, I'd say."

Black Bill tossed his head back and roared laughing. Blue flame shot twenty feet into the sky.

"You're in like company," Bill said. "We'll keep your wings out of the mud and in the air, we needs a dependable scout—not that lying crow. We'll attend to washing you up in the morning Mr. Mud-flap. Mud-flap, now that beats all."

Black Bill made for the Big House chuckling as he went. His gray and blue smoke trailed after him.

Mars felt like mud. They needed a flyer more than his scales. They'd keep him whole, and far removed from whatever fire-restoring magic was in the world. There was nothing else to do but to leave, and fast, before he was found out—but how? Run the gate or fly over the wall and into spears and arrows? Mars could not fight his way out, no. There had to be a better way but Mars had no ideas.

"We've got to get you out of here," Argolis whispered. "I'll show you how if you take me with you. I've planed my escape, but I need help. Partner with me."

Trusting a fool was better than trusting his luck against so many arms. Mars had little choice. At least Argolis knew the lands thereabout and although he wasn't book smart, Mars had hope. Of folks like Argolis, people say, 'Country folk perfect common sense.'

He's not as dumb as he looks.

"Agreed, but once we find a cross road, you'll depart from me, yes? I'm seeking the Inowise."

Argolis put a hand to his chin and thought until his crown stood, the first time Mars had seen any crown feathers fully upright in this dismal place. Blue flame slowly filled Argolis's mouth.

"I know the best road," Argolis said, "I've seen Inowise go that way, too. So happens, we must go much that same way or not at all. It is a dangerous road. What say you?"

"Deal, I'll follow," Mars said.

Mars' estimation of Argolis increased—Argolis was braver, or dumber, than any country dragon Mars had met before. Mars's mood flew skyward until Argolis laid out what he had in mind.

"Above the camp half up the mountain lays a road, not how I came. I found it mushrooming for the cook-pot. This here road rounds the forested slopes above and leads into a long valley. The Inowise Pass they call it—it spills out a-ways north of here into the Tangleswoods. The old Neff Road is beyond."

Mars knew of the Tangleswoods and nothing good was ever said of that land. It was a place along Neff's old northeast border on the Neff side of the Forbidden Mountains—A place nobody wanted where no intelligent dragon would go fireless. Lore said Tangleswoods was inhabited by cruel trees. Some were walking-trees; some were fixed to the earth. Dead trees haunted the scrub-land. The creatures living among their branches were full of bad intent. Fire was the only defense in such a place.

"That old Neff Road," said Argolis "Wasn't even safe in the days of the Garden. Last age folks avoided the Tangles, they tell. In them days tree-magic was worse. I hear there's a path through Tangleswoods that meets the old Neff Road away south. If we can get to Neff Road, it'll lead us to the Steppes cliffs up north or Vineland down south. That road splits the quicksand swamps and it keeps them black hearted guard-trees. It's a knife's edge road, if you take my meaning."

Mars closed his eyes and searched his memory and nothing in his learning spoke of this pass. Mars had no knowledge of this country.

"That's a desperate move," Mars said, "Why go in so treacherous a direction? Why can't we take the Giant's Road?"

"Iron Skins hunt it as do our companions, I'd sooner walk quicksand than get eaten, or taken into slavery again."

"The Inowise Pass is hard," Mars said, "Yet, I see it's the better option. If we make it to that mountain road above, without them knowing it, they'll assume we took the easier way. They'll waste time searching the Giant's Road. We'll be long gone before they figure it out. How do we get out of here unseen?"

"I'd been digging a tunnel under the back fence while tending the compost. With you in town, I've a better idea, if you take my meaning, Sir."

Argolis quietly led Mars away from the fire and brought him behind a ruined barn. He took one of Mars's wings and stretched it out.

"That's what I thought," Argolis said. "I'd never seen no dragon wrap around his wings like you. You got twice the wings of any dragon my size. And I'm half the dragon I used to be. This will work."

"What will work," Mars asked finding it hard not to laugh. Argolis's face was screwed up in concentration, his tongue hung to one side of his mouth like a child with a puzzle. White smoke streamed from his nostrils like a court jester.

"Ever see human folks play that game they play, what's it called? One gets on top of the other and they run to the finish. I mean, it's not easy, but we don't need to go far to get clear."

"It's a piggy-back race," Mars said. "I never heard of dragons doing that."

"Either has Black Bill, I'd wager," Argolis said. "I best be getting to serving the boys some red-berry drink, I mean them boys looks like they could use a nap…err… refreshments."

By midnight the guards had drunk what Argolis had supplied and felt the effects. Black Bill had given Mars a shack near the back wall and dung heap as befitting an untested newcomer. Argolis met him there wearing a plow harness, a thing no honorable high dragon would wear. Only dumb animals and criminals were fitted with such gear but Argolis wore it without embarrassment.

"You're quiet for a country dragon," Mars whispered.

"Aye, and I can jump too," said Argolis. "Get on my back, take the straps, and when I get to the wall, flap like mad. I ought to clear it on my own. The rest is yours."

Together they cleared the wall with height to spare—which was good because the tree line was near. Mars climbed until they made the high road a half mile above camp. For a mile or two they followed the road airborne. Mars set down and none too soon, the dark-scale spell had faded by the joy of flying.

Yet,Mars was spent. His feet and hands ached with the strain of holding the straps. But there was no time to rest. All that night they marched the crumbling road. It was an hour after dawn when they rounded the north horn. Mars found a cave there, and not smelling any bears or lions, and without a gnomes path in sight they lay up and slept a few hours before continuing alone the path. Then, that late afternoon, they left the high road for the valley. Mars spied a path far below winding downward through the upper valley like a white snake threading ant hills.

The valley proved fair, at first. The high valley was narrow between hills with no room for hunting Iron Skins to bank. There was a fast, narrow stream running the course of it along side the path Mars saw. It had good water and he found nicely rounded spitting stones along its banks and so he loaded his neck bag full. There was game to be had and it wasn't too late in the evening to take a pair of rabbits. Argolis knew much gathering lore and found wholesome greens and tubers which made a fine strew. The two travelers became fast friends as oft times those that cook and sup together do. That night they nested in a shallow cave on a hillside above the creek. They went to sleep early, tired but well contented.

FORTY

Emerald's War Room Idea

Emerald reclined near a cooking hearth smoking pipe-weed, it was seven days after Spring Breakfast. He had spent his week watching and feasting on the words of men and dragons rather than the plentiful food. Hunger sharpened his mind and so he ate little and rather endeavored to ferret-out what information he could use. Emerald realized that all the men, Outlander and Estate's men alike wangled their tongues foolishly although each faction represented a different sort of foolhardiness. What Emerald heard between brags was plan fact; Rogsin's wont for conquest spread like the spring floods. By now, Emerald supposed, even the Steppes got word.

The warriors were easily understood, 'Warriors are for war,' is the saying. The Estates men were landlords lusting for more land. But Rogsin, he was a different matter. Emerald found him complex, calculating, a good liar, and Emerald suspected some deeper evil gotten from Mordune. Rogsin's lips smiled easily but his eyes glistened with no merriments and rather shown as vague, dark pools. The way Rogsin treated his sister also told much. Rogsin feared her—but why?

The King loved nothing and no one that Emerald could see, save his own mad desires. The King may actually be mad, Emerald surmised, and thereby most unpredictable. *Even a madman can be played to suite me*, Emerald assured him self, *but first I must discover his game.*

Emerald wanted power and glories enough to better his brother, Draco. Unexpected opportunities arrived in plenty upon Hammond's demise, but Rogsin opened that door far too wide like a baited trap.

Rogsin took the news of Mars's escape in light stride. Rogsin never did say why he wanted Mars held captive. *This is all so strange.*

It was clear; Emerald should never trust Rogsin. Madness knows no honor or limits and there was naught but twisted logic within Rogsin—does madness ever make sense? Emerald searched for indiscernible truths inside the King's mind and heart. Thus, Emerald found his withered heart had rejuvenated somewhat over this past winter. Was it by the Golden's magic close at hand? Emerald's heart gave him warning for the first time in centuries but no good news. Emerald's innards felt Rogsin spinning his spider-trap yet in his own mind he reasoned it would take time to trace that web to its root cause.

"Who is bating who and who is the quarry?" Emerald asked his smoke ring.

Emerald decided he would go more carefully now. Foremost, he sought an excuse to leave Vinetop. Wizard to the King or not, a seat he longed for, is the place he must flee from. Emerald only trusted the safely of his caves.

At War Council, I'll pry open a crack and escape.

Rogsin called the War Council just past noon and the invited gathered within the War Room. Emerald was first to enter the sanctuary. Last he'd seen it, Emerald knew it different. Gone was the Tapestry. Gone was the wing table. Against the Tapestry wall at least fifteen sets of living dragon's wings hung like trophies bound face to face so not to float off. A table was set long-ways in the center of the room with places for twenty four men and one dragon. Hammond's old war table for twelve would not seat all who where invited, twelve estates and twelve Outland clans.

It was an odd sight although he'd only seen this place once before. The ring of the room was hollow and dead whereas before the air carried the weight of life. Emerald's gut rumbled and he was sorry he did not fill his tell-tales belly.

Emerald took a small jar of bees wax from his neck-bag and re-pasted his crown feathers. He was very glad, for once, that he couldn't make natural smoke and accidentally give away his thoughts.

Emerald took his place at the table well shielded and waited wide-eyed while the Outlander chiefs and Estate Marshals filed in with stern faces and suspicious glances. If eyes cut, they'd all be bleeding. Rogsin came last. The young scribe with him took the secretaries seat at a small desk.

"Harbor no formalities," Rogsin began, "Speak true and quick. Harsh words are best for war. Let us talk of invading the Steppes."

And fast talk makes for slipped tongues, Emerald thought as Rogsin eased into his chair. Despite Rogsin's directive, Emerald held his own words captive. War-lust did not influence or figure into Emerald's calculations.

All at once the Estate's men began yammering and calling questions while the Outlanders remained quiet—at first. The Outlander war chiefs wintered here so Emerald figured that they and Rogsin had already decided much. Even so, before long, the Outlanders joined in.

The Estate Marshals, less informed, inquired all at once such as; how to march armies against the Steppes so far away and with so few dragons, and how to support such a horde, and how to transport siege-engines so far, and other logistical concerns. Emerald marked that not one asked, 'what good reason is there for this war at all?' Emerald was glad for his home away from such nonsense. *What good are grasslands to farmers and miners?*

The local lands were rich, after all; the Outlands unsavory but quite productive after their own fashion. None in either place went hungry or naked. The Estates were spilling out, as usual, onto each other's lands and as such they forever fought over borders—this far-off war would not cure that strife. Land-lust filled the Estates Lord's hearts as surely as gold-lust filled dragon and dwarf hearts.

It quickly became apparent that the Estate's were glad for Rogsin's expansion plans—they were contemptuous of the Scroll's prohibition against such conquests. Common ground between former enemies was quickly founded upon the question; how best to invade their peaceful neighbors?

The greed of them is appalling—they forfeit ten thousand years of relative stability for the temporal wont of this generation. They deserve failure.

But still, it was an interesting problem Emerald thought. Even as the men wrestled with their quandary Emerald formed solutions in his mind. Their war was far from impossible as tradition had it. Emerald began to consider what payments he would realize form his services and lost track of the heated dialogues until an Outlanders loudly raised a concern that garnered Rogsin's attention.

"The Flatlanders have better bows!" The woodsman said. "They have countless horses and double-bent bows that shoot stronger and further whiles they needn't dismount to shoot. They'll cut us down before we get close enough to shoot. What of it, oh King?"

"That is why, my dear fellows, I've made Emerald here my wizard." Rogsin said as he stood up. "He is quiet cleaver you know, but none here have seen how cleaver. My Father's armory holds your answer. A device made by Emerald's design and I have other plans from him even more terrible than this. Behold, see what I have."

Rogsin took from behind his chair the very same crossbow Emerald had made. Although Hammond meant to destroy it as a danger to dragons, there it was, and a bolt missing from the quiver—the same bolt he removed from Mars's throat. Emerald could not help but shiver, his stomach went foul. Rogsin held it aloft as if it were an old, familiar keepsake.

Emerald's guess was that Hammond's crossbow was stolen and used by some robber. Now it was clear that Rogsin had shot Mars. Dragon kind's undoing was in the hands of a madman.

Emerald felt the trap closing, not on him, but closing on all of dragon kind. *Hammond was wise to hide it but he did not hide it well enough.*

"My ancestor's traditions are passing," Rogsin said. This is a new age…one that destroys the old way."

Rogsin called for his servants. They came and took down seven of the best famed armored suits and they stood all seven on their stands one behind the other in a line before a stone pillar. The older Estates men looked on with twisted red faces while the younger men watched with curious eyes. Rogsin cranked the bow ratchet and loaded a dragon-gold tipped bolt. He aimed and let fly. The bolt shot through all the suits and stuck fast into the stone pilaster with a chilling crack. Emerald was as shocked as the others. Emerald knew the bow's capability but not Rogsin's.

I must get out of here.

"This is only one of the many things Emerald will supply for us," Rogsin said with a wide grin. "I'd wager Emerald will invent even better devices for us. See him there so quiet, thinking—His mind is forever churning like a butter mill, so my spies tell me. Give us an invention Wizard; tell me what's on your mind now. Give me something I can use and I'll not cut your wings off today. I've taken to collecting wings, after all."

Emerald was taken aback. All eyes came upon him and so he had no time to think. Emerald began stammering and recklessly spit his thoughts out like over heated fire-rocks.

"You say and it's true too, that the Steppes are too far away to march Vineland's armies." Emerald said. "I think it can be done; only, it can't be done with dragons… Dragons eat too much and too often. Leave the dragons, gather horses instead. Horses eat grass, not human fare. They pull carts better than dragons. Lighten your food load. I'll design carts suitable for horses."

"Common wisdom," Rogsin said, "We need the advantage of air cover. Give me more, or feel my ax on your wings."

Emerald looked around wild-eyed—none were sympathetic. The fear of losing his wings ate at his better mind until a desperate thought struck him.

"Wings, wings that's the answer," blurted Emerald. "All the wings you gathered. Combine them in a harness of my design. We'll fix them to a basket and tethered it to the ground. You'll have an airborne observation station. Wings on wagons, too. Makes them easier to pull. Dragon wings need no food!"

Rogsin slammed his fist on the table and said, "Now that's more like it. Don't withhold your council again, Wizard, or suffer my wrath."

Emerald worried what might befall dragon folk. But then again, they rejected him and he owed them nothing. Emerald realized his way of escape. Emerald quickly contained his fears and brought forth a voice-spell, a spell fraught with seduction-magic. It worked on Penelope eighteen years ago. Would it work on Rogsin whose birth was a product of that same spell?

It must sound logical to keep the others off my tail.

"Oh King, I've accepted your mighty hand and generous station, and I'll honor your dictates. But I can serve you best from my laboratory. Spare my wings. I will perform quicker while working from home. There, I have all I need to serve you best."

The spell was cast and it took. All those at table were drowsy-eyed but none more so than Rogsin. The spell would not last long spread so wide. Emerald now knew the true lay—Rogsin's couriers were all spies. Emerald got all he could get from Vinetop and hoped Rogsin knew no more of him than Rogsin's spies provided. Rogsin was the enemy and yet, still, a precarious benefactor as well. Emerald would go as far as was good for his ambitions.

I must stay out of his reach.

Rogsin's one eye fluttered like a drunk's half-nap dream. It was time to make haste while the getting was still good.

"I will take my leave now, Lord," Emerald said bowing low. "In my study I will set to work on new engines."

Rogsin waved Emerald's leave as the stupor was still upon him. Emerald took no chances. Upon exiting the War Room, Emerald ran toward the landing. He passed Penelope and Praxis and other courtly folks in the Hall without slowing. He tracked for the gate like a wagon riding downhill ruts. From the landing he saw that Draco was coming in. As much as he enjoyed biting his brother's tail, Emerald did not wait, it was not a good time. Rather, Emerald took to the air and flew northeast against the wind as quick as he could. Emerald was not one for flying contrary winds but anything was better than facing the coming storm.

FORTY ONE

Penelope Waiting

Penelope was not surprised by Emerald's sudden departure. He never did remove his flight bags while on Vinetop. Like an auction-day pickpocket, Emerald remained ready to fly at a moments notice, and so he did. After the last few days, Penelope thought Emerald's dark wisdom had its merits. Emerald's fears must have come to fruition. Certainly, if Emerald, so enamored with achieving high status was eager to flee, then further evils awaited her court dragons.

Doubt filled Penelope. Praxis's report caused Penelope's fears to rise like fly-ash from the forge. Vinetop had become a dangerous place and there was no escape for Praxis. The intern's wings were tied. Penelope needed Praxis here but it was not safe. Penelope would take Praxis away if she could. Penelope normally reserved her judgment; after all, an elder shouldn't trust a young dragon's observations untested. Yet Praxis's assessments proved truer and graver by Emerald's hurried departure. Great evil was afoot.

Penelope stroked Praxis's mane and said, "Poor child, I would have you leave if it weren't for Rogsin's order. We cannot risk open disloyally."

Praxis had no time to comment. The guard sounded the Warlord's horn. They ran to the window. Draco approached flying in his full glory. His scales were polished, his mane was rewoven and hung heavy with his awards. His breast plate out-showed the sun. He did not wear the King's saddle. Penelope was awed at the sight. Her love for him, his glory, her deeper hopes and their old disputes fell on her all at once, but above all, she felt his life was in danger.

Draco entered the dragon's gate on the wing and fast. He landed within his own blast of flame and smoke as befitting a great warrior's return. Draco had missed the feast and the proceeding War Council. Draco landed dressed for war—a war of words.

"He looks incredible!" Praxis said.

"He should not have come," Penelope said. "He is not safe here."

"Hail the Warlord," cried the Captain of the Guards.

Everyone bowed. Penelope bowed lower than her station required. Draco stretched his head high quickly surveying the room. He went to Penelope and lifted her head gently with his hand.

"You are my right wing," Draco said in high dragon speak. "Walk with me."

Together they crossed the Great Hall to the War Room door with all eyes upon them. The guards threw open the door on impulse or by habit, Penelope did not know. The guards hailed and saluted him before calling: "Make way the Warlord."

Penelope could go no further; no females were permitted at War Council. So she stopped at the doors with her eyes and ears open. The foyer hallway beyond alighted with Draco's flame. She watched him enter with the red glow of his hue blazing as in war. Penelope's well trained gullet disobeyed her and she let loose a proud billow of smoke.

The guards did not close the doors quick and Penelope heard the voices within. The pitched laugh of Rogsin assaulted her ears, not the clamor of honors she expected. The men at table hissed and called insults.

As the guards closed the doors, Penelope knew Draco and all dragons were in deep trouble.

Had I only trusted Praxis sooner, things would fare better.

Penelope quickly retreated into the Hall. Many more human and dragon courtiers had come inside the Hall aroused by the blowing of Draco's horn. Penelope gathered the dragon's to her and addressed them in high dragon speech as no human present there understood it.

"This is my order," Penelope told them. "Go to the lands far and wide and do not come here again. Tell the dragon folk to stay clear of Rogsin's men. All you at courts must preen your ears and not confide in any human least Rogsin's spies hear it. It is time for dragons to hide our hearts. Darkness comes, nay, it has arrived: humankind turns against us. From where and how, the death blows come, I do not yet know. We must learn of it and fly from it. The end of the age is upon us. I fear for dragons. Now fly high and whisper low only into dragon's ears."

Before the hour chimed each dragon, save Penelope, departed flying off in every direction. Only Praxis and she remained. Penelope then spoke to Praxis.

"You must leave this place too. They will hunt you, but we will hide you."

"I cannot," Praxis said, "Nothing for Rogsin, to Onyx I am bound. She is bound to me and to all dragons. The Tapestry chose her, and we each other. Rogsin has her in the tower weaving, even now, and only I may visit her. Before Rogsin's decree, we spun the magic spinning wheel together and the knitting spell, the magic of familiars, took us."

"This is grave news," Penelope said. "Bonding magic makes its own way no matter the affairs of state. You cannot leave Onyx anymore than I can forsake Draco, impossible as he is."

"What should I do? If I leave, I will wither, if I stay Rogsin will…If I fail…He'll cut my wings!"

"Go careful; use what I've taught you. He cannot take your wings. The weaving magic won't work—tell him that lore so his cronies hear it. Stay away from Rogsin until Draco bond-mates you this next Auction Day. The familiar's bond will break then."

"Mars is the only one I want. I cannot bond-mate another…Pod mother what am I to do?"

"Your duty—keep your ears up, and, hope, hope in the Light. Draco and I will do our part…Mars may yet come home in time. But if not…"

Praxis began weeping. Penelope lowered her head and quieted. Penelope could not quell Praxis's tears any more than she could stop her own tears on the day Draco flew for War Camp. Praxis left the Hall leaving gray-black smoke behind. The perfect bond-mate for Praxis was Mars and Mars was nowhere to be found. Mars had until the fall to return. There was nothing to do but hope and wait while her flyers searched.

Draco emerged from the War Room dejected as never before. She wondered how any words could slay one as mighty as he. His head hung low, his mane scraped along the ground. He shuffled like a sickly grandfather. His tail lay heavy on the floor. Penelope fought within herself. She mustn't shed a tear—she mustn't run to him—she mustn't embarrass him in court. Too many of Rogsin's hired eyes watched. She stood like a distant stone.

Draco needed encouragement, not pity. Pity was a good salve for lowly folk but it was poison to warriors. Draco needed to resurrect his heart. Maybe it was time he warred within himself. For Draco's and dragon kind's sake, he needed a fight. She would provide one.

Draco paid no heed to his surroundings as he shuffled toward the landing. Penelope spat acid in his path, a dragon's challenge, gaining his attention. Penelope searched her mind for a way to antagonize him as he slowly straightened. Draco caste clouded eyes upon her. The Dragon's Gold breast plate he wore was gone.

Penelope's heart sunk. The golden breastplate—his badge of honor that was passed down to dragon warlords by the Kings of Vinetop from time out of mind—was gone. Draco was never without it.

Penelope looked upon Draco's Mark of Neff for the first time in countless years. There was no mistake; he bore the Mark and it was of perfect form just like Mars. Only, Draco's mark was red—the color of war, not gold the color of peace. She had forgotten its beauty. Even so adorned, Draco without his breastplate was half a dragon.

"I've lost my path," Draco said. "Rogsin dismissed dragons from the Steppes campaign. The Outlanders join with him. The Lords agree. There is no place for dragons on so long a march. I have no road before me."

"Draco, look into the Light and you'll find your way." She said, her planned antagonism forgotten.

"I've not had time for staring into the sun seeking revelations. That's Sages work. I was made for war and without war I am nothing."

"Are not all retired dragon's sages?"

Draco raised his head higher. The sunlight from an upper window caught his scales. Penelope thought his hue had changed, there was a new glint of gold, but oh so slightly, he was less red and more gold. Her heart began to beat a different rhythm.

"The sun is for all dragons, Draco," She said kindly. "We are all invited to look into the Light. Humans can't see as we do. It blinds them. They are too young, not pure hearted like we dragons were... are…Have you lived so long among men that you've forgotten? Seek the Light. It is not too late."

"I am not worthy. I've only had eyes for brown earth stained in red blood—true to my colors. Things of this Earth distracted me far too long. So much more than gold and glory lies within the Light. I was a fool."

Draco's tail fin suddenly knotted into a fist, he raised his tail to strike the floor. His eyes blazed with fire for a moment then glassed over turning to sky-blue. He did not dash the ground. His tail opened like a sunflower in the sun's beam.

"You are not a fool! You did what you saw best for dragon and humankind alike," Penelope said surprised at herself. "You honored the Light. Such great love often overwhelms wisdom…"

Penelope suddenly felt ashamed for all the years she worked against Draco. She had refused to consider him by the Light before now. Draco fought for peace in his own way. Rogsin was not the first King to lust after conquest.

"Bound as I am to war, I cannot bring dragons to rest. I'm no longer the King's Right Hand standing between human desire and unjustified war. Yet, I still have a duty. I have cadets. I will preside over the Auction and the fall games one last time. I am still the match-maker. As such, I can still do some good. Mars to Praxis…should he return."

Draco moved to a large window and looked out over the land. He splayed one wing as a gesture of joining. Penelope came by his side despite her old hurts. She was happy to do what he asked—like that day so long ago on Rookery Top when they overlooked Neff together. There he promised by the Light he would return to her once his duty was done. Penelope quoted the lore of love to him on that fine day. But she had no words for him now.

His time of duty would soon end and she should be happy but she was not. He put his wing over her so long ago, too. She rested her head on his neck as before. For the moment, as they watched dragons fly away from Vineland, she was young again. Age had robbed her of youthful hopes until Draco spoke saying.

"By the Light of the sun,'" Draco said quoting the blessing. "Praxis will wed Mars…"

"The sun has not set on your heart," Penelope said.

"Perhaps, but I fear that night falls on the Kingdom of Vineland and so falls the Dragon's Peace. I must go. I've warriors to train, search parties to send."

With that, Draco withdrew his wing, made his neck upright and moved to the landing with pride shown by his hue. He set out from the Warrior's Gate while Penelope watched from the window. He flew toward the War Camp. He was still commandant, after all. He still had duties to attend.

An omen seized her as he disappeared from sight—this was the last time Draco would ever fly from Vinetop, she felt. Then Penelope went to the same landing Draco used and took to the air herself.

She had her duties as well. There was much work to do before the end of this age.

FORTY TWO

Tangleswoods

The next day, before sunrise, Mars and Argolis listened from their hiding place. They heard and saw nothing of Black Bill or the Irons Skins. Thus they took to the over-grown path again and proceeded downward and west until they were below the northwest side of the mountain. After an hours march, the old path disappeared. If there was ever a path ahead it had washed out long ago. They picked their way downward through pine trees and thick underbrush until they reached the valley's bottom. There, they fast-marched half a day west until they found a clear spring and stopped to drink. Argolis gathered greens and roots while Mars hunted and spit-stoned a plump rabbit and two pheasants. Herbs were short but Argolis cooked a fair stew over a low, hot fire.

"It's a long way to Tangleswood," Argolis said picking his teeth. "They say this here pass runs sixty miles away west."

"We'll go slowly—stay under the trees," Mars said. "I don't think the bandits can see us from above, but all the same, keep your eyes sharp above, behind and ahead."

For two more days travel was easy. Argolis filled his loose skin along the way. The foraging was good so they ate often and much. On the third day the going got harder. The trees were fewer, the undergrowth became thicker and laced with thorns.

"We're nearing Tangleswood," Mars said. "The signs beseech it."

"I see why they call it that, if you take my meaning, Sir."

Scrub of all kinds invaded the valley floor and more of it appeared as they progressed. Gnarled trees thick with low thorn laden branches soon hampered them. Tangles of vines climbed the rocks and bent wholesome trees. Even the ground became hostile—sharp rocks lay wherever the ground was not covered by thorny brush, vine or stunted tree.

"Thorns or rocks, or what-all else I can't say, but they keeps wedging between me toes," Argolis cried with pain.

"We're stuck with it now," Mars said miserably, "If I had fire I'd burn it all down!"

"And us with it," Argolis said pushing to the front. "I'll keep me fires quiet, Sir. Let me stomp ahead a little. I've picked my way around a raspberry or two."

Argolis took the lead. Mars marveled at the lightness and speed of Argolis as he danced through the briers. Mars was hard pressed to keep up.

I'll never underestimate a country dragon again.

"I suppose country dragons, even fat ones, must also move about in tight places."

"Aye," Argolis said. "I came by it from woods-walking. I was hunting mushrooms long before I lost the wings. I must say, it's easier going without them, much as I miss them."

Mars thought it more akin to his station as a working class dragon. Country dragons had smaller wings than the highborn, and as such, Argolis wasn't suited for long flights or carrying burdens on the wing. Country dragons were known to be good on the ground. Mars saw the proof.

"Wish we could fly over this mess, "Mars said. "Even if we had room to get airborne, I couldn't carry you far the way you've gained weight." Mars said resigning himself to foot travel. "We're on the Neff side now. Iron Skins don't fly here. I wonder why."

"That's old lore," Argolis answered. "I'll sing the hearth song for you."

Once was Iron Skins were many and needed new roosts for a-laying.
And, so the males gathered and crossed the Forbidden Mountains from where they were staying.
Hungry from hard flying they attacked a village and feasted on men and dragons, goes the say-in.
There was nothing fore it but to go to war on it—on them leather birds who were straying.
For the first time, dragons let men ride them fore a dragon alone can't beat Iron Skin's-a-flailing.
Dragons bore men with long pikes so together they killed until skin-birds became failing…"

Argolis trailed off. He sopped a tear from his snout with a dry leaf and blew his noise.

"I'm not much for sad songs, Sir. But, that's why they won't cross, they remembers it still. Tis sad they lost all their men folk. You never heard this lore?"

"Of course not," Mars laughed. "They teach true lore at school, not silly hearth stories. And besides they are dumb animals. They can't pass tales from generation to generation. How could they remember the war?"

"Fact is," Argolis said, "It's the same ones of old what fly today. Even an old dog recalls his puppy-days beating. Those Irons is long lived, longer than Sages or wizards. That's why they are so few. Only the males went off to war—with the males gone, there's no egg-laying. There's plenty of space yonder for so few egg-less females. It's a sad thing."

Mars had heard their mournful calls. He realized that the sound was not a war-cry as he surmised. Their race was dying and the last of them screamed hopeless laments.

Mars's vision once again came to his mind. Hundreds of dragons and men flew together. Today, an Estate was lucky to have two dozen dragons. It stuck Mars that the warriors of his dream were flying to war against Iron Skins. Only male dragons fight and now, like the Irons, dragons were far fewer than they once were. Bile rose in Mars's gullet.

"Their fate will befall us," Mars said. He suddenly longed for Praxis.

"Not wiliest folks can fly to the Rookery and the Rookery stands." Argolis said snorting blue fire. "Now, if you highborn warring-types are too busy, or too dead, we country dragons will attend the highborn females, in your stead, if you take my meaning, Sir." Aegoolis winked.

"There is one I wont forsake," Mars said solemnly, "I'll not go as far-field as Draco did."

Yet even as he said it, Mars determined again to restore his fire and follow after Draco, thereby, becoming worthy of Praxis. She would never bond-mate an outcast despite her words, Mars felt. Draco's voice came to Mars's mind, 'A dragon proves honorable serving his duty.' Penelope's voice also spoke, but in his heart saying, 'there is nothing higher, no greater cause than love.'

No, to win Praxis, I must prove myself.

Mars found himself altogether lost—lost in a far away land, lost of hope, lost vocation, lost of love and mired with uncertainty. Mars halted at an up-righted long stone.

"Lost, we're lost," Mars cried. "Going in circles—I've seen this stone before."

There were many standing stones in this dismal place and Mars had scratched his name in that one two hours before. Argolis was taller than Mars standing upright on hind legs so he reared back, set his tail for balance and peered over the briers.

"There's a tree line yonder. Argolis said. "When I pass on, my star won't be the brightest in the sky, if you take my meaning, but that's a road I'd say. Trees don't grow in no straight lines save along roads or built waterways. Wild creeks ramble."

"If I could get air, we'd know better."

"I have a notion," Argolis said. "I'll pitch you the way them human acrobats do it at the Auction. Put your leg in me hands and I'll heave."

Argolis proved strong and easily thrust Mars above the thickets. Mars spread his wings and hung in the air. It was true. The trees stood side by side, all the same height like solders for inspection. Mars did not stay aloft long. There were other things beside Iron Skins that could do them harm. Mars half folded his wings and regained the Earth.

"Let us make for the road with stealth," Mars whispered. "Where there are roads, in theses parts, there are enemies."

The two slunk toward the tree-line quietly but not by the way between hills which is why they made circles all day, rather they made a bee-line over what terrain there was and so made for the tree stand directly. The thickets hid them at first until the land changed to a marsh dotted with clumps of brush. The footing got tricky. After an hour of sloshing from one bit of cover to the next they came upon an overgrown raised embankment. The road was ten feet above the marsh. Tired of slogging in bogs, thickets and mud felids, Mars scrabbled up a muddy bank to a new disappointment. The lane was impassable.

"We found the road, alright. It's more overgrown than where we came from" Mars said.

Argolis crested the bank and crashed into the tangles of the road, the flora thicker than before. But Argolis did not stand in defeated; rather, he put his head down and plowed into the undergrowth toward the trees. Mars followed doggedly longing for open sky until he found Argolis on a thin but well worn path that ran along the trees-line north and south.

"That's what I figured," Argolis said. "A deer run, it follows the old road. Critters make good paths in hard places."

Argolis's crown feathers splayed flat and he puffed a bit of white smoke at the good news.

"I guess that's it then, Mr. Mars. I mean, we said we'd part at the crossroad. I'll launch you and you can fly off…"

"Nonsense, I won't leave you here alone." Mars said. "Look at this track." Mars bent down and put his hand inside a fresh track on the muddy path. It was far larger then any he'd seen before. "That bear is twice Draco's size. Low, a dagger tooth lion passed here not two hours ago."

"You can't go to Vineland. That old elf told you they're hunting you. You should make for the Sages up north. I can't walk all that way. Nobody's hunting me away south. There's nothing for it then, you go your way and I'll go mine. I'll be alright, you go on and fly."

"No," Mars said firmly, "We'll go south. This road meets the Giant's Road on the outskirts of Vineland. You'll be safe there. I'll fly to Rookery Top and send help for you once we find a good hold-up."

Mars considered the argument settled and focused on how to proceed. Although they had not run into any dangerous trees yet, the possibility overhung their new path. The way they had just come seemed to have filled in.

"They must have been planted when the road was young." Mars said pointing down the tree-line.

Argolis went to a tree, scratched its bark, and licked his nail."These here trees are a friendly kind, slow growing and long lived. Eve's trees, they call them."

Mars had never seen such old, tall and big-around Eve's trees. Yet these trees did not sing or sway. The branches drooped and twisted and were tangled with vines. Mars supposed that good magic no longer passed this way which would keep them from slumbering. They had no apples, and no awareness. Mars examined the tracks again.

"Dogs and foxes also travel this way and often," Mars said.

"Nothing for it, then, we follow the wild things," Argolis said.

"And quietly," Mars added.

Before setting out Mars scratched out a bag full of the smooth river stones that pushed up from the muddy path. The road builders had used river gravel. Mars spent all the suitable rocks he had while hunting. With his neck-bag full, Mars felt confident as they moved out.

They marched all that day and into the next with quiet caution. Late on the second day, they came upon three great black carrion birds talking together high in a tree. Mars and Argolis were unnoticed. Scavengers have the sharpest eyes and good noses, but dragons hear further than any creature. As luck or Light had it, the birds faced away and down-wind from them. The giant vultures were looking out over the mud pits and scrubby tufts beyond the trees toward Neff. Mars and Argolis stopped and hid in the brush and listened to the bird's talk.

"We ought to wait for him to starve natural like. Tell me Willie, how long you think he'll last; they say Inowise go long without eats." A vulture said.

"Aye they do, But I say we kills him and eats him now, before his soul returns. I mean, how often you find a spirit-walker stuck, I mean, he can't do no magic on us without his spirit in him, can he now. What do you say Bert? Let's eat him now?" Another bird said.

"Willie'sss right, listen'sssss Dugan, if we kills him now, there's more meat on the bones-sss'. He aren't going no place in that tar pit, true enough. I'm say-en, how long you want-sss to wait for them vitals-ss? And say-in he sinks-ess we-sss out an easy meal."

The vultures went on with their debate for some time. It seemed to Mars the carrion birds grew increasingly pleased with the prospect of killing rather than waiting for a meal. They decided to attack although they hesitated. After all, such birds are cautious and as patient as they are dangerous. However known for waiting as such creatures were, Mars felt that time was rapidly shorting for the victim. The kindness of Bear Claw and Begoth's advice to seek the Inowise weighted in Mars's heart.

"We must save the Inowise," Mars whispered. "Let's jump them."

"Without fire? Argolis said. "Them three birds is all big as me, with beaks made for tearing out eyes—and me not flying and all, the fight's in their favor."

Mars felt cut to the heart, if only he had fire, he'd take them all on at once—feathers burn. No bird would face a warrior's flames. But, Argolis was right.

"I'm useless," Mars said with grave bitterness.

"Now, now Sir, don't fret. All I'm say-in is you can't take them alone. You know even the best don't fight alone. I mean, Draco didn't beat the Western-tribes all by himself—did he? I got an idea."

It was decided that Mars would take wing and keep the vultures distracted while Argolis ran to the Inowise and took up the Inowise's defense. In that way, the birds could not attack the helpless man. Argolis would protect him with his fire.

"I got a full gut," Argolis said. "I don't spit fire-rocks, but forge blowing was good practice for pitching fire long, far and hot."

"Once your position is secure, I'll come to your aid," Mars agreed.

Argolis has enough fire too cook a dozen birds.

Argolis and Mars stole to the base of the very same tree that the birds sat in. Argolis heated rocks in his mouth as they crept and handed them hot to Mars on arrival. Argolis then shot a hot jet as high as he could and set fire to the tree halfway to the top.

"Pray the Light they think it's all my doing," Mars said.

Argolis then tossed Mars into the air. Once aloft Mars beat wings and tail and burst through the flaming tree twisting in the air and spitting the rocks Argolis had fired. Each bird felt the sting of a fire-rock on their backs before leaping haphazardly into the air with loud squawks. They scattered in three directions as Mars topped the tree. Mars turned and dove for momentum while the vultures caught updrafts. The birds spiraled upwards five hundred feet. Mars came out of his dive and gained on them just as the birds turned toward the Forbidden Mountains. Mars banked and followed catching up; Mars bit one of their tails. One bird banked away. Mars glanced back. Argolis had broken the tree line and was slogging a slow zigzag between the mud-pots toward the Inowise.

That bird could double back and snatch up the Inowise. Argolis needs more time.

Mars used the wisdom he learned by flying the gauntlet. Fun as this was to be in the air again flying acrobatics, this was no game. He rolled and found another bird's tail. He chomped getting a mouthful of black feathers before banking away to bite another.

Had he fire, each would have gone down in flames before the first tail-bite. Mars's fun did not last long. Carrion birds are quick-minded, after all.

One called to his mates, "He's got no fire! He didn't burn my tail. Get him boys!"

Two birds folded smartly and dove at Mars from above while he chased the middle bird. Mars twisted his neck to see two sets of outstretched claws descending upon him. With an acrobatic twist Mars escaped the loss of his eye—yet a knife-edged talon raked his face. Scales fell away. Mars spat a rock as his attacker looked back. Instead of losing an eye, Mars took one.

"Fire or not," Mars cried, "I'm still the best shot!"

The attackers banked and came at him again. This time the one missing an eye, insane with revenge, tore at his wings and ripped Mars's wing tip. Mars rolled and spat another rock hitting another bird in the head knocking him silly but not dead. Yet with one damaged wing Mars's maneuverability was impinged. So he dove for speed, pulled up and made haste for Argolis's position with sure death riding his tail.

The tree tops were ablaze with a great smoke. Mars could not see Argolis's signal fire—did Argolis establish a safe landing? Mars had to stay in the air until he knew better and all the while, his enemies grew angrier and more brazen. Mars climbed and twisted and dodged but the birds got closer—they were on to his tricks. Mars was on the run. They swooped at him with abandon and scales fell with each attack. And yet Mars remembered Draco's teaching and did not panic.

'Desperate fighters make foolish mistakes.'

Mars banked, closed his wings and dove for the burning trees and flew along the flaming tree tops with the vultures on his tail. Mars saw a burning tree taller than the rest and flew lower going down into the flame.

Dragons don't burn like birds.

Mars suddenly spun, stopped and faced them as they rushed to strafe him. Two birds crashed into him, one then another, too close to pull up. They dropped into the branches and caught fire. They fell through burning branches and crashed onto the path dead. The third was behind and he veered around Mars and smacked into a lit branch. The bird sprang off and flew north with smoldering feathers. Satisfied, Mars flew high and spotted Argolis.

"Quite a time you had there." Argolis said as Mars landed. "Getting him out of this mire won't be such good sport."

Argolis rested on a tuft of dry bog near a small fire. He was covered in black mud from foot to neck. Argolis smelled of swamp-rot. Argolis pointed his tail at the mud-pot. A few yards into the oozing pool was the Inowise. He was not as fit or young as Bear Claw, the only Inowise Mars had seen. This one's hair and beard was gray, his body thin, his back bent, and his eyes were blank. There in the mire this Inowise's legs walked as if he treaded on dry land. His only progress was downward into the mud.

"No use calling to him. I tried. Spirits Walkers don't hear whilst their soul's out traveling around, so they say. Best we can do is get him out, and wait for his soul to come back. Look what I found."

Argolis tossed Mars a green stone set in gold. It was threaded onto a broken leather thong. The primitive must have lost it. Mars had seen this kind of stone at Emerald's cave. Emerald's scouts and traders wore such tokens around their necks. Mars held it to the sun wondering at its use. It glowed more as he brought it closer to his body. Mars pulled a strand of saddle lace from his bird-clawed pack and restrung the amulet and hung it on a bush.

"We better do what we can," Mars said, "before he sinks further."

The two made crude ropes from the plentiful hemp stalks. They cast nooses and tied off the Walker like mooring a boat. Then, they uprooted saplings and broke branches from the gnarled brush and made a solid path in the mud. It was well past first supper when they finally pulled the Inowise free. The man did not respond, rather his feet continued marching.

"He's like a dreaming dog chasing rabbits." Argolis said laughing at his own wit.

Mars tied a rope around the man's chest and the other end to a stump near the base of the bush where the green stone hung. Mars and Argolis were too tired and hungry to do anything more. Thus, they sat and watched as the Inowise walked around the bush winding the rope shorter with every pass. When the man met the stone, he stopped.

"I don't know any Wildman lore, but this seems fitting." Argolis said.

Argolis took the stone down and placed it on the primitive man's neck. He blinked once, then twice, his jaw jut out, and then he yawned.

"You found my path-maker!" The men said in perfect dragon speak. "My soul saw dragon fire. I found my way, praise the Light. You gave back my stone; lost it fair and square I did, that is a great kindness, indeed. Your hearts are true."

The Inowise crossed his hands over his heart. The mud in his hair, beard and deer skin tunic fell away like black snow flakes. He wore moccasins, a bag at his waste, and a small wood-handled stone ax trucked into his tunic's leather belt.

"I am Star Watcher, the war dragons call me," The Inowise then switched to human tongue. "My kin call me Starmere. I am from of old. Dragons and I tended the garden as brothers in my youth. Your kindness revives our kinship. For you, I am Starmere. The lesser folks, the new human people call me Pathfinder. Let us go, I have a dry place and stores of food nearby. Come."

Starmere abruptly disappeared into a thicket. The sun was low. Mars and Argolis did not hunt that day and they had nothing to eat. Mars having flown so hard was in sore need of food. Argolis, having waded through a mile of muck, was no better off. Their stomachs pushed them into the thicket after Starmere although there were easier paths full of animal tracks in plan sight. Argolis had gotten to Starmere by such paths.

"Pathfinder is a poor name," Argolis said without cheer. "Tis no path I'd find, if you take my meaning, Sir."

"How strange," Mars said. "Starmere leaves no sign, not a broken branch or nary a footprint."

The strange, bent man said nothing and rather increased his pace. Mars and Argolis followed. Starmere penetrated the flora without sound while they crashed loudly through brush and briers. One hour later an outcrop of gray rocks appeared ahead protruding twenty feet above the cat-tails.

Starmere pointed to the high ground and said, "This is my home."

Mars breathed relief despite the stench of rotting bogs. Argolis plowed through the reeds and onto dry ground praising the Light. Mars followed. That ground was not only dry, it was clear. Thin trees dotted the raised land while tangled thorns ringed the place. Clean water flowed from a small spring at the base of a rock.

Mars sprang onto a broad, flat rock and surveyed the land; they were deep within the deadly bogs. The tree-lined road was at least ten miles east of them and impossible to reach. To the north and west Mars spied the not so distant Black Forest.

"We're caught on a rock between two hard places." Mars said.

Mars realized the wisdom of traveling within heavy foliage, to do otherwise would mire a dragon like a fly in honey. Argolis was lucky to have reached Starmere at all. Why didn't Argolis sink? Mother's saying came to his mind. 'Light hearts touches not the earth but a little.'

Wet and muddy, Mars turned to the setting sun. He spread his wings and captured what sunrays he could. The sun welcomed him with warmth. Content, Mars's golden hue came forth unbidden. Long repressed, Mars finally let his light shine brightly. The flat stones around him shimmered like golden ponds of water. Then and odd thing happened, his crest shone as never before. It was as bright as a star. His chest became hot. His gullet burned as if he were blowing fire. Pride, magic and bravery welled up in him all together. Mars felt the glory of the station he was born for. Full of hope, Mars's crown arose and he spat. No fire appeared.

Mars hung his head and his light died all at once. Wrapping his wings about him, Mars plopped down on the rock with a wet splat.

"I'll never amount to anything without fire", Mars said. "I'm no good."

"What good is fire without Light," Starmere said emerging from a shallow cave with a bundle. "The Light came first. There can be no natural fire without it. No, fire is not necessary, a heart of Light is—that is the way of Neff. Seek that wisdom first. I am not a dragon. I have no natural fire. Watch this."

Starmere reached his hand outward and palm up. He closed his eyes and chanted a spell. A blue flame sprang from his hand like a candle wick.

"Teach me this magic," Mars cried. "Make me the dragon of Tapestry visions."

"We have watched you. Why do you forsake the Light for this lesser thing? Draco taught true, after a fashion, so too the Pod Mothers, yet you heard nothing. You will find far more than what you seek within the Light."

"I don't understand," Mars said.

"That is what prevents fire. The prophecy calls for a mighty seeker, one who has a heart of Light. Not a bringer of fire-death. The omens are clear. Whichever you become, a blessing or a curse, the end of the age is nigh. Save yourself for the Light then you may save the dragons, too, so say the Scrolls."

Starmere folded his hands over his chest, a sign Mars understood. Starmere had said all he would. Starmere took Argolis and gathered wood. Argolis lit the fire. Starmere opened his bundle and began preparing a stew in his copper kettle while Mars slipped out of his flight bags and laid out what cooking gear he had. Mars set down the empty honey crock Begoth had given him. It fell over with a crash but did not break. Starmere rushed to Begoth's jar, took it into his hands and marveled at it as if it were a treasure. Mars saw nothing but an ordinary stone jar fitted with an ordinary silver wire-hinged stone lid held closed by a wooden pin.

"Begoth the fairy gave it to me," Mars said, "I had forgotten it. There's nothing in it."

"This is a rare thing." Starmere said scratching his beaded cheek. "Begoth would not part with it easily."

"When did empty jars become rare? I've seen better in Black Bill's refuge heap."

"An elfish jar laid into the hands of a mortal is a strange omen. He foretells your journey, a journey long, hard and hungry. Behold."

Starmere removed the pin and opened the jar. He dipped his finger in and withdrew it laden with honey. Begoth lapped the honey from his finger. He dipped into the empty jar several more times drawing gobs of bee-nectar each time.

"My heart stands well," Starmere said, "lovers of Light eat their fill while those with lesser hearts, gets less."

Starmere handed the jar to Argolis who also found his dipping well rewarded with a thick drought of sticky pleasure around his finger. Argolis then passed the jar to Mars. Mars dipped too, but got a smaller portion with each dip. As many times as he asked, the jar gave Mars a small portion but such honey tasted better than any Mars had had before. Energy return to his worn body but Mars still felt hungry. The Mark of Neff on him felt warm and shimmered with each taste.

"It's good, but I'm not satisfied," Mars said.

"You have more to learn. Your Light has not reached its potential. When you fill up, your hunger will be satisfied," said Starmere.

"How can this be," Mars asked obstinately, "I am a golden? Why won't the jar give me the full measure that it gave Argolis—a low born dragon? I was hatched to lead the dragons!"

"Truth knows no status. The jar rewards Light. Argolis honors what light he has, you do not. The Golden of legend is more than color; it is deeper. You have, in body, what you need, but your heart is lacking. Your heart must be made pure."

A dragon is born with his heart, I cannot change it!

Starmere returned to the stew pot and dropped spices, roots, potatoes and herbs into the hot water one by one. He stirred it with a wood spoon. The smell of cooking caused Mars's belly to cry.

"My body doesn't have what I need, how can you say that? I'm fireless," Mars said bitterly, "Fire is all I lack."

"No, you lack much more."

Mars flopped down on the ground, scooped up a rock and tossed it into the swamp.

"Begoth confirms the signs are true. Darkness comes or he would not have parted with the Golden Honey Jar. I fear he gave it too hastily. The prophecy speaks of a dragon that brings golden fire. It tells nothing of that fire's nature or a dragon with gold scales."

Mars jumped up and cried "Help me find my fire then! You are wise. Surly you know a way."

Starmere laid his spoon aside. He looked upon Mars with eyes as deep as time itself and drew a slow breath. Sadness seemed to envelop Starmere.

"I have no art for what you seek. I cannot restore your fires, nor would I for it is not my station. We Inowise, the Giants gave another charge. Ours was the magic of peace. We tended the garden and taught men speech. We brought men and dragons together long ago as helpmates to one another. Dragons were more civilized then, while men were cruel. Our hope was men would become like dragons, but dragons have become like men. The garden was corrupted and so it fell."

Starmere sweep his long hairy arm gesturing toward the landscape.

"We can make no wars or lend ourselves to it. It is beyond my people. All creatures of the First Age are fading now. You of the Second Age grow weaker. Dragons may not survive the Third Age—the age of men."

"Then help me find my fire, so I may protect my people."

"No…it is not the Way of Neff. I am true to my vow. Men quicken the age-end. I say seek for the Light, not weapons, and then you will know the true fire of Neff. I have spoken."

Starmere puffed out his bony gray-haired chest and crossed his arms. He squatted and took up his spoon again. After and hour of silence Argolis came and dished the stew into Mars's cook-kit bowls. The three gathered closer to the fire. The sun was gone, the air was damp and cool. They eat quietly until Argolis spoke after several large helpings.

"Well that's all fine and good, fire or no, that's not our trouble now, if you take my meaning, a pickle isn't it Sir, I mean how's we going to find our way out of this place. And with trouble brewing at home we can't go by way of the Vineland's, no Sir. That Rogsin sure as dragon's fly will have your wings."

"I will help you," said the old Inowise. "I have a path stone, once lost, now found. You may have it—kindness for kindness." The primitive man thumped a fist on his chest."Go how the stone chooses. If you are true to the stone, it will be true to you. Go through Neff on the north side of Rookery Top. Rogsin has hunters every place, but fewer there. Make for the Highland. King Meric has no love of Rogsin."

Starmere removed the stone from his neck, kissed it and draped in around Mars's neck.

"The hills folk want no part of Rogsin, so the ravens tell me," Starmere said. "Meric will not march with Rogsin. He trades with the Steppes. King Meric thinks those folks good and their beer better."

Starmere cross his arms with a grunt. He touched his lips with a crooked finger before taking up his bowl again. Mars wanted to ask about the ravens, but thought it unwise to disrupt Starmere's thoughts.

Mars and Argolis stayed with Starmere two more days. On the night before they were to leave, Starmere spoke lost lore such as tales of the Garden that Mars had never heard before. Starmere spoke of how beautiful and plentiful the Garden was—every tree bore good fruit—every dragon was golden—every creature at peace, save one: man. Starmere spoke late into the night and conclude his tales with this advice.

"Before the Fall Inowise walked with dragons. We were not strangers then as we are now. There was no wont for anything! Even the Iron Skins, creatures of the primeval time, ate their fill and troubled no thinking folks until men invaded their sanctuaries. Hear what I say."

Starmere took up a stick. He scrawled images and letters in the ground for a time. Mars watched quietly waiting for Starmere's next words.

"Men twisted the Garden's promise. Even the words of the Giant's Scrolls were subverted. Dragons were ensnared—bound by the cleaver oaths and duties devised by greedy men. In that first war, Dragons won the day and defeated the Iron Skins but they lost their hearts to men. That is why the Garden died. This is the lore that ravens will not tell fore men and dragons have long closed their ears. It was written:

'The returned Golden brings forth dragon kind's lost heart.' Mars, you must find what was lost."

Starmere pointed his stick at Mars's breast. The Mark of Neff glowed once more.

"Where will I find it? How shall I seek what I don't understand?"

"I cannot say."

Starmere folded his arms over his chest. He spoke no more that night. At dawn Mars and Argolis awoke to find Starmere gone. Mars jumped onto the tallest rock and scanned the lands, but there was no sign of Starmere.

Starmere's pot was on the fire and filled to the brim. The two ate mightily before mounting their packs. Mars found their baggage was stuffed with dried fish, deer jerky, roots and bulbs. The path stone around Mars's neck glowed bright green.

"There's nothing for it then," Argolis said, "Best we hit the road, if you take my meaning Sir."

"I don't know the way," Mars said. "Meric must be 500 miles from here."

Argolis went to Mars, lifted the stone, and held it above Mars's head turning it in the sunlight. The stone glowed when Argolis pointed it in the direction Starmere said they should go—northwest toward the Black Forest.

"I'm not the sharpest plowshare on the farm, so to speak, but I'd say that's the way." Argolis pointed toward the Steppes with his tail.

Mars and Argolis set out crashing into the thickets behind Starmere's camp. They did not go far when they came to a substantial deer path. The stone shown its approval and so the two walked where no dragon had walked in ten thousands years.

Argolis bounced lightly along flexing his growing, but still very small wings. Argolis sang a merry country-inn song. Mars knew the tune but held his tongue.

They traveled good paths for two days when the swamp abated. Small trees gave way to larger tress of the type given to solid ground, and thorns and thistles became less. The land became friendly. Game and good eating plants increased. Whether it was late spring or midsummer Mars could not say but the sun shone hot and kind. They were not yet under the shadows of the Black Forest and so all was well.

"The stone leads true—gave us a safe road." Argolis remarked, "We'll not lose our way! No Sir."

But Mars still felt pathless. His heart pulled him in another direction. He was no closer to finding his fire than when he'd left Rookery Top. The Inowise gave not his answer. And now, he trod further from the land where the Sages lived and his last hope of an answer to his quandary. If the Inowise would not advise him on gaining fire, who else could but the sages?

"I've not yet found my road," Mars returned. "At this rate, I never will. The only road I seek is the road to my fire. That is what I wish most.

With those words, the stone on Mars's neck flashed in a most peculiar way. Mars ignored it and pressed on.

FORTY THREE

Rogsin Unites the Factions

Rogsin's first War Council was at Spring Breakfast. That meeting, ten days before, was for tradition's sake, not function. Even so, Rogsin had sprinkled seeds. Rogsin hated the old traditions but that one served his purpose. The planting was not yet done—the bulk of his seeds were unused. With Draco dismissed and Emerald sent away, it came time to plant in earnest.

Rogsin thought of Emerald as he watched the Council of Twenty Four pecking like vultures for fresh meat. Table positions fought over by birds of a feather, most unlike dragon-kind.

Emerald thinks his magic words moved me. I let the fool go. I have him where he can do me no harm. My gnomes ride his tail.

Finally, the war chiefs sorted-out their order—Outlanders to his left, Estates Men on the right and none happy about it. With each faction eyeing the other contemptuously, the room became quiet and Rogsin began sowing.

"It is not yet midsummer," Rogsin said, "And already the dragon's Warlord, a trader, attempts to supplant me, spreading words of dissent. Draco only advocates for dragons, not the wider needs of this land."

Rogsin pulled out his golden dagger and stuck it into the table.

"We don't need dragons in our affairs! They're always barking for peace whereas peace cannot come. How long have you shared your fodder, bathed them in gold whereas no amount of gold is enough for dragons—all for what? What have dragons done for us?"

A murmur of ill contented agreement traversed the room. The dwarf's war chiefs were especially rousted and stamped their feet or pulled at their long beards.

"For long ages dragons kept us from this alliance we now build. Dragons have gathered our gold unto themselves. Dragons are not our friends. They are worms eating our coffers. They grow fat and useless on our generosity, for what? For the sake of some obsolete dictate that doesn't concern men or our wellbeing."

Grumbles of disagreement came from the right while the left side cheered. Once the noise lessoned, Rogsin continued.

"Dragons insist that Giants had given them charge over us men. Has anyone ever seen a Giant? I say dragons gave themselves charge to steal the wealth of men. While our race was young and helpless they made themselves our masters. Our race is no longer helpless."

The men and dwarves on each side stamped their feet and pounded their dagger handles on the table. The Highland King was the least enthusiastic.

Of course, Meric has the most gold. He rather horde it then spend it.

"This is the dawning of the Age of Men. That is why you gather to me. Dragons will no longer take our due. Behold the power of men."

An orderly appeared with Rogsin's crossbow. The bow was already drawn and notched with a dragon-gold tipped bolt. Rogsin shouldered and aimed at a suit of armor made of only dragon scales. It was a famous suit no weapon had ever pierced.

Rogsin squeezed the release bar. The sinew twanged. The armor instantly clamored to the floor in ruin. The bolt passed straight through it and stuck fast into the stone wall. The one and only raven that was sunning itself on the high sill above squawked and flew leaving feathers and an old, gray crow behind.

The warriors at table gasped. Then, all at once, cries of marveling dismay and dread filled the hall. The nearest dwarf to Rogsin stood on his chair praising Rogsin.

"Bless Rogsin the joiner, the dragon slayer!"

Even the Estate's Men joined the praises. Men and dwarves cried their clan's or Estate's war-calls. They swore allegiances. Rogsin waited stone-faced-stern searching every face for disharmony. Rogsin raised his hand and they ceased their clamor.

"This is our key to independence," Rogsin said raising the machine aloft. "Dragons can no longer hold sway over us. But we must guard our advantage until the time is right."

Rogsin held the crossbow over his head.

"We'll make many more such as this. When we have war-wears in plenty, we'll take the Steppes. But first, we must deal with dragons. We still need Emerald's flying machine. We'll take their wings and thus their teeth. Wingless dragons are no obstacle."

Rogsin handed the crossbow to his right and motioned to pass it about.

"What say you?" Rogsin asked.

Voices arose in agreement, yet not all gave a resounding yes.

Rogsin cast his eyes upon each of the Estate Lords. Some looked away at his gaze. Some shed tears. Some bowed their heads obediently. Meric had fire in his eyes—fore or against him, Rogsin did not know.

Time I gave them a warning.

"I'll remind you that agreed or not this is a closed council—none of you can speak of this publicly. Join me or stand aside but don't try and stop me. If you stand against me, you will die."

Rogsin pulled scrolls up from under his seat and laid them on the table.

"You'll profit greatly by me. Each of you has a part I need. I have productions plans. I need ore from the hills and highlands, sinews and leathers from the pasturelands, hardwoods from the forested places, and all of your craftsmen's skills. Do your part and receive spoils ten fold!"

The pasturelands king, Loomis, stood up and threw his wool cape behind him revealing his prized dragon scale vest.

Loomis loves his dragon-scale protection but not his dragon protectors. I can rely on him.

"What of Draco and Penelope's influences. The rumors they stir dissuade the people. We cannot fight a war without soldiers, nor make ready a long march without the people's industry and consent."

"What rumors." Several Outlanders asked all at once.

"It is said that Rogsin is not the rightful king," Loomis said. "They say Hammond was not his father. People say Rogsin's blood is not fully of the King's line. Long have the people whispered that Hammond killed his brother wrongly for the rape of the queen."

I've got to satisfy the Outlander's superstitions for now.

"I have heard that," Rogsin said. "And, I have a solution. After Onyx makes the new Tapestry I will marry her. My rightful kingship will then be secured double. She will remain a maiden until it is finished, however long that takes."

They'll wait for the oracle they value so much. I've satisfied the legitimacy they require of me. Meanwhile, I get a dragon-killing army. Once they're in the Steppes, Onyx will fall from the tower leaving the Tapestry unfinished.

"What of the weaver's helper? Familiars cannot marry."

"Once the weaving is done, I'll kill that snake. They all will die soon anyway—if you trust the Scrolls. Praxis may be the last dragon, or the first to die if my oracle is finished sooner. If dragons must die to unify this, our new Kingdom, so be it."

The room became quiet as each considered the implications of Rogsin's words. The old crow on the sill cawed. Rogsin took his eating dagger, heaved it, and missed. The crow flew off as Rogsin's dagger fell to the floor with a clatter.

"If dragons stand in the way of our prosperity, then we'll remove them, by force if necessary." Rogsin said. "Dragons may not move any other way."

All at once the Council began debating. Some said driving dragons away was impossible. Some said that war dragon numbers were low and as such dragons were vulnerable. Others said there remained far too many. Others worried that dragons travel fast, and as such, news traveled fast between them. Kill one dragon and others will know. They will gather and fight. Even wingless dragons run fast and fight well. A man with a horse and lance was no match for a dragon's tail or fire. Many common people and warriors alike would side with dragons and not fight against them. Dragons live everywhere among people and were much loved. Only a surprise attack would ensure victory, most agreed.

This is going well. They want a preemptive strike without my prodding.

Finally, after much talk, the primary question was realized; how best to take the dragons? It was agreed that the killing must be swift and all at once—but, when, how? Rogsin was ready with an answer. He had thought long on that same question.

"There is a way," Rogsin said, "The Auction. When they gather for the games, distracted with food and match-making, we strike. Draco will be there; all but a few fighters will come. Whatever dragons don't come, we'll hunt them down later. It is a perfect plan."

"They come to Auction unarmed and unawares." Loomis said.

"They'll come expecting new life and we'll deal death." Rogsin said. "I will openly invite the Outlands. We won't risk defeat with dragon-skittish Estate's fighters. We have much to do, many crossbows to make before September! What say you?"

The Council of Twenty Four rose to their feet and cheered Rogsin with fists pumping in the air or banging on their breasts. Rogsin called for wine to close the deal. Rogsin's orderly ran to the pantry. Walters came with wine and mugs on a great silver tray. Walters pored for the men and stood aside ready to pour again. The servant was near but forgotten.

"What about the Golden," Digger the Dwarf said. "He is still a danger to us. We Dwarves cannot abide you fully while his magic is loose upon the land."

Rogsin understood well Dwarf's history and how they feared and hated dragons, most of all, they despised golden dragons. When every winged dragon was golden, they stole the Dwarf's beloved wealth, or so they wrongly tell it. No matter that the dragons had prosecuted their case rightfully. The Dwarf horde was given as recompense to the lowborn for the crimes committed against them. After all, it was the simple minded plow dragons, now all gone and not their masters the country dragons, whom stamped the mines. It was accidental. The Dwarfs never accepted the accident judgment which prompted the Dwarf's Revenge—the slaughter of nearly all land dragons. Dwarfs have not forgiven or forgotten the loss of their wealth and they still say that dragons got off better than they deserved.

Rogsin saw Mars as a threat too. That Golden could rally the people against him. Mars was the one dragon that was out of his reach and control. Rogsin needed the Dwarves as willing partners, yet killing Mars was as much Rogsin's pleasure as a necessity.

"My spies already seek him." Rogsin answered. "The first crossbows will go with my hunters to kill Mars. His head is my gift to Dwarfs. When I'm done with Praxis, you may have her head too. Will you join me?"

Aye, the answer came all at once. The Dwarfs raised their cups first. Everyone at table finished their draughts in fits of gulps worthy of fighters. Every cup was slammed on the table empty.

"Walters!" Rogsin called. "Don't stand there like a tree, more wine, bring the best I have."

Walters poured out what he had left then rushed to the pantry for more while the company celebrated their agreement.

FORTY FOUR

Bad Light

Mars and Argolis broke the underbrush two hundred yards from the edge of the Black Forest. A thick wall of tall, dark trees with black leaves draped in moss, vines, and webs stood before them—trees packed so tightly that a man could hardly press between them. The forest ran west and northeast as far as they could see. They started across the broad fields that edged the Black Forest. Mars and Argolis quaked in their scales.

"Let me light the way," Mars said recalling the lore, 'A dragon must light dark places.'

But try as he may, Mars could not make his hue light. Mars hesitated unwilling to go toward the shadows unlit. Mars spread his wings as a test.

"Not good. Magic doesn't work here, my wings are useless. This road is unwise."

"The stone got us here; must be some good in it, nothing for it..." Argolis's words trailed off.

They marched slowly onward over the increasingly browner field. The ground grew wetter and the air rancid with rotting grass as they progressed until they came upon a deep rushing stream which bordered the forest.

"There's no path yonder," Argolis said, "No fair landing on the far side either. Best we find a better spot to cross. I hear tell them black waters drive any who touches them mad. I'd hate to land badly—I can't swim be I crazy or in my right mind!"

Not too far for me to jump, Mars thought. Argolis with his bulk and bags would indeed falter. And, the water smelled fowler than the black-brown grass—enchanted or not. Mars patted the canteens slung over his bags.

"I've heard lore about this place," Mars said, "Draco told it as we flew above. There is no fit water or food within. Dragon magic has no power—no dragon should every land there, said Draco. Dragons that fly too low are never seen again; the forest binds those who enter it. There is no escape, not until magic itself flees the Earth. One who transverses it has no advantage but his stamina."

Mars held up the stone. It still worked. The stone pointed them west along the stream. Mars's crown lay half cocked in confusion.

"Should we trust the stone? It brought us here, but, can black magic skew its council?"

"That stone's First Age magic, Sir," Argolis offered. "They say the ages after the First Age can't ad or take away from First Time relics. There's nothing for it but go where it leads, I'd say."

"May be," Mars said, "But a stone maker two hundred thousand years dead couldn't have known about this forest. What if the stone points as the crow flies?"

"I don't suppose they had crows in them days."

"We'll follow the stone," Mars said, "Let's go."

After trudging many miles along the dark river Mars and Argolis came upon two great stone pillars set on flat land that was three feet above the river bank and back a pace. The stones leaned with age and rose twenty feet above the marsh field. They were spread west and east the distance of a common road. A great rusted iron ring was strapped onto each pillar near its top by a thick iron band. Mounted above the iron rings were heads carved from the same hard, black stone. The busts faced the far shore.

"Gnome kings, I make them," Mars said, "Look at their head dress. Only kings wear helms set with gems."

"Gnome or Dwarf who can tell," Argolis said?

Although the monoliths were weather worn, off kilter, and turned out of place, the statue's stony eyes were indeed fixed on the opposite bank. The eyes seemed alive.

"Well fancy that, a gnome to beat all gnomes, Sir, if you please. And look yonder. I'd say this was a ferryman's pull."

The travelers got nearer the bank for a closer look. The tops of rotted pilings from an old dock stuck out of the slick, black mud at the water's edge. Old paving stones protruded from the bank's cantilever. The far side was wide enough for a jump landing. The ribs of an old boat stuck up above tall, black-green reeds. Beyond that, a narrow path disappeared into darkness.

Mars held the stone aloft testing this way and that. The Pathfinder showed best when Mars pointed it across the river. It also shone in other directions but it glowed weaker—behind them it went dark.

"I don't like it," Mars said. "Gnomes spirits guard this pass. Look at the guardian stones. They're laughing. Laughing at whoever comes here."

"What's in your heart?" Argolis asked. "That's where the Pathfinder takes you safe. If you trust your heart's desire…we go that way."

"Fire is in my heart," Mars said steadily. "We'll cross."

The river was narrower there and so the two made the jump with ease. Mars judged the leap well and landed on his feet in soft marsh grass. Argolis jumped too hard, lost his footing and rolled like a ball until he crashed into the remains of that old boat. But it was not a boat.

"Look at that, will you!" Argolis cried as he jumped up in a start. "It's the innards of a dragon, naught left but his bones!"

Mars was twenty paces less inland scrutinizing the path when Argolis cried out. Mars twisted around and ran to Argolis, jamming rock into his mouth as he went. But there was no cause for alarm. The bones were old, turned into stone. The dragon was eons dead. This creature was huge, twice the size of Draco. Mars examined the bones carefully while searching his learning.

"I don't like it Sir, not one bit. Not a scale left here and will you look at that lance tip! It's as big round as my arm. Who wields such a pike?"

"Must be a land dragon," Mars said. "Plow dragons I've heard them called. Their foolish kind died out at the dawn of Vineland's kingdom. The Dwarfs killed them off in their Revenge War."

"Looks like gnomes had a hand on the dwarf-ax, if you take my meaning."

Mars reached into the ruin and brought out the spear point. It was not a man-made thing; rather, it was a horn and not a unicorn's horn. It was thicker, black and two feet long, its tip hooked slightly, and, although it was as hard as stone, it weighted no more than a dry stick and it's point was quiet sharp. It wasn't made by any magic Mars knew. He pondered it from hand to hand until the answer came to him.

"It's a stinger—Giant spiders roomed these lands before the Garden. No one knows what became of them. I don't know much of their lore."

"Seeing how it did what it did, begging your pardon Sir, I don't want to know its lore. Old bones chill my soul."

The two then checked their packs and gear making sure nothing came loose or lost. Mars loaded the stinger into his flight bag's sword holster as a keepsake.

"Nobody's seen it's like, I'd wager. Not even Merilbe." Mars said.

Mars tested his wings again, still no lift. Rather, when Mars opened his wings, he was pulled downward. Mars's soul chilled. He tried to light his hue but that only made him colder. And yet the pathfinder still glowed but that light gave him no comfort.

They took the path side-by-side and had not marched one hour when the path behind them disappeared. Only the path ahead appeared through the low mists. Although it was mid day, darkness surrounded them as a thick, blackish fog while the true fog glowed like green ghosts. The trees healed over the path every which way blotting out the sky. And, all about them, noises came from the forest such as the evil screams and mournful laments of ghosts and yet Mars felt they were not ghosts at all. A wind blew above the tree tops…or was it ghost riders causing the crackly calls of tortured birds. As the hours passed they lost all sense of time.

The road became no wider than a gnome's path. Mars felt crushed as the proper road narrowed with thorns. Yet the pathfinder insisted on staying the course. Every step became a labor as no dragon suffered dark places well. Mars couldn't tell if it was night or day. Finally they ceased their march too weary to go on. They disrobed their packs, and gathered what wood was at hand, careful not to tarry away from the road. Mars, seeing Argolis discouraged offered council.

"I've heard about safe roads that cross this black land. Emerald's traders come this way. We're safe as long as we stay on the road."

"I'm not feeling none too safe, Sir. I can't get my fire up."

Argolis's magic fire was gone, of course. So Mars brought forth his flint, steel and tinder. The tinder fired but the rotting wood would not stay lit. They lit a small fire with what wood they brought, cooked quickly and snuffed the fire to use the fuel again. And so they ate hard bread and under-cooked salted meat in the dark.

"Tis a pity," Argolis said, "We got the makings of proper stew but I can't cook it proper."

Argolis's bright nature and country dragon appetite was so oppressed even he ate little. Argolis then made his pack into a pillow and he lay down on the thorny path. Mars watched as his companion slept fitfully.

Mars sat with his flint and steel striking sparks for comfort until yellow eyes appeared glowing in the woods. Mars set his flint aside, stuffed rocks into his mouth, and readied himself for a fight. The eyes moved about and blinked in and out of sight, but never came near enough, or stayed long enough for a decent shot. Finally, exhausted, Mars decided to trust the pathfinder. 'Good roads repelled evil things.' Mars curled up next to Argolis. Dreamless sleep took him and Mars got no rest that night.

In the days and nights that followed, the forest never changed. The eyes always watched. One thing changed. They each lost more of their appetites as their hopes wavered. They walked until tired and sleep without rest one march after another never knowing if it was day or night. Mars gave up striking flints to steel as even the bright sparks seemed dulled. Not even the idea of regaining his fire lent Mars any pleasure.

It was the fifth day or so they thought when Argolis threw himself onto his belly and cried out."If I don't get some light soon, surly I will die."

From then on Mars could not stop thinking about light. The less they had the more he wanted it. It seemed the darkness would never end. The sick glint of the watcher's eyes began to seem fair and good to him. He took notice that the eye were of many different creatures. Mars felt he must go to them, or go mad. But whenever he wondered from the path, Argolis slapped Mars with his tail snapping Mars out of his trance.

"No Sir, I'm not going on alone, highborn or not I'll slap you silly if you leave me."

On the tenth day Mars cried into the darkness.

"Give us light! Bring us light—my soul for a candle!"

And with that, the eyes fled. Critters big and small ran through the woods—away from them. No more eye-light was seen. Mars sat upon a rock along the roadside, hands to face and wept bitterly for his wont of light.

"Begging your pardon, Sir," Argolis said quietly after a time, "I'm either a gold dragon or that's a lamp yonder. We're near the end, I'd say. It's about eleven days, I recon. Lore says the Black Wood is eleven days walking wide."

Mars pushed Argolis away and bounded to his feet straining in the direction where Argolis had pointed. There was a small light one hundred yards off the path into the woods.

"It's just a hop, skip and a jump away." Argolis said or my scales are gold.

"It is a lamp," Mars said, "and your scales aren't gold. He's got to be just out of the woods, a homestead I'll wager. Let's go. We've nothing to lose."

Mars held the stone toward the direction of the light and it went dark.

"Now, now, Starmere said, 'don't leave the stone's way.' This here's a wicket place. Starmere said stick with the stone to the bitter end. I mean you're the highborn and all, but I think we best do like Starmere says."

"I'm the Golden," Mars snapped darkly, "I'll keep my own council. I'm going to that light, with or without you."

"Well, there's nothing for it then, Sir," Argolis said hosting his pack. "You're too riled for me to tail-slap any sense into you."

Another mile and they would have found wholesome trees and a wider road. Even there, black trees were fewer and the air fresher although they hadn't noticed. But Mars had lost his wits. Once off the narrow way, he ran toward the light crashing thought the woods with wild abandon.

Argolis followed struggling to keep pace. The hundred yard sprint became a five hundred yard run and still they got no closer. Finally Argolis called for rest.

"That light is moving," Argolis said puffing for air. "It's a trick, Sir, we should go back."

But, despite their destructive run, they could not find the way they had come. The road was lost. So they followed the light. When they stopped the light stopped too but always the light stayed ahead until it bounced up a steep rocky rise and disappeared near the top. Mars and Argolis scrambled up the slope after it using small green trees as handholds. They crested a small landing and faced a cave entry. An unseen lamp within reflected and lit the rough rock walls.

"It's around that bend in the cave," Mars said confidently. "Let us go in, whoever owns that lamp can't be far."

Mars rounded the bend with Argolis close behind; they passed under an arch and found the lamp placed inside a carved niche on the far side of a room. The polished floor and walls magnified the tiny oil-lamp's light. The cave was a dead end. Mars and Argolis move inside for a closer look.

"Gnome's lamp, I'd wager," Argolis said, "Why'd they put it here and where'd the little fellow go?"

"I've gone dragon hunting," A small voice replied.

With that, a great slab of dressed stone rolled into the entry archway with a crash—the escape tunnel was cut off. Mars rushed forward and slammed the stone to no avail. Together they pressed against it but it would not move. Frustrated, Argolis roared and his flame shot upward and so they discovered that the ceiling in the center of the cave-room was open and that their magic was restored. Like a smoke stack it went straight up one hundred feet, and beyond that, were stars.

"We're out from under the wood," Argolis said, "but not out of the woods!"

Mars was not amused by Argolis's accidental pun, but others were. All at once many small voices laughed from above. Small heads peered over high ledges inside the stack silhouetted by a moonlit night sky. Mars sprang upward and opened his wings. He floated but not well enough. The tunnel above was too tight to flap or open his wings fully enough to rise at speed. Mars had no running room to launch either.

Mars tried rising slowly on three quarter wing. But a hail of darts and stones rained down and forced him to fold his wings. Mars landed and moved away from the opening.

"That'll do you no good," A gnome said. "If you get past us you still got to deal with Webweaver. He's hungry too, he's not had a taste of dragon since we gave him that ferry puller. You met Palmer's bones on your way. This here's no smoke stack; this here's Webweaver's house."

"Let us go," Argolis cried, "Gnomes got no dispute with dragons. We got nothing you want!"

"Rogsin wants that Golden's head. We're in it for the pay if you understand me. You just sit nice until Webweaver gets back. Rogsin's man will identify your bones later. You won't deny Webweaver an easy meal, will you?"

Argolis roared so ferociously that Mars jumped back against the wall in fear. His fire shot half way to the top— quite a shot for a country dragon. A high web was set ablaze and it burned all the way to the top in a flash. The gnomes retreated and taunted them no more that night.

"We aren't anybody's easy meal! This country dragon's nothing to fool with! Let that old spider come down here, I'll bash him with me tail, I'll make pulp of him. No ordinary living thing stand's against a dragon's tail."

Argolis swung his tail against the wall and smashed a great lump of hard rock into gravel.

"Quit so," a loud hissing voce said from above. "But I am not an ordinary spider. My kin are long dead, that is true, and yet I remain. Does that not cause you to wonder?"

Mars moved to the center of the shaft encouraged by Argolis's outburst. A back blob clung near the top of the vertical wall; eight red eyes glowed like bloody ruin. But there were stars shinning beyond the monster thus hope reentered Mars's heart.

The sun will shine upon us in the morning—if we last the night.

"I am no ordinary dragon," Mars said evenly, "I am the Golden told of legend. My magic is great. Can a spider stand against two great dragons? I think not!"

Mars's eyes were used to the dark and he noticed an oddity. The spider wore a crown on its head. Not the crown of a dragon or man, it was a unicorn's crown—its spiraled ivory spike and golden headband contrasted the night.

"That may well be," the spider said, "but I can wait. Dragons without food can't breathe fire, or swing their tails well. And I have magic of my own—Magic greater than yours."

"He's right on that, Sir. We got to eat. But look here, will you—I've wood in my pack and plenty of food. That beastie will have a long wait, if you take my meaning."

"We won't stay long," Mars said.

"As long as it is my pleasure, you'll stay." Webweaver said.

Mars and the spider traded many more barbs while Argolis cooked a meal. Mars grew weary of the conversation and paused to eat, and yet, the spider continued bragging. Mars thought the spider rather enjoyed conversing. Mars then recalled something Mother had said, 'Where weapons fail, words may win.'

"I've got an idea," Mars whispered. "He likes to talk, so let's keep him talking; maybe we'll learn something useful. Ask him questions."

And so it went late into the night. The spider did indeed say more than just his brag. Webweaver enjoyed speaking his wisdom and said so. He told tales of how cleaver he'd become in so long a life. The monster became more and more caught up in the sound of his own voice while speaking the lore of his kind from ages long past. Mars learned giant spiders don't abide sunlight. They have no magic of their own except their stinger which can kill any living thing.

Webweaver bragged he often stole magic and that accounted for its long life fore the wearer of a unicorn crown received many magic protections. Thus, Webweaver was the last of his kind, and in his mind, unbeatable.

No wonder he is so confident!

No magic save that of his own kind could kill him, although Mars did confirm that dragon's fire and bashing tails would cause Webweaver unpleasant injuries.

"Begging your pardon, Sir," Argolis whispered, "Look at the stone."

The pathfinder glowed lightly. They were not far from a sound path. Mar pointed it here and there but it only shown brightly when he held it aloft in the shaft.

"What does that mean," Mars hissed, "That way is blocked."

Webweaver's knowledge was indeed wide and deep. Mars realized his next question. But first, Mars brought the pathfinder out into the open shaft and he whispered asking it for the road to his fire. The stone intensified when Mars pointed it at Webweaver.

He either knows the answer, or I must go through him to get it.

"Whatever toy you have there, will soon be mine," Webweaver said. "Come you are an educated dragon, ask me harder questions."

"Saying a dragon lost his fire by means of injury, how may he regain it? Whose magic or healing art could repair such damage?"

"There was only one," Webweaver said, "The Unicorn Princess; she once healed such wounds but no longer. She is a prisoner of the horsemen. Without her crown, she has no power. I'm quite sure she won't recover it, it is quite lost to her, indeed, but not lost."

On the answer, dawn finally came. Webweaver moved deeper into the shaft to avoid the infant daylight, but not so far that Argolis's fire could reach him. Mars longed even more for sunlight but climbing was impossible. Webweaver knew better than to give a dragon light and so he placed his body in the middle, spread his legs and blocked the shaft.

"Useless," Mars exclaimed dashing the pathfinder to the ground, it bounced and landed on Mars's flight bags unharmed. There it lay and glowed more brightly that he'd seen it glow before.

"What's that supposed to mean," Mars said, "Mount up and fly from here?"

"No Sir, but it means to say something, and I think I know what its saying. I got an idea."

Argolis gathered up the old bones left by Webweaver and the last of his firewood. He placed it all on the edge of the shaft fire-ready.

Argolis kept the longest bone, a leg bone of a great elk. He jammed the bone inside the stinger's fat, hollow end and secured it with sinew. Argolis tested it away from Webweaver's view. It made a stout pike. Argolis whispered his plan to Mars and Mars found it good. The pathfinder did not disagree.

While Mars brought forth his best spitting rocks, Argolis lit the small pyre he had arranged. Argolis stacked the fuel so that the fire smoked greatly. The shaft began filling with smoke. Dragons can breathe smoke, but not forever. They did not have much time.

"Smoke harms me not," Webweaver said, "Yet, I smell a rat cooking within it."

As smoke filled the shaft, the giant splayed his legs wider coving every side. The spider must be preparing for his assault. Mars placed a hand full of good rocks into his mouth feeling well pleased.

Inflexible targets suffer greater blows!

All at once, Argolis and Mars jumped into the center of the smokestack. Argolis's made his hands a cradle and Mars put one foot into Argolis's launcher. Argolis thrust Mars into the air. Mars opened his wings three quarters, lit his golden hue, beat his tail and pointed his lance. Mars became a shot arrow spiting stones. His brightness blinded Webweaver. Mars's lance struck the spider mid-body cleaving him terribly. Mars let go the sting letting it fall and rushed upward into the light unscathed as the spider screamed. But, all was not well.

Mars flipped in the air and twisted his neck in time to see the monster slipping toward the bottom and then it let loose. Webweaver fell down the shaft nearly hitting Argolis. From the shaft's edge Mars watched the monster thrashing its legs savagely while ranting curses.

Argolis will be killed!

Before Mars could think how to give him aid, Argolis stabbed the creature's eyes with a burning bone. The spider rolled to its back screeching as Argolis disappeared from view. Argolis returned with the unicorn crown and jammed the crown's spike deep into Webweaver's head.

The spider moved no more.

Mars raced to the entry cave to find the slab at the inner cave's arch had rolled back inside a slot in the wall, what magic that held it was no more. The entrapment spell wrought by the crown's last wearer was broken. Argolis came out of the prison licking his teeth with glee. Argolis had the crown in one hand and the stinger-pike in the other. Argolis offered the pike to Mars.

"This dagger is what killed that old ferry-puller dragon; Webweaver's own sting is what laid him low." Mars said. "Yours was the killing blow" Mars held out the stinger. "Keep this as a trophy."

"I won't, not this, so evil a trophy." Argolis said. "Poor old Palmer!"

Mars took it from Argolis, wedged it between two boulders and yanked. It splintered into a cascade of shards. Whereupon, before their eyes, the unicorn crown glowed white and the headband shrank small enough for a human to wear. The long unicorn horn mounted on the headband shrank to the length of a boot-dagger.

"They say Unicorn People are shape shifters and there goes the proof," Mars said. "You won that prize, keep it well."

"I'm not one for such things." Argolis said carefully placing the crown inside Mars's worn-torn pack. "Carry it for me till we find its rightful keeper. My bags are full of holes."

The two left the tunnel and climbed to the top of Webweaver's hill seeking clean air. There, they took stock of their surroundings.

"This place, although much smaller, is not unlike Rookery Mountain," Mars commented. "The higher we move above the Black Forest the stronger I feel. Let us make for that cliff base yonder. I won't rest until I'm well away from this cursed woodland."

"I supposed then, we'll be going to the Steppes," Argolis said, "Rogsin's got a price on you. We'll never make it to Meric's safety. We can't go to Vineland, no Sir. Over yonder is where that crown belongs anyway."

The White Cliffs of the Steppes were fifteen miles north. Mars had never seen this boarder land from the ground. He saw it once from afar while flying Draco's tour. But now, Mars had a better look and the cliffs were beautiful. The face rose shear fifteen hundred feet above green fields. Fields that began beyond the Black Forest. The cliffs sparkled with pinks, blues and grays in the sun. At various points distant and near waterfalls cascaded over the cliff's edge leaving rainbow mists against white stone.

"Not too far to fly tandem I suppose." Mars said.

Argolis had gotten thin again and Mars felt strong with the excitement of battle still upon him. And from this height, Mars could gain the air without running—they had only to fall from the shear side of this parapet for momentum.

"We can't make the top, but we'll surely fly clear of these woods. We'll land below the cliffs. Come Argolis, let us fly together."

The day was bright and the promise of flight gladdened Mars's heart. They quickly sorted their packs to make ready, leaving much behind to lessen the load. They flew to the boarder of Neff below the White Cliffs carrying little else but their bags and wits. But Mars also carried his hope. Hope that the Unicorn Princess would heal his fire—if only he could find her is this wide and hostile land. Mars realized that the stone showed true, it brought them safe through dangerous places but would it show him the Unicorn Princess? Lore said she herself was a danger.

FORTY FIVE

The Weavers

Onyx and Praxis made their way quietly from the top of the armory tower, where they weaved together, to the guards practice grounds below and behind the tower. Rogsin rarely visited the solders of Vinetop. It was said that Hammond knew each warrior by name and called each friend. Rogsin paid his men no such respect that Praxis ever saw.

How strange that one so given to war knows nothing about his fighting men?

Here the citadel's guards lived in wooden barracks built against Vinetop's thick-stoned rear wall. The men ate, dressed and stored their polished parade weapons in the outbuildings around the field. And here too was found practice gear and a large grass field. Straw targets and dummies used for training were set on the grounds. It was Onyx's favorite place.

"After Father died," Onyx said as they stood on the tower's exit landing, "These men took up fatherly pride for me and my upkeep."

"Such men of war-craft have great skill," Praxis said. "Yet, their love is the greater skill. They love you dearly. I have seen it."

Onyx jumped from the stoop and raced to the center of the grassy court where wooden swords and pikes were neatly bulwarked for the next match. Onyx hefted a brass-coated wooden shield and took up a wooden practice sword. She swung it expertly dancing and parrying with the grace of a joyful war hero.

A small group of men reclined on one of the team benches and were sharpening their long swords with stones. Upon seeing her, they bespoke their approval with grunts and knee slaps. Praxis joined the men as they were commenting on Onyx's forms.

"Who is brave enough to fight the daughter of Hammond?" Onyx proclaimed pointing her sword at the party.

"Not I," said one veteran, "You so small, who can strike points upon you? You're as fast as a dragon's tail and harder to hit. Nay, I've enough bruises for today!"

One after the other, five men declined Onyx's offer to spar with good humor but true reservations until one young recruit stood up accepting the challenge. The men gave warnings, but the young man called Robmere laughed saying;

"She is but a girl. I'll show no mercy. That is why you feel her sting. You give quarters allotting her size and status. I shall not."

Garson, the eldest of them laughed in return. He then thumped his chest causing his armor to ring.

"Size matters not! Training and practice makes a fighter's steel. Onyx is the daughter of her father, a natural, to be sure. More so, she's practiced all her years. I say she smites you in two moves."

"Three moves," someone said.

The men gathered close and whispered their bets so not to taint the fighters. Praxis held the coins while Robmere donned practice gear. Robmere was small as men go, about the size of Rogsin. However, Robmere was fitter. The men said Robmere was agile and strong, as far as new fighters go.

He's no match for Onyx.

Praxis wished she had placed a bet.

The two met on the field, touched swords, and took up defenses. Robmere sprang first. He charged savagely hooting and swinging wild with fearful cries. Onyx stood fast unflustered and within a hare's breath, she ducked under his charge quick as a shot arrow. She scored a wounding point striking his backside as he stumbled passed. Robmere landed face-first in the grass.

"She playing with him," Garson said, "Wounding points don't count!"

Robmere jumped to his feet spiting clovers. His face was red according embarrassment rather than from injury. Onyx raised her sword and posed ready, her face grave, her shield behind her slung as a backpack. It was then the Captain of the Guards hearing the commotion came out of his office. Boomax ran to the field and stood between them.

"You should be weaving," Boomax said. "The King gave orders. My duty bids me I stop this."

"I wasn't going to hurt him," Onyx cried, "Come on, Captain. I've had enough weaving. Praxis and I weave day in and day out, and too little avail. A maiden needs fresh air!"

"I know otherwise, young Queen," You spend far more time here than in yonder tower and if the King finds you here, he will be most displeased. Do not tempt his wrath."

"So what," Onyx said, her face screwed up in disdain. "I will not heed him. He treated me poorly far too long. You know how he abuses me. Why should I help him please his miserable Dwarfs? My skills are better than his. If he punishes you for my independence, I will cut him down!"

Onyx spun and pitched her wooden sword sticking it into the archer's target fifty paces away and dead center, too. The dull oaken spike penetrated the tightly woven straw target like iron into flesh. The men scuffed their feet with bowed heads while Boomax tensed. Onyx had spoke treason and not for the first time. But Robmere was fixed on Onyx's sword toss and so he closed his slack-jaw and exclaimed, "By the Light she is good! She is good!"

"Too good," Rogsin said from inside the tower's open door. "Did I hear a threat to my kingship?"

Rogsin and an outlander came out onto the playing field. The man held a dwarf's throwing-ax. Without warning he raised it to throw. Onyx sprang and twisted as the ax flew. The ax clanked off Onyx's shield and grounded. She rolled, scooped it up, and was ready to attack. Rogsin stepped behind the disarmed man. The guards rallied to Rogsin's side as duty called leaving Onyx alone in the field. Praxis moved to Onyx's side.

"You always wanted to follow after Father, fancied yourself a warrior-princess. You learned war-craft in secret. What other secrets do you harbor? You men, you see the danger, don't you? You heard what she said. I should cut off her head. But alas I cannot, fitting as it may be. I cannot kill my wife-to-be."

Onyx dropped the ax. Her face became as pale as limestone. Praxis, likewise, felt sickened to her bones.

What madness is this?

"Boomax take her to the tower." Rogsin said. "Lock her up with the loom in the topmost cell. She may not come out. And you dragon, I thought you a friend, but, of course, your allegiances lie with your familiar. So be it. Have the stonemason open the window for a dragon. Praxis must attend the weaver or the weaving will have no magic."

"What is this," The Outlander said, "What keeps them from flying off? We need that oracle. What if she escapes and rallies the people against our cause?"

"No need to fear, my friend" Rogsin said, "Female dragons are too small and untrained for a rider. They aren't going anywhere. We'll keep watchmen on the parapets. Hear that Boomax? I want men up there. If they fly together shoot them."

"Yes, oh King" Boomax said gravely.

Boomax gave orders while Rogsin departed. The guards ushered Onyx away leaving Praxis alone on the field while the ravens on the walls above squawked in disapproval. Boomax, having dispatched his men, went to Praxis and spoke quietly.

"I am sorry. I have no choice but my duty. I must serve the King."

"What if Rogsin proves not to be the rightful king?" Praxis said."You live here; you heard the rumors. Why did Hammond kill his brother? Rogsin looks nothing like Hammond. He cannot be Hammond's son."

"I serve the house of Vinetop. I will slay Rogsin myself, if evidence proves him a usurper. Yet, once he marries Onyx, Rogsin seals his right…alas…I am at a loss."

Boomax gritted his teeth. Boomax's family had served Vinetop for centuries. Praxis knew well that Boomax, much like Draco, would not shirk clear duty. And yet, these days, no duty appeared clear not even to the likes of Boomax. The Kingdom was changing in so many profound ways not written in the Scrolls. Praxis thought it hard for Boomax; even 'Boomax the rock' was crumbling under Rogsin's mud-slid deceptions. It was unfair to press him further.

This good man walks in Light where naught but darkness is found.

"Onyx and the King—they must not…I cannot stop it." Boomax said.

"Rest your mind dragon-friend. I will ask no treachery of you." Praxis said, "This abomination will not transpire whilst I remain Onyx's Right Hand. Reckoning will come—I will say no more."

Praxis spoke brave words, and she meant them, but she had no idea how she would keep them. But a slim hope lit Praxis's heart.

When the time comes, she and I will do the unexpected. I need help, but not so much help as to alert Rogsin. I'll walk upon this sword blade alone.

"Boomax, will you teach me how war-dragons carry riders? It's a matter of academics, of course. A courtly dragon such as I must understand many such things. I must serve my duty to Vinetop and learn all I can."

"Aye, aye, after all, it is my duty to train dragons and men in the greater ways of Vinetop." Boomax said with a one sided smile. "I would be remiss otherwise."

FORTY SIX

On the Steppes

Mars and Argolis flew tandem from Webweaver's hill two miles over the thinning Black Forest and landed well on the other side in a wholesome green field rife with summer wildflowers. Grasshoppers and honey bees fled like splashed water as they touched down. The trip was easier than their escape from Black Bill's hideout. This time Mars's grip on Argolis's harness was less strained as the country dragon's wings had grown to one quarter size and lessened the load.

The fields on the northwest side of the evil Forest were much different than that of the southeast side. There were no rotting marshes. Red deer grazed in the broad flat fields between low rolling hills. There were groves of nut trees and berry bushes in the dales between grassy hillocks. The grasses were taller and greener; the trees that dotted the landscape were healthy and full. Game was in the air. Mars smelled rabbits, wild pigs, and squirrels. Argolis pointed out many good-eating plants. A distant pronghorn grazed contently with swinging tail and flickering ears while her two fawns pranced nearby.

"My heart longs for home," Mars said as he watched the fawns at play.

Mars took a deep draught of the air and confirmed it was indeed a good land. Argolis's crown stood tall as he too surveyed the place. Although the narrows between the forest and cliffs was only five miles wide there was a feast of water and food at wingtip.

"A dragon could live well in this place," Argolis said. "The ground is fair for planting and look! There are caves on them cliffs. A dragon's abode if I ever knew one!"

"If Neff was ever a paradise this is the proof," Mars agreed. "What magic keeps this edge whole?"

"Must be spillover from her uncorn-ness up there." Argolis looked at the cliffs and swallowed hard.

They moved toward the cliffs and finding a little creek they walked down stream along it until they came upon a waterfall. Fish jumped in the pool before the cascade. There were no signs that men ever went there. They made camp along the pool under a rocky outcrop.

"I think we'll have no visitors here," Mars said, "We're a long way from the frontier land. The Steppes trade road is at least a few hundred miles west of here. We're safe for now."

Mars and Argolis stayed several days eating often. Argolis regained a measure of his girth. They caught and dried fish for their packs. They found salt-rock in the cliff face and so they salted meat as well. With packs and bellies full Argolis spoke of parting while roasting a rabbit on the open fire.

"We've come to it now. I mean, Sir, we said we'd part when fair roads find us and this here is a fair place. I mean, you can fly and all and your way is over them cliffs. As for me, I'll walk west along the cliffs until I find the trader's road. I figure the cliffs are 1500 miles from end to end and I figure we are well past the middle. I'll find my way alright. I can walk forever with easy vitals along the way. My wings are growing, and all, so I won't walk the whole way. I'll find that traders road and…"

"Hush!" Mars commanded with a tone of good humor. "You don't suppose I've come all this way to part with you, do you? Don't be foolish Argolis. As Mother says, 'A dragon alone is half a dragon.' Either we find a passage or we'll walk the cliff line together. I cannot carry you to the heights but I won't leave you behind either. I once made that mistake—leaving loved ones behind favoring my wont. I'll not do that again!"

"Yes Sir," Argolis said, his smoke blushing pink.

"For the sake of Light Argolis stop calling me sir. Highborn, lowborn, who cares? We are brothers of the road. If we ever get out of here, I'll forever forgo these foolish castes."

They broke camp and traveled west until late in the day they came upon a zigzag road going up behind and between two great rents in the cliff's face. It was a path long ago made for men and horses. It could not be seen from the air or ground unless one knew exactly where to look—it was a very cleaver path…and recently used. The footing was tricky for one as large as Argolis but his baby wings lent balance and lighter footfalls. Mars ferried the packs to the top first then joined Argolis on the climb.

It was afternoon when they set out thinking it a short distance. But, it was an hour after nightfall when they crested the rocky edge exhausted. Fearful of the Steppes people, they moved off the bare rocks and made a nest under tall wheat grasses and made no fire that night.

The earth was warm and the stars were endless. They lay on pillows of soft grass and admired the heavens. The dragon constellation was directly over head—it was past midsummer.

"There are but two prime stars missing before its whole," Argolis said, "They say the last spot's for the greatest dragon lord of all. Begging your pardon, but I hopes that place isn't for you, least wise, if so, a long time coming."

"If Rogsin finds us, my star will rise sooner, not later." Mars said.

"Funny how the old constellation seems more filled in since last I looked."

Next day, after filling their bellies with what fresh meat they had, Mars and Argolis set off into the interior with no idea of where the Path Stone would land them. They had not gone many miles inland when the grasses reached five foot tall and tickled their shoulders. The land was broad and flat although the terrain rolled somewhat. The cliff's edge became lost in a sea of green and golden brown. The fields were not easy walking. Among weeds, wheat and barley stalks were twisted ground vines and briers. They often snagged their feet and tripped as they went.

"Surly the locals have a road," Mars said. "Why would the stone lead us thus? It leads as if we were flying."

"Mayhap the paths are not safe. There's nothing for it but to go flying—time you have a-look-see."

As before, Argolis launched Mars into the air. Mars opened his wings and rose easily on warm updrafts. He circled upward careful to keep track of Argolis. Delighted to fly again, Mars let his golden hue shine. He flashed in the sunlight like a day star. Mars saw no paths, but he did see large flying creatures in the distance and they saw him too—they moved in his direction. From every direction small birds flew toward him as well. Below Mars saw Argolis standing on his hind legs waving his arms frantically.

Mars dove and landed. Once on the ground Mars knew why Argolis waved. Hoards of locusts and other insects had descended on him followed by an army of small birds. Did the birds attack Argolis as well? Mars had no time to consider it.

Scales or not, they were not safe. Bugs attacked Mars's eyes so he closed his flight lids and joined Argolis who had his tail fin opened wide fanning the air. Mars flapped his wings to add to the wind torrent but that only drove off the birds allowing even more insects to converge and find their way under scale where they bit unceasingly.

"Use your fire," Shouted Mars, "burn them!"

"Nay," Argolis cried, "I'll set flame to the grasses—it's too dry here. Even dragons roast in fire storms!"

"It's hopeless," Mars shouted above the buzzing. "What's worst, getting eaten alive one tiny bite at a time or burned all at once?"

When Mars thought he could stand it no more Argolis cried out.

"Light your hue, they didn't attack you aloft, light your scales!"

They both did so. The insects immediately withdrew but not far. Dark clouds of them hovered near giving the wrens and sparrows an easy feast. But, a dragon can only stay lit brightly for so long.

"We've got ourselves in a bog, if you take my meaning, Sir. How long can we last?"

It was then that Mars noticed that not all the ground shadows were cast by clouds of insects. New shadows appeared—shapes much like that of the Iron Skins. The silhouette of great wings folding for a dive fell on the ground before Mars.

"To the ground Argolis, lay flat!" Mars shouted.

They thrust themselves onto the ground, Mars facing up, a hare's breath before two great winged creatures strafed where they had been. The birds were the size of Iron Skins with white feathers and opened bills big enough to swallow a man. They flew head long into the swarms with beaks agape while the small birds scattered before them.

"They're after the bugs," Mars shouted, "Let's move out, and head down!"

Running on all fours, they gained distance quickly. They topped a rise overlooking the fields. Mars looked back and realized they had escaped the swarm. They were a mile from the carnage looking down into a dish of lower land. The birds, as large as any dragon, continued to eat until the remnants were utterly scattered. Then the birds soured high and circled as if waiting. Searching along the way they had come, Mars saw no end to the plains. Lost, Mars thought as he grabbed for the Path Stone.

"I've lost the stone," Mars cried.

"It's in the low places where bugs gather," Argolis said. "We can't go down there."

"We must stay to higher lands." Mars said, his tone not hiding his misery at losing the stone. "It's a depression, a heat trap, the insects must favor it."

The dozen giant birds swooped down and landed on another ridge-line and transformed into white unicorns. The unicorns then filed one behind the other and ran atop the parallel rise in the direction that they had come from. Mars watched until they faded into the distance.

"I'd say if it is the Unicorn Princes we want then we best follow them unicorns."

"So be it," Mars said. "The rise we're on meets that one ahead. As a wise country dragon I know often says, 'there's nothing for it then,' come on let's go."

Mars had a hope that one of the unicorn folks had snatched up his stone, but it was a fanciful notion and a very unlikely one at that.

FORTY SEVEN

Onyx's Question

Onyx stood near her tower-prison's makeshift dragon-door shivering. Although it was past midsummer, the tower's thick walls kept the sun's warmth out while retaining the cold air that rose from the ice stores below. Each tower level had four rooms radiating off the open stair well at center. Every door was shut against the cold mists that ascended the stairs like a procession of apparitions. Onyx's door had a barred window which allowed the cold's egress.

On the very top floor there was the King's armory and Onyx's small cell. Her only window, now a landing, never saw direct sunlight. An unlighted dragon's door was a dismal thing and Praxis loathed entering that way Onyx knew. The stair was too twisted for a dragon.

No warmth ever comes by way of this window save what Praxis brings.

Onyx always hated the tower while Rogsin loved it for its royal armory just beyond her locked door. Onyx never visited there although Father wanted her to see his trophies. As a child, she avoided any place Rogsin favored and would not go where he tread. Onyx regretted refusing Father's invitations now. She longed to hear what glories he would have told. Mother instructed Onyx from her deathbed saying, 'Do as Hammond does—fight with honor, rule by wisdom.'

'But Mother," Onyx said long ago. 'If I can't ride, I can't rule.'

'You will take his seat,' she said, 'Follow after him…you are the last of our line.'

Mother saw my assent. Can a Prophetess misspeak?

Onyx shivered all the more. Hammond was a master warrior whose armor no one could fill.

How can I equal him? I wish Merilbe were here.

Onyx pondered how Father, so fleet footed in battle, could have fallen to his death from the window next door.

Impossible, Rogsin lied.

The truth was known. The birds saw it, those same ravens that forever sat on Vinetop's roofs and sills watching. Ravens were said to speak only truth. Yet, the birds for whose color she was named would not speak to her while Brother, the only other witness, spoke naught but lies. Even so Rogsin had his men harry the ravens whenever they were within bow-shot.

"How did you die, what evil befell you Father?"Onyx cried.

No ghost answered. And it seemed the tower extruded Onyx's memories from her like wine from the press. There was no comfort in recall and no answers trapped within her cell. She had only the loom, spinning wheel, stool, straw bed, and sideboard for company. Praxis had not yet returned from gathering. Suddenly lonely, Onyx rushed to the locked door and called through the barred window.

"Give me quarters! Companionship is all I ask. Won't you talk with me?"

"I cannot," called Robmere's faint voice from the lower floor. "King's orders, sorry."

Ten days in this place and it felt like a year. Rogsin denied every request for leave. At least Praxis could go. Onyx was glad for the news Praxis brought on each return although whenever Praxis flew out again loneliness redoubled. Human familiars separated from their dragons did not fair well. Praxis stayed less long each day, and for good reason they agreed.

The ravens on the roof called excitedly as they usual did whenever a flying dragon came near. Onyx rushed back to the window. Praxis's blue-gold hue flashed in the sky. Onyx's heart raced as Praxis approached for a landing.

"Yes dear Praxis, we are true familiars; Sister, I cannot weave without your magic but more so, my soul pains me when you are gone. Yet you must fly."

Praxis gracefully swooped in and landed softly but her leg muscles were as taught as clock windings—typical for war-dragons who are always ready to spring.

"You're flying and landings improve every day—no courtiers compare."

"Boomax teaches well," Praxis said.

As Praxis moved into the room three ravens landed on the landing's edge. They bobbed their heads this way and that listening as they often did there. Onyx left them alone as a comfort to her as were the ravens that perched on the roof above. Even the chattering bluebirds roosting in the eves were welcome. Love for all flying things grew in Onyx's stone cage—a love Onyx could not account for.

"Not much canvas to be had," Praxis said removing her pack, "Rogsin's Steppes war eats resources like country dragons at morning meal. There's hardly a scrap left. We'll have no backing for the Tapestry at this rate."

"Craft-wears matter not," Onyx said, "There is no magic in this loom. These dragon's gold treads will not mate. The oracle is lost. You know it, too. Our weaving is for naught."

"The gold bobbin we spooled is far too dull." Praxis said taking up the cloth and examining it. "I've never heard of dragon gold tarnishing. Something is definitely wrong."

Praxis held up the work and shook it lightly. Ten days work and it was no larger than a towel and just as unremarkable.

"It looks like an hours worth of work." Praxis said. "The golden treads of the original where undetectable but caused it to shimmer. No matter how finely we stitch the golden threads show and don't shine."

"No matter what we do, it doesn't mesh," Onyx agreed.

"Lore says the Tapestry can't be remade. Your Brother has another purpose. Of what, only he knows."

"But the Tapestry chose me; it blessed me and repelled him. What does that mean?"

"You ask the correct question, Oh Queen," The raven at the sill said. "I have not spoken to humans in a thousand years. I will now. The right time and hearer has come."

"What! What have you seen, what do you know," Onyx cried.

"We know much, Oh Queen, long have we kept watch over the last rightful heir. The golden thread has failed, it will shine no more. Your weaving is the proof. Long have we been the Tapestry's eyes. You are the golden thread now. You will shine. I will speak to you."

"I don't understand! I am not a queen." Onyx fell to her knees before the ravens.

"Oh but you are, as Hammond's wizard knows. That is why Rogsin locked Merilbe in this very tower. Merilbe read the signs correctly. The Tapestry chose the last rightful ruler of this age. You are not a magic-weaver. Your mother named you after us, that is, our color, as she foresaw the new age and your glory in it. Only now will our race speak but only with the golden tread. The changing is night—time straddles the abyss. Dragons must depart from where magic was first given or they will be destroyed. And you must take up the sword."

Praxis's crown shot tall while rainbow smoke poured from her mouth. Onyx's heart pounded in her ears.

"Speak plainly," Onyx cried. "What riddle is this, why must birds speak in puzzles?!"

"I give you the puzzle parts, Emerald, Merilbe, and Walters they understand intricacies. We speak of the ages, not of the days—time is a circular. Our understanding is not your understanding. We ravens will not remain another season. My people are old. Our souls will go to the stars and fly with our brothers—on the last dragon's day, magic-ravens will be no more."

The raven opened his wings and fluttered, but he did not fly.

"A brother saw Rogsin shoot the golden and lay ruin to dragon's hope. Rogsin killed Hammond, my brothers and I saw it. A royal son cannot kill his sire. Rogsin is not the rightful heir. Murder is the omen. You are the rightful ruler. I will answer once more."

"I will not ask it lightly," Onyx said. "As yet, I do not know what to ask."

"I am Roecon**,"** the raven said "I will perch above until the last days. I will speak with you and fulfill my days in your company, Oh Queen. Yet I will only answer one more hidden thing. Seek the persons I named who have had a place in this tale and you will have clear sight. You will know your path."

"There is one thing we need to know," Praxis said, "Where is Mars. If he is the golden foretold then he'll save us. We must find him…if he is still alive."

Onyx, with her head reeling, sat upon the stool to reason out her quandary. Praxis loved Mars and so her judgment was skewed. But, if the Legend of Neff were true, Onyx thought, Mars was the key. But, a lost key opens no door. And Mars has no fire. Dragon's never lead without fire. What could a small fireless dragon do? How could he overcome Rogsin's army? There were too many variables, too many questions.

There is something as yet unseen in all of this.

A deeper turning of the wheel was at hand, Onyx was sure of it—more than Rogsin's games were in play. What was said in legends, signs and omens were truths only in part. How the parts fit Onyx could not tell—that was wizard's work. A great change was in the air and Mars had a part in it she could not see. Rationales spun within her mind like the spinning-wheel before her. In the end Onyx decided to trust her heart.

"I will ask of Mars," Onyx said slowly. "Roecon what news do you have? Is he the one written of in the scrolls—the savor of dragons?"

"He is," Roecon said, "He is the Golden of legend. How or if he affects the coming days we cannot know. The legends say nothing of a wounded dragon. What news I have is thin. The brothers saw him at Emerald's cave. He wintered there. But he left Emerald high winter, a most dangerous time to travel. And crows say, crows not trust worthy, mind you, they say he was in Dreglands. A lone dragon there is no match for the Iron Skins."

"From there we are less sure. Vulture's rumors, less trusted than crows, say a great dragon attacked and overcame three stout vultures below Forbidden Mountains. They say two dragons on foot entered the Mires of Neff in the north east and crossed the Black River. Vultures are shape eyed but not even they see who travels under the Black Forest's canopy. It could be him."

"If it is Mars," Onyx said, "he is going in the wrong direction."

"We need to find out, "Praxis said. "I'd wager Emerald knows."

"Seek the puzzle pieces and you'll know better," Roecon said.

Roecon and his two brothers then flew from the dragon-door. Moments later their talons were scratching on the thatched roof above. Then, a great many ravens spoke together in their own language. The bird song gave Onyx new confidence. She no longer felt trapped—an end to her imprisonment would come but she knew not how or when.

"When Walters brings the meal we'll learn more." Onyx said.

"He will help," Praxis agreed. "He has no love of Rogsin. His oath is to Vinetop. He spent a season with Emerald. He'll know something."

"Yes," Onyx said, "We also need a wizard's advice. If we cannot reach Merilbe, Emerald may do."

"Penelope says, 'there are no secrets among the house staff' Walters was and is the King's butler." Praxis said.

Onyx thought of day to day life on Vinetop. Walters was always on hand but never underfoot. He knew Father's need before he asked. He was not a man of words, letters or magic, but his eyes and ears served Hammond well.

"He could help us, but would he? I sit not upon Vinetop's throne but on this stool."

They waited until Robmere announced lunch and unlocked the door. Walters appeared with the midday meal and bowed. Onyx bid Walters enter with a friendly greeting. Robmere lingered at the door watching but not with suspicion. Robmere's attention was not for security's sake. His easy smile and red cheeks bore affection. Onyx likewise felt an attraction and her heart beat as such. She decided to take advantage of his affection and felt badly but showed no misgivings.

It is for the good of Vinetop. Forgive me Robmere.

Onyx approached Robmere and touched his cheek with her fingertips saying, "Robmere, my dear, brave guard, I would have words with Walters in private if you please. Won't you allow him a short stay?"

"Orders me Lady," He said. But his voice was soft.

Onyx stroked his arm and leaned closer to him. She felt him unravel. His neck went stiff his eyes blinked rapidly and his muscles flexed. She did not wish to let go. He smelled fine, his arm was strong. Onyx almost swooned.

By the Light he is hansom.

"Please," Onyx said kissing him on each cheek. "He is a father to me."

Robmere's face flushed as he ran a hand through his hair then staggered backward beyond the door. "A short stay," he said closing the door without latching it. Robmere danced to the stairwell. His footfalls faded downward with a happy cadence.

Onyx wasted no time. She beseeched Walters to tell what he knew of Mars's stay with Emerald. He confirmed what Roecon had said and added details of Mars's escape—helped by a dragon-ghost's push no less! Praxis's hue glowed pride on the telling.

Mars was brave, indeed. I see why she fancies him.

"Mars's intent was plain," Walters said. "He sought Emerald's help for his fire. But Emerald, ever the game player, would not tell. Thus Mars went seeking elsewhere. I do not know all they said together or where Mars had flown to. Emerald may know if you can con it out of him."

Walters looked to the window and lowered his voice.

"Mars is in danger. Rogsin means to kill him. Hunters with that dragon-slayer bow are after him. And Rogsin employs gnomes as spies and none are better spies. Rogsin hates dragons, most of all Mars."

"We must warn him," Praxis exclaimed, "We must save him!"

"Emerald has the means to find Mars," Walters said. "He possesses an Inowise seer bowl. Not even Rogsin knows this. Go to Emerald and you will find Mars."

"How," Onyx said. "Rogsin will not let me leave nor do I know the way. Nobody knows the way."

"Rogsin is not here. He has gone on business," Walters said. "I know the way."

Walters reached into his waist band and took from his charm pocket a small green stone mounted on a gold chain and handed it to Onyx. She marveled at the depths of its facets. It glowed so beautifully. She had heard of such things but never thought to see one much less hold one in her hand. As she held it, the path-stone warmed. By intuition she held the stone aloft and it then flashed brilliantly toward the window. Stone-faced Walters smiled as he set down a bowl of stew from his serving tray.

"Bear Claw asked me to mind it until it found its rightful user. The stone chooses you," he said. "It will take you wherever you ask it. Ride before Rogsin returns."

"There are no dragon's here suitable for a rider. Who will take me," Onyx said.

"I will," Praxis said. "I'm ready now."

Waters dropped his jaw followed by his serving tray. Robmere returned due the clatter and made Walters go.

FORTY EIGHT

The Unicorn People

Mars and Argolis endeavored to follow the unicorns with stealth at first and so they dashed from tufts of high grass to standalone boulders or other cover with their heads low and hues muted. Lost as they were they hoped to discover the Unicorn Queen's whereabouts—and their own. But whenever Mars and Argolis snuck close with ready eyes and ears up the unicorns shape-shifted into great eagles and flew forward; always in the same direction, and never beyond the hunter's sight.

"They want us to follow them," Mars said, "A trap or salvation we won't know until we get there."

Thus, they followed the unicorn three days along the ridgelines in plain sight. On the forth morning they lost them while crossing a grassy hollow. Trudging up the far side they broke the ridge and looked down upon a wide, rocky dale, spotted with large boulders and short green grass.

"I'm tired of wading though grass seas," Argolis said. "The going just got better. Come on."

"Hold still," Mars whispered. "I don't like it. This is the place for an ambush if one there ever was. They can hide easily among those rocks. It is better we lay up and watch awhile."

Mars and Argolis backed away until only their heads breached the hill's crest. Unicorns soon emerged and began grazing with tails whipping and hooves stamping. Past them, in the center of the dale Mars spotted a distant spring. Mars's parched tongue rolled out from his mouth uninvited.

Mars rolled up his tongue and whispered."We're over one hundred miles from the cliffs and the last water I've seen. My canteen is near empty and they led us to water. What game is this?"

"I'm no student of war, Sir, but I'd say they're up to no good. I mean…they must know we're here, and need water: they aren't stupid—I'd slap tail back where we came from, if I knew the way."

Argolis is right; they led us here but why? Curse loosing that Path Stone.

"A stout horse can't keep pace with running dragons. Yet unicorns run faster still, and eagles surly out-fly dragons," Mars said. "They set a snare, and we stepped on the trip-line."

Mars's crown feather flared wide and flat.

"Mayhap they're not so bad, Sir. I mean here we are out of that nasty bug country. If they wanted us dead they'd of let those bugs have at us. Look at their crowns, they could run us through."

"They don't look evil no matter what men say about them." Mars said. "This is the closest we've gotten, they allowed it. My heart says they are good creatures. Let us approach. Slowly, Argolis, don't slap your tail."

The two dragons slowly rose on the hillock. They remained still there until Mars thought they were seen. The unicorns did not startle as deer or elk would, rather, their tail-swishing and foot-stamping settled. Mars took it as a good sign and they descended softly. They made for the nearest unicorn and it moved out of reach. After several attempts with the same result the hot sun and Mars's thrust beckoned him to drink. The unicorns stopped grazing and watched as the two moved toward the water.

They are not blocking our passage. This is an invitation.

Mars quickened his pace toward the spring. Mars fell to the ground before the waters and drank deeply while Argolis filled water-skins. The water tasted unnaturally sweet, and he drank so long that Mars forgot the unicorns. Mars's thirst was satisfied but he could not leave the poolside. His reflection began to swirl like the Tapestry in the ripples he had made. Once the waters stilled, Mars appeared old. His mane was short and gray. Eagles appeared above his head in the sky. Long-pike tips shown behind him as if Calvary filed after him. Then the spears trained downward—on him.

Mars fell back from the pool. He was surrounded by men mounted on great lean horses whose manes were cut short. The riders wore leather leggings and boots, and loose gray woolen shirts under leather vests tied with leather belts or thongs. Tanned, stern-faced men drew counter bent bows or leveled long pikes at the dragons. The man sitting upon the only white horse spoke while unsheathing a long curved sword.

"What rights have you? Outlanders cannot drink from this sacred pool, not without permission!"

Mars lowered his head and knotted his tail ready to answer tail-to-iron. Argolis moved first and reared fully onto hind legs above the saddled men—a poor fighting stance—and spoke with billows of black smoke.

"By the permission of them unicorns that brought us here, you seen them fly off, they got us here and gave us to drink."

"They have no claim on this water. Not while we have her cloistered. Yield or die!"

The men tensed on the word of their Captain but by hesitated awaiting an order. Mars loaded a handful of rocks into his mouth. The Steppes men, two dozen in all, although without armor were well equipped. Mounted pike-men could penetrate a dragon's hide. Mars still had room to fly even without cutting a fire path. But, Argolis unable to take to the air knotted his tail and dropped to ground with his head low and tail high.

Argolis will club himself silly. He doesn't know how to tail-fight.

Argolis doesn't fly and Mars had no fire. The wisdom of Draco flashed in mind, 'Never show your weakness.'

"Stand down," Mars said in dragon speak so the fighters would not understand, "We'll yield, go with them. Learn what we can. We escaped Webweaver; they'll not hold us. Stand down! No jail holds dragons long."

The men hearing the growling dragon-speak backed away. The Captain was unmoved and spoke his war language. His troops moved closer.

"I hope you know what you're doing," Argolis said in common speech.

"We yield," Mars cried.

The two dragons bowed. Mars put his spiting-rocks back into his neck bag.

"Come then, walk with us," the Captain said. He gave further orders in war-tongue. The men lined before and behind the dragons, the white horse and rider first.

They moved over to the far side of the dale, up the slop and over the crest into a wider, rocky valley landscaped with short green grass. They marched ten miles across the basin to a village, of sorts. It was an odd mixture of sod houses, round stacked stone huts without mortar, and animal skin tents with corrals of woven vines and saplings which altogether made a rambling town.

Some fencing contained horses and others contained sheep or goats. Hens, kid goats and children scurried about. The children cried out with glee, "dragons have come, dragons are here!" Women in long woven coats of many colors and black braded hair came out from the houses. Several hundred men women and children soon gathered.

After the clamor subsided, the old men gathered nearby and talked in a tongue Mars did not know while Mars and Argolis sat on their tails waiting at the central fire-pit. The villagers kept their distance, but not far enough.

"We have room to run and fly for our escape," Mars said. "They're not the warriors of rumor. This is bad strategy on their part."

It was not long before the men at arms rested their gear—another opening for attack. Curious adults came and greeted them in the Vineland language. The children, boldest of all, brought them cheese and fruits and plopped down on the dusty ground to eat with them. In return Argolis entertained the children with smoke rings and country lore. All was peace until a group of young fighters mounted their stallions and charged off in various directions. The horsemen's Captain then approached.

"You have broken the law, that is true, yet we have no argument against dragon-folk. We here won't decide your repayment. The Council of Chiefs is called. Until they rule, you will remain corralled. Think not to leave for our bows are sure and strong, unlike the long bowmen of your land, we seldom miss."

In a flurry the Capitan drew his bow off his back, notched it, and fired at a fence post fifty yards away sticking his arrow deep into an eye-knot. The target was no larger than a dragon's eye. It was a deadly strike. Indeed, this Steppes bows was far more powerful that any Mars had seen. Such a bow may even penetrate his scales. Such aim would take out his eye.

"Then we are prisoners," Mars said. "Is this the hospitality of your people? Our sin is thirst. Is drinking a crime in your land? How would we know?"

"It is not, save but the enchanted pool. None may drink from it. Yet we are not uncivil. You will be well cared for. Your kind is given to barn living we hear so you will house with the hornless unicorn. She will testify to the treatment of our captives and teach you the way of our land. Come."

He led Mars and Argolis to a building made of sticks woven like cloth but it was such a weave that Mars could fit head and neck through it. The building had a sound thatched roof. Such a place was no dragon enclosure. Yet, it was a homely place like the summer shelters of a hunting-camp. The gate was tied shut by a leather thong. The man bid them enter but he did not go in.

"The maimed one will keep you company. Make yourself to home."

The Chief tied the gate and strode away.

"That I will," said a pretty voice from within.

Mars and Argolis saw a talking horse, the first they ever heard of. They stood together slack jawed as a beautiful white mare pranced lightly into the enclosure from a rear opening. Beyond was a yard hemmed in by a stick-woven fence.

"I trust Jawlsa found you at the pool," the mare said. "I am Lea. Welcome to my captivity."

"How'd you know we were at the pool," Argolis blunted out.

"Argolis," Mars said, "remember you manners. Forgive him. He is but a country dragon as such not given to formalities. I am Mars. This is my brother of the road Argolis. Thank you for your hospitality."

Mars then bowed. But Argolis puffed pink smoke and stood with eyes blinking and tongue hanging. Mars slapped Argolis with an open tail. Argolis bowed too.

"If that don't beat all," Argolis said while rising, "A talking horse, I mean I never heard tell…"

"I am no horse," Lea said kindly, "But I understand your confusion. A unicorn without a horn is a strange sight, indeed."

She was not a usual horse in other ways. Her body was longer and less weighty. Her eyes blue not brown, her tail, legs and neck were much longer; a cross between a sea dragon and a horse but she had no scales.

A horn would be fitting.

"Now that's a pity, it is. A unicorn ought to have a horn, if you take my meaning, me lady."

Again Mars nudged Argolis with his tail and Argolis closed his mouth. Mars feared he would give away too much too soon. Draco and Penelope did not agree on much but both taught him the danger of a loose tongue. Mars needed to know more before he would ask his burning question—where is the Unicorn Princess.

"Tell us Lea, if you will, how did you come to such a state? We saw the unicorns. How any man could capture one such as you is beyond hope or skill."

"I will tell you Mars the Golden. It is said of old that Golden dragons are worthy of trust. We unicorn are shape shifters, no doubt you saw my brothers and sisters changing. Alas we cannot change without the magic in our crowns. I lost my crown so I am fixed in this form. Without it I cannot fly nor change. The men caught me crownless."

"That ain't right," Argolis exclaimed, "Why'd they do that, I mean, can't they leave a body alone."

"Shush Argolis. Let her speak, for the sake of Light. Remember your manners!"

The Unicorn Lady threw back her head and whinnied in laughter.

"No, it is all right. I don't mind. I was captured as you were; drinking from the pool. We unicorns always drink there. The men, who live here and guard that place, are enchanted. They must protect it without understanding why. It is not their fault—the Princess made a spell beseeching its protection. But, the spell was not intended to stay forever. Until she unmakes her magic, the spell holds. These poor men are bound by that magic. The last to drink of it was she, and she is no more."

"Won't the Princess return? Where did she go," Mars cried.

Mars's crown fell low—there was no finding the Unicorn Princess or his fire now. Hope ran from Mars like blood from an egregious wound. Mars lowered his head to the ground.

"No one knows how to find her." Lea said. "The prophecies are muddled. The Pool of Light tells nothing. She went to war on Webweaver and never retuned. She must be fighting still. Her bones were never found and no omen of her death is known. I have hope."

Mars thought of the fire Argolis had made of wood and old bones in the spider hole. The longest bone, the leg bone of an elk, he thought then, was his pike. Mars suddenly realized that bone was far too long for any elk. The Princess's bone laid Webweaver low. Her crown finished the monster. Mars thought it fitting—the unicorn princess's bones and crown defeated Webweaver after all. The Princes got her revenge. Her soul would rest. Mars lay down on the straw. He cared no more for hearing or telling lore having what he thought of as a full account of a sad story.

"We know that spider and of unicorn bones," Mars said. "Tell it Argolis my heart pains me too much."

Argolis then told the tale of how he and Mars met and made their way to the spider's cave. Argolis told of Mars's quest, and the doings in Neff. All the while she listened and asked no questions. Argolis's speech was round-about but she never interrupted. He told how they got the idea from Webweaver to seek the Unicorn Princess. He told of the fight and gave himself no glory. Argolis stopped the telling where he jammed the horn into the spider's eyes. Argolis slipped out of his flight bag and put his hand inside Mars's bag rooting around as he spoke.

"Well there's nothing for it then. Seeing how we was on our way looking for her and seeing how she is no more, as you say, I suppose I'll give you what I mean to give her, if you understand me, Miss. Being as you got no crown and all." He looked at Mars and Mars nodded agreement "Well here it is. Take it with our blessing."

Argolis brought forth the crown and set it on the head of the Unicorn Lady.

"You give it freely?" Lea asked with ears tall and neck straight.

"I do." said Argolis. "That's why I came. We found it sure enough, and I killed the spider with it. Well, Mars here, he did the bravest blow, I just finished him, on reflex, if your take my meaning. But I'm not one to keep what's not mine, Miss. It belongs here. Seeing as you lost yours, well there you have it."

"The monster is dead. Long had he hunted and killed my people. For your kindness, Argolis, and your free will giving," Lea said. "Your folk, the dragon folk, forever have my leave to travel this land. The Steppes will never harm dragons."

Mars picked up his head, his crown stood. "How can you give leave? Only royalty may do that."

"Behold, I am whom you seek."

Suddenly, a great light radiated from Lea. The crown became one with her. Lea began transforming before their eyes. Her mane became long golden hair that rose around her head like dancing smoke. Her dusty gray fur became milk-white skin. Her eyes became smaller and turned from deep blue to the color of summer sky. The Unicorn Princes became human.

Her white robes glowed like a sunlit dragon. Mars sprang to his feet. Then, in a flash, she became a normal girl clad in a simple gray village dress, her long hair was braided. Mars staggered then fell and prostrated himself. Argolis followed likewise without a tail-slap motivation from Mars.

"Stand up my heroes," she said, "you shall not bow before me. Nay, you have restored me. My magic is whole. The spell I set is no more. The people are whole again. My blessing goes forth."

She waved her hand and the walls of the corral fell to the ground. All at once the people came running. Shouts went all around the village. War calls were not shouted but songs of celebration erupted. The people came all at once and set Lea into a great rattan chair lifting her into the air, they carried her about the town. The people danced all around her.

Mars and Argolis danced, too. Fires were lit. Meat was put on spits. Riders went out. And unicorns came from every direction. Some came on the wing as eagles, some on the hoof. Each unicorn transformed into whatever form most pleased it and they joined with the people. Lea went to the elder unicorns and humans and conferred with them.

Then shouts went up again. A great feast was declared for the next day and food for the moment as well. At her bidding, Argolis was invited and so he tapped the first barrel of barley-malt beer. Mars was handed the first mug which overflowed with frothy-brown pleasure. Mars drank and ate beyond his fill and he did not see Lea anymore that day.

All that night they ate to their hearts delight with foods such as wheat and nut breads, roasted meats, goat cheeses and yogurt mixed with sweet berries. They drank the Steppes' famous ale in plenty. Late that night, they were given the largest stone barn, a solid, clean place not unlike the dragon barns of home. In it was everything a dragon wanted for a nest-bed, good hay and sweet smelling grass, and huge soft pillows of goose down. As Mars lay his head down in comfort fit for a warlord, Mars did not forget his quest. He rolled half the night thinking of how, or if, his fire would return.

Mars awoke late the next morning to Argolis snoring and the song of a village crier; "By word of Lea all hail the dragons…honored guests they are…Come and feast with them tonight…by the word of Lea…!"

As the crier's words faded, there was a knock on the barn's door. Mars regretfully rousted from his sweet-grass bed to find a covey of maidens at the door. The women entered and opened the shutters letting in a bright day where upon Argolis rose. They quickly set plates laden with food before the dragons.

Argolis blinked his eyes many times; his crown rose and fell, while his hue reradiated.

"If that don't beat it, I mean breakfast in bed, I mean…I cannot accept…I mean..."

Argolis was hushed by the laughter of his servers. Mars thought it unwise to comment with his mouth stuffed full with sweat-cake. Mars raised his cup and winked at Argolis instead.

"Nothing for it then I suppose."

Argolis drove into his vitals and did not look up until hot water and soft towels were brought. The women took away the plates, washed each dragon's hands and snouts then disappeared leaving long pipes and tobacco.

Groomers, older boys, came to them that afternoon as they stood on their tails in the sun watching the villagers make ready. The lads bathed them, polished their scales, and trimmed their nails. Mars and Argolis's tangled manes were unfurled, brushed and braided. The two resumed leaning back on tails afterwards, but now they gleamed brighter in the sun and did not stink!

A great tent without sidewalls was erected in the round. The three center poles were forty feet high reminding Mars of the tents used at the Auction's fair—the same kind of tent were used for wedding feasts all over Vineland.

"These folks are the same as any other folks," Mars said, but he got no response. Argolis had drifted off to sleep and was puffing white smoke as he snored.

"Wake up Argolis, its past three. Get up you silly lout!"

"Must I," Argolis replied sleepily, "I'm dreaming of flying, a fine dream. I miss it, Sir. Flying that is."

"It's no dream Country Dragon, it's a prediction, I'd say, unless, that nasty spider steered us wrong."

With that, Argolis came full awake and jumped to his feet nearly hitting his head on the roof's overhang.

"You suppose Webweaver told true? I mean he might-a-been playing some cruel sport."

"We'll soon know." Mars said. "Jawlsa and a unicorn-made-bear, unless bears have taken up wearing crowns, are coming this way."

Argolis got off his tripod with knees shaking while Mars stood wary. Bears, after all, are the only creatures that might kill a dragon in a hand-to-hand fight. Mars moved from the stone barn's wall wanting room for tail swing—just in case.

The bear came up onto its hind legs with a grunt while Jawlsa greeted them with a kindly smile and his palms up. Jawlsa's previously stern face was nowhere seen. How a man so hard could appear so soft was a mystery to Mars.

"You must have some unicorn in you," Mars said.

"Aye, I do, we all do. Unicorn magic inhabits us just as dragon magic inhabits the Estates men. Is that not so Wingfoot?"

"It is so," said the towering black bear. His voice was kindly, too.

"If it's all the same to you," Argolis said with his whole body now twitching in fear, "I'll stay here; I mean, I'm not accustomed to supping with bears. I'm a bit unleveled, if you understand me."

"Nothing to fear from Wingfoot," Jawlsa said. "He led you here. He was among the bug catchers. He saved your life."

"Tis true," Wingfoot said. "We've been watching since the dragon's Ghost Star went up last winter. Lea said 'when you see the Ghost Star bring the gold dragon,' so was her words at her last Light Pool reading. She spoke it just before going off hunting for that spider. Three hundred years back, I'd say."

Argolis's body relaxed, but his eyes darted wary and his teeth chattered still. The four started toward the tent. Argolis hung back unsure.

"Why go to meal as a bear," Mars asked.

Wingfoot roared and beat his chest in such a way Mars knew the laughter of it.

"I like to eat. Dragons eat much, they say, but not so much as unicorns. When there are bugs I am a bug catcher, when the grass is new I am a horse, when fish are plenty, I am a kingfisher. This feast is great, so, I bring hunger as great. Thus, I become a bear!"

"I'm no sage," Argolis said, "But there's wisdom in that."

"Let us talk further under yon tent." Jawlsa said. "There is food aplenty. Let us eat and await Lea's return. She's gone to consult the Light Pool. She will have news of the world. The Pool's guidance is at hand!"

Argolis finally appeared at ease. But restlessness rose up in Mars—his tail threshed unasked for. Argolis's fear was answered while Mars's question still burned unquenched and the wrong answer was what Mars feared more than bears. Dragons love food, but Mars hungered more for healing.

What will I do if she cannot cure my fire?

As they made for the eatery tent Mars thought a stranger sight was never written in lore, a bear walking with dragons! Many children fell in behind them as they marched the two hundred yards. One child jumped onto Argolis's back, a great insult to high-born dragons at court but Argolis took no offence whatsoever, rather he invited the rest of them to do likewise.

"The smallest first," Argolis commanded and Argolis instantly became a wagon full of small, gleeful travelers.

Upon entering the eatery, the children dispersed but not because they were made too. Mars's hue came instantly on and flashed brightly unbidden. He glowed like a burning ember. A dragon calls his own hue at need or pleasure but Mars called it not. Argolis, too, was lit. The people about them bowed.

Lea stood at the further side at her chair in the form of that radiant woman Mars first saw as she transformed. Her crown shone gold at the band and the spiral horn of it was purest white. Her arms were held aloft and when she lowered them, after many bows, theirs and her hue dissipated. She became a plain but naturally beautiful woman again.

"Rest," She said, "All rest, be at ease, and all you that hear bend your ears. Mars, Argolis come and sup with me. I have much to say. Behold, the Golden Dragon has come."

Mars and Argolis settled at a low table suitable for humans and sat upon great pillows with tails straight out behind them. They reclined, as dragons typically do at table, on either side of Lea. Men and women of various forms of dress filed in and took seats at long tables. Their appearance bespoke many different tribes. The unicorns in human form wore white robes. Wingfoot did not transform. Lea, once everyone found a place, stood to address the assembly.

"The deeds of our guests are by now well known to you all. I will not retell their tales. We gather to give them due honor and gifts. We gather to hear the first reading of the Pool since Webweaver came. Much is grave news and none too soon for had the crown not come now, the people would be scattered. Hope is night!"

The people stamped their feet and hooted or clapped until Lea raised her hand once more.

"The Kingship of Vineland readies for war against us, and not with dragon's consent. Dragons are not our enemy. The King, Rogsin, hates dragons. Rogsin means to do dragons and unicorns harm alike."

Jeers and hoots and pounding on the tables filled the air.

"Neff walks a sword's blade. Evil has Vinetop. The Golden Thread breaks. We must make ready for war. The Council of Chiefs convenes."

Men beat their chests and women wailed laments. Daggers were stabbed into tables.

"We will convey Argolis and Mars to safe land. Eat all of you, while I decide their rewards."

Girls and young men rushed in from outside where the cook fires were. They brought food and drink. Once Lea sat the feast began. The room's men and women began talking and eating all at once. But Mars ate little and said less as his unanswered hoped chewed his guts. Two hours passed before the feast slowed.

Pipes were lit and the tables were already cleared when Lea spoke to Mars and Argolis saying, "It is our custom to give gifts after the meal. I'll hear your requests. Whatever is within my wisdom or wealth is yours. Before you ask consider that none know what will befall your race after the Age. You may stand the tides or be drowned. What is your foremost need? Argolis will ask first as 'the least is first.' Argolis with less gave most."

"Your pardon, Queen Lea, I'm just a simple dragon. I want nothing but to get home. Highborn dragons should go first anyway."

"Argolis, ask her." Mars said. "The laws of Neff don't matter, not anymore, not here."

Argolis let out a jet of pink smoke—his crown feathers parted in disarray.

"Well, then, I'd like to fly again, but that will come in time. I mean my wings are growing and all. I'd like to help them dragons what lost their wings. I mean what's a dragon what can't fly?"

"Dear, dear Argolis," Lea said, "You have your wish. I need not give magic fore magic dwells within you always—the heart keeps magic, not wings. That is what will heal them."

Lea tossed back her hair and laughed.

"I will tell you this secret. Wings are not the source of dragon magic. Argolis, you need nothing but inner Light. Love is the Light and the Light is magic. Believe and you will fly."

"You mean I could-a done it all along?"

"I do."

"If that don't beat all, I mean no wonder I didn't bust that narrow path or ground Mars when he carried me. I had no weight! Now, if that don't beat all! I got to go tell them sad dragons at Black Bill's camp."

"And so you will, nothing can stop you."

Argolis got up from the table and went directly outside. With a mighty running jump he was airborne. Mars heard Argolis sing songs of joy as he flew above the camp.

A shout went up from all the children outside as Argolis circled above. The people at table banged copper mugs and shouted 'here, here!'

"You need not ask," Lea said, "I know what you want Mars. Belly-fire is natural, not magical. I cannot replace destroyed organs. Hear this wisdom and have hope. Magic brings Golden-Fire, but, not for war-craft. Fix your heart and the body will then follow. When you breathe Golden-Fire you will be a true Dragon Lord and you will then heal naturally."

Mars's crown went low. His shoulders slumped. His scales dulled. There was no easy road and Mars cried, "Everything Draco taught was wrong! How sad I followed him!"

"No, your expectations were wrong. Draco lost his way yet even he taught the Light. You took from him only what you thought best for fighting. Seek the Lighted Way. It is in all dragons, even Emerald. Overturn your heart then you will have fire."

"I don't understand. I was born to be Warlord—I can't fight without fire. How can I bring peace without fire! This makes no sense. Fireless, I'm not worthy of respect."

Mars knotted his tail to bash the floor but did not raise his tail.

"Practice peace in heart and deed and win respect." Lea said. "Spread the Word of Light and become worthy. Show yourself approved!"

Mars thought in silence for a time while everyone ate deserts. Lea took a small seed cake and a mug of black tea from a serving girl. She ate casually while Mars struggled to understand her words.

This is what Mother had taught, too. How foolish to resist Mother's teaching.

Clearer sight fell on Mars like cold rain—thoughts and visions rushed into his mind. Even Draco spoke Light Lore. Draco taught Mars the Silence of the Ravens as they flew the heights together. Did not Draco tell the tale of the Dwarf Wars as they flew over the Black Forest? He even spoke of the Garden of Neff with a tear under his eye. The truth was always there. Draco and Mother traveled in the same direction but by different paths.

Mars remembered a small part of his Tapestry vision: a man-made basket woven of gold and textiles was placed over him. It dimmed his hue. And an elf said, 'Whereas dragons once kept men, men will sway dragons.'

I cannot be a captive any longer.

Mars knew not how he would live but he would not live by his former hopes. No man would ever weave his mane with the clutter that Draco wore.

No iron will weight my neck!

"I will teach the lore," Mars said. "Cut off my warrior's mane. I'll go as the Sages and unicorns go. I will not seek glory. I will go to the frontiers and speak peace."

"The turning of your heart has begun." Lea said. "I will give you a magic gift. You may restore the life of one person that is struck down. You will raise the dead but once. Cut your mane and receive my gift."

"How will I know when to use it," Mars asked?

"Your heart will know." She said. "Let not your mind decide."

Mars took an eating dagger from the table and went outside. He hailed Argolis from the sky. Whereupon landing, Mars handed over the knife and had Argolis cut off his hair. Argolis mane had grown while on the road so Mars cut his as well. The country dragon never did like it long.

"Never will tokens of war adorn my locks," Mars said. "I will not fight save for the defense of innocents."

"That's good country wisdom, Sir. It's like they say, 'treat them others like you wants them treating you.'"

Mars smelled the air. There was still food to be had. With the weight of his worry no longer filling his stomach Mars felt hungry.

"Court-wise dragons have no wisdom greater than a country dragon's lore," Mars said, "One other saying I've heard country dragons speak is worth repeating now."

"What saying is that," Argolis asked?

"'Lets eat while the eating is good!'"

Together they reentered the feast.

FORTY NINE

Rogsin Fires Emerald

Emerald looked over the nearly finished airship drawings that were spread over his workshop table and licked his snout with pleasure. A picture of winged ores, dragon tail-like rudder and cloth sails filled the page.

"Bear Claw, come and see this," Emerald said. "Even Starmere would admit my genius."

Bear Claw remained in the hall arms over chest not willing to enter any place where weapons were wrought. Emerald needed only to illustrate how to control the airship on the wind to finish the design but he could not bring himself to draw the rigging detail.

I'm not getting paid well enough for such wizardry as this.

But payment was not what stopped Emerald; there was an odd gnawing in his gut that he could not account for. Emerald nervously fingered the opened scroll that Rogsin demanded and would soon come for. Rogsin's flying ships required one thousand wings to move his troops. Emerald could not bring himself to write down that calculation either.

This deal is out of control. Rogsin must take the wings of five hundred dragons. How many innocent dragons will pay wings?

A pang of grief overcame Emerald. His wings shuttered and his bile gurgled.

Rogsin already has the model and so the basic concept.

Emerald's throat constricted as he choked-back bile. He never thought it was possible—he agreed with the Light Lore that forever attacked his logic. The same Light he beat down with the hammer of his pride all these years now agreed with his empirical judgments. All in all, his guts and mind screamed together; *Flee from Rogsin!*

"Don't let it get to you old boy, stay the course! Glory will be yours."

His words drove the Light back, but only for a moment. The pit of Emerald's stomach reacted with hurt. Emerald invented what Rogsin desired—but the cost was too high. Emerald got news of a great many lost wings—dragons leaving their homes hiding in fear—Outland sheriffs preying on hapless dragons. *'Dragons don't kill dragons,'* echoed in his mind.

"Nor do we cause unjust harm."

When Emerald agreed to design the King's machines, he did not expect Rogsin to go about collecting wings in this accelerated fashion. Rogsin's obsession would destroy the kingdom's wealth. How long before all dragons flee their fields and industries? Rogsin demanded ships capable of carrying a great force. It would take one hundred years to gather so many wings, even unjustly. But Rogsin doesn't like to wait.

Rogsin makes ready to march next spring. How can this be?

No, the news Emerald's spies brought did not bode well at all. Rogsin promised fame and fortune and the highest dragon seat, but would he be true to his word? Finally, Emerald would better Draco,true. The thought tasted good in his mouth. And then again, what good is the Dragon Seat without dragons to rule?

"You know, Bear Claw," Emerald called, "I only want my long deserved due."

"All that is due is what is earned well.' Bear Claw quoted.

Emerald came out into the main tunnel, his crown feathers ruffled.

"Don't quote scripture to me Bear Claw. Speak plainly or speak not at all."

"As you wish—Rogsin will pay but with treachery fore he pays in like kind. Deceivers receive deceit."

Bear Claw's words struck Emerald like a clapper on a bell and his legs felt weak. Emerald decided it was time to leave. Rogsin was due the next day.

"Prepare my bags for a long flight, I have business with the Sages," Emerald lied.

"By the smell on the air—Rogsin comes now. His stink was on the wind all morning. He is close to hand." Bare Claw said. "It is too late."

Emerald and Bear Claw moved to the landing and looked out over the mountains. It was a fine summer day, quite warm for so high a place. Far below the foliage was lush. The snow was gone excepting the mountain peaks. All around the burial caves that were cut into the mountain faces were easily discernible. Rogsin was not far off. The sight broke Emerald's hope of escape. Rogsin, two Outland men with crossbows and a dwarf flew toward him in a lake-boat under sail. Under sail! Opened dragon's wings were mounted on the gunnels. Rogsin had copied his model!

"He cheated," Emerald said, "We had a deal."

"I take my leave," Bear Claw said. "You should never have given Rogsin a path-stone."

Bear Claw slipped over the landing's edge and vanished. Emerald thought to take flight but the dragon boat came on fast. The men trained their crossbows on Emerald. They were in range. They could catch him on the wing.

I mustn't show myself weak.

Emerald controlled his crown and rushed back into his liar. His plan was still the better. Rogsin's boat was crude. He quickly removed his scrolls and placed them in a store room hid by magic. He had improved his traps and covers when Mars was there. Rogsin would never find his secrets.

I must keep my advantage.

Rogsin and a guard found Emerald in his workshop; his best books already well hid. Emerald's writing implements, known parchments and small tools, common enough, remained. The guard came ready for battle, a dagger in his belt, a dwarf's ax in one hand and a crossbow slung on his back. Rogsin was dressed for court but he held a new crossbow finer made than Emerald's prototype. Rogsin stroked the release bar like a pet snake.

"I've come to see what you have for me, Rogsin said, "You are late with your promises. My informants tell me your efforts wane. What of it? I see no industry here."

He is searching me out, I cannot show my hand. Go careful, he casts a net.

"The invention process is fraught with tests and small steps. I will surly complete the airship's plans long before you move on the Steppes."

"As you no doubt saw," Rogsin said, "I have mastered the sky boat. That is not of which I speak. I want the ballista; the weapon you spoke of that can launch greater bolts a further distance than this toy."

I have not even begun working on it!

Rogsin held up his crossbow in one hand, his finger along the release bar. Rogsin improved Emerald's model with a thicker bow and better twine—a more powerful device, indeed, but still a limited range. Emerald's ballista would be a hundred times more powerful and kill at ten times the distance.

What use could Rogsin have for it?

A dark realization formed in Emerald's mind. Rogsin would destroy the Estates. The ballista will topple walls. Boarder disputes were fought hand to hand, properties were never laid ruin—it was a waste. With dragons gone, and the Outlands in Rogsin's charm pocket, Emerald's greatest engine was the perfect tool to impose absolute power.

"The Steppes have no forts." Emerald whispered.

"What's that," Rogsin asked?

"I have not yet begun to make it," Emerald said, "I saw no need for it, it was just an idea. Even so; you cannot mobilize until next spring. I will design it over the winter. There is time."

"No, time is nigh." Rogsin said with a twisted grin. "I need it now and as you don't have it, I have no more use of you."

"Will you destroy your own properties and peoples?!" Emerald cried.

"I think not, unless they refuse me. I want it for the Auction. Such a thing would make short work of you dragons."

Rogsin pointed the crossbow at Emerald."This and the like will have to do."

Emerald stepped backward. Rogsin pressed the bar. There was a great twang and the bolt flew. Emerald looked down and saw it was buried up to its feathers in his chest. Emerald was shot in the center of his Crest.

A sickly realization shook Emerald as he slumped to the ground—all he had worked for, all his hopes, had come to naught. Emerald rolled half a turn, and lay on his side facing his murderer. Rogsin laughed as Emerald gasped in pain. Emerald touched the shaft with his hand. It was a grave blow. His heart was stuck yet still passed blood.

I don't have long.

Emerald laid down his head. The room became darker and the wizard saw nothing but the dirty sandaled feet of the Outlander and his own reflection in Rogsin's polished boots. Emerald watched as his eyes dimmed from bright to pale green.

"Take his wings," the guard asked?

"No," Rogsin answered, "Let his wings and bones lay among the dead he defiled. His soul will never join the stars while his wings remain here. Let him rot."

"You betrayer," Emerald hasped spitting blood.

"Now that is funny. Let me mint a new saying in your honor—it takes one to know one."

The voice of another man called saying there was a dragon and rider in the distance. The guard reported that he had found nothing of value in his search.

You will not have my best.

"Make ready to sail," Rogsin ordered. "We'll top the peak and drop below the far side out of sight. I won't expose my ship."

With that Rogsin and his man departed. Emerald heard Rogsin's merry gait eco as they quickly walked away. The steps faded as did Emerald's strength. The cold stone floor seemed to grow hot although this floor never warmed.

The end is near.

Emerald closed his eyes never expecting to see another living being. His blood and life-remembered mixed together and poured from his heart with each beat. He listened to this ragged drumming within as it spilled the errors of his life onto the floor like draining a river of mud. His life all at once became as pictures within the Tapestry of Neff. His mind became clearer; the desire for vengeance and retort burned away with a golden fire. And so, the Light filled him.

"I was…a…fool…forgive me."

Emerald prayed the Light that the Dragon whom approached was Draco and that he lived long enough to make peace with his brother.

FIFTY

Emerald's Salvation

Early that morning Onyx and Praxis peered from the tower's landing. The tower edged Vinetop so the fall was over three hundred feet to the plain. The training saddle that Walters had smuggled from the stores did not fit well adding to Praxis's unease. It was made for a young bulky male not a sleek female. Onyx made new strap-holes and choked the harness as best she could. Praxis had never carried such an odd thing on her back. It weighted more than any flight bag she had wore before.

"Don't know if I can do this," Praxis said.

"I am confident. You'll do fine," Onyx said. "Did not Boomax teach you flying a rider?"

"I have yet to actually host a rider. And Onyx, you have no training at all. You've only sat upon Draco as a child. This is no child's game."

"We must fly or else we'll never know whatever Emerald may tell us. I'm for this adventure."

Onyx's face was grim like when she spared. However, her eyes held mirth, too.

At least one of us is having fun!

"You are always for adventure," Praxis said, "and so, forever in trouble."

"What a strange sight we'll make," Onyx said tossing back her hair with a laugh, "A girl rides a female dragon! Ha, that's ripe for a silly country song. Lighten your heart, this will be fun."

"Perhaps we'll laugh all the way to the ground," Praxis said, trying her best to sound as well humored.

"Time is nigh," Onyx said, "No saying when Rogsin will return. Let us fly!"

Onyx bowed and spoke the traditional permissions with due reverence which pleased Praxis. *Onyx must have learned it from Boomax.* Praxis prayed the Light she too learned as well from him. Onyx mounted and Praxis felt better—the rider weighted little. Then a new worry sprang forth as Praxis readied to leap.

"You must hold tight, once I jump we'll fall fast gaining speed until I open my wings full—you might blow right off."

"I've ridden war horses twice your size and they and I were not friends. Let us fly!"

Praxis jumped and pulled up expertly only to fly as awkwardly as a yearling. Her wings and tail beat out of time as she tried to find balance. Dragons and riders were a common sight, and so not worth a closer look, unless flying erratically. Unstable flights caused alarm and bespoke a hurt rider or steed. Yet, this early, only the farmers were out and their eyes were on the ground.

Onyx rode like a practiced rider—she crouched when streamlining and sat full upright when sail was needed. Although Praxis struggled Onyx was no hindrance. By the time they reached Singing Rocks Road Praxis had control. She flew smoothly along the road and with pleasure—it was good to be on the wing—until they reached the boarder of Vineland.

"This is Rock Point where Mars was shot," Praxis said. "Wish I'd seen the shooter's face. He deserves punishment."

"Curse the shooter. May he fall low," Onyx shouted into the wind.

There they changed course and followed the edge of the Neff swamp north-east. Walters had instructed them on the route's landmarks. He had gone to and fro many times in the last days of Hammond. The up-drafts along the swamps edge made for easy travel. Hot air gave lift and the winds blew right so Praxis didn't need the High Stream.

The distance to Emerald was two hundred miles. Due to good wind it only took three hours. As they skirted the low hills of the Forbidden Mountains Praxis closed both sets of her clear eye lids against the bugs. The cold wet wind from above met the hot dryer air from below and so insects were in the band seeking water droplets. Praxis's sharp eyes so guarded did not see what Onyx spied.

Onyx spoke to her ear saying, "Some flying thing just went over that mountain. Not an Iron Skin or a dragon. Open your lids, sister."

Praxis did not see it, but she did see her destination. It was just as Walters had described. There was a series of three mountain peaks of about the same height standing in a line like solders at attention. If Onyx had not pointed where the flyer went, Praxis may not have found Emerald's cave. Caves were everywhere and all alike and each with a stone landing protruding from the mountains' sides. Emerald's particular landing was only one among many. Praxis noticed telltale stacked firewood at one cave entry. On closer examination she saw a fire-pit surrounded by charred stones—easily missed against gray mountains. The fire-pit smoldered with terse white smoke.

"The dead don't use fire," Praxis said pointing out the spot.

Onyx leaned forward and looked where Praxis instructed while holding the path stone Walters had given them. Such a lesser stone only gave direction while in close: Now, it shone brightly.

"It's Emerald's," Onyx said. "Are we expected?"

"Why burn hard-gotten wood in the open," Praxis asked? "Emerald is frugal. It's a signal-fire—lit hours ago. Why waste wood?"

Praxis saw a man moving down the mountain head first far below the landing—only Inowise descended like that. Praxis took it a good omen. The fire must have been lit for the Inowise and so they stumbled onto confirmation of Emerald's location. Praxis pointed to the man below.

"It was for him, not us," Praxis said. "Walters mentioned Bear Claw's visits."

Praxis circled once around as was the custom for a friendly landing before touch-down. Unlike the custom there was no greeter waiting. Onyx dismounted quickly and searched the landing for signs.

"This is the place," Onyx said, "There are footprints, men and dragon. Where is he? What does your nose tell?"

Praxis took a drought of air and said. "It is his smell, and the smell of his industry is here…That is odd…dragon's blood…wet blood…what is this?"

"Let's go," Onyx said. "Emerald works for Vinetop. Emerald must have taken up cutting wings for Rogsin. The wizard will give us nothing. He'll expose us."

"Fear is upon me," Praxis said. "My mind beseeches leaving. Yet my heart draws me hither.

Praxis pointed to the open cave door with her tail saying, "A healer runs to dragon's blood not away from it. Let us enter."

They proceeded slowly. Although torches were lit they did not trust the way. Many side tunnels and doors were there and despite Walter's descriptions, they knew little of the place. There was no choice but for Praxis to follow the scent. As such the smell of lamp oil, mental working, and potions mixed with living blood led them to Emerald's workshop.

They found him lying in a pool of sticky gore. Emerald's blood was drying.

"He's dead!" Onyx cried.

"No, he yet lives, but just barely. He still bleeds." Praxis said. "Unlatch the medical kit from my saddle."

Praxis immediately set to work. Emerald's shelves were well stocked with the herbs of healing. But there was nothing she could do about the bolt. It was a far worse wound than any wound she had seen before. Pulling it out would cleave his heart asunder. It was the same type of barb that had done Mars wrong. Praxis, seeing the futility, slowed her efforts.

"He is done, let him go." Onyx said. "No creature survives such a sting."

"I must awaken him." Praxis said. "We've come for his words. I mean to hear them. Whoever shot him likely shot Mars! This we must know."

Praxis mixed a potion and blew it down Emerald's throat with a long reed. He woke coughing blood. His eyes opened slowly and came clear although his Light was greatly faded. He smiled and croaked, "I am not lost."

"We've not come to save you," Onyx said coldly, "We come for answers. Tell of the coming days. Tell us. Redeem yourself, and Praxis will heal you."

"Too late…The brink is…it is black beneath me."

I cannot preserve his life. Healers mend souls as well. I must try.

Emerald wheezed and his breathing became shallower. He lifted his head with great effort. Blood and bile drooled from his mouth as he came up onto one elbow thus tearing his wound. Emerald cried out in pain. Praxis turned away and took up a pain remedy. She faced Emerald with great pity whereupon his eyes flashed golden light and her heart softened toward him.

"This will ease your passing," Praxis said.

"Only truth will do that," Emerald said. "Hear me…find me deserving and bring my wings outside…that...I may join our fathers. I will answer all."

"No dragon deserves this," Onyx said. "I will release your spirit."

"Said by the true Queen…wise you are," Emerald said his voice low but clear. "You're the heir—Hammond's last child. Rogsin is half blood."

"How do you know," Onyx asked?

"I gave Mordune…the potion…Your mother did no wrong…She saw Hammond in her mind…" Blood poured out but Emerald continued. "Tricked by the seduction spell, same I used…on Penelope… Mars is my son."

Outrage welled up in Praxis and she blew a jet of black smoke into the ceiling releasing her anger. Yet, Praxis would not forgo her healer's duty. Rather she invited the pity of Emerald's ruin into her heart and so over-wrote her anger.

"What of Rogsin," Praxis asked. "What will he do?"

"He will destroy all dragons. I just learned…so he shot me…with my own invention…Rogsin will attack I know not when…for hate…machines wrought of dragon's wings is not what he's after. He cuts wings…to ground… ambush…"

Emerald spate a clot of blood onto the floor and much coughing ensued—his eyes went from pale green to gold and fire breath came forth as he spewed.

Magic Fire, he has no natural fire. His soul is healing.

Praxis and Onyx waited for him to settle. Praxis trusted his words for the first time; the Light was within him, his eyes and fire shown gold.

"He'll kill Mars—he's sent hunters…Warn the dragons...save my son."

Emerald then laid his head down and rasped his last breath whereupon the green Crest of Neff on Emerald's breast turned golden and shone brightly. Emerald's body crumbled into dust leaving naught but his wings and a previously hidden Dragon's Gold dagger.

"It is the twin of Rogsin's dagger, one for good one for ill." Onyx said picking it up.

Onyx held up the dagger saying the warrior's Oath of Promise by swearing to use it against the decease's enemies.

Then Praxis and Onyx carried Emerald's wings to the landing while chanting the death blessing. Praxis led Onyx to the edge of the landing and let the wings go. Emerald's wings floated upward and disappeared into the sun.

"He is redeemed," Praxis said. "I will tell his lore."

The travelers stayed that night to morn his passing as tradition allowed not caring that they would be missed and as such likely caught. They camped on Emerald's landing without a fire as was fitting. That night a new star appeared in the dragon constellation proper. Only important dragon's rested within the body of the Sky Dragon while other dragon spirits gathered around it. The dragon's eye was still left, the last great star needed to complete the constellation and fulfill the prophecy of the Dragon Age's ending. Praxis prayed that the next dragon-star would not be Mars's.

A great dragon must die, and soon.

FIFTY ONE

Trapped in the Tower

Praxis and Onyx took wing at dawn with vain hope that they were not missed. It was the third hour past dawn when they arrived above Vinetop. Praxis's hopes were dashed even before landing. On approached to the tower she smelled Rogsin's scent fresh in the air.

"He is waiting," Praxis warned Onyx.

"Time to kill that snake," Onyx said. "I have Emerald's dagger."

Although unnerved by Rogsin presence, and the thought of bloodshed, Praxis managed a solid landing. The door of their cell was wide open and cold air poured through. Onyx dismounted with her newfound dagger in hand. Onyx moved to the door with her knife high and ready to stab the first person that entered.

"What are you doing," hissed Praxis "You aren't really doing it!"

"Let Rogsin taste what he dishes, steel for steel." Onyx's voice was hard as iron.

Footsteps then pounded up the stairs and Onyx braced for ambush. But the footfalls were heavy—not the patter of Rogsin's feet. Before Praxis could cry a warning, Robmere burst through the door with terrified eyes and empty hands. Onyx hacked once in the air pulling her thrust while backing away. She barely missed Robmere's neck.

"You run block for that, that monster." Onyx said, "I shouldn't have pulled my strike."

"Orders, I had to," Robmere said and cast his eyes on the floor.

"Oh Robmere, how could you." Onyx's voice wavered.

Onyx's red cheeks turned white and she crumpled to the floor, her vigor was lost.

"I cannot harm Vinetop's guards." Onyx whispered. "They are…kin of my heart."

She loved them as family, Praxis knew. But Onyx loved Robmere not as a brother. Robmere so stern-faced on the field—his face was now racked with confusion and fear.

His weapon sheathes were empty, he wore no mail. He likewise fell to his knees and took her face in his hands saying, "I am heartily sorry."

"I forgive you Robmere." Onyx said.

"How touching," came Rogsin's voice sailing on the cold air from below.

Two Dwarfs clad in full armor plowed over Robmere. They stood back-to-back with axes raised ready to chop. Onyx could do nothing. The Dwarfs had Robmere underfoot and he was helpless.

'Warn the dragons,' Emerald's last words rang in Praxis's mind. Thus, Praxis moved to take flight. But a Dwarf was quickly upon her. She dared not fly. Quarters were tight, fire would not do and she was no fighter besides.

Two Outland men rushed through the door with Rogsin behind. Onyx kneeling on the floor flashed her dagger and cut an Outlander's leg—his calf gushed terribly. But the man was hard-bitten and bore down with his bloody leg stepping on Onyx's knife hand. The fight was over.

"Well then, I see my betrothed is not so much the warrior she thinks." Rogsin said his tone amused. "I can't trust you. Yet, I've learned my fears regarding you were for naught, you are no threat."

The injured guard wiped his blood from Onyx's dagger and handed it to Rogsin. Rogsin looked the knife over tracing the blade and handle with his finger.

"Last I saw this it was in Emeralds' possession. You know my justice, no doubt. The bird is out of the coop. Pity, the Auction is in three days and you'll miss the fun. I will contain you here."

Onyx sprang to her feet and screamed, "You are no king, impostor. You trader!"

She spat in Rogsin's face.

Rogsin's man backhanded her knocking her to the ground. Onyx's lip was spilt. She quickly stood spitting blood and faced her attacker. She spat again and her blood spattered the man's beard. He did not flinch.

"Have respect for the King," the Outlander demanded raising his hand to strike her again.

"Enough," Rogsin said. "Robmere, run, get the masons; have them stone that window shut. The rest of you watch them. Any trouble, take her wings."

Robmere leapt to his feet and ran off. Rogsin laughed and followed at his ease. By midday the masons had closed the landing and the guards departed. Only a small square window remained. There was no good light save the lamps. Praxis already missed the open air. Her loss was made worse by an old crow landing on the new sill because he was free. Praxis thought of the ravens, too—no doubt driven off by the clamor. At least they two were still alive.

"How will we warn the dragons? The ravens have gone and we are trapped." Praxis said.

"What would we tell them? We don't know where Rogsin will strike. That crossbow is powerful but short ranged. Rogsin needs an ambush, but how, where, when?"

The old crow squawked and bounced its head rapidly up and down as crows will when they wished to speak. Praxis didn't pay it any heed. Crows were known for half truths and double speak. Even other birds, ravens especially, often drove them off.

But Onyx looked on it kindly and said. "The ravens tolerate this star-headed crow." Onyx went before it and bowed. "Speak, you are welcome here. Tell me your name."

"Merilbe calls me friend, my bird-name you could not pronounce."

"Merilbe," Onyx said. "He disappeared on the day he called me Queen. There are roomers that he lives. I've heard a raven say as much, but ravens can't be trusted in theses times. "No, if Merilbe were alive he would act. He must be dead."

"He is not—he is imprisoned in this tower."

"How do you know this," Praxis demanded. "What crow trick is this?"

"Hush," Onyx said quietly, "Let him talk. He is not like other crows."

"Quiet right," The crow said. "I am not like my kin. The Wizard and I are associates. I am his eyes on the lands. Merilbe bid me say the name he called you as a child and know I speak truly. He named you Dragon-Mort. He told you, you will dragon-ride."

"He is right, Merilbe said it."

"The courts were open then, any crow could have seen or heard that," Praxis said. "I don't trust him. He could be with Rogsin. Rogsin has spies everywhere."

"I will hear you," Onyx said.

"Rogsin will attack the dragons at Auction as many will gather unready for war. Merilbe sends me for Mars and to beseech Roecon and Penelope to warn dragons. Time is short. I must fly."

"I saw no army," Praxis said. "How can this be?"

"Look to the wood beyond the low hills. They gather on the far side of the fairgrounds under the cover of trees in the King's preserve."

The crow tuned and spread his wings. Praxis called for him to halt and bent her neck to him. She spoke to the crow in a low voice so none but he would hear saying."Tell Mars this or he will not believe you. On the day we parted, I promised him my love fire or naught. Tell him that and I love him still."

With that the crow bobbed his head agreeably and took off. She prayed the Light the crow would find his way. Then the clamor of men echoed from the walls. A captain, it was not Boomax, ordered, "Shoot the ravens!" Rocks and arrows pilfered the tower roof. The birds cawed and screeched and fled. No birds were heard upon the roofs thereafter.

"Rogsin is not taking any chances," Onyx said, "He drives the ravens off. So goes our hope of sending word."

Praxis, filled with hurt and longing, and regret on the telling of her love-promise to the crow, thrashed her tail up and down venting fear and frustration.

I so nimble a dragon, a swift flyer, I could give aid.

But she was caged and helpless. Her people were in danger with nothing more than an old crow to save them. Worry and panic rose up in her.

"I'm useless. I can't stand it!" Praxis cried.

Praxis balled her tail and bashed the floor. A large chunk of stone flew and smashed the wall with killing force. The destruction scared Praxis—she did not know her tail was so powerful. Only male fighters were trained to use it and only sparingly fore a dragon warrior's tail was terrible. Praxis suddenly realized her tail was just as deadly although she would never hurt any living thing. Praxis slumped to the floor exhaling black smoke, her crown feathers low. A new sadness filled her heart.

A healer cures, not kills. Curse my tail!

Onyx's face shown well pleased although that dashed stone nearly struck her. Onyx bent and examined the floor. She traced the divot with her fingers and smiled.

"This stone is very hard," Onyx said, "That was a deadly blow."

"I can't…I can't bring it against men. Beat down the door, and I'll have to fight. I can't…I won't," Praxis cried.

"This stone is not alive," Onyx said. "I have an idea. We will fly again.

FIFTY TWO

The Borderline Inn

On the morning after the week long feast, as summer waned, Mars and Argolis bid Lea and her people farewell. A compliment of unicorns became winged horses and flew the dragons across the Wheatland's to the White Cliffs. Mars and Argolis descended from the steppes and landed just beyond the north-west frontier. Their guides did not follow because the curse of Neff would impinge their magic. Rather, they turned into eagles and raced back the way they had come.

Mars and Argolis landed in a fair wilderness field lying within an old forest. They camped two nights in sight of the cliffs. Argolis, wanting to fly every possible chance, surveyed the lands from above and so they plotted their course. Crude man-built frontier roads and homesteads were near. And so they walked this land for two weeks finding woodsy people and preaching the lore of Light to them that would hear. Some were dragons others human, many they found were hunters, mushroom gatherers or woodsman not gathering their trade goods but seeking staves for pikes and arrows as the market for such things had increased of late, so it was said. Pressing further from the Cliffs, they passed larger farming homesteads and trappers camps as they moved inland toward the Kingdom proper.

Mars dulled his hue and wore the woolen hooded cape Lea had given him. Like the story tellers of old, Mars traveled as a beggar trading stories for food. Everywhere the people greeted them well and received the Lore of Mars with open ears, but rugged hearers always took heart-medicine with salt. In the wilds trust untested wasn't practical.

Everyone enjoys stories. Yet, these folks don't take the message seriously.

"Redeeming fire won't come quickly, with so few hearers, and the hearers so doubtful, unfortunately, they're not much moved." Mars said as they walked an overgrown path. "This is hard ground for sowing ideas. Yet, I care less now. I like this raw country—it feels homely.

"'Home's where your heart is,'" Argolis quoted. "This here's where Black Bill comes from. Dragons hereabout are hatched local, as Bill told it. They get no Rookery education; highborn fertilizer can't seep in, if you take my meaning. But, good folks all around, I'd say."

"They are kindly," Mars agreed, "Not thick-headed like the highborn say."

They came upon a fork in the road, if a road is what this forest path was, and turned left for no reason other than the call for going that way in Mars' heart.

"Common sense smarts," Argolis said, "makes them leery."

In this part of the world every dragon had traces of gold within their colors—when Mars let slip his color there was no alarm but Mars kept his hue hidden as Lea had advised, 'The way of your healing is humility.' Word got around of Mars's travels so folks took to calling Mars the Neff Monk, but they often laughed at the Monk's peace-wisdom, and for good reason. Away from Vineland peace was fleeting. Mars learned that boarder wars, robbers, outcasts and Outlander raids were common and more so since Hammond died. This place was called the Wild West for good reasons.

He and Argolis stayed to the safer footpaths as the locals did and avoided wagon roads. Argolis took to the air less as more and more wingless dragons hurrying away from the Kingdom and into the deep forest appeared. The wingless would not speak of their condition, due their shame, or tell Mars any meaningful news of Vineland. The local dragons avoided the wingless ones altogether as their hospitality stopped short at the sight of cut off wings.

"Let's find out why inland dragons are fleeing into the wilds," Mars said on the third week. "We'll make for the trader's outpost; they say it's a small town."

As they traveled south the trail became wider, wagon ruts appeared, and fewer woodsy locals were seen. Late that day they came to the crossroads.

"Lay low," Mars said. "The outpost is near. Rogsin's Outland sheriffs are there—rumor has it they've been shooting down flying dragons."

"I could do without an arrow in me eye," Argolis said.

They entered the fort-town called Tree Branch where more trade roads met, one road to the Steppes, two roads were Estates border roads, and the Wilderness Road they tread converged there along with lesser paths. The fort was like Back Bill's camp but larger and well kept. Outside the wooden pole stockade were a dozen moss-covered stone buildings. The largest was a slate-roofed inn called the Borderline. The door was large enough for dragons—a good sign—this place accommodated dragons and men together. The two approached the door with good cheer.

"Strange," Mars said, "I neither smell nor see any dragons."

"Don't look so good. I mean them sheriffs up on the wall been looking us over all steel eyed. I don't like it."

"I'm for changing hearts, Argolis. Let us go inside and see what good we may do." Mars said. "People from everywhere gather here. Let's give wisdom and get news."

They entered a large foyer. The innkeeper, a thin, bald, jittery man greeted them with halting speech and shifting eyes. He led them into the dark hall all the while chattering, "Oh dear, oh my, oh bother." Yet the inn was a comfortable place. A huge hearth was lit and burning apple wood. There was an iron pot over the fire and meat on smoking racks above the kettle. *Taters and sheep stew by the smell.*

"This way yes, this way, it's been some time since dragons come in—with them wing hunters about, dragons…oh dear. I like dragons. They eat their fill. Dragon are good for business, like I like to say. They've gone to the fair I hear, the Auction they call it, the games, yes, the games are three days off."

The innkeeper stopped to pull empty mugs off a table. "So many have gone away—the King calls all dragons, you know. What are you doing here, might I ask? I mean no harm, just curious. I've food and drink if you got money. You got money? I'll take trade…"

"I got money," Argolis interrupted cutting off the man's chatter.

The man sat Mars and Argolis at table suited for dragons. It was built low for reclining—considered a crude way to eat by high born dragons but favored by country and frontier dragons. Mars flopped down like he was born to it and took in the room by gawking like a country-bread dragon in town for the first time.

Outland solders wearing the sashes of Vinetop were there for a meal. A few locals sat nearby nervously fingering stoneware mugs while their eyes flitted between the Outlanders and two over-armed royal huntsmen. *Do they worry a fight might break?* Both hunters bore odd, strung weapons like what gnomes use. Their clothes were worn ragged by long exposure. Mars swallowed bile and deepened his color blacker.

"I've some money, also" Mars said, setting a few silver coins on the table. "We need good eats and I'll pay what I have. But I'll give you, and any that will hear me, good council, too, an added payment free. Is this not a place were a story-teller may speak freely?"

"Well freely, yes, well no, I mean…oh dear…I mean…some ale for you then? Say, you aren't that Monk I hear tell of, are you?"

"Stop you're babbling," The taller of the two huntsman said coming to the table with his mug in hand. "You're that Neff preacher I heard about, not the first or last I've seen in this miserable backwater."

The man took a deep swallow from his tankard. Mars realized he was drunk.

"Tell me—I seek a certain dragon, by the King's orders. You travel hereabout. Tell what you've seen and I'll not cut your wings. I see your brother has already lost his."

Mars humbly lowered his head, and bobbed shallow bows. The tall, thin Outlander relaxed. The plump one at the next table became attentive tracking his partner's words. Mars saw an opportunity for news.

Why are royal hunters so far from the King's reserve?

"Would you harm this crimeless beggar unjustly?" Mars asked.

"I harm who I chose, King Rogsin gives me leave."

Argolis rose onto his rear legs suddenly agitated. Black smoke billowed from his snout. The men around the room put hands on their weapons. Argolis winked at Mars.

Argolis thinks he is helping. This is not good.

"Now see here, this here's a holy dragon and a cripple, leave him alone, I mean picking on such a small dragon. You ought to be ashamed. He's harmless. He's got no fire. We're just simple missionaries."

"No fire, eh? No fire! I'm looking for one such as him. Morton, train your bow!"

"Oh bother," the Inn Keeper said scooping up the coins before running for the kitchen.

The standing huntsman drew his sword. A battle plan raced through Mars's mind. He had room to swing. Nobody expected tail-play. Mars's tail knotted on the thought. The dozen men there had no advantage and no chance…as long as Argolis stayed clear.

I don't want to kill anyone!

He would kill them all if he fought the way Draco had taught. Mars struggled to loosen his knotted tail.

Strike the crossbow man first and quick—easy range—if only my tail-fin would open.

A warmth filled Mars's breast beneath his hidden crest. It was not the heat of war-rage, rather he felt peaceful. Mars's tension abated and he determined to fight this battle with words first. He took a long breath.

"What is so unusual about a fire-cripple," Mars said, "Surly you have heard of my kin Black Bill. He was hatched without wings, I without fire and nearly as black. It is my family's trait, bad eggs, one after another."

"Aye, I've seen old Bill," said Morton, "This one is no golden warrior, look at him. I'm not wont to waste another bolt on the likes of him."

Motrin lowered his bow half to his waste. A puzzled look came to his face. His eyes went wide and he snapped the bow back to attention.

"Never heard of old Bill having any relatives," Morton said.

Argolis, sidelong to the shooter, suddenly thrashed his balled tail fin. Morton swung his bow one hundred and eighty degrees onto Argolis.

"Hold still," Mars cried. "Peace, peace I say!"

Swords weren't effective against scales, but that bow would kill Argolis. He was an easy target. Mars reared up making himself a decoy. The bowmen pivoted and aimed at Mars.

"Look at me," Mars said; throwing back his cape and pushing his breast forward. "I am not a golden."

The bowmen squinted at Mars and relaxed his grip on the stock.

"No," the tall hunter said, "Yet, you have the mark—the Crest of Neff, and all aglow. You are him, it is Mars. Shoot Morton, Shoot!"

Mars blazed golden with blinding light-force while Argolis slammed his tail into the stone floor. The bowman was knocked off his feet. The shot flew over Mars's head. Argolis's great tail swung again sending three onrushing soldiers flying. Another Outlander charged Argolis with a dragon-gold knife. The man stabbed, Argolis dodged and the dagger got jammed into Argolis's tail. Argolis roared fire and swung wildly.

Tables, men and chairs flew in every direction as the tall hunter ran for cover. The local men backed away not willing to fight while the Outlanders rallied for a charge. Morton regained his feet and worked to reload.

It was all like a dream remembered from Mars's vision. Mars did not join the fight; rather he stood entranced, his crest was hot as a brand and shone like a forge. Argolis furry was not wild or foolishness. In between his attackers launching furniture missiles, Argolis bashed the wall until it crumbled.

"Don't just stand there," Argolis shouted, "Let's fly!"

They ran outside. They were below the fort wall and took the air with a leap and a bound while long bowmen let loose. Arrows glanced off Mars's back. Many ripped the leather of his wings. No serious harm was done save the dagger stuck in Argolis's tail. Once out of bowshot range, Mars spoke as they flew.

"I, I just couldn't fight—Lea's words…I'm sorry…Almost got us killed."

"Even a sage has got to defend himself. I mean what good's wisdom if nobody hears it? Didn't kills nobody, anyhow, we just scared them."

"I'm glad for that," Mars said, "Let's set down…see about your wound."

"I'm fine, it's best we beat tail out of here!"

They flew thirty miles east until they were out of the forests country. They flew onward another twenty miles over grass and scrub hills avoiding the patchwork of low wooden dales between fields were shooters could hide. Here, in the scrubs, sheep and goat herders kept flocks and camped under the lee of spotty woods. Mars didn't care to dodge the slings or arrows of outraged shepherds either. The shadows of dragons on the wing upset flocks so they flew wide of them.

They continued until trees were fewer and the sweet grass gave way to rocky hills laden with thorny brush and gnarled oaks which dotting the land. It was the edge of the cured land. No camp fires were smelled nor sign of man or dragon seen. They flew until nothing but red deer and jack rabbits moved below.

Spires of rocks like dragons teeth appeared between ranges of low hills. A dirt road snaked around spire and hill. Satisfied that the lands were uninhabited, Mars sought a high place to land. No spire had good landings while the hilltops were too exposed. Mars finally spotted a mesa—its flat top was bathed in sunlight. Thus, they landed there. Below it there was a profusion of green foliage.

It is a fresh water spring.

"This is good," Mars said. "We'll see far from here. An Estate's road is in view—any that pass here will take that road." The two landed well and Mars popped his head up high. "From this lookout, we have cover and so hidden, time enough for mending you, Argolis."

"I'm glad your better sense hasn't deserted you," Argolis said as he plopped down on the ground with his tail in hand. "You had me wondering at the Borderline."

Mars slipped his flight bags off and brought out his spur kit. He took a close look at Argolis's tail. The knife did not tear any scale but wedged sideways between two. The blade did not go deep but rather ran painfully under the skin sidelong. Mars brought out a small tool like a blacksmith's tong.

"You may loose a scale or two." Mars said.

"What have you there; I don't like the look of it, oh no Sir." Argolis said with the voice of a fearful child. "Will it hurt!? What is that thing?"

"Scales are hard," Mars said. "Still, marching dragons oftentimes get burs under scales or between toes. A fighter can't be distracted. This is my spur-puller."

"I washed out early," Argolis said, "I never got a War Camper's kit."

Mars worked a wedge tool back and forth slowly spreading the scale, then with the tongs he gripped and wiggled the blade out. All the while brave Argolis gritted his teeth and squirmed like a human child with a splinter. Once removed, Mars handled the knife. It was Outland make and good quality steel, the blade was polished. "Good for trading," Mars said.

"How'd they get dragon gold for the tip?" Argolis said.

Mars threw the knife and it stuck into a bark-less dead tree. It glittered in the afternoon sun.

"Glad that's done," Argolis said, "Now I'm for vitals, only, we don't got any. That stew would have been the best meal we've seen in weeks. It's a pity—we lost the money too. Nothing for it, I suppose we'll have to gather roots and greens and catch us a rabbit or two, boils us a nice stew. Least ways we have fire wood up here." Argolis pointed at one of the dead trees.

"No fire," Mars said, "This is the highest place for miles. They'll spot us. We must lay low with sharp eyes. Those two aren't the only ones out for wings. Its grass seed and grubs for us."

"The eating's been cooked lately," Argolis said, "I don't know if my poor stomach will take kindly to so raw a turn, if you take my meaning...What say you bring out that honey jar?"

Mars had forgotten Begoth's crock. It only ever gave him a frustrating taste which only made him hunger for more. Argolis got the better of it then. Now they both could use some goodly fare.

"'Food a-plenty is best for healing.'" Mars quoted.

Mars searched the pockets of his bags, found the small jar and tossed it to Argolis who ate from it ten times the jar's size before stopping.

"Aren't you having none," Argolis said, "Plenty here, I mean, I've naught seen it so full."

"It doesn't favor me."

"A little taste is better than no taste," Argolis said as he passed the jar.

Mars flipped the top and found the jar full whereas before when he looked inside only a smattering was stuck on the sides. Mars dipped his finger and brought it to his mouth. It was sweater than any honey he'd had before. Mars dipped again and again and ate much. With each dip his breast warmed more and more until finally his golden hue burst forth like a watchmen's beacon.

"So much for laying low," Argolis said with a snort of blue fire. "Fortunes have changed."

Mars quickly set the jar aside and roused onto his hind legs and mustered himself for blowing fire—he huffed and yawned and strained his guts, but not even a puff of smoke appeared.

"The magic crock finds me worthier than before, yet not worthy enough." Mars said, spitting out the bile. "I'll take no more honey else it gives us away. I'm glowing like a fire fly!"

Mars slumped down next to Argolis with his back against the natural parapet wall that ringed the mesa's edge. The mesa's top was depressed and lowest at center. The hedged edges were like a low stone fence. Only Mars's head poked up into the open air where he reclined, so he flipped up the hood of his cape against the cool wind.

"Fall is coming," Mars said, "We'll miss the Games."

"All that fresh harvest food too," Argolis said glumly.

They sat in silence together until they heard the low voices of dragon long-speak on the wind. They listened intently for a time. The voices became louder but Mars couldn't make it out.

"If that don't beat all, it's the Brimstone brothers, they was in my pod. Why I'd know Dar and Puffin anywhere."

"I know them too," Mars said, 'They were first year guards when I was at the Rookery. They got sent to War Camp before I ran."

"Seems they got riders and they're walking patrol," Argolis said, "There taking in long-speak. No low born human knows it, them two is a rip."

"You've better ears than me, what are they saying Argolis? Where are they?"

"I'd say they're about two miles apart and heading toward each other and us. Seems they work for different Estates and their King's don't like each other. Puffin says he's the only war dragon left, just him and some court dragons in King Ackerman's Keep… Dar say's King Evens sent all but two dragon's to the games…something about… Puffin says his rider means to fight Dar's rider at Broken Tooth. I think that's where we are. Dar says his man wants revenge—both men are out for blood."

Mars turned his ears out of the wind and the conversation became clearer. Mars also heard agitated birds. He guessed they sensed danger. An old crow flew in from the south and landed with a squawk on the mesa's largest dead oak tree and the bird quieted. The crow tilted his head toward Mars then bobbed up and down for attention.

"Now that's a rip, if I hear right, Dar and Puffin's going to charge, stop short and toss their riders. No wonder them two was always in trouble, always playing they was."

"They aren't looking for me," Mars said. "The Neff Monk should speak with them."

"I smell vitals," Argolis said." Seems them dragon riders could use some wisdom—spare a bit of food for a good word."

"Outlanders, don't share," the Crow said. "You best keep hid and let them pass, there is little time, you must fly…"

"Hush, Crow, don't spoil it," Argolis said, "He knows what he's doing: Stupid crows."

"The riders don't sound like familiars," Mars said. "The Crow is right. The Brimstones carry Outlanders, hear that accent? They couldn't throw sanctified riders."

"Aye," said Argolis, "The Brimstones don't sound any too happy about them riders."

"That's right," said the Crow, "You know me Mars, listen. I've come with news you must hear. Belay your actions. You must listen."

"How do you know my name, speak Crow or suffer my flame."

"You have no flame," the Crow said, "Remember the Iron Skin attack, I was there. Did I point you wrong?"

"Don't bother with him, Sir, he's just a crow, they talk riddles. You can't trust them."

Mars's attention swung to the crow. It was that same old Crow—the Crow with the white star on his head. It was that same one which saved his life.

"Why should I heed you," Mars said keeping his voice low.

"I am Merilbe's helper; his magic has grown fit again for there is a dragon where he is prisoner. He speaks from me. Last we saw you, Merilbe was weak. Away from dragon magic, we could speak but little. Hear us Mars. We've news for you."

"How is it Merilbe speaks now? Where was he when I was lost?"

"Rogsin caged him in the tower. Praxis and Onyx are locked there, too. Rogsin will ambush the dragons at Auction…kill them all…he's called every dragon to assembly. This is no celebration. The Outlanders have the dragon-killer…Rogsin made many… You must warn Draco. Draco will not listen."

'Praxis is trapped! Save her,' screamed in Mars's heart. He wanted nothing more than to fly to her. But, was she truly in peril? A clever trickster would know his weakness—Emerald surely knew. Nothing could send him into danger quicker than love. Yet that was knowledge any trickster would use: Tricks within tricks within tricks.

"Answer me this. If she sent you, tell me what only Praxis and I know."

"She loves you, Mars. She loves you even without fire, so she said on the day you parted."

Mars's Crest flayed at the words. So busy with his quest Mars seldom thought of her due the desperate days of the past year. Her promise was reborn in his heart and his crest became hot. Praxis would not tell such a thing to any old crow, and she would not speak it openly so passing ears could hear.

"Sir Crow you speak true," Mars said, "We must warn the dragons—in country and court, not every dragon is at the fair! What of the frontiers?"

"You cannot save them all," Mars Hammertail, "Race to Draco's War Camp, there is little time. The war begins. I will spread the warning as I may."

"Begging your pardon, Mr. Crow, but near as I can tell there's four good dragons hereabout and four corners of the kingdom. I mean dragons aren't much for talking with crows, anyway. Mars should have a talk with them yonder dragon's, seeing as they are about to toss them Outland riders and all."

The Crow cocked his head toward Argolis. The star on his head shone.

"Yes, go to your brothers." The Crow said. "It is time—The Golden returns! It has begun. The raven's silence has ended—they will speak to dragons and I will send them forth. Do your part and I'll do mine!"

The Crow took wing and was gone.

Mars slipped over the back side of the mesa and glided to the ground landing with no more sound than a leaf. Mars made for the front side hidden by foliage where a great boulder overlooking the road below Broken Tooth rested. Mars's perch stood ten feet above the road. He jumped up onto it as Puffin and Dar charged.

The calamity of armored riders skidding in the dirt was his queue. Mars leaped from the rock with blazing gold—his Crest shown bright. Dar and Puffin's laughter stopped instantly and they bowed. The Outland riders, each in a heap on the road, covered in dust, jumped to their feet and ran away wildly in the directions that they had each come from leaving their swords and pikes behind.

As Mars commanded the dragons' rise small-winged Argolis floated down from above. No dragon save Mars had ever seen or heard of such a thing before; a dragon flying with nothing but baby-wings. Dar's tail shook while Puffin jetted purple smoke from his nose.

"Hear me," Mars said, "I am Mars. I am the Golden. I have work for you. Argolis will explain. I must fly. Heed him. He is your pod brother, but more, he is my Right Hand. What he tells you is true. Are you for dragons or are you for men?"

Argolis said as he landed. "What say you?"

Dar and Puffin looked at each other then at Mars and then again at Argolis.

"We were getting tired of guard duty anyways," Dar said.

"I'm for dragons," Puffin said. "Count us in."

Mars stopped his glow and the four dragons came together. Mars quickly told the story and gave instruction for Argolis and them to spread the word— all dragons must run for the Rookery.

"Should one of you fine Draco," Mars said. "Tell him to gather all able dragons to arms, tell of their peril. I'm shooting straight for Vinetop. I'll spring Praxis and warn the Auctioneers."

Mars, leaving Argolis to plan further, took the air and beat for Vinetop as fast as his wings would carry him praying the Light, the winds would bring him in time.

FIFTY THREE

The Games Begin

Draco came in from the northwest with six new War Camp graduates trailing behind. Draco banked until Vinetop's causeway was directly below him. The fairgrounds beyond appeared in the distance as he over flew the Great Hall. The fair was already in progress. Draco slowed and sharpened his eyes.

Fair Avenue ran due east two miles from the King's stables situated below the rear towers and ended at the gaming grounds. Along the road and at the playing field's entry were vendors. Dragons and humans sold every kind of wares and food. Large tents stood as makeshift pubs and inns. The grounds were already full of dragons and people—their camps established in the pastures surrounding the sports field. Estates banners and town or family standards fluttered in the warm breeze. Outland tribe standards were present but few tribesmen were seen.

Thousands were reported to be traveling throughout Vineland.

The doings of common folk did not concern Draco but he saw that dragons were many more than usual while people were fewer than before—strange indeed. Rogsin invited the Outlands this year. Draco expected great numbers of humans.

Where are the Outlanders?

Draco and his charges circled Vinetop three times as tradition called for. But tradition was not on Draco's mind. With each lap Draco viewed the playing field where parades, mock battles and contests of skill would take place next morning. By habit, Draco sought his gaming advantage.

The grass is tall, hard running for big dragons.

The main sports field was an artificial landscape. It was a great elliptical earthwork like a horse shoe that the Giants had made and for what reason no one knew. It served well as a theater. Mounds of earth were heaped eighty feet high around the playing field save the entry. The tops of the grassy mounds were flatted forty feet across while the Giant-built hillside sloped thirty five degrees.

Important dragons and men sat low on the stair-hills, as people called them, upon leveled wooden benches while lesser folks sat upon the hill's grass, the least of all people watched from the top. Draco supposed that was why Outlander banners were erected there.

'Least of the invited the further seated,' Penelope would say.

Like Sky Top, this place served well for flying games. The gauntlet racers flew between and around the tall standing stones that the Giants had set in place. The wind blew downward off the artificial hills keeping flyers down and thus from over shooting the course. These down-winds also made for a difficult takeoff. A big dragon with armor-clad rider could only gain the air by charging headlong toward the entry. It was the only way to defeat the downdraft. This arrangement never bode well with Draco; it was too much like a fish trap—easy in and no good way out.

Draco banked and descended toward the stables spitting acid to calm his churning gut. Something was amiss, he felt, and he didn't care to trust his feelings of late.

He landed below Vinetop at the Dragon Stables and moved off the runway. One after the other by rank his six new warriors touched down on the Warrior's Landing as tradition called for. Draco paid scant attention to his crew.

A dozen highborn dragons were gathered at the near-by civilian landing. Penelope's scent was on that air. Draco turned his snout to, but only for a moment.

Keep to your duty. Steady.

From here he and his cadets would walk the road to the fairgrounds arrayed in fine coverings. The cadets bowed as several veteran dragons and riders landed. Draco's cadets would soon have riders, too, as decided at Auction. Draco had not taken any rider since Hammond nor would he. Warlords only fly deserving royalty. He exhaled black smoke on seeing one particular touchdown.

That spineless King Bromere rides Hillguard of all dragons.

"Why must we land so far from the game field?" Corporal Timor asked.

"Tradition, war dragons and riders have always landed here," Draco said. "We remove our war-gear here out of respect for Vinetop."

Rogsin's respect is not mutual, Draco thought as his nose wrinkled with disdain.

Draco smelled horses. The smells of leather working, smith-working fires, but the smell of carpenter's shavings from making breakaway pikes that he expected were absent. Never had he smelled so many horses here. Rogsin's lawns were fenced in and full of them whereas dragons had traditionally camped there before. The dragon plots were pushed miles away down the avenue.

"Dragon grounds remade for horses!" Draco's hue flashed red and he jetted fire.

The local animals accustom to dragons continued grazing while the war-scarred steeds behind fences stamped hooves and flared their nostrils. Draco rumbled. His charges lowered their heads.

"Sorry Master," Cadet Timor said. "I mean no disrespect."

"My discontent is not directed at you," Draco grunted and hailed the waiting attendants saying, "Bring these fine cadets to their tents."

Festival changing tents were always made new to honor the graduates, but these booths were old and tattered. No respect for the cadets was evident.

No matter, respect is earned. These graduates will outshine pageant decorations.

Draco singled an attendant to help him out of his flight bags.

"Only six warriors this year for twelve kingdoms," the attended said, "The bidding will add much to the coffers of Rookery Top."

"Money concerns me not," Draco said. "The public proving of my dragons is reward aplenty for me."

"Fine dragons they are," the man said. "But, I need money. How shall I place my wager? Who will win the over-all?"

Draco's mood suddenly improved. He always looked forward to testing his cadets against each other and experienced fighters. In his youth Draco bested all comers in every contest. None had done so well since. This time, no one would win every event—everyone would surly win one or two. Draco thought of Mars's magnificent win at Last Games Day. Mars would win all again if fireless dragons could compete.

"Each has merit. Good athletes all," Draco said. "Your best guess is no better than mine."

Draco allowed his hue to glow. His pride was full. Yes, he thought, tomorrow is anyone's game. There is only one dragon he knew as a sure bet, and Mars was far and long out of the running. Still, in all, this small class exceeded his expectations.

"Fine dragons all," Draco muttered to himself as he made for his tent trailing blue smoke.

FIFTY FOUR

Game Day

Praxis awoke before dawn on Game Day although the night before she and Onyx looked from their prison's window late into the night. Camp fires sparkled in the King's distant Game Reserve like fireflies in a field. Such thick and privet woods gave cover enough to hide any army—the crow had told true. Arriving dragons would not fly over that forest nor fly at night. With all the clamor of Game Day, who would hear this army advance?

The trap was set.

The sound of men mounting the defensive walls which intersected the tower rose up from below. She bid Onyx to wake. Together they confirmed the dragon's peril. Rogsin was on the parapet addressing his men.

"The dragons have betrayed us to the Steppes. And so, they must die. Together, Dragons and Unicorns will make war on Vinetop. You of my royal guards…"

Rogsin paused as there was a murmuring. Praxis imagined Rogsin looking them over for disagreeable reactions.

"You will do as my loyal Outlanders do. In the eleventh hour, when the dragons are assembled in the game-bowl, I will sound the King's Horn and the army will attack. At the sound of the King's Horn we move against them…all of them."

A clamor of angry words were shouted at Rogsin by the Vineland Guards.

"There are many more Outlanders on the walls then royal guards," Praxis whispered.

"Vinelanders won't shoot dragons," Onyx returned, "They can't. We love dragons."

Boomax's voice rose up among the clamor. "Nay, nay, this cannot be, dragons have never…I will not fight them."

"Then you will die," Rogsin called loudly. "Your oath is to Vinetop. I've instructed my allies to shoot any man that refuses to fight, or support the dragons. My loyalists have many crossbows. Do you wish to die first Boomax?"

"I'll honor my oath." Boomax said.

A familiar voice hailed the King. It was Robmere.

"What of the fairgoers, the innocents who stand between factions'—old men, women, children, country dragons. Not every man will get word. Will we kill our innocent brothers?!"

"It cannot be helped," Rogsin said. "There will never be another like opportunity. Respect your oaths. Defend the walls. Set pikes. Loose your arrows against any flying dragon, with Vineland rider or not. Dwarves will take the wings of any that fall."

Boomax gave orders to spread out about the walls. The clanging of men at arms dispersing rang in the still air. Praxis stood stiffly—she could not believe her ears. Praxis told Onyx all she was able to hear with her long dragon ears. Grim determination was set on Onyx's face.

Onyx went to the door and looked out the small window.

"We are alone. No guards on the stairs" Onyx said. "They're on the walls—there is time enough to swing your tail before they can react."

"We won't make the parapet," Praxis said, "We can't fight our way down to a jump-off."

Praxis's crown fell, her blue-gold scales darkened. But Onyx stood taller, her face shown with mischievous mirth.

"Yes that is true. The parapet door is four levels below," Onyx said. "Fully armored men running upstairs with ungainly weapons won't arrive here quickly or ready to fight or equipped to bash this door down. You'll have time. Break the wall. Use your tail."

"I am many days without sunlight," Praxis said, "and weak. But I think I can do it. The new mortar is soft. I'll not fly well. I don't have the strength to flee. I must rise into light above the shadows and refresh…"

"And, before they shoot. It will be a near thing," Onyx said. "The sun will still be low when Rogsin blows his horn."

"There is naught to do but wait till then." Praxis said.

"My Father's cunning moves within me," Onyx said. "The horn will serve us. He'll have fewer men on the wall as all eyes will turn to the blower. Down there they'll see stone fly and be warned."

Onyx and Praxis wedged the chair under the latch and heaped all the furniture in front of the door. Even the magic spinning wheel was jammed there. Last of all, Onyx placed the incomplete Tapestry on the heap.

"Textiles make great smoke." Onyx said.

What unwoven material there was, they made wicks and placed each so when lit the pile would go ablaze all at once. Praxis tested her fire and found it weak.

"We'll use the lamps, save your fires," Onyx said. "Our Tapestry burning will keep them back, the smoke will detour them."

"We might die before I get the bricks out. Those wooden ceiling beams are tinder-dry, the whole tower will burn and us with it…what if I fail."

"You dragons are tolerant of fire. Should it consume me, fly out alone. Fire cracks stone. Let the tower fall!"

Onyx's grim face produced a little smile—the cover fire already danced in her eyes. It dawned on Praxis that she beheld the face of a warrior-queen, not the pale, fearful child Onyx was not so very long ago.

"If bringing down the tower of the dragon's enemy cost me my life, so be it. I am ready."

"Surly you are your Father's daughter."

And as is true of one familiar to the other, Praxis garnered the strength of her counterpart. Praxis would not leave Onyx behind, dead or alive.

*****

Mars had flow all yesterday, and all the night he traveled the High Streams in bitter cold with only the light of stars to warm him. It was midmorning when Mars spied Vinetop far below and ahead. Was it too late? No warriors were yet in the pastures but troops moving fast were in the woods beyond the fairground. The stands were full. The dragons were gathered. No dragons were in the air. Draco would not see troops moving in from where he stood on the playing field.

There was no time.

Mars let loose his golden hue hoping the dragons would see him and take warning. All eyes in the stands must be on the field. The men on Vinetop's west wall spotted him. They shouted an alarm but blew no horn. Mars closed his wings and fell steeply toward Vinetop. Ice dust trailing bespoke Mars's coming like a comet's tail. A horn sounded.

That's not a landing horn.

Moments before reaching the castle's lookout, all the while arrows flying at him, Mars opened his wings and shot over Vinetop. The west wall archers fired as he passed, then the east wall's missiles came. A great many arrows flew so Mars twisted away losing momentum. He beat his tail and pressed onward calling in long-speak as he flew.

"Ambush, ambush. From the woods, the woods!"

Mars was a mile from the fields when pandemonium struck. Mars flapped and beat his tail and climbed. A mass of Outlanders and Estates men poured out from the woods and charged across the camping grounds toward the entry shooting as they ran. Dragons and men fell like corn stalks.

Dust rose up and all was confusion. The vendors' tents caught fire. People and dragons stampeded in every direction. Outland archers picked them off from atop the game ground's hills. Still, the Outlanders were out of sorts. Mars forced their hand early. Some charged while others stood back. Country dragons waded into the disorganized charge thrashed their tails while peasants took up fallen weapons against the Outlanders. The slaughter on each side was sure to be great.

Mars gained enough height to dive but he had no rider or weapon save his foot-claws. He turned and dove. Mars strafed the Outland line long-wise. He tore off many helmets with heads still attached. Mars banked and healed over wanting to land with tail and teeth raging. But he heard Draco's command.

"Too me, to me! Dragon's to me!"

Mars answered and swooped into the Bowl of Death. He found Draco shouting orders from the center of the grounds. Bolts rained from the hilltop. Many dragons were dead or wounded. Draco and his fighters were scrambling to protect the civilians.

"Bash down the stones, make cover." Draco shouted. "Arrow above, heads low! Save the civilians!"

Mars joined the effort rounding up panicked civilians. The war dragons backed everyone into the furthest field behind fresh fallen stones. All the while, bolts and arrows crashed about them. Country dragons and courtesies rushed to the makeshift shelter from the stands. Many fell while others arrived wounded. Out onto the fields ran Dwarves with axes. They cut the wings of the dead and living alike before retreating with their trophies.

Ignoring the mayhem, Draco rallied his fighters. The men with Draco took up the bows of dead Outlanders and shot whatever arrows they found. War dragons spewed fire and fire-rocks and so a dozen Dwarves soon burned with a putrid smoke.

Footmen charged but dragon fire forced them back. The war dragons pressed forward and were beaten back three times all the while more and more men joined either faction. After many forays of fight or rescue, Mars rested behind a great stone. Draco found him panting there.

"Your warning saved lives," Draco said. "Many flew safely away. Yet, we here are pressed, outnumbered. They only need lay siege to take us. We must fly before they organize. The entry is the way out. Our escape is well covered."

"Escape, escape!" Mars said, "Praxis is captive in the armory tower! I must go to her."

"Too late, look the tower burns." Draco said.

Who would light it, it must be her doing.

"Hear that," Mars asked?

They both focused their ears and there was an alarm on Vinetop. Even Mars's eyes, not as good as Draco's, saw stones flying from below the tower's burning roof.

"She's bashing the walls. She is alive." Mars cried.

"Go, get her. Then, rally what dragons you find and attack the entry. Make a diversion. Give me a clearer runway. I must get these fat dragons airborne else they die!

Draco then called out in long-speak. "Small dragons take air. Gather. Attack the gate archers!"

Timor jumped to the call and got away with nary a glazing arrow while spitting fire-rocks as he went. Others were less lucky. A small country dragon, running for air, fell dead as Mars took wing. Mars beat tail for the tower and saw that dozens of dragons and men were trapped in the bowl while a thousand Outlanders fought their way toward the game field. Dozens of dragons and many more men lay dead and dying on the pastures. Groups of dragons bashed and burned left and right in the outer fields out of range for the hilltop archers; such a disgraceful thing was never heard of. Yet, the Outlander force would soon overcome the free-roaming defenders—they cannot last, nor the trapped dragons Mars saw.

Time was waning.

Anger rose up in Mars yet he wished not for fire. The stench of burning men sickened his heart. Mars swallowed his bile and bee-lined to the burning tower. He had a life to save. On the Avenue, dragons and men ran for the Keep. He called as he flew, "Attack the game field! Rally to Draco!" Some turned others did not. Mars flew on. *There is time to turn the rest; first, Praxis.*

Archers fired on Mars as he drew near Vinetop. Mars ignored the King's longbows. Their arrows flew wide—they wanted to miss. The crossbow archers were Outlanders.

Their bolts were forewarned by a distinctive twang. Mars flew by twisting loops and stone-drops narrowly evading mayhem.

Close to the tower the archers lost line-of-sight. The arrows stopped. Mars hovered at the window blinded by smoke.

Praxis could not see him between the smoke and wall bashing.

"Praxis, I am here!"

"Mars," She cried. "Get us out of here."

Praxis backed away, turned and wrapped her wings around someone. Her tail was a bloody mess.

"Hit the wall. Hit the wall!" Praxis screamed.

Mars swung his tail mightily three times and cleared the barrier and dropped inside. There was no time for reunions. A fire raged at the opposite end of the small room. Mars fanned back the smoke with his wings and so the flames shot higher. Onyx fell to her knees before Mars coughing.

"Get out of here Praxis," Mars shouted above the roaring fire, "I'll take her."

"We fly together as before. I won't leave her," Praxis said.

"No," Onyx called hacking smoke, "Go, go, you'll…fly faster without me. I'll ride Mars."

Praxis moved between the fire and Onyx instead of toward the window. Her hue shown greatly radiating her confidence—Mars saw arguing was futile.

"Praxis, take her" Mars shouted. "Dragons are trapped on the field. Turn the rout. Attack the gate. They'll obey Onyx. Turn the fleeing fighters. I'll distract the archers. Then Go."

Onyx jump-mounted Praxis like a practiced warrior. The humans face was steel. Mars moved to the window and said, "Count to thirty and fly. I'll storm the wall and turn the shooters. Fly rightward."

Mars launched but did not fall far before banking hard left under the archer's wall. He spun and raced upward beating his tail only two feet from the face of the wall and burst over the top. He flipped in the air and landed between longbow archers with tail swinging. The Vineland men did not shoot. No crossbow-men were close.

A Dwarf ran at Mars with a lance. Mars swung his tail and the small man was launched over the wall. There wasn't much room to swing, but room enough for that. The longbow archer tossed his bow over the side, shrugged his shoulder and smiled queerly.

Another guard ejected his arms and ran up the stairs to the lookout station which was a small round tower twenty feet above the top-wall and built into the side of the main tower. Others ran for the descending stairs. Mars faced off with the remaining dozen Outlanders and King's guard. The wall top was narrow, eight feet across, not suited for tail swinging. Mars took up a long pike.

Arrows flew at him from the further lookout post. Mars ducked his head protecting his eyes. He was hit yet no arrow stung. Mars shook like a wet dog throwing off arrows; several remained embedded in his wing-leather. Men called for crossbows as Mars moved toward the swordsmen.

Surly they will not shoot their own men.

Mars charged wishing he had his mane. Mane-woven maces were made for this. He crashed into the group, with head and tail swinging. They were too bunched-up to swing their long swords. Mars knocked all but a few to the ground. He could have crushed them dead, but he did not. Mars backed away toward the lookout post and called out in long-speak.

"Come on Praxis fly, I cannot hold them long. Where are you?"

Soldiers charged up the stairs calling, "Dragon on the wall." Fighters emerged from the further lookout tower intersecting the wall. More raced up the wall's main stairway. Three Outland men charged with short pikes. Mars swung and tail-bashed the parapet wall sending chunks of stone at them. Several fell, the other one backed away. Mars still held the long pike. He did not thrust it into the wounded as Draco taught.

"Praxis, what's taking you?"

"He won't kill," the surviving pike-man cried, "He didn't follow up—get after him."

The men were less exited now. They closed on him slowly and in better order. Fire would have won this fight. And there was a torch at hand yet Mars did not spit or light his bile. Mars backed away until his tail touched the lookout tower behind him.

"He's a coward, naught but a child, hold him boys—hold him for the King."

Mars swallowed his bile and all at once leapt straight up onto the lookout block behind him. The exterior stair was narrow; they would have to come one-by-one. He landed and readied himself for an onslaught, there was room enough for his tail, but none charged up the stair.

"Mercy dragon, have mercy, I'm with you." A voice from behind called out.

Mars spun about ready to strike and found a young man dressed in apprentice guards gear cowering against the wall. He looked no more than seventeen and had no weapons.

"Spare you," Mars hissed?

"I'm Robmere, friend of Praxis and Onyx. I mean no harm."

"So be it," Mars said, "Stay clear, I've grim work ahead."

Calls went up then, "Hail the King, Make way the King. Hold fire, hold fire."

Mars ventured a peek over the lookout wall. Rogsin walked prideful toward his position as the troops parted for him. A finely made crossbow was on his shoulder. There were now many more troops on the wall including crossbow and longbow archers. Two crossbows were trained on Mars. Praxis still had clear air. The mob's attention was on Mars. Yet, with so many archers on the wall their escape window narrowed.

Why have they not flown?

This entire fight took no more than a few minutes. The smoke from the burning tower above was now thicker in the air. The armory tower's roof was near collapse and flames were punching though the eves licking the sky. Smoke billowed from the lower levels, as well.

Praxis must have descended setting fires—to bring down the tower—she needs more time.

"Ho there dragon," Rogsin called. "I'm coming to see you. Stay your place. I will have words with you. Act against me and you will die."

What could he want? I'll let him speak. Talk gives Praxis leeway. The men's attention is here.

"Come up and I'll speak with you," Mars said. "On my honor, I won't kill you."

"I trust no dragon's word, but I do not fear you either. I will come up. You cannot escape."

"So be it," Mars said, "Come, but know this, The Golden Dragon's word is law."

Rogsin climbed the semi-circular stair laughing. Two guards followed close behind. The passageway was thin. Rogsin held them on the stair beyond Mars's tail reach.

"Should he attack, kill him." Rogsin told his guards.

Rogsin then stepped off the top stair onto the stone lookout's platform. A deadly dragon gold sword hung from his belt and a notched crossbow lay in his steady hands.

"Well, well, what have I here, it is Robmere hiding like a mouse. I see you have a pet Master Mars. Before this day is done, I will make this child into a man…or a corpse."

Keep him talking.

"A man he is," Mars said, "He honors his promise to dragons. He is no coward."

"He is a trader then," Rogsin said. "But I will give Robmere an opportunity to prove his loyalties."

An alarm sounded from below, "dragon, dragon."

Rogsin quickly side stepped to the out-look wall, never pulling his aim.

"Shoot them," Rogsin ordered, "Why have you not."

"Tis Onyx, your sister, she rides a dragon!"

"I don't care, shoot! Kill her." Rogsin commanded.

A distraction was needed. Mars bashed his tail on the wooden stair top landing. The stair collapsed sending the bowmen crashing down. The men on the walls turned toward the commotion but arrows did fly. Yet, Praxis must have banked on Rogsin's order. What arrows flew missed save one. Onyx fell forward onto Praxis neck with an arrow in her shoulder. Mars charged Rogsin. Rogsin screamed. Mars stopped. All eyes went to the King and Praxis flew on. Rogsin faced Mars with his crossbow ready.

"That was a good trick. My sister got away. No matter, I'll find her. You and I have business to complete. Let us finish what I started on Singing Rock Point."

"You," Mars said. "You were the shooter! How?"

"Indeed, I shot you—Emerald's crossbow. Father never intended to use it, you know. He hid it away. But nothing escapes me. Did you know Emerald was your father?"

Mars's jaw hung agape, his crown flared in disarray. His crest glowed hot. Rogsin spoke true!

Was? Or is? He distracts—keep focused.

"I thought not. Yet, I see, you know it now. The Crest of Neff doesn't lie." Rogsin said smugly.

A war plan flashed in Mars's mind. Yes, he could kill Rogsin. But then, on the thought, his crest went cold. Mars loved his inner fire more than he hated Rogsin. Mars, just minutes prior, swore not to kill him.

I cannot do it.

"I am not disingenuous. I did promise Robmere his chance at redemption. Take my sword and hack that dragon's head off. Do so and I'll know you're loyalty."

Rogsin unsheathed his sword with one hand while keeping his bow on Mars. Rogsin bid him come. Robmere took the sword and backed away. There they all stood spaced as a tripod. Robmere's tan face turned sickly green as he looked from Mars to Rogsin.

"I am no murderer. I am of Vinetop, an honorable man."

Robmere spoke it loudly. The troops below heard him.

"I will not kill this dragon." Robmere proclaimed.

A rumbling agreement from the guards of Vinetop rose up. There were many more of them than Outlanders on the wall now. Rogsin's eyes became arrow slits.

"Then die." Rogsin said.

Rogsin aimed and fired. Robmere was hit square in the chest. The bolt passed through him and stuck fast in the armory tower's wall. The golden sword flew over the front-side and Robmere fell dead. Rogsin's weapons were spent.

"You are defenseless" Mars said.

Rogsin felt for his sword, found only a dagger. His folly turned sour on his face. He fell to his knees and cried out.

"My vision comes alive! The Golden kills me, I don't want to die!"

Mars moved and stood over Rogsin filled with outrage. Mars's fisted tail ready. Rogsin's life was his to take and none would say it was unjust. Rogsin confessed his guilt openly—none would stop Mars's retribution.

Mars's tail came down like lighting bashing the stone floor next to Rogsin. Rogsin wet his breeches. Mars raised his tail once again but took pity. Rogsin's weeping made him a small, sick man in Mars's eyes. Mars decided he would not strike and lowered his tail. The Crest of Neff flashed a blinding light that bathed Rogsin with gold-fire. Rogsin screamed but he did not burn.

The promise of Lea is upon me.

Mars turned to the body of Robmere and breathed forth a golden light. Robmere awoke, his wound was gone. Mars stood tall on his hind legs above Rogsin so that the men on the wall saw and heard.

"He deserves death yet I am a creature of Light. I will not deal death—that is the way of men. Dragons will serve men no more."

Mars stood down and went to the edge of the lookout bidding Robmere to come. Robmere mounted. They took wing leaving Rogsin sprawled on the lookout floor. Mars dove and pulled up, But rather than a clean escape he bank-turned to convey a message.

"I'm flying over the walls one last time," Mars said to Robmere, "We must give the men of Vinetop hope and courage. Hang on!"

Circling once while calling, "repent, honor be yours." Mars passed over the lookout before making his exit. But Rogsin had regained his feet. When Mars was only a hundred feet beyond the wall, Rogsin yelled, "FIRE!"

A hail of arrows came. Mars twisted midair toward the missiles and spewed a mighty flame. It was not a common red-fire but a jet of golden light. Every arrow and bolt, and every bow or pike crumbled to soot. And yet, not a man was set aflame.

Mars raced to the battle front and there he found Onyx leading a charge against the bottle neck. What men and dragons she had were too few. The Outlanders were the larger force and holding their ground at the gate. Mars landed and set Robmere to fighting with Rogsin's golden sword. Robmere went to work even as escaping dragons got air. Some flew out while others fell.

It was then that Argolis appeared in the sky with a contingency of wingless dragons. Black Bill himself led a flight of outcaste dragon riders while Puffin came in low with a small contingent of war dragons. Dar came in from high above with others. The Outlanders turned direction and concentrated fire at the new force. Argolis landed near Mars.

"We're outnumbered," Argolis said, "We can't engage them long. How do we beat them? We can't get close to the woods. Them there crossbows got reach."

"We don't need to win, Mars said gasping for air, "Give cover and we'll get the trapped dragons out, once they are away, retreat. Fly for the Rookery. I'll go and tell Draco. Count three hundred…then attack the gate's archers."

"Aye, that's what I call a plan. Light your beacon sir, times a-wasting. I'll pass the word to Dar, Dar's got the mouth, he'll long-speak the message."

Mars took flight and dropped into the Bowl of Death with arrows flying. As before, he burned them to soot with golden flame. Of the dragons and good men on the ground many were fighting hand-to-hand below the back hill as Outlanders dropped in from above. Many Outlanders were shot by their own archers. Draco was there with many deadly bolts in him; his left wing was damaged beyond repair. Mars quickly explained the plan.

"Good work," Draco said. "I and my war-dragons will charge the footman yonder. We'll draw fire and fighters to us. The civilians are already near the runway. Lead them up."

"I will pass the word," Mars said, "I will stay and fight."

"NO," Draco billowed. "I need a leader they'll follow. Keep them together or they'll flee haphazard, or not fly at all. Get them out of here. Do as I say. I am still the Warlord but for a little time more. I cannot fly. Mars do this for me."

Biting back tears, Mars bounded to the covey of dragons among the fallen stone. He rousted them to action. Penelope was with them tending the wounded. Dar's call was sounded. Mars led the dragons running down the Avenue. One after the other, they got air and quickly rose above arrow range upon Mars's urging.

The courtly dragons, now safe, made for Rockery Top while Mars hovered high above the fight seeking an opportunity to help. All the commoner dragons were away or dead. Thus, Argolis called his troops. They strafed the archers spitting fire-rocks and giving the last of Draco's war dragons their escape. Mars joined the fray giving cover with blasts of Golden fire. What war dragons were still able thundered down the runway and into the air.

Rider-less warrior dragons and Argolis's misfits, on Mars's command, came about, landed, and took Onyx and her men onto their backs. Mars and a few others gave air cover. From aloft Mars saw Draco's remaining wounded warriors unable to fly but still fighting.

"We are coming for you," Mars cried in long-speak.

"No," Draco returned. "The people are yours, keep them well. Obey my last order. FLEE!"

Draco's well trained war-dragons banked for home without hesitation. Argolis and his motley crew followed. Mars hung back and floated high above.

I'll witness his last glory.

Draco was mid field surrounded by burning Dwarfs and men. Draco roared with pleasure and fought with abandon until a Dwarf jumped on his back swinging an axe. Draco's broken wing lopped off. Draco rolled and crushed the axman. Spiting fire, Draco sprang to his feet and charged into the largest group of fighters. The last Mars saw of Draco, he was engulfed in the pyre of burning bodies that he had wrought.

Draco is no more.

Mars turned away and flew for the Rookery alone.

FIFTY FIVE

The Parting of Ways

Dragons and human gathered at Rookery Top as refugees and set to mending each other's hearts and bodies. Many dragons had come earlier on the word of ravens and landed unharmed, while other's arrived from the horror of battle. Mars spied dragons he knew from the frontier and from Black Bill's camp, yet glad reunions were far from his mind. Thankfully, many dragons heeded Dar's, Puffin's and Argolis's call to arms.

Word spread: A great many dragons were lost. There was a great wailing and sorrow on the air. Mars had no time for mourning. He busied taking stock of the dragon's remnant and went about organizing the healing. He sent unharmed dragons, event the highborn into the kitchens to make food in plenty sparing no stores. Persons of healing skill were put to labor tending the wounded. Mars found Praxis already at work stitching Onyx's wound.

"Onyx's shoulder was torn badly yet she fought long and hard on the field." Praxis said with her hue shinning pride. "Thankfully it was not her sword arm."

"What delayed you, Praxis," Mars asked weary of voice, "I was on the wall far too long."

"Merilbe," she said. "He was in the tower. We tried to save him. But, we didn't find him." Praxis did not look away from her bloody work.

"Let us hope...he escaped," Onyx said. Her face was grim and sweat streaked her dirty face yet her eyes were clear. "The tower fell."

Mars left Praxis to her task and came upon Hillguard whose many wounds were not serious. Mars had Hillguard assess what fighters were there. At dusk Hillguard reported.

"I count seventy war dragons here and sixty dragon-loyal fighting men and...one woman at arms."

"Seventy dragons," Mars said." Is that all we are? In the estates alone there were five hundred without the boarder patrols. We cannot defend against Rogsin with so small a force."

"Surly Rogsin has hostages," Hillguard said. "Argolis says many common dragons haven't got word yet. There are still dragons in the lands unawares. Messengers seek them now. The ravens search too. Argolis says his lowborn and misfits stand ready for war. Between us all we have a force to recon with. Draco would have us strike back fast and hard as soon as may be."

His last sight of Draco appeared in Mars's mind. The burning of Draco cooled his heart.

"We may defeat Rogsin's Outlanders, but at what cost? I must think on this."

Mars left and saw to the food procreations glad for a mundane concern. He directed the resident chief cook, whom resisted the order of letting go the winter stores, to opened more fully the larders and feed the people a feast as a comfort to them.

With so many refugees there was a great need of food's comfort. The stoves and ovens were soon overwrought and so Mars ordered cooking fires lit on Sky Top proper; a thing never before done. There people and dragon gathered and told their stories and they ate under bright stars without much joy.

The dragon constellation was directly above; many more stars surrounded the sky dragon than before. As many watched a great flare raced across the sky and became the dragon's eye. The sky image was thus completed.

"The Great Sky Dragon looks like Draco," someone cried. "I never thought so before."

"Draco is among the fallen," another said. "That must be Draco's star."

"Behold the last War Dragon." Many said while others were uncertain it was Draco's star.

Mars jumped onto the Teacher's Rock and called for assembly and there Mars told of Draco's last fight. Penelope fell to the ground and cried in great pants and sobs as Mars finished the tale. Weeping and laments filled the air as never before on Rookery Top.

"Forever more the Sky Dragon will be called Draco!" Mars declared and no one disagreed.

Some cheered while others, like Penelope wept more bitterly. Penelope then went to her chambers and shut the door not eating or speaking until Mars came for her on the third day as was proper. Many more dragons had arrived by then. Some came uninhibited while others told tales of escape and death. Rogsin's men were on the hunt and dragons their game. Mars thought it time to address the people still not knowing what should be done.

"Mother," he said, "Time is waning. Your wisdom is required."

"Yes, we cannot stay here long, although Rogsin will not attack with ease, he will find a way." Penelope said. "We must decide our course."

And so a council was called. Senior dragons gathered on the game grounds. All along the rim ravens sat with lowborn dragons and men. Fairy lights appeared among them, too. Each important person spoke in turn. Some wanted to fight, other wished to depart the land. When Onyx held the floor she and Praxis told of Emerald's salvation and Rogsin's illegitimacy.

"As for me," Onyx said finally, "I am the heir of Vinetop and I mean to take it back, or destroy it. Should dragons go, I will stay and fight. Any that wish to fight with me are welcome, yet not obligated. The treaties between dragons and men are no more. I don't know how yet, but I will smite him."

Argolis jumped down from the rim and bowed to address Onyx. *Most unlike a humble country dragon,* Mars thought.

"Rogsin has numbers. Vineland's people are divided, for and against him. You need a dependable force. I know where to get one. Seems the Steeps weren't wont for war, but they know Rogsin means to have at them. Me and Mars is friends with them folks, I'll take you to the Queen. Birds of the same feathers you two are, if you take my meaning."

"I will go to Lea and accept any of her people that will fight with me." Onyx said and then yielded the floor.

There were no more important speakers save Mars and Penelope. A cry went up and Mars was called to speak. Many called, "Let the Warlord speak!" Mars declined and rather he gave the floor to his Mother saying.

"You are the senor dragon. I am no Warlord. You know the lore of how we should choose."

"I have loathed this wisdom," Penelope said and she came forward. "It breaks me to say what I must. On the passing of the Warlord, who has not chosen his replacement, lore has it; 'he who carries the Crest will rule dragons.' Emerald is dead, Draco is dead and Black Bill, whom few knew has the Crest, is missing."

"Old Bill weren't none to sup with highborn, if you take my meaning," Argolis said. "I knew him; He's off in the wilds, if you ask me."

Calls for news of Black Bill rose among the assembly. By all accounts, Bill fought like three dragons in one—tooth, tail and flame all at once. Bill fought with the tenacity of Draco. No one knew what became of Bill on the field until one man stood.

Aye, that Bill's a fighter. I saw him chasing Outlanders into the woods. He'd gone after them like a hound running deer. The dragons were aloft, the retreat sounded, but he kept fighting."

"Bill turned tail on dragon society long ago; he swore he'd never land here. I don't blame him. Look how we treated him." Penelope said. "Bill has gone home…There is only one dragon here with the Crest. The one told in legend; however much I tried to deny it...Forgive me—Warlords die bitter deaths. Mars is the last of the Crest Bearers. He is our patriarch."

Calls and cheers went up for Mars. Not a dragon or man in the house held back. Save Penelope and Praxis who bowed their heads with flayed crown feathers. Staffs and swords were pounded on the floors and walls for Mars as the females who loved him most shed sad tears which did not go unnoticed by Mars.

The clamor continued until Mars jumped upon Teaching Rock.

"I am not for war. The Dragon Age is ended," Mars said. "I say it is an end to the laws we forged with mankind. I will lead you, if you'll accept the Light Way. I will fight no more, save for self protection. I will fly away as foretold and fulfill the Scrolls. Who will fly away with me?"

The gathering hushed. Mars looked to the sky searching for his next words. Even the ravens on the rim sat quiet and allowed the old gray crow room to land. The crow looked upon Mars with head cocked. No one answered Mars's call as vengeance was their wont.

"I will not be Warlord. I fly for Light." Mars called. "Join me."

"Hear the wisdom of the Golden!" The crow squawked so loudly all heard.

"We'll fly brothers and sisters—no highborn or lowborn—all dragons as one. Dragons wherefore will bond-pair for love not bloodlines. No more matchmaking for war-breed dragons. We will be one people." Mars proclaimed.

"Accept this wisdom or you will fail utterly," The crow squawked.

The gathering held silent a time then stirred. Such an ideal was never before heard. The highborn scuffed their tails on the floor while lowborn heads bobbed up and down with agreement although their feathers were askew with doubt.

"I will fly with you," one called, and then another and others called their allegiances. Many voices rose all at once then. Many hard-bitten dragon warriors took up the call, too. The gathering cried praises. Yet some did not. The humans among them were divided and some dragons blew worried smoke. Murmurs came, "How will we live, where will we go, when shall we fight?" Argolis then spoke above the din.

"I'm with you, but…There's dragons unaccounted for, Sir, I mean we can't leave them." Argolis said. "Some here got family missing."

"If you are willing become my Right Hand." Mars said. "Stay and seek the lost. Bring them home. What dragons that are willing, will you stay and help Argolis?"

"I'll do it," Argolis said. "The missing needs an accounting."

"All of you are free!" Mars exclaimed. "Come with me, or stay. Fight Rogsin if that's your desire. As for me, I'll go east to the Sage Dragons first then I'll leave Neff forever."

"Well said," The old gray crow squawked. "Well said!"

The crow flew to Mars, hovered six feet above the ground, and began to glow. Dragons and men backed away. No crow had ever acted so strangely. It changed shape and grew until meeting the ground as a bubble the size of a man. The bubble popped.

There stood Merilbe the wizard.

"Never is a long time," The Wizard said. "Anything is possible in a life as long as yours. That is wisdom Sir Hammertail. Yet, you have spoken wise this first day of the new age…an age of dragons separate from men. Depart as foretold. The Golden is here. Leave Neff or perish. I will remain and help dragon kind as I may."

All at once the ravens hailed Merilbe. Long had the ravens feuded with crows but now they foreswore a brotherhood whereas Merilbe chose the crow race his familiar kin. Merilbe then bid the ravens to continue and find what dragons there were and say this to all ears, "The Golden has come, retreat to the Rookery."

And so they did. Inside a week all the dragons they found were on Rookery Top. But not all were accounted for. On the seventh day of the raven's rescue, the ravens flew to the stars as their magic was spent and their age finished.

Mars and his dragons assembled on Rookery Top then. Twenty war dragons, two healers, and a dozen of Queen Onyx's men stayed behind to give aid and protection fore many wounded remained on Rookery Top. All Mars's dragons that were able ascended into the high stream with flight bags laden. They flew in formation to the Steppes and set down like flocks of geese near Lea's village. Once there, Onyx and her fighting men disembarked and Onyx and Lea formed an allegiance against Rogsin.

Mars had brought for the unicorn people a portion of Rookery Top's horde of gold and before everyone, Mars gave it to Lea saying he had left the greater part of the dragon's treasurer behind within Rookery Top.

"It is my gift for the men, unicorns, and dragons that fight Rogsin. Of Queen Onyx I ask she share it with her allies. All pay heed," Mars called. "I warn dragons beware: Gold, the bane of man, was the downfall of dragons. Keep it not, don't love it or it will destroy your soul. Here are your war chests Queen Onyx and Princes Lea, take what's on Sky Top as you may."

Praxis came forward with a dragon gold knife saying. "Behold, Mars asked my hand. I will bond him in marriage. He had cut his mane here, and with it, the entanglements of human concerns. I do now as my beloved did."

Praxis cut from her mane what gold charms were woven there by human hands and left them at Lea's feet. Praxis left her valuable knife in a low stump between Lea and Onyx. Other lowborn dragons came and took up the knife. Then the highborn came until one and all they cut away their human wrought status. From their manes, a bounty of gold was laid before Onyx and Lea's feet.

"It is finished," Mars said, "What is wrought by men let men keep."

Lea ordered a great feast. All that day everyone ate well. There was much celebration as was befitting of Mars and Praxis's wedding. Thus eleven days after the ambush the unlucky number Mars was born under became a charm for dragons. On that day, with full bellies, Lea's blessings, the weight of gold was cut from their hearts and manes. As such they flew east from the Steppes with great lightness borne of hope and freedom. Into the sun the dragon flew as one family. The newlyweds Mars and Praxis led the way.

EPILOGUE

Rogsin Burns

Clive Villas was in no mood for pesky children. If he was not clad head to toe in steel armor, or if he were a younger man, he would simply have turned about and run off the children following him. At his age, however, he wouldn't waste his energy. He needed all his strength to fight that one-wing dragon that was menacing Rock Point.

Clive was sixty years old. He figured this was his last season, and last chance, to finally kill a dragon. The woodsmen said this one-wing dragon was very large, a brown and red, the most fearsome kind.

I have the advantage, Clive thought, *it can't fly off and cheat me of glory.*

Clive tried to work out a plan as he clanged and clattered his way toward the stables. But the children distracted his thinking with their unrelenting questions.

"Hush, be going, I'm thinking!" Clive cried.

But, the children gave him no quarters and rather called all the more saying, "Going after a magic dragon? See any unicorns? Are the Dwarves warring? Find any dragon's bones?"

Clive wanted quiet to set his mind for hunting. Thrashing the children would give him peace now, but only at the cost of his wife's retribution later. After all, these are his kinsmen's children. Clive noticed the old man as he passed—that fool who lived in the rubble of Queen Onyx's Tower. Clive had an idea.

When he was a boy that same old man sat in that same place—Clive and his friends had delighted in harassing that wrenched pilgrim. The beggar had since stacked up more blocks around his hovel but was otherwise the same.

If the children took an interest in this gray-beard, they'd let me alone.

So Clive stopped at the beggar's small fire—the old man was roasting a rat on a spit. Clive addressed his followers.

"Children, I've naught the wisdom to answers your questions, I am but a humble Knight, and no lore-keeper. Ask this grandfather here. He was already old when I was a boy. He knows dragon-lore. Is that not so grandfather?"

"Can't have been old when you was a lad," A boy of about ten years said, "Nobody's that old. Can a man live so long?"

"Good question." The old man said, "And I have good answers."

I've never so much as asked his name.

Clive decided to hear the answer himself. The child was right, no one lived that long and yet this man hadn't changed since Clive's grandfather's time.

How could this be?

"Well then," Clive said, "Before I go kill this dragon and take his magic, I'll hear your answer."

"Villas, you aren't getting any dragon-magic fore no dragon in Neff still has any." The old man said. "When Mars left, so went the magic. Any dragons that are still here have none to give. I know why, too."

"That's not the answer I'm after," Clive said.

"In good time, mercy for an old man, Light knows I've got time, 300 years so far, but listen."

The old man turned the rat over on the fire spit. The children drew nearer. Clive thought this could work. Get the old man talking and slip away. Old Draco would wait a little longer.

"You can't find no dragon's bones," the beggar said, "No wings either, cause when that nasty Mars took off all the dead dragons turned to dust as did their wings. There are no dragon relics, not in this cursed land, least you look into the night sky. Curse Mars! He ruined me."

"I haven't all day," Clive said, "No more foolishness. Tell me how you got so old and I'll be on my way. You children stay with him, learn what you can, report back me on my return. You are hereby my honorary bards. Old man, tell me, how do you live so long?" Villas kick at the fire, "And, on such food?"

"It's not food that keeps me, its magic." The old man said.

"Now that is foolish. There is no magic in this rubble—come now old crow."

The graybeard's cheeks became red. He plucked at his long beard and threw down his dirty felt hat. Standing up with a creak, he reached into his charm pocket and withdrew his angry brown spotted fist.

"Now see here, I have a name," the toothless man said as spittle fell into his beard. "I am Rogsin, Rogsin the Great. I have magic!"

Clive could not help but laugh. This was good entertainment after all. Rogsin was run off more than three hundred years ago when Queen Onyx won the war, or so the fable goes. Rogsin tried to kill the Steppes people. What foolishness, if true. Why kill the makers of the best beer? No decent person would claim the name "Rogsin" much less call that name great. The Steppes and Neffland were parts of the same wider country, after all. Clive even had relatives up in Wheatland.

"There is no magic here old man. Only unicorns and dragons have magic."

"I have the last of Neff magic right here in my pocket." Rogsin seethed. "I'll show you. It's from the Tapestry of Neff, I cut it out myself. Even such fools as you have heard of it."

Rogsin dug into his charm pocket and pulled something out.

"Here it is."

Rogsin thrust his dirty hand forward and opened his bony fingers. On his filthily palm was a perfectly clean scrap of shimmering textile. Clive thought he must have torn if from a lady's laundry. It was fine material, indeed, nothing peasant made. Clive thought to snatch it up and find from where the beggar stole it. Clive Villas grabbed at Rogsin's hand. Rogsin recoiled and the cloth fell into the fire.

Rogsin let forth a horrid scream.

Clive stepped backward tripping over a child and fell onto the ground. The children screamed and ran off while an old crow came in and landed on the rock pile. Once Clive had regained his composure he noticed that the old man was gone. He moved forward and looked where the beggar had been. Clive only found a circle of fine black ash upon that ground. A queer feeling came over Clive as he kicked the ashes. The ash swirled and became a small dust-devil before collapsing into nothing.

For reasons he could not explain, Clive decided he would not hunt for Draco that day. *No,* Clive thought standing in the ruins, *this is a bad omen.*

"Today is a bad day to go hunting dragons," Clive Villas declared. "Draco can wait."

But only an old crow with a peculiar white star on its head remained to hear Clive's pronouncement.

"Draco lives? Draco lives!" the old crow squawked.

The crow flew off and Clive went home with a new heart. He never took up arms against dragons again, but he did live to become a very, very old man.

THE END

ACKNOWLEDGEMENTS

The idea for this story germinated in an adult education writing class at Northampton Community College, Bethlehem Township, Pa. so I must first thank Kathy Coddington who taught the class and otherwise encouraged me. Rita Bitner, a class mate there, was first to get behind the idea and she spent much time helping me work out the plot and served as a sounding board along with various member of the Greater Lehigh Valley Writers Group (GLVWG.org) who critiqued the work in progress and gave me many suggestions. Angel Ackerman, my longtime friend and editor did much to keep this story straight. Beta readers along the way are too many to list, thank you all. It took years to write *Dragon Fire* and more years to perfect it and I could not have done any of this without my life mate and primary story editor, proof reader, and bottle washer, Lisa Cross for without her help and encouragement I could not write.

ABOUT THE AUTHOR

Rachel Thompson, writing fantasy and sci-fi as R.C. Thom, began her writing career after surviving a devastating motorcycle accident in 2003. She has since published non-fiction pieces in newspapers and magazines, cartoons, and a handful of short stories. *Soul Harvest* is her second novel but first published. The sequel, *Aggie in Orbit*, will follow in the fall of 2018. Look out for her short story anthology, *Stalking Kilgore Trout* and novel *Book of Answers* due for release late in 2018. *Dragon Fire* is her first novel but is only just now published. Email her at rc@rcthom.com or visit her website at rcthom.com

CPSIA information can be obtained
at www.ICGtesting.com
Printed in the USA
LVHW081354290621
691467LV00012B/343